TOWN IN A
Cinnamon Toast

B. B. Haywood

BERKLEY PRIME CRIME, NEW YORK

BERKLEY
PRIME
CRIME

An imprint of Penguin Random House LLC
375 Hudson Street, New York, New York 10014

TOWN IN A CINNAMON TOAST

A Berkley Prime Crime Book / published by arrangement with the author

Copyright © 2016 by Robert R. Feeman and Beth Ann Feeman.
Excerpt from *Town in a Blueberry Jam* by B. B. Haywood copyright
© 2010 by Robert R. Feeman and Beth Ann Feeman.

ISBN: 978-0-425-27855-0

PUBLISHING HISTORY
Berkley Prime Crime mass-market edition / February 2016

PRINTED IN THE UNITED STATES OF AMERICA

10 9 8 7 6 5 4 3 2 1

Cover illustration by Teresa Fasolino.
Cover design by Diana Kolsky.
Interior text design by Kristin del Rosario.

Penguin
Random
House

This one is for the fans,
and for the many dedicated bloggers
who provide invaluable support to
cozy mystery books and their writers

PROLOGUE

It was a tragedy, he thought, a terrible tragedy.

He'd been so looking forward to the wedding, and regretted that he'd miss it. But he'd never make it now, because he was dying.

At least he was wearing his favorite cardigan, and that gave him some small comfort in the final moments of his existence.

At one time the cardigan had been light blue in color, but over the years it faded to a pleasant silvery gray. Down the front, a trio of worn bone buttons were usually hitched into their corresponding buttonholes—he'd always prided himself on the neatness of his appearance—but he'd neglected to fasten them over the past few days, leaving the sweater open, revealing a wrinkled shirt underneath. He'd also forgotten to comb his hair, shave his whiskers, and clean his shoes, which were often untied as well, all because of his preoccupation with another matter.

That "other matter" had brought him to this point, he thought fleetingly as the last few sparks in his brain began to extinguish. He'd acted too carelessly, misplaced his suspicions, and unleashed a force he had never seen coming.

Now he was paying the ultimate price. He'd triggered an unexpected attack, which led to his untimely demise here in this place he loved so dearly.

It was all because of the land deeds, and what he'd found out about them.

The deeds.

He wished they had never come to him, those yellowed, crinkly old documents, though the historian in him had initially leapt at the chance to study them. But they'd turned out to be more trouble than they were ever worth—and they could be worth a lot if they fell into the wrong hands. That's what he'd been trying to prevent, but he had failed.

They had also led to his other discovery, a dark, dangerous, largely forgotten place.

Foul Mouth.

It was an ominous-sounding name, one he had puzzled over when he first saw it in the pages of the deeds. He'd only recently confirmed its existence through his discreet inquiries, and had planned further investigation. But someone had beaten him to it. Someone had already been over there, sneaking around, digging into the past. He'd watched it happen through the binoculars, and had intended to reveal what he knew. But he'd waited too long. And that, in the end, had been his undoing.

Now he'd never have a chance to warn others about his misgivings.

At least, in his growing concern for his safety, he'd taken the time to leave behind a few clues hidden in the books, identifiable only to a particularly curious eye.

But in doing so, had he endangered someone else?

That ragged thought—or perhaps it was just the devastating blow he'd received—sent a startling chill through him as his eyes began to glaze over and his breath rattled in his throat.

He only hoped the message he'd left behind wasn't too obscure, too difficult to decipher. He'd debated the matter until the very end, but decided there was no other way. He hadn't been certain whom he could trust. There were spying eyes all around. He'd had no choice but to hide the clues from those who might be searching for them. He only hoped they'd do what he intended.

And he'd taken two additional precautions, passing the copies to his friend, and making a call this afternoon. In hindsight those had been good decisions. But he hadn't had time to follow up on them. Now he never would.

In the last few thumps of his heart, he recalled the attack, trying to figure out what he could have done differently. He knew it hadn't been planned; it had happened in the heat of the moment. Neither of them had expected it would end the way it did.

One of the final images burned into his mind was of the blurred shoes of his attacker. They'd looked uncommonly large and misshapen when viewed from this odd, low angle. As the shoes retreated, headed back the way they'd come, down the stairs and out of the building, he thought he'd heard someone speak, perhaps directly to him. He thought the person said *sorry*. But ultimately it had just been an indistinct rumble in his ears.

He'd also heard that loud thud, as if an object of some weight had dropped to the floor nearby. Out of sight, it had bounced once or twice and rolled a little before settling. He had felt the heavy vibrations through the rough wood upon which his left cheek, and his entire body, had come to rest.

Now he was alone. He wanted to shift his head around so he could see what had fallen nearby, but his body wouldn't respond to his mental commands. Instead, the effort brought up an unfamiliar cold that coursed through him, along with a pain so sharp it would have made him wince and cry out, if he could achieve such actions.

The creak of the door downstairs should have alerted him. The brush of footsteps on the stairs, the flicker of light above the second-floor landing, the strange silence that followed, as if a ghost were approaching. The odd, awkward conversation, the tensions rising. Perhaps he could have protected himself better, fought back more. But he was too old and frail, and he'd never seen the attack coming. It had been too unexpected, too swift, and in the end, too overpowering.

But it made no matter now. It was over. He knew that, and accepted it. He had no regrets. He'd lived a long time, accomplished all he'd set out to do, and then some. He couldn't complain about anything that had happened to him over his long life—or even in the last few moments of it.

He would have liked to have seen this whole matter through to the end, to make sure it turned out properly—to protect his village and perhaps a life or two, including his own.

But it was all slipping away. . . .

Now someone else would have to pick up the baton of inquiry and investigation and carry it through to its conclusion. Someone who would follow the trail he'd followed and finish what he'd started. Someone who would see the danger he saw, decipher the clues, alert the right people, and stop the chaos he believed was about to happen.

Someone like Candy Holliday.

That gave him some small comfort as he wheezed out his last breath—that, and his favorite once-blue sweater, gathered so comfortably around his body, fighting back against the unrelenting cold that finally, inexorably, engulfed him in its icy embrace.

From the *Cape Crier*
Cape Willington, Maine
May 6th Edition

THE CAPE CRUSADER

by Wanda Boyle
Managing Editor

LOVE IS IN THE AIR!
Calling all romantics! Along with May flowers come wedding
showers, and we have a big one coming up this month. Our
own lovebirds and bakers extraordinaire, the gifted Herr Georg
Wolfsburger and his delightful fiancée, Maggie Tremont, are
finally tying the knot after a long engagement (and it's "knot"
the kind you'll find on those scrumptious Bavarian pretzels
they sell in their shop, the Black Forest Bakery on Main
Street!). As we've discussed endlessly in this column, the afternoon wedding ceremony, with the Reverend James P. Daisy
presiding, will take place at Holliday's Blueberry Acres on Saturday, May 14th, with the Boyle family in attendance (I practically had to *steal* an invitation, but that's another story!). I'll
be among the forty or so wedding guests (that's all they can
fit in the barn!), and I have it on good authority from new
wedding planners Ralph Henry and Malcolm Stevens Randolph that the bucolic (and hopefully well-cleaned!) venue will
be positively *transformed* for the event! Expect photos and
tweets galore, plus a full report in the May 20th edition!

MYSTERY BUYER SCOOPS UP WHITBY ESTATE
In a surprise announcement, the Whitby family, previous
owners of the Lightkeeper's Inn here in the village, have
sold their family estate across the bay, on Whitby Point.
The house and property, which reportedly encompass some
dozen acres on prime oceanfront land, has been in the family's hands for several generations, although we have it on
good authority that the place has fallen into disrepair over
the past few years. No word yet on the identity of the buyer,
though we're told it's someone with close ties to the

community. Who could it be? We've got our money on Martha Stewart! Who do you think bought the place? Sound off, Capers, and as always, send your scoops and latest tidbits to us, so we can report it to the world!

SPRING HAS FINALLY SPRUNG

After some iffy (and at times drenching!) weather through April, spring has finally arrived here in our little corner of Down East Maine. Yay!!! Activities around town are gearing up as we prepare for the busy summer season just ahead, which kicks off on Memorial Day weekend. That's just THREE WEEKS AWAY, folks! (Let me repeat that: THREE. WEEKS. AWAY! Okay, you've been properly warned.) You'll find a list of shop and restaurant opening dates on page 11 of this issue. This is my second-favorite time of year,* when we plant our gardens and clean out that old stuff from our garages. Time for love, and time for fun in the sun. So get ready—summer is almost here! And before you break out the gardening shovel or tiller, be sure to check out columnist Candy Holliday's gardening tips later in this issue.

A PLUCKY TALENT

Speaking of summer, be on the lookout this season for *Sumner*, one of the village's newest and most innovative talents. Local artisan Sumner Kent must have music in his artistic soul, because he's crafting beautiful jewelry out of used guitar strings and glass beads! Yes, you read that right! He got the idea for the jewelry when he kept breaking strings on his guitar, and they got caught around his wrists and ankles. Clearly not a seasoned musician, he turned his klutz into craft (a talent I can wholeheartedly admire!). The finished creations practically strum themselves (just don't let Sumner do it!). I'm wearing one of his guitar-string ankle bracelets as we speak, and I must say it rivals Tiffany's! (Well, almost.) It has me singing a happy song.

RUN FOR THE ROSES . . .

No, wait, we mean for the geraniums! Next year's graduating class at Cape Willington High School will sponsor a

"Run for the Geraniums" race to raise funds for the 2017 prom and graduation season. A truckload of beautiful potted geraniums will arrive at Town Park at 1 P.M. on Saturday, May 21st. Members of the Class of 2017 will then run through town carrying a geranium or two and meet up at the high school gym. The geraniums will then be set out on tables, where they will await eager buyers! That's you! So hurry on down, support a great cause, and take home a beautiful blooming plant for the season. For more information, call or e-mail the high school.

THE BIRDS ARE COMING! THE BIRDS ARE COMING!
Some, like most sparrows, are already here, with yellow-throats, American redstarts, magnolia warblers, and rose-breasted grosbeaks right on their heels. (Note to self: Do birds have heels?) To help you keep up with all the latest ornithological news as the annual spring migration comes to a rustling crescendo, join local birder Jody Dumont of the Down East Audubon Society at the Pruitt Public Library on Sunday, May 15th at 2 P.M. During her presentation, she'll discuss spring migration paths of Maine birds. Light refreshments will be served afterward, so you can even eat like a bird. Jody promises not to ruffle your feathers, and instead will leave you chirping with delight!

TASTY TIDBITS
Who doesn't love growing ornamental grasses in their gardens? Or growing bounties of berries in a small fruit garden? You can learn about both during two workshops to be held at Hatch's Garden Center on Saturday and Sunday, May 28th and 29th. Both workshops are open to the public, whether you're a beginning or advanced gardener. Space is limited, so grab your trowels (your phone would work too) and reserve a spot today! . . . Speaking of nature, everyone in town knows that local landscaper Mick Rilke is a force of nature himself! (The type that makes you want to head inside when you see him coming!) Mick has been spotted with his hands in more than one flowerpot this spring, and the season has barely begun. Good thing there's more than

one gray pickup truck in town! . . . Jeff Hall and Betsy Frost are taking charge of the community bulletin board outside Zeke's General Store on Main Street. Jeff lovingly repainted the trim, and the two of them set to work to organize the mess. They sorted through piles of faded business cards, announcements, and torn posters from events long past. Now the board is all cleaned up, and there are new posting rules. Here are just a few:

- No posting anything on the wood trim. Stay within the confines of the corkboard, folks!

- No more gigantic posters that take up all the room! Smaller is often better!

- Keep the business cards with the business cards, posters with posters, etc., etc., blah blah.

- No displays of affection in front of the board! It's a public place, remember? (This means you, Mick Rilke!)

Okay, so enough with the rules! Just be kind to the board—and to Jeff and Betsy. They worked hard to clean that up!

THE BOSWORTH REPORT
Official Judicious F. P. Bosworth sightings for the previous two weeks:

Visible: 8 days
Invisible: 6 days

Thanks for flying out of the nest, Judicious. It's great seeing you flocking into town this spring, along with the birds!

* My favorite time of the year, of course, is HARVEST time, when we get to EAT what we planted in the spring. And as all of you know, I LOVE to eat—more than I love to plant and garden! My burgeoning waistband proves it! Diet time, I hear you calling to me!

ONE

"A toast!" said Henry "Doc" Holliday enthusiastically as he reached for his champagne flute and hoisted it in a ceremonial gesture. "Or, to be more precise, a *cinnamon* toast!"

Around the table, the laughter, joking, and lighthearted conversations dwindled to an attentive hush as the other dinner guests reached for their glasses as well. All turned toward Doc, who cleared his throat and waited a few moments before launching into his remarks.

"Now, I realize we're currently missing two important members of our party—including our best man, who never showed up tonight, and our maid of honor, who went off looking for him—but I think we need to get the festivities going here. So in their absence, if no one minds, I'll step in to fill their shoes."

Hearing no objections, and instead noticing smiles and a few nods of encouragement around the table, Doc took a breath, considered his next words, and continued.

"Of course, I'm calling this a cinnamon toast, because that's one of the colors you'll be seeing everywhere during the biggest social event of the season. I'm talking, of course, about the impending wedding of two of my favorite people"—and here he angled the champagne flute toward the happy couple, seated across the table from him—"the beautiful and vivacious Maggie Tremont and her incredibly talented and debonair soon-to-be husband, Herr Georg Wolfsburger!"

Several of the guests around the table applauded, as well as they could while holding their glasses of champagne, and offered a few words of encouragement and congratulations. The bride and groom beamed, their hands clasped tightly together. Doc noticed they were both blushing a little at the sudden attention, especially Herr Georg, who could turn bright red due to his ruddy complexion and white hair and mustache.

"As the story goes," Doc went on, "Herr Georg often made the comment around the bakery that the color of Maggie's eyes reminded him of his favorite spice, cinnamon, which he uses frequently in his recipes. And, in turn, Maggie noticed one day that the color of Georg's eyes is remarkably similar to that of a ripe blueberry. So it was an easy decision to make cinnamon and blueberry-blue the official colors for their wedding—which, by the way, is only *three days away*!"

This statement brought looks of anticipation and a few whistles and catcalls from around the table. Doc acknowledged them briefly and plunged on.

"Now, I've known both Maggie and Georg for a long time, and I don't mind telling you they're two of the finest people I've ever met. Maggie, of course, is an outstanding member of our community, who's lived in Cape Willington for most of her adult life and raised her daughter, Amanda, here."

Amanda Tremont, seated to her mother's left, along with her longtime boyfriend and fiancé, Cameron Zimmerman, affectionately clapped her mother on the shoulder. Cameron pumped his fist lightly in the air and gave out a low whooping cry of approval.

"In addition to being a fantastic mom," Doc said, "Maggie is a hardworking businesswoman, having spent many years as an administrative assistant at the Stone and Milbury Insurance Agency, which was right across the street from here, before it closed down due to the, shall we say, nefarious practices of its former owner?"

"May he roast in Hades," Doc heard Maggie quip under her breath, in a somewhat facetious tone, though with an edge to it. "You know as well as I do, Doc," she said, her voice rising, "that that man was a liar and a cheat, and a few other things I won't mention in mixed company!"

Several folks around the table chuckled in agreement, and Doc smiled indulgently, raising his glass to her. "Hear! Hear! Since then," he continued without skipping a beat, "Maggie has held a number of positions around our community. She's worked at the dry cleaners, managed the local pumpkin patch, and currently helps run the famed Black Forest Bakery, along with her betrothed, Herr Georg."

Doc pronounced the German baker's name the way he preferred it, calling him *Gay-org*, as did most of those in town, though there were still a few holdouts who simply called him George. The baker didn't seem to mind, though. "I'm just glad they call me something," he'd often been heard to say.

"Now," Doc said, "it was shortly after Maggie started working at the bakery that the romance between her and Georg blossomed—which, of course, will happen when you're surrounded all day by all those fragrant wedding cakes Georg makes, along with the spicy ingredients he uses!"

That brought a few more chuckles, and Doc sensed he was on a roll, but also knew it was about time to wrap this up. "Georg proposed to Maggie shortly after she started working at the bakery, and while it's taken them a while to make it to the altar, that day is finally upon us. So please raise your glasses and join me in wishing good luck, continued success, and much prosperity to our soon-to-be newlyweds, the future Mr. and Mrs.—or perhaps I should say Herr *und* Frau— Georg Wolfsburger!"

That brought more laughs and applause, as well as a few good-natured cheers as the dinner guests drank in the couple's honor.

There were ten chairs in all encircling the oval table, which was set into an alcove off the main dining room at the Lightkeeper's Inn, but only eight were currently occupied. To Doc's right were two empty chairs, reserved for Candy Holliday,

Doc's daughter and the maid of honor, and Julius Seabury, the elderly best man. To the right of Julius's chair were Cameron and Amanda. On the other side of the table, to Herr Georg's right, sat his future mother-in-law, Ellie Chase, who was Maggie's vivacious widowed mother, now in her mid-seventies. In between her and Doc, completing the party, were the two wedding planners, Ralph Henry and Malcolm Stevens Randolph, smartly outfitted in the wedding's colors.

As the enthusiasm around the table died down, Herr Georg picked up a spoon and rapped lightly on his champagne glass. When he had everyone's attention, he spoke up.

"First of all," he began, rising to his feet, "I'd like to thank all of you for coming today. Those of you gathered here are our nearest and dearest friends, and we couldn't have made it this far without your help. As you know, we still have a lot to do out at Blueberry Acres before the wedding on Saturday, but I'm sure everything will be squared away in time. Of course, we couldn't have done any of this without the assistance of Doc and Candy, who allowed us to hold the ceremony out at their farm. And with the blueberry fields just coming into bloom, it should be a spectacular setting."

"The tent for the reception went up yesterday," Doc quipped, "so all the heavy lifting is done."

"Except for the chairs, tables, lighting, flowers, decorations, food, and of course, the guests!" quipped Malcolm with a mischievous smile.

"Right," Herr Georg acknowledged. "As I said, there's still a lot to do, but Doc will address that shortly. For now, let me again say a hearty *danke schön* to all of you. And to my beloved," he added, turning to Maggie and raising his glass, "I would like to say that you've made me the happiest man on this planet, and all the others in the universe!"

That brought a roaring round of applause, as well as a few heartfelt *ahh*s from the dinner guests, and even a tear or two. It was Cameron, acting as instigator, who turned to his future mother-in-law and said, "Speech! Speech!"

As Herr Georg resettled himself with a broad smile, the call was taken up by others around the table. Maggie playfully waved them away until Amanda reached over to persuasively hoist her mother up, and Maggie finally rose to her feet.

She quieted the crowd with a motion of her hands. "Okay, okay, keep it down, you banshees, or they'll throw us out of this joint!" There was more laughter as Maggie smiled, and she placed a gentle hand on her betrothed's shoulder.

"Now, I would just like to echo what Georg said. Both of us are incredibly fortunate to live in a town like Cape Willington, with good friends and loving family like all of you. You'll never know how much you all mean to us, but we'll do our best to tell you in every way we can in the years to come."

Turning to look at Herr Georg, she continued, "And to you, my cherished German baker, *I* would just like to say that these two years working alongside you in the shop have been among the most creative, most rewarding, and most glorious ones of my life. You've taught me so much, like how to make pretzels and fudge, not to mention *Blätterteig* and *Franzbrötchen*, that I can never thank you enough. But no matter how expert I become at making all those things, I'll never achieve one tenth—one hundredth! one thousandth!—of your level of skills with a spatula and a mixing bowl. I can think of no other way I'd like to spend the rest of my days than to work beside you, rubbing elbows with you, learning from you, baking with you, eating with you, living with you, and loving you. And to finish, my *Kuschelbär*, I'll simply say, *Du bist die Liebe meines Lebens*, which means," she added, turning back to the table, "'You are the love of my life'"!

Amid the resumed applause and supportive calls, someone around the table asked, "What does *Kuschelbär* mean?"

"It means," Maggie said as she returned to her seat, "he's my cuddle bear," and she leaned over to give him a big hug.

"Hey, Georg," Malcolm called from across the table, "how do you say *congratulations* in German?"

The baker finished swallowing a sip of champagne and turned toward the wedding planner. "Well, you would say *Glückwunsch*, or perhaps *herzlichen Glückwunsch*, which would add a superlative, such as *hearty* or *sincere* congratulations. Or you could say *viel Glück* for *good luck*."

"Well, then, *herzlichen Glückwunsch* and *viel Glück*!" said Malcolm jovially, and the others around the table echoed his words, though most of them stumbled over the pronunciations.

"Well," Doc piped in, "now that the remarks are out of the way, let's get on to the food!"

"Speaking of food," Amanda said as Doc signaled to a nearby waiter, "I've heard Herr Georg is going to make quite a wedding cake for the reception."

"It will be the most important one I've ever made," the baker said as he looked over at Maggie, "because it's for our own wedding, of course."

"What's it going to be?" Cameron asked. "Like eight feet tall?"

"Are you going to use cinnamon?" Ralph asked.

"Tell us about it," encouraged Ellie, Maggie's mother.

But the baker simply raised a forefinger. "It is, so far, top secret," he said, "but I will tell you that it's from an old family recipe, one handed down to me by my mother. And, of course, its colors will fit with the theme of the wedding. But I'll not say anything more, other than to promise you it will be special when it is unveiled on Saturday." He squeezed Maggie's hand. "Wait until you see it."

"He says he won't let me in the shop while he's making it, because he wants it to be a surprise!" Maggie added, beaming.

That got them started, and they began to discuss the various details they had yet to accomplish before Saturday. But as they talked, Maggie suddenly went silent as she looked over at the two empty chairs. She caught Doc's eye and mouthed, "Where are they?"

Doc just shrugged and tried to put on a nonchalant air, but it wasn't hard to see the concern in his eyes.

TWO

The place looked deserted.

It was the last house at the end of a winding dirt road, a weather-beaten wood-framed cabin with a small front porch and a peaked roof, sitting on a rocky spit of land that jutted out into the dark sea. White-framed windows, graying cedar-shake siding, and a red-painted front door gave it a rustic appearance. A single rocker swayed back and forth on the porch. Windblown trees, a dwindling pile of firewood, and a few ragged lilac bushes dotted the property, which had been in the Seabury family for generations.

The cabin's windows were dark. Even though the sun was setting, there were no lights on inside. No car sat in the double-rutted parking spot at one side of the building.

It seemed no one was home. So where could he be?

With a concerned expression on her face, Candy Holliday pulled her teal-colored Jeep to a stop in front of the cabin and shut off the engine. As she opened the driver's side door and stepped out, a sudden sea breeze tossed about her honey-colored hair. Absently she brushed it aside, squinting into the gathering dusk as she surveyed the oceanfront property with an inquisitive gaze.

It was certainly a prime piece of land, isolated and private yet within a short driving distance of downtown Cape Willington. A grass yard, still dull and flattened by the heavy snows of winter, extended a couple dozen feet behind the cabin, eventually giving way to dense shrubbery and a mixture of deciduous and pine trees. Spring wildflowers poked tentatively through the grasses and foliage in places, and Candy spotted a few wild raspberry and blueberry bushes along the back edge of the property, just coming into bloom.

As for the cabin itself, it wasn't anything fancy. Probably just a couple of bedrooms, she surmised, with a small kitchen and a living and dining room combination. But she imagined the ocean views from the porch, or from anywhere inside the cabin, were magnificent, and she had no doubt the place was cozy and comfortable inside.

After a final glance around, she walked up onto the porch, stepped over to the red-painted door, and rapped on it several times. "Julius," she called out, "are you home? It's Candy Holliday. I've come to check on you."

She waited a few moments, leaning forward, her ear turned toward the door, but heard no response, nor any other sounds from inside.

She knocked again, louder this time. "Hello? Mr. Seabury?"

As the cape's unofficial historian, Julius Seabury was a fixture around the village, and a favorite with tourists. For more than a decade, on weekends and holidays, he had settled himself at the foot of the towering English Point Lighthouse, seated in an old wooden folding chair at a card table he'd set up to display multiple copies of his self-published books. Most were short hundred-page histories of the lighthouse, its lightkeepers, the attached museum, prominent local citizens past and present, and the village itself. The books were filled with insightful commentary accompanied by vintage photographs pulled from the museum's archives, and they sold like hotcakes—several dozen on a good day in the summer, when vacationers flooded into the area, thanks in no small part to Julius's ebullient, chatty nature.

Candy had known him for years and had talked to him on many occasions. During their conversations she'd always learned something new, and he'd provided important information that had helped her solve a mystery or two. He was a kindly soul with an active mind. Perhaps more important with the upcoming wedding ceremony, he was also the best man.

And he was missing.

He was supposed to have joined them for dinner at the Lightkeeper's Inn that evening, but he never showed up, so Candy had volunteered to go out looking for him. He was getting older, she knew, becoming frailer. He didn't get around as well as he used to, and he could be forgetful at times. Maybe he'd mixed up the date or time, or maybe he was just working on another book and everything else had slipped from his mind. She'd tried to call him but his phone just rang, unanswered. So she'd jumped into her Jeep and driven out to his cabin.

She knocked a final, halfhearted time on the red door, then backed away, stepping down off the porch. She walked the entire way around the cabin, peeking in the windows to see if she could spot anyone inside. But it was too dark to make out much, and she saw no shadows moving around. She wondered if she should try to find a way in, but decided against it for now. Breaking and entering was frowned upon by the Cape Willington Police Department. Best not to overreact—at least, not right now.

Just to make sure he wasn't meandering outside somewhere, she walked a long, wide circle around the property, going all the way back to the edge of the yard, and finally checked down by the water. But there was no sign of Julius anywhere.

Where could he be?

Only one other place, she thought.

After a final look around, she climbed into the Jeep and drove back into town. But rather than return to the Lightkeeper's Inn to rejoin the dinner party, she headed to the

English Point Lighthouse, which was located near the inn on Route 196, known locally as the Coastal Loop.

The lighthouse and its attached museum were a second home to Julius. Perhaps he was there conducting research.

Since it was after five P.M., the buildings were closed, and the parking lot was nearly empty. But she thought she recognized Julius's old red station wagon parked off to one side, where the employees and volunteers liked to park their cars. It was just a short walk from there down to the lighthouse and museum.

She loved coming here. It was always an impressive sight, the whitewashed lighthouse tower standing tall beside the red-roofed Keeper's Quarters, a two-story Victorian-style cottage housing the town's historical museum on the first floor. Upstairs were the historical society's archives, where Julius spent quite a bit of time conducting research for his books.

As she came down the walkway toward the rugged shore, she noticed that a light was on upstairs at the Keeper's Quarters, visible through one of the windows.

She felt a sense of relief. *So he is here*, she thought, and hurried down the slope toward the small compound at water's edge. It consisted of several buildings, including a separate wood-framed garage, a maintenance shed, and a low brick structure that housed the foghorn, in addition to the tower itself and the Keeper's Quarters.

She wasn't expecting to find the door to the Keeper's Quarters unlocked. Usually it was kept locked after hours, even when people were still working inside. But she hoped she could attract Julius's attention if he was upstairs, or perhaps she could get a key from Bob, the maintenance man, if he was still around.

So she was surprised when she climbed the wood steps to the side door of the Keeper's Quarters and found it not only unlocked, but ajar.

"Well, that's unusual," she said softly to herself as she pushed the door farther open and stepped inside.

The last light of the day still leaked in through the windows, so it wasn't completely dark inside. Still, shadows gathered in the corners and along the back walls, so she turned and looked for a light switch. She found it on the wall near the door and flicked it on. A row of fluorescent lights stuttered on overhead, illuminating the main exhibit hall.

Still standing by the door, which she left open behind her, she looked around and listened, but saw or heard no one. There were several rooms on this level, so she thought she'd take a quick look in all of them before heading upstairs—just so there weren't any surprises. Finding the door unlocked and open made her feel a little uneasy. Best to proceed with caution.

To her left was the Long Desk, a front counter stacked with informational brochures and handouts. She took a few steps toward it, leaning over to get a look behind it, but saw no one.

Farther back, on the other side of the counter, a shadowy hallway led to the lighthouse itself. The door at the far end of the hall, which opened into the tower, was locked at all times. Still, she rounded the counter and checked the door just to make sure. As she suspected, it was indeed locked.

The door to the office of the museum's director was locked as well—again, as it should be.

She checked the other rooms, flicking lights on and off as she moved from one area to another. They were all empty. No one in sight. And no sounds from the floor above her. If Julius was up there, she was sure she'd hear him rustling around.

She was beginning to think the place was empty. She'd been mistaken in her suspicion that somebody was there. Someone must have just forgotten to turn off a light upstairs and lock the door. Still, she had to check, just to make sure. Maybe Julius had fallen asleep while doing his research, or maybe he'd been injured somehow, though she tried not to let her mind jump to conclusions.

She passed through a doorway on her right, which led to a small exhibit room off the main hall, and took the wooden stairs to the second floor. As below, there were several rooms up here, including a narrow one under the eaves that served as a lab for identifying, cleaning, cataloging, and maintaining items in the museum's collections. A single overhead light was turned on at the top of the stairs, which she'd seen from outside. Two of the larger rooms, to her left and straight ahead, were dark, but she knew they were equipped with shelving and tables to accommodate some of the archives and the needs of researchers like Julius.

She checked the larger room first, on the cottage's ocean side. She flicked on a light switch just inside the door and took a few steps into the room, but a quick look around revealed nothing.

She turned off the light and moved to the smaller room next, which contained many of the town's older records.

And that's where she found him.

He was sprawled on the floor, lying in an awkward position, belly down, one hand thrown above his head, as if he'd been hailing a cab—or trying to defend himself. He was wearing dark brown pants and a threadbare gray cardigan sweater, which was bunched up around him. His gray hair was disheveled and sticking up in places. His head was turned sideways, so his left cheek rested on the hardwood floor. The one eye she could see was closed. His feet were at odd angles.

Candy gasped and hesitated for a few moments just inside the door as her mind registered the scene before her. Then, with a mixture of shock, concern, and surprise, she rushed to his side, falling to one knee.

"Julius," she called out, and touched him gently on the back shoulder. There was no response. She jostled him, pushing him with increasing force on the back, and called his name again, several times. Finally, reluctantly, she checked the pulse at his neck.

There was none. He was already growing cold and clammy.

She was closer to him now, and her gaze shifted. He kept his white hair cut short, and there was a bald patch on top, which made it easy to see an indented area at the back of his skull, concave and a few inches long.

Suddenly spooked, she backed away, moving swiftly in a low crouch. Her left foot hit something heavy and knocked it off to one side. It rolled across the floor with a harsh clatter.

Candy dropped into a sitting position and twisted around,

her heart thumping as she searched for the object. Finally she spotted it as it bumped against the far wall.

It was an unopened bottle of champagne.

She stared at it in confusion. What was *that* doing here?

Something about its shape jumped out at her. Her eyes were drawn to the curve around the label, the roundness of the bottle. It seemed, oddly, to match the indentation in the back of Julius's skull.

Then she realized what the bottle of champagne was. . . .

The murder weapon.

THREE

For a few moments everything became a blur as the surrounding silence and stillness quickened into a loud rush
that seemed to storm through her ears. Instinctively she
scooted backward even farther, shuffling across the wooden
floor on all fours toward the far wall of bookshelves, putting
some distance between herself, the bottle of champagne,
and the body sprawled before her.

There she stopped and took several deep breaths to calm
herself. Her mind whirred and her gaze jumped from place
to place, bouncing around the room as she struggled to
understand what she saw.

Giving herself some time to think, she studied the low,
yellowed ceiling, the rows of thick wooden shelves lined with
dusty volumes, the dark window opposite her that peered out
over the shadowed landscape, the table and chairs, the
antique lighting fixture above her, and the pockmarked, well-
varnished floor, before she could finally turn her eyes once
more back toward the body, forcing herself to focus in on it.

Julius Seabury, wearing his favorite sweater. He'd been
more than an acquaintance over the past few years—he'd

been a friend, a scholar, a man of good humor and sharp intelligence, someone who loved history and the written word . . . and this building in which he'd been found, as well as the village itself.

It was a loss she could barely comprehend.

She hoped, somewhere in the back of her mind, that she was mistaken, that she'd jumped too quickly to the wrong conclusion. She watched him for a long minute or two. But as much as she hated to admit it, she saw no signs of life from him. No movement, no fluttering of the eyes or flexing of the fingers. No rise and fall of his torso that might indicate he was breathing. No sighs or sounds coming from him. Nothing to indicate he still clung to life.

She looked toward the champagne bottle. Maybe she'd been mistaken about that part of it. Maybe it had just been an accident of some sort—he'd fallen and hit his head on the table, or died of natural causes.

But the concave wound in his head and the shape of the bottle were too similar, too perfect a fit. It wasn't hard to draw a conclusion.

It appeared someone had murdered Julius Seabury, as shocking as it sounded. But who could have done such a thing? And why?

The champagne bottle, she thought, was the first clue. Its presence here was no accident. Someone—perhaps Julius, perhaps the murderer, perhaps another person—had brought it here and used it for a terrible purpose.

She'd had a quick look at the bottle's blue and gold label, in that second or two it had scuttled away from her, rolling across the floor. And she had a pretty good idea where it came from, because she'd seen it before.

It was the same brand of champagne being served— probably right this moment—at the pre-wedding dinner party she'd just left at the Lightkeeper's Inn. Herr Georg, she knew, had selected the champagne personally when they were planning the event a month or so ago. It was a lesser-known brand from a smaller, independent producer located near the town of Épernay in the Champagne region in northern France. It was a favorite of the baker's, he'd told them at the time, and thought it would make an interesting addition to tonight's party.

She suspected there weren't too many other bottles of that exact champagne floating around town—if any. So, most likely, it was one of the bottles from the dinner party. But how did it get from the inn's dining room to this second-floor archive at the Keeper's Quarters?

As she mulled over that thought, she shifted slightly so she could pull her mobile phone out of her back pocket. She was about to dial 911, but before she did, her gaze wandered once more over the crime scene before her, and her attention was drawn away from the call as she noticed several things at once.

There were definite signs of a scuffle. One of the chairs was tipped over, and the table was pushed off-center. Also, an old book had tumbled or been pushed from the table; it was lying in a splayed fashion, facedown on the floor. Several more ancient-looking tomes were scattered across the top of the table, as were various notebooks and papers.

The disarray around her raised all sorts of questions in Candy's mind. Had Julius tried to defend himself? Had he been surprised by an unknown attacker? Or had he known the person who had wielded the bottle? Could the two of them have arranged to meet here for some reason? Did they have an argument about something that resulted in the attack?

With the phone still in her hand, forgotten for the moment, she began to notice other things. For instance, there seemed to be a bit of sand attached to the bottoms of Julius's shoes. And, she realized, the shoes themselves were scuffed—unusual for someone like Julius, who prided himself on the neatness of his appearance. His slacks were wrinkled as well, and the sweater looked unbuttoned. He wasn't wearing a bow tie, as he often did, and which he certainly would have donned today if he'd been planning on attending the dinner party at the inn.

Sand on the bottoms of his shoes, twinkling with sparkles that might be bits of sea glass . . .

Where had he picked that up? she wondered. Obviously somewhere outside, probably down by the water.

Finally, spurred by that thought, Candy forced herself to move. She lurched upward, clutching her phone tightly, and got her footing underneath her. Giving the body a wide berth, she stepped around the far side of the table and crossed to the window in the opposite wall, pausing there to look out.

The view faced north, so she could see the mouth of the English River directly in front of her and part of the village to her left. Lights were coming on, illuminating the docks and buildings that squatted along the river. The lighthouse tower was to her right, though the light atop it was hidden by the window overhang. Farther right was the edge of land and the dark sea.

Could the murderer still be out there somewhere?

Her next thought gave her a jolt: Could the murderer still be *inside* the building?

Possibly, though she'd already checked much of the place. Still, someone could be hiding in a closet, or in an alcove she hadn't searched yet, or even behind one of the larger exhibits.

Just to make sure she wasn't surprised by someone who might be lurking around, she angled around the table again, crossed to the inside wall, and shut the room's heavy wooden door, sealing in herself and Julius. The door, which was rarely closed, had a keyhole but there was no key in it. Turning around and leaning her back against it, she finally dialed 911, reporting what she'd found.

Once she was certain the police and an ambulance were on the way, she keyed off the call and made another one, to her father.

"Brace yourself, Dad," she told him after he'd asked where she was. "I have some bad news. And I need you to do something for me."

FOUR

Doc was so surprised he nearly blew bubbly out his nose.
He could scarcely believe his ears. He wasn't sure he was
hearing properly.

"Say that again," he murmured into the phone, turning
away from the other dinner guests and sticking a finger in one
ear to block out the sounds of the conversations around him.

But, at the other end of the line, his daughter warned him
not to overreact, to stay low-key for the moment to avoid
upsetting everyone at the dinner party, so he did his best to
keep his cool as she explained what had happened.

"You're kidding me," he said softly when she'd finished.
His heart sank at the news. This was something he'd never
expected to hear.

"Afraid not, Dad. We've lost our best man."

Doc could barely comprehend what he was hearing. Julius
had been a friend and an intellectual colleague. Doc had always
treasured their time together, and he was devastated to think
they'd never get to talk again. But he tried to keep his emotions
in check for now. He didn't want to interrupt the dinner party's
lighthearted atmosphere—at least, not until he had to.

But everyone would know soon enough, and Doc hated to think how Julius's death would affect them, especially Herr Georg. The two had been close friends, and certainly Julius's loss would be a shock to the baker. But beyond that, Doc had no idea what it might do to the wedding plans. It could change everything.

Doc's first concern, however, was for his daughter's safety. Lowering his voice even more and shielding his mouth with his hand in an effort to remain as inconspicuous as possible, he told her that.

She did her best to reassure him. "I've called the police and I've closed the door to the room, so for the moment I'm sealed in with the body."

At first Doc wasn't sure if that was a good idea or not, but decided it was her best move, given the circumstances. "Lock yourself in," he said "just in case whoever did this is still around."

"I can't. There's no key."

"Then stick something up against the door. A chair, maybe, or a table or a bookshelf."

"I've got my back against it. That will have to do for now. I don't want to disturb the crime scene too much."

"Don't move until the police get there." Even as the words left his mouth, Doc could hear the first siren in the distance. "Sounds like they're on their way. I'm on my way too."

"Not yet, Dad. As I said, there's something I want you to do first."

"And what's that?"

As she told him, Doc listened carefully, his face a tight mask. "Are you sure we should be thinking about that right now?" he asked when she'd finished.

"It's too suspicious a clue to pass up. You have to check it out and put a hold on everything before someone messes with the evidence."

Her father paused, thinking it over. "Okay, I'll see what I can do."

"Just be careful who you talk to, and try not to disturb the bottles too much. The police will be following up, I'm sure, but since Herr Georg is involved, I thought we should at least try to get to the bottom of this as quickly as possible."

"Got it," Doc said. "I'll let you know what we find out. And take care of yourself. Don't get into any more trouble than you already have."

"I'll keep that in mind," Candy said, and there was a pause, as if she'd held the phone away from her mouth for a few moments. "I think someone's here. I'll call you back as soon as I can."

Then she was gone.

As Doc flipped his old clamshell-design mobile phone closed, his brow crinkled in worry, he heard a voice behind him ask, "So who's in trouble?"

"Huh?" He swung around.

Maggie stood behind him, a half smile on her face. "I said, 'Who's in trouble?' Was that Candy?"

"Um, yeah, yeah." For the moment Doc couldn't think of anything else to say.

"Is everything all right? Did she find Julius?"

Doc hesitated before he nodded and said as noncommittally as possible, "She did."

"When will she be back? They're going to start serving dinner in a few minutes."

Glancing at the table, Doc saw that the appetizers had arrived, and the other dinner guests were munching, drinking, and talking among themselves.

"She . . . she's been delayed," he said softly, and rose. "I'll tell you about it shortly, but right now I have to talk to your fiancé."

"Why? Is something going on?" Maggie's gaze sharpened on him. "You look stressed out."

Doc shook his head. "Must have been something I ate."

"But you haven't eaten anything yet," Maggie pointed out as Doc excused himself and walked around to the far side of the table. There he bent over and whispered something into the ear of Herr Georg, who listened attentively before looking up at Doc with widened eyes. The baker nodded stoically, rose stiffly, and followed Doc from the room.

They found a relatively quiet place to talk in the hallway outside the dining room, back near the kitchen. Looking around to make sure they were alone, Doc filled Herr Georg in on their mission. "We need to keep this between ourselves for the moment," he began in a voice barely above a whisper, "but something's happened to Julius. Apparently someone knocked him in the noggin with a bottle of champagne. Unfortunately, it was a fatal blow."

A look of total disbelief crossed the baker's face. When he spoke, his voice was low and coarse. "But that's not possible. There must be some mistake."

"Candy found his body at the museum," Doc said softly. "The police are on their way to the scene."

Herr Georg became distraught. "But that's incomprehensible. How can something like this happen? He can't be gone! I just talked to him a few days ago and he was fine."

Doc nodded in understanding as the baker continued, giving him a few moments to process this information before he continued with the rest of his news. "Here's the thing: The bottle of champagne Candy found near the body had a label from House Villers-Moussy."

Upon hearing this, Herr Georg's normally reddened face went deathly pale. "But how can that be? Are you sure?"

"That's what Candy says."

"But . . . that's the champagne I ordered specially for tonight's dinner."

"Exactly," said Doc, "and we have to count the bottles that are here to find out if any are missing from the stock you ordered. Do you remember how many there were before we started opening them?"

The baker tugged at his white moustache and stammered about a bit, still in shock, before he answered. "But of course. I ordered two cases, six bottles each. Twelve in all. I thought that should be enough, since none of us are heavy drinkers—though Ellie's put down several glasses so far."

"Did you bring the cases here yourself?"

"No, they were delivered directly to the inn. I believe we've opened four bottles so far, though we can quickly check what's

on the table. The rest must be back in the kitchen somewhere."
He glanced toward the set of double doors near them, at the
end of the hall, through which the waiters emerged.

Doc followed his gaze and nodded. "Okay. Let's see what
we can find out. Hopefully the bottle that killed Julius wasn't
from your stock. But if it was, we could have a mess of trouble
on our hands."

FIVE

Maggie watched, curious, as her fiancé and Doc Holliday walked quickly and solemnly from the room, their heads bent together, talking in low tones.

"Well, that's odd," she said to herself, her gaze following them until they disappeared out the door and into the hall beyond. "I wonder where they're off to."

Why would they leave the dinner party so quickly like that, especially with the entrées just about to arrive? And without saying anything to anyone—especially her?

Almost immediately her curiosity gave way to suspicion. "Something's up," she muttered under her breath as her brows fell together. In her mind, she added, *And I'm going to find out what it is.*

Could it have something to do with Candy? Doc had said she'd been delayed. What did that mean? Could it have something to do with Julius? Or with Blueberry Acres? Or could it be something else, something she hadn't considered?

What was going on?

As her mind whirred, she felt a flutter in her stomach and

a rising sense that something bad was occurring that would disrupt their wedding plans.

No way, she thought. *I'm not going to let that happen.*

So with her jaw firmly set, she glanced around the table, trying to decide on her next move. She had to know why their pre-wedding dinner party was being interrupted in such a strange way, but reasoned that she couldn't just waltz away from the table, leaving her remaining dinner guests unattended. That would be rude.

She needed a pretext—a reason to excuse herself from the table for a few minutes. And she decided to go with the most obvious one, since it was the only thing she could think of at the moment.

"Oh, all that champagne! It's so delicious, isn't it? But I think I drank too much too fast!" she said to no one in particular, and she leaned over toward her daughter. "I have to go to the little girls' room. Would you keep an eye on everything until I get back?"

Amanda, who was munching on a stuffed mushroom cap, nodded absently, and looking around the table, Maggie saw that the others were contentedly enjoying their appetizers as well. No one seemed to notice that anything was wrong. If she was going to go, now was the time.

Without any further hesitation, she rose from her chair. "I'll be right back!" she said, holding up a finger. "Don't go anywhere!" And with that, she hurried out of the alcove, across the dining room, and into the hallway beyond.

She looked in both directions. They were, somewhat surprisingly, empty. No sign of Doc or Georg.

Where had they gone?

To her right, at the back end of the hall, a set of double swinging doors led to the kitchen. At the other end, the hall emptied into the inn's lobby area, lounge, and front entrance.

She turned first in one direction, then the other, trying to decide which way the two men might have gone. After a few moments of indecision, she turned toward the lobby first and started off.

It was a Wednesday night in mid-May, with the summer

season still a couple of weeks away. The calm before the storm. Not surprisingly, the inn's lobby, like the hallway, was deserted. She heard voices and the sounds of soft music and clinking glasses from the lounge, but a quick glance through the doorway revealed no Doc and no Georg in there—just a very subdued atmosphere and a few people talking in low tones.

She made a quick sweep of the general lobby area, peering into alcoves and even glancing behind the main desk, before heading back the way she'd come, toward the kitchen. It was, she surmised, the only other place they could have gone.

But she stopped just outside the double doors at the end of the hall and wondered if she should enter. Were civilians like her allowed inside that inner sanctum? Would she be breaking some sort of unspoken protocol? Would they kick her out or cause a scene if she wandered in there uninvited?

"Only one way to find out," she said to herself, and pushed through the swinging door on the right.

She entered the warm, well-lit, gleaming kitchen, a cacophony of stainless steel tables, shelves, racks, drawers, work spaces, ovens, cooktops, and refrigerators, as well as pots, pans, and cooking utensils hanging from pegs and hooks along one wall. The place was dominated by a large center island, over which hung a huge commercial-sized ventilation hood. Its fan gave off a mild hum as it drew out the heat, smoke, and cooking odors.

There were several people working in the kitchen, wearing white aprons or chef coats. One or two also had on tall, narrow chef's hats, which she knew were called toques, although she'd learned that only when she started working at the bakery. Georg often wore one when he was baking.

No one seemed to notice her, or even look around to see who had entered the kitchen. She realized that waiters, waitresses, and staff members probably came and went so often that no one bothered to pay attention.

She was going to announce her arrival but hesitated. No point in disturbing anyone. She'd just make a quick search of the area and see if she could find her soon-to-be husband.

But at first glance, she saw neither Doc nor Georg.

They seemed to have disappeared. Again, she thought, where could they have gone?

On an impulse she started across the kitchen, walking quickly and confidently, as if she belonged there, eyes pointed straight ahead as she went. She headed toward a doorway in the opposite wall that seemed to lead back out of the kitchen, toward the rear of the building. Maybe the two of them had gone in that direction.

At first she thought she'd simply make a fast exit, before anyone noticed she was there. But then she realized she was missing an opportunity. So, instead, she stopped beside a young blond-haired man in his early twenties who was chopping vegetables at a stainless steel table. "Excuse me," she said. "Did you happen to notice two white-haired gentlemen pass through here a few minutes ago?"

He stopped chopping and glanced toward her. Then he pointed toward the far door. "They went back to the storage rooms with the chef."

She patted him on the shoulder. "Thanks. And great job, by the way. The food here is terrific."

He smiled easily. "Thanks!"

She headed off again, through the doorway and into a green-tiled corridor beyond, much starker in appearance than the front carpeted hallway. Here she saw several doors on either side, and another one at the opposite end of the corridor, probably leading to the outside.

But still no Doc and Georg.

"Hmm," she said, pondering her options.

Most of the doors that lined the corridor were closed, and possibly locked, but one stood ajar, toward the end on the left, and she thought she could hear voices coming from inside that room. She approached it somewhat stealthily, as if she were a spy creeping up on an enemy discussing military secrets. With her ear cocked she could hear snatches of conversation.

"One's definitely missing from this case," she heard a male voice say. It didn't sound like either Doc or Georg.

"Are you certain?" That sounded like her husband-to-be.

"I'll double-check, but yes, that's my impression."

"We have to make sure," said a gravelly voice that could belong only to Doc. "And we need to seal this room until the police get here. This could be evidence, and we have to make sure it's undisturbed."

That stopped Maggie in her tracks.

Evidence? Evidence of what?

She thought she heard movement then, the sounds of shuffling shoes, coming from the storage room at the end of the hall, and the door opened farther, as if someone was about to emerge into the corridor. That spooked her for some reason, and an instinctive flight response surged through her. She decided in a split second that she didn't want to be spotted here, since she was afraid it would look like she was eavesdropping, sneaking around, even stalking her fiancé. It was an impression she didn't want to project, so she shifted around, looking back the way she'd come. It was time to retreat.

But she was too late. Someone was emerging from the room at the end, talking to someone else who still remained inside. She didn't catch the words, for her head was swinging back and forth as she sought a place to hide. She reached out and tested the knob of the door closest to her on the left, and was surprised to find that it opened. Without giving it a second thought, she pushed through the door, darted inside, and closed it quietly behind her.

She stood in total darkness with her back against the door, holding her breath as she heard someone walk hurriedly along the corridor outside. The person quickly passed her door and, she surmised, went into the kitchen.

She waited in the darkness, her heart beating strongly in her chest, wondering what to do next. But after a few moments of thinking it through, she decided that she was probably just being silly. Who was she hiding from? Georg? Doc? And why? She had nothing to hide. She'd done nothing wrong. She'd simply been trying to find out what was going on.

"Maggie, you're overreacting," she said under her breath. "And why are you standing here talking to yourself in the dark, you ninny? At least turn on the lights."

Tentatively she reached out with her right hand, feeling

along the wall beside her, fingers probing for a light switch.
It took a few moments but she finally located it, and moved
the switch upward to the on position.

Overhead fluorescent lights flickered to life, casting an
eerie green glow. She relaxed a bit as she took in her
surroundings—mostly metal shelves that reached from floor
to ceiling, stocked with a variety of large canned goods. Her
gaze slid around from shelf to shelf, and then angled downward toward the floor . . .

Where she saw the body sprawled out before her, lying
facedown on the cold tile in the middle of the room.

SIX

Not too far away, Candy also stood with her back against a different door, hesitant to move. While she'd been talking to her father on the phone, she thought she'd heard sounds from downstairs—the creak of a wood floorboard, the echoing shuffle of footsteps. At first she'd been certain the police had arrived. Now she wasn't so sure.

Other than those few obscure sounds, she'd heard nothing to indicate someone else was in the building. No one had called out to her. No one had rushed up the stairs to her aid. She hadn't seen any flashing lights coming through the window, but she could hear the siren of an approaching vehicle—probably the ambulance, she surmised. It sounded as if it was still a few blocks away, coming through Fowler's Corner or over the bridge across the English River.

So if the police and ambulance hadn't arrived yet, who was downstairs? Who had made those sounds? Had she imagined them—or was someone sneaking around down there?

She had the fleeting thought that the killer might have returned to the scene of the crime. But that didn't make any sense. Who would be dumb enough to murder someone and then hang around until the police showed up?

Unless something had gone wrong. Unless the killer had come back for *her*.

But she shook that thought away. Ten minutes ago, no one knew she'd be here. She hadn't known herself that she was stopping by.

Unless the killer had hung around and watched her enter the building—and knew she had probably discovered the body.

But still, the pieces didn't fit. Why would the killer be concerned if the body was found? It was bound to happen sometime. So why would someone want to kill her?

Unless some sort of evidence had been left behind.

Once again, her gaze swept around the room, but from where she stood, she couldn't see anything that would incriminate anyone, other than the bottle of champagne.

Maybe the killer had come back for *that*.

Candy, you're jumping to conclusions, she thought, trying to calm herself. It was probably just the maintenance man, or a cleaning person, or someone who had wandered in through the cottage's front door, which she'd left open when she'd arrived, allowing herself a quick escape if she needed it. Just someone checking to make sure everything was all right.

Yes, it was probably something like that, and she toyed with the idea of calling out. But any words she might form in her brain got stuck in her throat, which had become dry and raspy, and refused to come out.

So she waited and listened.

And then she heard, through the closed door at her back, what sounded like footsteps coming up the stairs to the second floor. More than one or two of the wooden steps creaked when weight was put on them. The sounds were faint but she could still hear a slight sliding noise echo up the stairwell as someone's shoes moved hesitantly from step to step, a few at a time, pausing often.

Someone was definitely out there. But who?

Right now, she wasn't about to open the door to find out. She remained with her back against it, though now she could feel her heart beating strongly, and her breathing sounded loud in her ears.

The footsteps reached the top of the stairs and paused there, on the landing. After several moments a voice called out—a man's voice.

"Hello? Anyone up here?"

Candy's body tensed. Whoever he was, he was on the second floor!

It took several beats of her heart as her mind worked, but she finally realized the voice sounded familiar. She might know who it was. Still, she was uncertain, so she said nothing.

"Hello?" the man repeated.

Through the door, she could hear the footsteps approaching, growing closer and closer.

Then someone knocked, sending small vibrations through the wooden door at her back. "Anyone in there?" A pause. "I saw the light on and the door open downstairs." Another pause. "It's Owen Peabody, the museum's director," he clarified.

"Owen?"

He must have heard her voice through the door.

"Who's in there?" he called from the other side.

"It's . . . it's . . ." Finally able to speak and move, she shifted awkwardly. Her hand reached for the doorknob, but it was already turning, so she backed away a few paces.

The door opened a foot or so, and a florid face peeked into the room.

"Hello?"

With some effort, she finally managed to push a few words out of her mouth. "Owen, it . . . it's Candy Holliday."

Standing just outside the doorframe, he was a short, squat, balding man wearing a tweed sport jacket and an open-collared shirt. He had a thick neck, heavy jowls, and close-set dark eyes partially hidden in the shadow of an overhanging brow.

"Candy?" he said, sounding confused.

Owen had served as the museum's director for several years now. He'd taken over the position after the unfortunate death of his predecessor, Charlotte Depew. Early in his tenure, Candy had interviewed him for an article in the village newspaper, the *Cape Crier.* At the time she'd been its community correspondent, before being promoted to interim managing editor. She'd left her full-time job at the paper just a few months ago, after the beginning of the year, wanting to spend more time out at the blueberry farm. She didn't come into town as much as she used to, so she hadn't run into Owen in a while.

"What's going on?" he asked, recovering from his surprise at seeing her. "What are you doing up here? The museum is closed, you know."

"Yes, I know, but . . ." Candy had to swallow several times to ease the dryness of her throat before she spoke again. "I'm afraid there's been a terrible accident."

His eyes narrowed and his voice took on a hard edge. "What kind of accident? What do you mean?"

She moved aside then, and the director pushed the door fully open. He took a few commanding steps into the room, then stopped in shock as he saw the body.

"Who is that? What's happened here?" His words took on an accusatory tone.

Candy explained quickly, telling him how she'd found the body while searching for Julius after he failed to show up for their dinner party. "I was worried about him, and discovered him here, just like that." She pointed toward the body. "He was dead when I arrived. I've called the police. They're on their way, and an ambulance," she finished. "I actually thought you might be them—but, of course, you're not."

"No, no, I'm not," Owen finally managed to say, working his mouth strangely, which set his jowls jiggling. He looked as if he wanted to move closer to the body but couldn't. "But . . . how did this happen? How could such a thing take place here, at the museum?"

"I don't know," Candy said, "but I think *that* is the murder weapon." She indicated the bottle of champagne, rolled up against the wall.

As the realization of what had happened began to sink in, Owen let out a small, unearthly wail. "But this is a terrible tragedy," he said. "Just terrible. Julius was, well, I just can't believe it."

His gaze shifted away from the body, glancing around the room. It settled for a few moments on the champagne bottle, before moving to the table and the dusty old volumes scattered across it. "But what was he doing up here?"

"I don't know. I've been wondering that myself."

On an impulse, Owen crossed the room, stopping to look at the books arrayed on the table. His head tilted to one side so he could read the words on one of the spines. He leaned forward in curiosity. "Land deeds," he said.

"What?" Candy wasn't sure what he meant.

Owen pointed at the books on the table. "Historical records of some of the early land transactions and deeds here on the cape. Mid-eighteenth century. He must have been conducting research on them, though I have no idea why he was up here this late at night working on it."

"Was it for a book he was writing?" Candy asked.

Owen waved his hand dismissively. "No, no, nothing like that. This is most unusual." He looked as if he was about to say more, but his gaze shifted again, and he spotted something that seemed to horrify him. Moving quickly for such a heavy man, he walked around the table to the far side of the room, close to the window. "What is *this* doing on the floor?" he asked as he bent over to retrieve something. "It could become damaged."

Before Candy could warn him not to disturb the crime scene, he had plucked up the book that had fallen to the floor. It had a black, battered cover, she saw, and looked very old. He lifted it gingerly and turned it over in his hands so he could examine it. "Fortunately the spine's not broken. It must have fallen from the table." He fanned the pages a little, checking them.

"Owen, don't—" Candy began, but stopped when a folded slip of paper fell from between the pages of the book and fluttered to the floor.

"What's this?" Owen asked, stooping again.

"We shouldn't touch anything," Candy cautioned. "It's a

crime scene. It needs to be preserved so the police can conduct an investigation."

But Owen didn't pay any attention to her. Instead, he straightened. With thick fingers he unfolded the paper, removed a pair of wire-rimmed reading glasses from his jacket pocket, settled them on his nose, and studied the writing on the paper.

"Just a bunch of names," he said, unimpressed. "Bosworth. Ethingham. Whitby. Rainsford. Palfrey. Sykes." He made a face. "Old family names, some of the early settlers here on the cape. And, of course, descendants of most of those families still live here. Three of them sit on the board." He paused and adjusted his glasses. "Then there are two initials below that: *L. B.*, underlined twice. And these words here." He frowned as he pointed with a pinky at some writing at the bottom of the note. "'Foul Mouth,' it says." He crinkled his nose as he spelled it out, as if it were something distasteful to him, then shook his head and refolded the paper. "I don't know what any of it means. Just odd scribblings, probably. Nothing important, as far as I can tell. It's probably been stuck inside that book for years."

Absently, he slipped the paper into his jacket pocket and closed up the book reverently as Candy heard dying sirens outside and saw flashing lights reflected through the windowpanes. The lights flashed vividly on Owen's face, which turned alternately red and white. She could hear car doors opening, a rush of movement. Moments later, the police and paramedics entered the building in a dense clatter of footsteps and voices.

SEVEN

At first Maggie couldn't quite comprehend what she was seeing—or maybe, she thought, she *hoped* she wasn't seeing it. She blinked several times, thinking the figure lying prone before her might simply disappear in a *poof!* It certainly would make her life a lot easier if that were to happen, if it would just go away.

But it didn't, much to her dismay. It stayed right where it was, there in the center of the room, facedown, unmoving. So she'd have to deal with it somehow.

She gulped and thought of calling out, or maybe letting out a hearty scream, which surely would bring someone running to help. Doc and Georg were somewhere nearby. They'd know what to do.

But before she could muster up the vocal power needed, she heard, much to her surprise, a low moan echoing through the room, like the sound a ghost might make.

She froze. It took her a few moments to realize the moan was coming from the body.

"Oh!" was all she could manage to say.

The person was alive then. She hadn't been certain earlier. Now at least she knew.

Eyes wide, fingers feeling cold, her throat choked with uncertainty, she took a step toward it. And then another.

She stopped when, suddenly, the body moved. The shoulders shifted slightly, the eyes fluttered, and the head, resting on its right cheek, slid a micro-inch across the cold floor.

He was young, maybe in his early twenties. Longish dark hair, with thin black eyebrows. A pale face, straight nose, wide mouth with reddish lips. A long, thin frame, wearing black pants and a white shirt.

It was one of the waiters, Maggie realized as she took another step closer, though she didn't know his name. He hadn't served their table tonight, but she'd seen him earlier scooting around the dining room, waiting on other guests.

"Um, hello?" she called to him gently, still a short distance away.

Another moan, as if in answer.

"Are you . . . okay?"

She waited, and when there was no reply, said, "Okay, I admit, that was a dumb question." She hesitated before moving any closer. "I suppose I should . . . go get someone?"

The eyes fluttered again.

"Yes, I'll go get help," Maggie said, answering her own question. She finally moved quickly, back across the room and out the door, where she almost ran headlong into Doc, who was walking along the hallway.

"Maggie!" he said as he jerked to a sudden stop, narrowly avoiding running into her. "What are you—?"

"There's a body!" Maggie said, interrupting him. And she pointed back the way she'd come. "In there. A waiter. You'd better go take a look at him."

"A waiter?" Doc's brow dropped as he processed this new information.

"He's alive," Maggie said urgently, "and he needs help!"

Doc's head swiveled toward the door through which she'd just emerged. He nodded, shifted on his heels, and disappeared into the room.

Before Maggie could follow him back inside, she heard a familiar voice behind her. "What's this about a body?"

She turned and saw her fiancé at the other end of the hall-way, just coming back from the kitchen. He looked worried about something. Seeing the expression of concern on his face, she ran to him and threw her arms around him. "Oh, Georg! I'm so glad to see you!"

It took him a moment to compose himself, as he seemed startled by her sudden appearance back here, but he quickly returned her hug. "Maggie, *mein Liebchen*. I thought you were still at the party. I went looking for you. When I couldn't find you I . . ." He let his words trail off, and Maggie filled in the blanks.

"I wondered what you and Doc were doing," she said, talking quickly, "so I followed you. I heard your voices and I didn't want you to think I was snooping on you, so I hid in that room back there." She turned slightly and pointed. "And I found a body lying on the floor. One of the waiters. Oh, Georg! I didn't know what to do. Doc's looking at him right now."

As if on cue, Doc emerged from the room, spotted them, and hurried in their direction. "The boy was knocked uncon-scious," Doc informed them. "He's the waiter we've been looking for—the one who moved the cases of champagne into that back room. I'm not sure what happened to him yet—he's still groggy—but I called an ambulance. They're on their way. I'll stay with him until they get here. But would you inform Alby, who I think is at the front desk, and Oliver, if he's still around? They need to know what's going on." Alby Alcott was the assistant innkeeper, while Oliver LaForce was the proprietor of the Lightkeeper's Inn.

Georg nodded. "I'll let Colin know as well. He's out looking for that waiter right now."

Maggie knew that Colin Trevor Jones was the inn's exec-utive chef, but the names and details were flying by so fast she could barely keep up with them. "What's going on?" she asked, turning back to her fiancé and looking him in the eyes. "What happened to that waiter? And why are you both sneaking around back here?"

Herr Georg kissed her lightly on the cheek. "I'll explain right away, as soon as we inform the inn's staff." He turned his attention back to Doc and gave him a nod. "At least there haven't been two deaths tonight."

"You got that right," Doc said as he headed back into the room.

"Two deaths?" Maggie said, her breath leaving her in a rush. It appeared her instincts had been right. Something bad had happened. "But—"

She never got any further, for Georg took her by the hand and led her toward the kitchen and the lobby area beyond. "Come, my dear. We have people to see first, and then we have much to discuss. All your questions will be answered in good time."

"But . . . what about the dinner party? What about our guests?"

"The guests will have to take care of themselves for the moment," Georg said over his shoulder as they made their way across the kitchen. "We'll return to them as soon as we can. But first, I'm afraid, I have some bad news, and then you and I have some important decisions to make."

"Decisions? About what?"

Georg turned back to look at her, and by the expression on his face, she knew their upcoming conversation was going to be a difficult one.

EIGHT

"Okay, Ms. Holliday, let's go over it all again," said Chief Darryl Durr of the Cape Willington Police Department. "From the beginning, if you don't mind."

Candy took a long breath and checked her watch. Nearly an hour and a half had passed since the police had arrived at the museum. Almost immediately they'd ushered her and Owen away from the crime scene, out of the upstairs room, and downstairs to separate first-floor rooms, where they'd both been sequestered. Candy hadn't seen Owen since, but she guessed that, like her, he was being extensively questioned about everything that had happened that evening.

She'd already given a statement to one of the police officers, Molly Prospect, whom she'd known for several years. Molly was professional as always, and relatively understanding and consoling.

"I know it's difficult, Candy," she'd said at one point during the initial interview, "but I just have a few more questions for you. Now, when you discovered the body . . ."

After about an hour or so, Chief Durr had entered the room and Officer Prospect had left, closing the door behind her.

Candy had gone over everything again for him, and when she'd finished, he asked her for another recounting.

She was tired. She was hungry. She was still in shock about the loss of Julius, and felt a hollow place inside her. Who could have done such a thing to such a sweet man? She wondered what her father had found out about the bottle of champagne, and if he'd told Maggie and Georg about Julius's death. How would they take the news? Obviously, not well. And what would it do to the wedding? She wanted to get back to them and commiserate with them, tell them what had happened, what she'd found, and figure out how to get through this together.

But, she knew, that would have to wait until the chief was satisfied with the account of her involvement in the incident here tonight.

So she started again, from the beginning, explaining how Julius had failed to show up for the dinner party, and how she'd gone looking for him, first at his cabin, then here at the Keeper's Quarters. As she talked, the chief questioned her about every detail.

"Was anyone else in the building when you arrived?"

"No, I don't believe so. I checked all the rooms down here before I went upstairs. Owen showed up a little later."

"What position was Mr. Seabury lying in when you found him?"

"Facedown, with his cheek against the floor."

"Did you touch the body?"

"Only to see if he was still breathing."

"And?"

"No, he wasn't."

"Did you disturb anything around him?"

"No, I tried not to."

"What about the champagne bottle?"

"Well," she admitted, "I might have hit it with my foot and knocked it aside."

"Do you know where it came from? Is the label familiar?"

Candy admitted that it was, and explained about the cases

of champagne Herr Georg had ordered for tonight's dinner party.

The chief nodded at her admission. "Yes, we're checking out that connection right now. We've talked to both Georg Wolfsburger and your father, and for the moment they both seem to have pretty good alibis for tonight, since they were both at the dinner party. But there's been another development." He paused, and after a few moments said, "I suppose I can tell you this, since you'll find out shortly anyway, but apparently they found one of the waiters unconscious in a storage room off the inn's kitchen."

Candy was suddenly alarmed. "Who found him?"

"Your friend Maggie Tremont."

This added to her shock. "Is Maggie all right?"

"She's fine."

"What happened?"

"I can't give you the details right now."

"Who is he—this waiter she found?"

"We're not releasing his name yet, but we're trying to find out if he's connected to this whole episode."

"Were any of the champagne bottles missing?"

He gave her a stoic look. "Again, we're not releasing that information just yet. But I'm sure you'll find out soon enough." Another pause. "Do you know anyone who might have wanted to harm Julius Seabury?"

Candy didn't hesitate before she shook her head. "I've racked my brain about that, Chief. He was such a kind person. I don't think he ever had a cross word with anyone. I can't imagine why anyone would want to do this to him."

The chief's jaw tightened as he looked at her with a more scrutinizing gaze. "You realize, of course, that you were at the inn earlier in the evening, and you could have had access to those cases of champagne."

"So could a lot of people," Candy countered.

The chief nodded, accepting her response. "Yes, that may be true, but so far you're the only person we know of who was at both the inn and here at the museum tonight."

Candy's face tightened but she said nothing.

The chief continued. "According to Owen Peabody, you were up here alone with the body. Is that correct?"

Candy nodded hesitantly. "Yes, but—"

"He says he saw you standing over the body."

"He what? I wasn't—"

"Let's be clear about this, Ms. Holliday," the chief said, cutting her off. "You were the only person up here, alone with the body, when Owen arrived here tonight. He saw no one else in the building, nor was anyone else spotted on the premises around that time. And as we both know, you have a history of stumbling into these sorts of situations. It's happened several times over the past few years. And to anyone with a suspicious mind, this makes one time too many."

Candy felt a chill go up her spine. "What are you saying?"

The chief leaned forward and put his elbows on the table between them. When he continued, he was businesslike and somewhat distant, even though she thought they'd developed a somewhat respectable professional relationship over the past few years.

"I'm just stating the facts, Ms. Holliday. So far we're not accusing anyone of anything, but your continued involvement in this series of murders that has taken place in the village, well, frankly, it's troubling. Do you have any explanation as to why you seem to be at the center of these events that have been plaguing our town?"

As a matter of fact, Candy thought in the back of her mind, she did—or at least, she had an inkling of an idea. But she wasn't ready to admit that to the chief just yet. Most of what she believed was circumstantial. She had no direct evidence of anyone's involvement. But the very fact that Julius had died while apparently researching old land deeds was . . . *troubling*, she thought, to borrow a word from the chief.

During all her accounts of this evening's events, she hadn't mentioned the slip of paper that had fluttered out of the book Owen had picked up off the floor, uncertain whether it had any relevance or not. But at least one of the names on that list raised her suspicion.

Sykes.

She'd had several encounters with members of the Sykes family over the past few years, and most of them had been unpleasant. Some of her encounters with them had been downright dangerous. The idea that a member of the Sykes family might be involved in Julius's death gave her greater concern than she wanted to admit. But she also felt she couldn't come right out and make an accusatory statement about them to the police—at least, not right now. She had to think about it first. She had to assess all that had happened tonight.

And she had to determine if that slip of paper had any real link to Julius Seabury.

There was an easy way to do that, she knew, but now was not the time.

And what about the other family names on that slip of paper?

Bosworth. Ethingham. Whitby. Rainsford. Palfrey.

L. B.

And what about the words written at the bottom of the paper, according to Owen?

Foul Mouth?

Had Owen mentioned to the police that he'd found a slip of paper in a book in that room? He'd said it wasn't important—"odd scribblings" was the phrase he used.

Yes, but *whose* odd scribblings?

She looked up at the chief, who was waiting for a reply to his last question. Finally, after thinking it all through, she answered him.

"Right now, Chief, I have no idea."

He held her gaze for the longest time, as if judging her response. Finally, he nodded, placed his palms on the table, and pushed himself to his feet. "Somehow I knew you'd say that," he said, looking suddenly weary. He reached up, lifted his cap, and scratched his head with a few fingers. "Why do I get the feeling we're playing a game of cat and mouse here?"

Candy shrugged innocently. "I'm not sure I know what you mean."

That made him smile, but there was no humor in it. "No,

I'm sure you don't." He started toward the door, opened it, and turned back toward her. "You're free to go, for now. But stay close, in case we need to talk again. And I'm sure you know this, but if you think of anything that might aid in our investigation, contact myself or someone at the department immediately."

"I'll surely do that, Chief."

He nodded. "Just do me a favor, Candy, and take care of yourself. And whatever you do, for the sake of both of us, don't get into any more trouble, okay?"

Now it was Candy's turn to smile. "I'll try my best, Chief. Just like I always do."

NINE

Once out of the building and into the cool night air, Candy paused, took in a few deep breaths, and looked around as she considered her next move.

Myriad thoughts ran through her mind, most of them focused on Julius. What had he been doing up in the archives? Why had he been researching deeds? How did the champagne bottle get up there? And what about the list of names? Did that have anything to do with his death? Was the Sykes family somehow involved in his murder?

And what about the unconscious waiter, the one the chief had mentioned? Did he have anything to do with this? If so, what was the connection?

There was a simple answer to that last question: the champagne bottle. Someone must have walked it over to the museum. A waiter was the logical person. Had Julius asked for it for some reason? Had he been drinking? Or planned to drink? It might explain his disheveled clothes. But what about the sand on the bottoms of his shoes?

Sand.

Where had it come from?

Her head twisted to her right, eastward, toward the sea. From where she stood, she could hear the waves slapping gently against the shoreline. She was tempted to head down that way, to the waterfront, to perhaps get an idea of where Julius might have picked up the sand on his shoes. Much of this part of the coastline was rocky, especially the wedge of land upon which the English Point Lighthouse and Museum stood. But she knew there were also small stretches of sandy coastline just south of the buildings and parking lot, a few hundred steps away. She wanted to check the area and see if she could spot anything suspicious, possibly turn up a clue or two.

But, she decided with some reluctance as her gaze shifted around, this wasn't the right time. Not only was the place crawling with police officers, who would notice her movements, but it was also too dark to make any sort of an effective search. She might slip out on those wet, black rocks, fall, and break something. Or completely miss anything that might be useful. Better, she thought, to wait until daylight, when she could see where she was going and what she was doing.

Besides, there were other things she needed to check on first.

So, instead, she hurried up the sloping walkway toward the parking lot, where a couple of squad cars with lights still flashing flanked her Jeep. Off to one side of the lot, several officers were bunched together, talking amongst themselves. She eyed them surreptitiously as she unlocked the Jeep and climbed inside, but they paid her no attention.

Deciding to move on quickly while she could, she started the engine, flicked on the headlights, and made a beeline for the Lightkeeper's Inn, which was only a block or so away. She made the trip in just a few minutes, found a parking spot along Ocean Avenue, and headed into the inn.

The dining room was dimly lit and somewhat subdued, though still busy enough for a weeknight. But as she'd expected, the alcove where the pre-wedding dinner party had taken place was deserted. The table had been cleared off, and a new crisp white linen tablecloth laid upon it.

Unused place settings and silverware were set out. But no Maggie, no Herr Georg, no Doc, nor anyone else she knew.

She glanced around and flagged down a passing waiter. "Do you know what happened to the folks who were eating in here a little while ago?" she asked.

He looked around at the empty private room. "They've finished," he said simply, and nodded toward the front of the inn. "I think they moved into the lounge."

Candy thanked him and headed in that direction. Like the dining room, the lights in the lounge were turned down low, making the burning logs in the open stone fireplace along the far wall even more eye-catching. Candy paused in the entranceway as she scanned the room. And there, sitting in a wood-and-leather booth to one side of the fireplace, were the people she sought—her father, Maggie, and Herr Georg, along with Maggie's mother, Ellie, Amanda and Cameron, and Malcolm and Ralph.

Her father glanced around, spotted her, and waved her over, rising from his seat as she approached. "Hi, pumpkin, glad you finally made it back," he said, giving her a tight hug and a kiss on the cheek. "We've been so worried about you. Are you all right?"

"As good as can be expected," Candy replied as Maggie came over and gave her a hug also. Herr Georg scooted aside, making room for her in the booth.

"So, is it true?" Maggie asked after Candy had settled herself, voicing the question they all seemed to have. "Is Julius really gone?"

Candy nodded. "I'm sorry, but yes, it's true. I saw his body myself."

"It's still hard to believe," said Herr Georg, his voice cracking a bit. "He was such a wonderful man, with a zest for life, and never a harsh word for anyone. Why would someone want to harm him?"

Candy had a ready answer, as she'd thought about that question a lot over the past couple of hours. "Because I think he was onto something," she said. "Something he uncovered in his research."

"What could it possibly be?" asked her father.

Candy shook her head. "I don't know exactly, but according to Owen Peabody, Julius was apparently looking through records of old land deeds."

Maggie made a face. "Land deeds? Why would he be interested in that?"

"I thought he was writing a book about the founding families in Cape Willington," Doc said. "At least, that's what I heard. He also told me a little while ago he was thinking of writing a book about the controversy over alewives."

"Alewives?" Maggie said, sounding confused. "What's an alewife? Like a tavern owner's wife?"

"In the Middle Ages, yes, it had that kind of meaning," Doc said. "But here in Maine it's a type of herring that lives in the ocean but spawns in rivers, like the St. Croix, which serves as the boundary between us and New Brunswick. Apparently they've had a negative effect on the smallmouth bass population."

There was silence around the table as everyone tried to digest this curious bit of information.

"But why would he write about that?" Herr Georg finally asked.

"Sounds fishy to me," Maggie agreed.

Doc just shrugged. "I don't know. That's how Julius was."

"Did he ever mention a book about land deeds—local property?" Candy asked.

Doc shook his head. "Not that I can remember."

She looked over at Herr Georg. "You were close to him. You two talked a lot. Did he tell you anything about what he was working on?"

The baker scrunched up his face, as if thinking hard. "Well, I, um, I can't recall," he said noncommittally.

Candy studied him for a moment, then turned back to her father, changing the subject. "Dad, have you ever heard of someone—or someplace—called Foul Mouth? Does that ring a bell?"

Doc didn't have to give it much thought before he answered. "Sure, it's a fairly common name in the Northeast. Falmouth was an early name for Portland. The settlers took it from a seaside town in England. Of course, when it was first established, the city we know today as Portland was called Casco, but it was changed to Falmouth in 1658 by the Massachusetts Bay Colony. Then in 1786 the portion of the city out on the neck was split off and rechristened Portland, after a town on the southern coast of England. Part of the original town of Falmouth remains today, just north of Portland, and there are also towns called Falmouth in Massachusetts and Jamaica."

Candy had known most of that—well, not the dates specifically—but let her father confirm it all for her. When he'd finished, she hesitated before she said, "Thanks, but I'm not sure that's what I'm looking for, Dad. It's pronounced the same but it's two words—Foul Mouth." And she spelled it out, just as Owen had done a few hours earlier. "It sounds like something that, well, something that smells funny, I guess. Or maybe someone who swears a lot?" She was just speculating at this point, and the tone of her voice communicated that.

Doc gave her a blank look. After a few moments he said, "Are you sure it's not just a misspelling?" He paused. "What has this got to do with Julius anyway?"

Candy sidestepped the question for now. Instead, she asked, "What about some of the town's founding families, like the Whitbys, the Rainsfords, the Ethinghams, and the Palfreys? Oh, and the Bosworths. And, um, the Sykes clan. How familiar are you with their family histories?"

"Whitby?" Herr Georg asked. "Rainsford, Ethingham? Sykes? And Bosworth? As in Judicious F. P. Bosworth?" he asked, referring to the local town mystic. He looked a little confused by this line of questioning. Candy noticed a lot of confused expressions around the table.

"I don't know, pumpkin," Doc said, his face tightening as if he were in pain. "I've heard of all of them, of course. I could give you specifics on all those families, though I'd have to do a little research and check out some of my old notes first. But why? What's this all about, anyway?"

Candy shook her head. "I don't know, really. Just wondering."

There was an uneasy silence around the table. Candy

could hear the crackling of the fire, the tinkling of glasses, the quiet conversations going on around them. No one seemed to know what to say.

Maggie finally broke the silence, speaking softly in a voice barely above a whisper. "So . . . what are we going to do about it?"

"About what?" Doc asked, roused from his deliberations.

"About everything! We've just lost a good friend and our best man! That's terrible news, of course—we all loved Julius dearly—but his passing leaves us in an awkward position."

"Which is?"

"What should we do about the wedding? About all the preparations and last-minute planning and setting up?" She couldn't help but sound a little exasperated as she looked around the table, and she pointed at Malcolm and Ralph. "These two have done a lot of work on this, so we have to let them know what's happening. *All* of us have to know what's happening. So . . . what are we going to do?"

Herr Georg reached out, put his hand on hers, and squeezed it lightly. "What my beloved is trying to say," the baker told those seated around the table, "is that she and I have been talking, and, well, we're wondering if we should postpone the wedding—given what's happened to Julius, out of respect for him."

Doc harrumphed at that. "Well, I know Julius—um, *knew* Julius, I suppose—fairly well, and I can tell you he was really looking forward to the wedding, and to being your best man. I have no idea what happened to him, why he's no longer with us, but I think he'd be devastated to know that the wedding was postponed or canceled because of him."

"I agree," said Maggie's mother, piping in. "I think it would be a shame to cancel or postpone it at this late date, after all the preparations you've done."

"Everyone in town is looking forward to it," Malcolm said, joining in.

"And you've waited so long for this moment to arrive," added Ralph passionately.

"He's right," said Amanda, touching her mother's arm.

"You've spent months getting ready. Your dress is beautiful. Melody's all ready to go with the catering. The reception tent is set up at Blueberry Acres, and Candy and Doc have been working for weeks to get the place in shape. We've ordered all the tables and chairs, which will arrive tomorrow. Everything's all lined up. It would be a shame to postpone the ceremony at this point."

When they were all finished, Candy turned to her best friend. "Those are all good points," she told Maggie softly, "but you should really do what your heart tells you to do. Whatever decision you make, we'll support you."

All around the table agreed.

Maggie wasn't quite sure how to respond, so Herr Georg spoke up again, turning to look at his bride-to-be. "We need to consider another issue, my beloved, which we've already discussed. As you well know, we have a very small window here. We're opening the shop in a couple of weeks. We have barely enough time for a quick honeymoon trip to New York. If we postpone the wedding now, all our plans will have to change. We'll probably be too busy over the summer and well into the fall to reschedule the ceremony anytime soon. Of course, we could postpone until Thanksgiving, I suppose, or Christmas, or push it back to next year. . . ."

He let his words trail off, giving that thought time to sink in.

Maggie responded by squeezing his hand and giving him a weak smile. "I know, Georg, and you know I love you. I don't want to delay the wedding any more than you do," she said, "but it just seems like there's so much going on right now that's out of our hands. And there's still so much to do! We both have cakes to make, we have to set up the barn and tent, and decorate, and we have a wedding rehearsal, and I have to get my hair and makeup done. . . . It's all just making my head spin!"

"That's why we're here," said Malcolm reassuringly. "Our goal, as wedding planners, is to take all the stress out of your big day. You won't have to worry about a thing. We promise."

"And the rest of us will help out too, Mom," said Amanda. "That's what we're all here for. Like Malcolm said—you shouldn't have to worry about a thing."

"I know, but I do, I do! And now we don't even have a best man!"

"Ah, yes. The best man." Herr Georg held up a finger. "We can never replace Julius—he was truly one of a kind—but I've been giving that issue some thought as I've been sitting here, listening to everyone, and I think I might have a solution—one I'm sure Julius would approve of, if he were still with us."

The baker looked over at Doc. "You were a good friend to Julius, and you and I have known each other for many years. You've always been kind and welcoming to me, and have never failed to pitch in and help any way you can. Perhaps, if it isn't too much of an imposition, you wouldn't mind stepping into Julius's place, at this late moment, and serving as my best man?"

Doc looked surprised by the suggestion—and a little saddened by it. "Well, Georg, I . . . I don't know what to say. I wish it hadn't come to this. I wish Julius was still here, as all of us do. But he's not . . . and of course I'd be honored to stand in for him." He paused, and his expression subtly lightened as a smile slowly spread across his face. "Yes, that's certainly something I could do."

"Wunderbar!" exclaimed Herr Georg, his face brightening as well. Candy leaned toward her father and laid a hand on his arm. "That's very gracious of you, Dad."

"I guess it's all settled now," said Ellie, and she slapped the table with her palms. "We're going to have a wedding!"

But Maggie still looked skeptical. "But what about the murderer? We have someone running around town who killed Julius—with one of our champagne bottles! What if he or she strikes again?" Her face grew a little paler. "Or what if the police think one of us did it? After all, we *did* order those bottles. Any one of us might be a suspect!" She turned toward her fiancé, alarmed.

At her words, the smiles around the table disappeared, and all eyes turned inevitably toward Candy.

"Well," she said after a few moments, leaning forward and lowering her voice so only those around the table could hear her, "I think that's a very real possibility, Mags, and something they're considering down at the station right now. From what I've heard, Herr Georg and Dad seem to have alibis, at least right now. But unfortunately I'm currently at the top of their lists of suspects," she continued, "and, honestly, it makes perfect sense. As the chief pointed out to me just a little while ago, I was at both the inn and the museum tonight. I easily could have carried that bottle over there myself. And Georg was the one who ordered those cases in the first place, so I'm certain he's still under some suspicion. But, honestly, we all know that none of us was involved in Julius's death, right?"

When she heard no disagreement from anyone around the table, she took a breath and continued. "So, that means one of two things happened. Either Julius took that bottle over there himself for some reason, or someone else had access to those bottles, someone who was here at the inn over the past day or so—maybe even tonight—and removed one from those cases without anyone noticing. Then that person surprised Julius at the museum and deliberately used the bottle to end his life—perhaps with the very intent to implicate one of us."

"But why? Who would do such a thing?" asked Maggie.

"I don't know," Candy said with a determined tone in her voice, "but I have a few suspicions of my own, and I promise you I'm going to find out."

"What about this unconscious waiter Maggie found?" Herr Georg said. "Maybe he can help us solve this."

"Does anyone know what happened to him?" Candy asked. "He was working here all evening. Could he have taken the bottle of champagne over to the museum? Or did he *see* the person who did? Is that why he was knocked out?"

"We don't know yet," her father answered, "but we're working on it."

Candy nodded thoughtfully and turned back to Maggie.

"There are a lot of smart people sitting around this table. We'll figure this out, Mags, if we all pull together. So don't you worry, because one way or another, we're going to get to the bottom of this, and we're all going to make sure your wedding goes off without a hitch!"

Ellie grinned at that. "Or, rather, *with* one, I hope!" she said, and Cameron raised a glass. "To the bride and groom!"

"To the bride and groom!" they all echoed.

That brought a somewhat lighter atmosphere back to the table, Candy noticed. But she also saw the concerned look still on Maggie's face, and knew she had only a couple of days to solve this latest mystery if she was going to make sure her best friend's special day was one they all would remember.

TEN

The following morning Candy was up early. There was a lot to do. And a lot to think about.

The night before seemed like a dream. She ran over in her head all that had happened, trying to make sense of it, wondering how all the pieces fit together. She still couldn't believe Julius was gone, but she had seen him with her own eyes. Now she wanted to find out what had happened to him.

She checked the calendar on her phone and began to formulate a plan. She had to be back at Blueberry Acres around noon, since Maggie, Herr Georg, the wedding planners, and other friends and family were stopping by in the afternoon to set up the barn and tent for the ceremony on Saturday. But she had nothing else planned until then, so she had time to do a little snooping around.

She had two simple questions on her mind: Who killed Julius—and why?

Time to get a move on and see what she could find out.

She wasn't surprised to find her father already awake, working downstairs in his home office. Doc often worked late at night or early in the mornings when he was on a mission, and he appeared to be on one today.

Still in her stocking feet, Candy entered the office quietly, so as not to disturb him if he was deep in thought. An old beige radio, tuned to an AM station, was playing the local farm report. A cup of coffee in a white mug steamed at his elbow. He was sitting at an old oak desk, pushed up against the opposite wall, with his back to the open door, surrounded by piles of papers and wall-length shelves filled with old books, photos, mementos, and awards of recognition from his years as a college history professor. But he must have heard her coming, because he said to her without turning around, "Hello, pumpkin. How are you doing this morning?"

"You always can hear me coming, can't you?" Candy crossed the room and plopped in a chair beside the desk. "I'm doing okay, considering everything that happened last night. How about you? How long have you been up?"

Doc checked his watch. "An hour or two now. Couldn't sleep. Thinking about Julius, I guess. And I wanted to see what I could find out about those families you mentioned last night. See if I could turn up anything that might help you out—whatever it is you're planning on doing."

Candy smiled at that. "And?"

"Well," Doc said, leaning over to turn down the radio, and pulling out a folder, which he opened, "might as well get into it. Let's start with the Sykes family, since we've both had some experiences with them in one way or another. As you know, they were among the original settlers here on the cape, going all the way back to the eighteenth century and Captain Josiah Sykes. They were seafarers, traders, and often scoundrels and thieves, though they became quite respectable landholders as the decades passed, and made a name for themselves around here. But they also ran into hard times, especially when they came up against the wealthier and more powerful Pruitts. Those two families have had some bitter clashes over the years."

"I have a feeling those clashes are still going on," Candy said.

Doc nodded. "You could be right. As you've no doubt heard, rumors about a resurgent feud between those families has been widespread for years now, though sometimes it's hard to tell fact from fiction. Evidence is sketchy. Of course, there was that burned-down foundation we found out at Crawford's Berry Farm a couple of years back, and the treasure box that once belonged to Silas Sykes, who lived around here a hundred years ago or so. Julius did some research on that box a while back, when we first found out about it, but I don't know if he ever came to a satisfying conclusion about its contents."

"You think that treasure box could have had something to do with Julius's death?" Candy asked, feeling a sudden chill.

Doc shrugged, missing his daughter's reaction. "Don't know, pumpkin. At the moment, we have to keep every option open, I guess." He shuffled through a few papers before he continued. "Daisy Porter-Sykes, the current family matriarch, is still alive, though she's well into her nineties by now. I've heard she's having trouble getting around these days but she's still as feisty as ever."

"And probably still as dangerous," Candy muttered under her breath.

Doc arched an eyebrow but let the comment slide, continuing on without skipping a beat. "She lives in the old family house down in Marblehead near Boston, which she inherited through her mother's side of the family, I believe. Roger, one of her grandsons, remains in the Maine State Prison at Warren, where he'll be for a long time. Another grandson, Porter, is a developer and was the primary force behind that new hotel and convention project they built down on Portland's waterfront a while back. And then there's the granddaughter, Morgan, who we ran into a couple of years ago."

Candy tilted her head, picturing in her mind a dark-haired woman in a flowery print dress, standing on the porch of a modest chocolate-brown bungalow on a side street in Cape Willington. "I remember."

"She seemed like a pleasant-enough person at the time," Doc said, "though I haven't run into her around town since

then. I'm not sure she's ever returned, after what happened
to her aunt." He was referring to Rachel Fairweather, an
elderly town resident who had died under mysterious circumstances a couple of years earlier.

"She has made herself scarce, hasn't she? They all have."

"Especially since one of their last major holdings, Whitefield, burned down a few years ago, and they sold the property,
including the remains of the mansion and nearly a hundred
acres or so of land. I suppose it made sense, since the old
place had been abandoned for years. They haven't actually
occupied a property here on the cape for a decade or more.
Just about everything they owned was lost or sold off long
ago. The Pruitts saw to that."

Candy glanced at the papers spread out on the desk. "Any
information on whether they're trying to get back into the
real estate market around here?"

Doc shook his head. "Not that I've heard, though I'm
looking into it. What about you?"

Candy admitted she'd heard a few rumblings but nothing
specific. "I can ask Wanda about it. She might know something. She keeps her ear pretty close to the ground." Wanda
Boyle, whom Candy would best describe as a frenemy, had
been her co-worker for years at the *Cape Crier*. Recently,
Wanda had been promoted from her role as community correspondent to managing editor, a position Candy had held
before she'd made the difficult decision to leave the paper so
she could spend more time on the farm.

"Sounds like a good idea." Doc closed the file,
reached across the desk, pulled another one toward him, and
opened it. "Okay, the Whitby family. Another familiar name
around the cape. We both know of Elliot Whitby, a fairly
cadaverous villager who likes to dress up like Edgar Allan
Poe and give annual readings of 'The Raven' in Town Park
on All Hallows' Eve. His impersonation is pretty popular with
tourists and locals alike, as you know, and he usually attracts
large crowds for his readings. And, if you recall, a few years
back, we ran into Oliver LaForce at the Lobster Stew Cook-off

contest, who provided us with a quick history of the Light-keeper's Inn, and the Whitbys' involvement with it."

Candy nodded. "I remember. It was for that book you were working on—the history of Cape Willington."

"Still working on it," Doc said with a slight grimace. "I'm up to the early twentieth century. Hope to finish it sometime this year. There's more material than I thought to work with. And I keep getting distracted."

"Happens to the best of us," Candy acknowledged.

"Anyway, as Oliver pointed out, the inn dates back to 1791, which was also the year the town was incorporated. It was one of the cape's original buildings, but burned down in 1811. It was rebuilt and burned down again. The current structure dates back to 1902, when Elias Whitby, Elliot's ancestor, took over ownership of the place. The Whitby family continued to run it until the mid-eighties, when they sold it. And just recently, of course, they put their old mansion across the bay up for sale."

"The Whitby estate," Candy said, nodding. "Wanda wrote something about it in this week's issue. Apparently it's been sold, though I haven't heard anything about the buyer yet."

"No one has, far as I can tell. It's all hush-hush, for some reason. Maybe some big celebrity bought it or something like that."

"Maybe. But it's pretty isolated out there on that point all by itself. And it's half an hour or so from town, since you have to drive around the bay to get there."

"True," Doc said, "but I also hear it has amazing ocean views, and a good view of Cape Willington as well. As long as the weather's clear, they say you can see both lighthouses, the docks, and even the opera house from that side of the bay."

"Hmm." She thought a moment, her mind working. "Are you aware of any connections between Julius and the Whit-bys? Or any of these families?"

Doc saw right through her question. "You think it's possible someone from one of these families could be involved in Julius's death?"

"I don't know, Dad. That's what I'm trying to find out." And briefly she told him about the list of names that had fallen out of the book Owen picked up the night before, and how it included the words *Foul Mouth* and the initials *L. B.*

"Ahh, so that's where all these names come from," Doc said, a look of understanding spreading across his face. "You didn't mention any of this last night."

"I didn't want to discuss it in public—and I wanted to give it some thought before I said anything."

"Makes sense," he acknowledged. "So you think that list had something to do with Julius's death? Or this Foul Mouth thing? Or this L. B.?"

"I'm considering all possibilities at this point. You have any idea who—or what—L. B. might be?"

"Not off the top of my head but I'll think about it."

"What about the families on the list? Could there be a connection between one of them and Julius?" she asked again.

Doc answered quickly. "Sure, it's possible. Over the years Julius probably talked to people from all those families you mentioned, as research for his books. I'm sure he knew a lot more about them than I do."

He leaned back in his chair and indicated a row of slim books on a shelf above his head, all written by Julius. "I haven't had a chance to go back through them in detail today, but it's on my to-do list. There might be something useful in one of those."

Candy glanced up at the row of white-and-blue-spined volumes. There were seven or eight in all, thin self-published trade-sized paperbacks authored by the elderly historian later in his life, primarily for sale to tourists.

On an impulse, Candy rose and plucked one from the shelf, opening it to the first few pages. Julian had included a short inscription to Doc and signed his name in black ink on the title page in a flowing yet sure hand. "'To my good friend and fellow lover of history,'" Candy read. She turned the book around to show her father. "When did he sign this for you?"

"A few years back, I guess. Why?"

"Do you mind if I take this one with me? There's something I'd like to verify."

Doc made a motion with his hand. "Sure, be my guest, if it will help. You see something interesting?"

"Maybe," Candy said, mulling over some thoughts in her head.

They went on to talk about the other family names listed on the piece of paper that had fallen out of the book the night before. The Rainsfords, Doc told her, had family roots in Cape Willington going back generations, to around the time of the Civil War. "They were loosely affiliated with the much wealthier Pruitts, and there has been some intermarriage between the two families, though not for quite a while, to the best of my recollection."

They talked briefly about Alice Rainsford, a descendant of the original settlers, who was now a member of the Cape Willington Heritage Protection League. Candy recalled her encounters with Alice, a reserved and reliable woman. She couldn't see any real link between Alice and Julius, though. She knew they'd been acquaintances, but probably no more than that.

"The Ethinghams were early landholders and foresters around Mount Katahdin, north of here," Doc went on, continuing down the list of names. "Some of their holdings adjoined those of Percival P. Baxter, the wealthy governor of Maine back in the nineteen twenties. The association was lucrative for the Ethinghams, who acquired other lands and properties throughout the state, including some in Cape Willington. They've always worked behind the scenes, though, and were never a truly prominent family, either locally or statewide. One of the current residents from the family is Gilbert Ethingham, whom I'm sure you've heard of."

"Of course," Candy said, "but we've never met."

"I'm not surprised. He's no exception to the family's trait of avoiding the limelight. He's something of a recluse."

"A bachelor for as long as I've been in town, if I recall."

Doc nodded. "He rarely mingles at community affairs

and prefers his own company much of the time. But I've heard he turns up occasionally."

"Have you ever run into him?"

"Once or twice, shook hands with him but didn't talk much, other than to say hello. Quiet guy, not really heavyset but he has a pale, puffy face. I don't think he goes out in the sun much. Despite his aversion to social events, he does tend to stand out in a crowd, since he likes to wear expensive jewelry, things like silver bracelets and expensive watches. I'm honestly not sure what he does with his time, but it's really none of my business, is it? Anyway, moving on. The Palfreys."

He paused a moment, leaned forward to take a sip of his cooling coffee, and continued. "The family hasn't been in town as long as the others, but they've had some impact locally. Samuel Palfrey sat on the town council for a couple of decades back in the fifties and sixties, his wife, Shirley, was a schoolteacher here in the village her entire career, and their son, Plymouth Palfrey, is something of a local celebrity, though he hasn't lived here in town for many years."

"I've never met him in person either, though I've seen him at a couple of his speaking engagements. He started his career here, with the paper, right?"

Doc nodded. "As a volunteer reporter many years ago, when he was still in his teens. After college he worked his way up through newspapers in Ellsworth, Bangor, and Booth-bay Harbor before segueing into magazines and then book publishing. He started his own small publishing house, the Kennebec Press, out of the basement office at his home in Boothbay Harbor, and he's achieved some level of success by focusing on regional subjects like lobsters, lighthouses, history, and local mysteries."

"When was the last time you talked to him?"

"It's been a while," Doc admitted. "Probably close to a year ago now, when we discussed that history book I've been working on, and some of my other projects, like the book on Devil's Half Acre up in Bangor."

"He seemed to like that idea."

Doc nodded. "He did, and I'm sure we'll talk again as I get

closer to finishing one of them. But he hasn't been around town much lately, and I've been too busy to follow up."

"What about the rest of his family?"

"The parents are gone now, and the kids have scattered. He has a brother in Vermont and a sister in Detroit, both with families of their own."

"So none of them are living in town right now?"

"Not that I'm aware of."

They discussed the Palfreys a little longer before segueing to the Bosworths. They started by discussing Judicious F. P. Bosworth, a villager who lived in a small cabin by the English River just north of town. Shunning the family tradition of a career in the legal or political fields, Judicious took a different path. Considered the town mystic by some, and a few bricks shy of a full load by others, he'd gained a certain amount of notoriety for his alleged ability to turn himself invisible. Candy wasn't sure she believed it or not, but she'd seen Judicious pop up, and disappear, in some surprising ways over the past few years, so she simply accepted him as a friend and fellow villager, and left it at that.

When they'd finished, Candy leaned back in her chair, wondering what it all meant—if anything. "That's quite a long list of characters," she said, thinking out loud, "but it makes sense that Julius would have crossed paths with most or all of those folks over the past few years."

"It does," Doc agreed.

"So the next question is, which one or ones did he talk to recently? And did someone from one of those families have a reason to cause Julius any harm?"

"Right."

"What about you? Can you think of someone who might have wanted to attack Julius?"

Doc rubbed his fingers across his chin. "I've thought about that, pumpkin. It's what kept me awake all night. But I honestly can't think of anyone. As far as I know, he didn't have any enemies."

"Everyone has enemies," Candy said. "We just have to figure out who they were."

Doc closed up the final file on his desk. "Well, you have plenty of places to start. I'll keep digging around and let you know if I come across anything of interest."

"And Foul Mouth?" Candy asked before they broke up. "Find out anything about that?"

Doc shook his head. "Nothing so far. Of course, for something like this, the first person I'd go talk to would be Julius. He used to have all kinds of tidbits about stuff like that floating around in his head. But now that he's gone, we'll have to figure it out on our own. We still have his books we can go through, of course, and the archives over at the museum might provide something useful, though I doubt we can get into those right now."

Candy agreed with him. "I'm sure the police have that whole upstairs area blocked off, but I'm going to head over there anyway and see if I can talk to Owen. Go over what happened last night with him. See if anything jumps out."

Doc checked his watch. "It's about time to adjourn to the diner for breakfast. The boys will be gathering. I'm sure we'll have plenty to talk about. You going to join us?"

"I might stop by," Candy said, her gaze growing distant as her mind focused on her next move, "but first, duty calls."

ELEVEN

Outside, the day was sunny and a little windy, with the temperatures rising slightly above normal, headed into the high sixties. It was glorious, Candy thought as she headed back between the house and barn, past the recently tilled but yet to be planted vegetable garden, to the chicken coop. As she went, she relished the warmth of the sun on her skin. She just hoped the good weather would last a few more days, until the wedding was over. So far the forecast seemed promising, with no rain and a slight warming trend expected into the weekend. With any luck, the temperatures would climb into the low seventies by Saturday, the day of the wedding.

Good news, indeed.

The fortunate stretch of spring weather—which was also good for the blueberry fields, a week or two into bloom—was better than Candy dared hope, especially after another long, harsh winter, when temperatures plunged far below the freezing mark for several consecutive weeks in late January and into early February.

Candy and Maggie had fretted for much of that time, and well into March and April, wondering if the weather would turn in their favor in time for an outdoor wedding in Maine in May. They both knew they were playing the odds, and remembered many years past when clouds, rain, fog, and cool temperatures lingered along the Down East coast well into June and even longer, making it seem as if summer would never arrive. This year, thankfully, warmer weather had made an early appearance, and would stick around for at least a little while longer.

With the warmer temperatures, the bees had also arrived at the farm, trucked in "from away"—places like Florida and Texas. The hives were now arranged in "beeyards" around the blueberry barrens, which were literally buzzing today. Trucking in the honeybees was an expensive proposition, one Candy and her father debated and planned for each year. It certainly stretched their budget, but the productive little insects would increase the wild blueberry yield by as much as a thousand pounds per acre, and would pay for their cost five or six times over come harvest time.

Making ends meet until then was always the challenge.

The bees would be around for several more weeks, since the fields were only about 30 percent into bloom. They tended to stay to themselves when left undisturbed, but they could become defensive around their colonies, which is why the beeyards were positioned away from the house and barn, around the center of the barrens and farther back, along the top of the southeast ridge.

During their early years on the farm, Candy and Doc had relied on native bees to pollinate the fields, but they'd decided to try a more commercial process in recent years in an effort to boost their yield and revenue. They'd considered becoming beekeepers themselves, but had decided to postpone that decision for another few years. They had enough to do as it was.

Just the sight of the honeybees working the sunny barrens made Candy herself buzz with activity as she went about her chores. They'd have a profitable year indeed and, at least for the moment, she felt relatively upbeat about their future prospects.

The bees, black flies, and other spring insects, she

thought, were a good reason to hold the wedding inside the barn, rather than out in the fields, something they'd toyed with early on. Heaven forbid a wedding guest—or, worse, the bride or groom—became the target of some aggressive stinging insect. However, the closest beehive was more than two hundred feet away, and the black flies and mosquitoes weren't too bad yet, since the weather had been relatively dry lately, so she didn't anticipate too many problems.

With the chickens fed and watered, and carrying a wire basket of freshly laid eggs on her arm, Candy turned to survey their two newest structures at the farm. One was temporary, while the other was semipermanent.

Behind the barn, occupying a flat, cleared spot of land—which in a few weeks would become the back half of their vegetable garden, nearly doubling it in size—stood a recently erected twenty-by-thirty-foot framed white tent, closed in by flaps on three sides to minimize intrusions from both flying and four-footed creatures. The open side faced the barn's back door, which would make it easy for wedding guests to move between the two.

The tent had arrived a day earlier on a flatbed truck, and a team of two assemblers set it up in short order. It would provide a place for the reception following the wedding.

That had been an almost endless debate as well, with alternatives such as the Lightkeeper's Inn and Melody's Cafe considered as possible reception sites, until they'd decided to keep everything associated with the ceremony out at the farm, for the ease of everyone involved. But they'd found ways to incorporate the other two venues, with the pre-wedding dinner party held at the inn, and the upcoming rehearsal dinner tomorrow night scheduled to take place at the café on River Road.

Farther on, around the barn on the other side, was the farm's other new structure, the semipermanent one. It was their new hoophouse, which they'd finished putting up just a month or so ago. It was a big improvement on the farm, and they were still getting it up and running. But over the next few years it would help them greatly expand their crops, and their revenue stream as well—or, at least, that was the plan.

She was proud of what she saw. They'd done a lot of work around the place recently, and it showed. As she surveyed her surroundings, she thought about Julius, remembering the last time he'd visited out here the previous fall. They'd had a wonderful time together. He and Doc had talked for quite a while about their writing projects, and they had even tossed around the idea of collaborating on a project at some point in the future.

That brought her back to the problem at hand.

Why was he murdered? Who would do such a thing?

She thought back over the conversation she'd just had with her father, pondering all the names they'd discussed. It was a curious list, she thought, and knew something must link all the names together. But whether a member of any of those families was tied to Julius's death, she had no idea.

A better exercise, she thought, would be to try to reconstruct Julius's activities over the past few days. Where had he gone? Who had he talked to? Who saw him last? That would give her better information, she thought, and might help her get a grasp on who killed him, and why.

Although she was still working on the *who* part, she thought she had a possible motivation for the *why*. Owen Peabody had given her a clue last night.

Julius has been researching old historical books about local land deeds.

Deeds.

She'd heard that word before in connection with the cape's history, from a few different people around town. And here it was again, leaving another murder in its wake.

What was so important about land deeds? More important, why would anyone care enough to murder someone over them—if that, in fact, was what had happened?

But she already knew the answer to that question: It was all about property. It was about the land, about Cape Willington itself.

Was someone, she thought, *really* trying to gain control of the land around Cape Willington, as she'd come to suspect over the past few years? Trying to get hold of the original deeds—those that preceded and superseded all other existing deeds—to gain ownership of local properties? Could someone claim to own the land upon which the downtown area stood? Or Pruitt Manor?

Or Blueberry Acres?

It gave her a chill.

Could someone take their property—their land—away from them? Or someone else's land?

It was, she thought, a very good motivation for murder.

She'd heard rumblings of this before, several times, in fact, over the past few years. She could recall a conversation she'd had a couple of years earlier with the late Rachel Fairweather, who was born a Sykes before she married Mr. Fairweather:

"Oh, yes, those famous deeds," she'd told Candy one night in a whispery tone as the two of them sat in the kitchen of a chocolate-brown bungalow not too far from here. *"Those are part of the legend as well."*

She'd been referring to the legend of Silas Sykes, the nineteenth-century scoundrel and thief whose treasure box had been discovered two years before at Crawford's Berry Farm by Miles Crawford, then owner of the property. He'd been murdered because of it. The box had contained gold and jewels—which they'd found after Miles's death—and also allegedly a set of old deeds, which they hadn't found.

"Deeds to what?" Candy had inquired of Mrs. Fairweather at the time.

"To property, of course," the elderly woman had said. *"Here in Cape Willington."*

"What properties?"

"All of them."

The deeds, Candy had been told, were allegedly written before all existing deeds for properties in the village, but had disappeared long ago, lost in the fog of time—until Miles had dug up the treasure box. If he'd found the deeds inside, he'd told no one about them before he died—at least as far as she knew. So far, no one had discovered what had become of them.

Mrs. Fairweather's words echoed in her mind:

". . . All the businesses, all the properties—all this land belonging to someone else . . ."

Had Miles really found the deeds? If so, what had he done with them? Had he destroyed them? Had he given them to someone? Had they even existed at all?

Miles's son, Neil, who had inherited the berry farm from his father, had tried to find out, with Candy's assistance, but they'd run into a dead end. The deeds were nowhere to be found.

And now here they were, popping up again, causing trouble.

Causing murder.

And it appeared Julius had somehow wound up right in the middle of it.

What had he found out? What secrets had he uncovered that led to his death?

Her father had said that Julius had researched the treasure box and its contents. Had his research been successful? Had he located the deeds? Was that why he'd been murdered?

But what about the champagne bottle? Why would someone hit him over the head with *that*?

Could his murder have anything to do with the upcoming wedding? With Maggie or Herr Georg?

What about the unconscious waiter? What did he have to do with all of this?

And what about the list Owen had found, with names of some of the village's founding families?

L. B.?

Foul Mouth?

It was a lot to think about, and Candy pondered the ramifications as she turned back toward the house. Doc had already left for the diner, his old Ford pickup truck gone from its parking spot next to the barn. So she grabbed her trusty old tote bag from the kitchen, locked the door behind her, climbed into her Jeep, and headed off to find some answers.

TWELVE

The parking lot for the lighthouse and museum was relatively empty today. But she spotted a couple of squad cars parked at the opposite end of the lot, near the top of the wide walkway that led down toward the lighthouse, and, sitting nearby, a white oversized van with the words MOBILE INVESTIGATION UNIT stenciled on its side panels in bright blue letters.

Candy cautiously avoided them, circling around the outer edges of the lot before parking in a far corner, some distance from the squad cars and van. Despite the presence of the vehicles, she could see no police officers or other official-looking people in the lot or down toward the lighthouse and museum buildings, so there was no one to prevent her from leaving the Jeep parked there and having a quick look around.

Before she locked up, she pulled her tote bag from the front seat. Inside, she'd placed the signed copy of Julius's book she'd brought from her father's office. She hoped it might help her out later.

She thought it best to keep a low profile, so rather than march straight down the main walkway to the cluster of build-ings at water's edge, right in full view of anyone who might be looking out a window of the Keeper's Quarters, she decided to take a smarter path. She headed in the opposite direction, toward a narrow dirt track that led off the back side of the parking lot, away from the buildings, down a steep bank to a narrow stretch of rock-strewn coastline.

But before she left the parking area, a sudden thought stopped her. She twisted around, her eyes sweeping the lot.

Yes, there it was, still parked right where he'd left it yesterday.

Julius's red station wagon.

From what she could see, there was nothing to indicate the car had been searched by the police or examined in any way. It hadn't moved. The windows were all rolled up. It looked totally undisturbed, as if it had sat there for years.

Subtly, Candy flicked her gaze left and right, and left again.

No one around. No one to notice if she took a little peek inside. She wouldn't bother anything . . . just look. No harm in that, right?

Moving as nonchalantly but as quickly as possible, she crossed the lot and sidled up beside the wagon.

Not surprisingly for a busy man's transportation, it was a bit of a mess inside. In the trunk area she saw a few opened boxes of Julius's books, a long-handled window scraper, an empty bag of rock salt, a few empty burlap bags, and a couple of snow tires.

She took a few steps forward along the car, still peering in the windows. In the backseat were a jacket, a pair of gloves, an old but apparently functional umbrella, papers, half-read magazines and newspapers, a battered yellow industrial-sized flashlight, and a few old books. History books, they looked like to Candy, though she couldn't quite make out the titles.

On the front passenger seat were a half-used box of Kleenex, sunglasses, a map, binoculars, and a fairly new digital camera with a long lens.

An interesting collection, she thought—functional for a historical researcher who drove in Maine's tough winters, and who no doubt ran down a lot of his stories in person, no matter the time or season. A camera for taking photos of interviewees and buildings. A flashlight to explore those dark places he no doubt had sometimes wandered into. A pair of binoculars to . . . what, watch birds?

But, overall, nothing really out of the norm, nor anything that might help her uncover a murderer.

She moved on, back across the parking lot to the dirt path and down the bank to the waterfront.

She'd explored this section of the coastline before, and knew the shale and rocks eventually gave way to a coarse sand beach, possibly flecked with small shiny bits of sea glass, where Julius might have wandered prior to his death, picking up that sand on the bottoms of his shoes. It was not a place for ocean swimming, since the water was too cold and the undercurrents too treacherous in this area near the mouth of the English River. But it was a picturesque and somewhat secluded spot and might yield a clue or two.

As she walked, the ocean shimmered to the east, and waves lapped gently on the shoreline. She skipped carefully over black, wet rocks, doing her best to stay to the dry patches of land so she didn't get her shoes too soggy. She was all alone in this part of the cape, except for the gulls floating overhead. Even they were quiet right now.

The rocks soon gave way to the narrow beach, only a few yards deep from shore to slope. Here she slowed, looking down and studying the ground as she walked, focusing in on the mix at her feet. She saw a few stray footprints, some made by shoes, others by bare feet. Paw prints and bird tracks as well, meandering across the sand. An occasional discarded paper cup, some larger bits of sea glass, strewn brownish-green seaweed, broken bits of shell, even a few nice pieces of driftwood. But nothing that caught her eye.

She stooped and scooped up a handful of the coarse, pebble-inflected sand, letting it run through her fingers as she rose. In the bright sun she could see the smaller flecks of sea glass mixed with the sand. The mixture was damp and a bit muddy, but it could be the same thing she'd seen upstairs, dried out a little . . . possibly.

She flicked the rest away and brushed her hands together to

clean them off as she walked to the far side of the beach, turned, and retraced her steps. Her gaze continually swept across the ground in front of her. At the far side she paused and sighed.

Nothing.

She heard the blast of a horn and looked out toward the sea. A powerboat swept past, breaking through gently rolling waters, leaving a churning white stream in its wake.

The view beyond the boat drew her attention. From here, she realized, she could look directly across the bay to the shore of another finger of land, which stretched down from the mainland, much as the cape did. Though it was some distance away, it was a surprisingly clear day, and she could make out rocky cliffs and a few oceanfront houses on that stretch of land. One seemed to sit all by itself out by the point, near a rising, forbidding headland.

She'd seen this view before from other spots along the shore, but for some reason it looked different today, possibly because of the light or the clarity of the air, or maybe because of the angle and the curving coastline. The view from the Keeper's Quarters was more to the northeast, but here she was looking almost directly east, across the bay.

The Whitby house was over there, she thought, remembering what her father had told her. It must be that last one out on the point. She squinted into the bright sunlight, holding a hand over her eyes, trying to get a better view. But it was too far away to make out much.

She might be able to see it better, she mused, if she'd brought a pair of binoculars along with her. . . .

Hmm, now there was a thought.

She toyed briefly with the idea of heading back up to Julius's car to see if the doors were unlocked, but quickly decided that was a bad idea. There'd no doubt be loads of trouble if she removed the binoculars from his car. She'd just have to bring along her own pair next time—or, better yet, drive over to that distant peninsula herself to check out the place, she thought as she headed back the way she'd come, toward the lighthouse. It rose majestically above the land before her like a giant white tapering candle.

In a little more than five minutes she was approaching it from the ocean side, and not the landward side, where she'd be more visible. Here she was somewhat hidden behind the bank and rocks to her left. Again, she saw no one around the lighthouse or museum buildings, so she climbed the bank to the walkway that led along the lighthouse and Keeper's Quarters. Again, she tried to appear as casual as possible, just an average person out for a morning stroll as she approached the gray-painted wooden steps that led into the two-story cottage.

Much to her surprise, the door stood open, just as it had the night before. Curious. With quick glances in either direction, she climbed the steps, gently pushed the door farther open, and ventured inside.

THIRTEEN

She heard voices the moment she crossed the threshold.

She paused, peering through the dim light, trying to figure out where the sounds were coming from. She saw no movement, could see no one around. The overhead lights were turned off, so the place looked like it might be closed, but Candy could see no sign indicating this, and there was no one behind the Long Desk on her left to inform her otherwise. So she took a few tentative steps across the worn wooden floor, gazing left and right into the other rooms, trying to get a sense of who was in here, and where.

She heard a creaking sound above her and tilted back her head. Someone was upstairs in the archives, walking around on the old floorboards—the crime scene investigators, no doubt, and probably the police officers as well.

They'd accessed the second floor via the wooden staircase in the exhibit room to her right. She turned in that direction, but hesitated. They would have removed Julius's body—and the offending bottle of champagne—the night before, and were probably conducting a final search of the area. Had they found anything new? Any additional evidence? She heard only occasional fragments of hushed conversation drifting down the stairs but couldn't make out any of the words. She sharpened her senses, trying to listen more closely, but finally shook her head. They were too far away for her to hear what they were saying, and she doubted they'd fill her in, or even allow her onto the second floor, if she headed up that way.

But there were other voices, more prominent, though still hushed, coming from somewhere closer, on *this* floor.

From straight ahead, Candy realized after a moment.

The museum director's office.

Owen's office.

It was a small room tucked into a far corner of the building, and someone was in there.

More than one person, from the sound of it.

The door was nearly closed, though it stood open a couple of inches, allowing the voices of those inside the room to filter out. She could identify three distinct individuals, though there might be a fourth, or even a fifth. It was hard to tell, since there was a lot of cross-talking going on. But again, because the voices were so low, it was difficult to make out any of the words. Still, it sounded like a fairly tense conversation

Small wonder, since a dead body had been found upstairs the night before. That alone was shocking enough, but she imagined it was causing the museum's director a big headache this morning, for a number of other reasons—the security of the place, whether to close or stay open, how to honor the victim, what to do about nosy visitors like her . . . and, of course, what about the lost revenue if the place shut down for several days.

And then there were the two questions on everyone's mind: Who murdered Julius, and why?

For a fleeting moment she thought of leaving, but dismissed that idea. Instead, she reached into her tote, pulled out the book Julius had signed, and hefted it briefly. Her business here was with Owen, and she felt it was fairly important. No sense leaving without at least attempting to talk to him, no matter who was in there with him, and what important decision-making might be going on.

She paused a moment to collect her thoughts and, with a determined nod of her chin, crossed the room to the office door and rapped lightly a couple of times.

"Owen, are you in there?"

She pushed the door open a little and stuck her head inside. She spotted the museum director sitting behind his desk, and smiled at him.

"Oh, hi, Owen, there you are! I was hoping I might find you in here." She tried to sound as easygoing as possible, and almost succeeded, she thought. There was only that slight tightness in her tone that might give her away. She tried to relax and appear normal—not as easy as it sounded.

The director, sitting behind his desk, twisted toward her. His expression changed rapidly, tightening in confusion. "Candy? Is that you? What are you doing here?"

"Well, you know, I just thought I'd drop by to check on you and see how you're doing this morning. Make sure everything's okay, you know?" She pushed open the door a little farther. "I'm not interrupting anything, am I?"

In response, he gave her an annoyed glance and waved a hand around the room, as if shooing away a fly, to indicate he was not alone.

She poked her head around the edge of the door and finally got a good look around his office.

Three individuals sat in front of his desk, a woman and two men. They were looking at her with blank stares, frozen in mid-conversation. She knew one of them, had seen another around town, and thought she might know who the third was, but she'd never met either of the two men face-to-face.

The person she knew, the one sitting closest to her in an office chair, was Edith Pring. A thin, stern, straight-backed woman, conservatively dressed, she had facial features as sharp as her name, led by a nose that could cut through a block of ice. Her prominent cheekbones stuck out like diamonds above her hollow cheeks. Dark circles under her eyes gave her a menacing look, which she used to her advantage.

Edith, one of the museum's board members, wasn't the type of person one crossed on purpose. Candy knew most folks around town gave her a wide berth whenever possible. She was a strongly opinionated woman who wasted no time correcting whatever she felt was wrong around town, and letting others know when she was unhappy. Candy had heard Wanda Boyle at the paper talking about Edith on more than one occasion, usually beginning with the words, "You won't believe what's got Edith riled up now. . . ."

She looked like she was ready for a skirmish this morning, and Owen obviously had been the object of her antagonism . . . until Candy walked in. Edith's blank stare quickly turned to a disapproving look—which Candy tried her best to ignore.

The other two individuals didn't appear quite as confrontational, though the man sitting on the far side, near a small window overlooking craggy rocks and a seascape, seemed less than bemused by the interruption, though tolerant of it. He had a fleshy face, nondescript features, and wary eyes that seemed to avoid looking directly at people. But he was well dressed, wearing a starched blue cotton shirt, nice leather loafers, a silver bracelet on one wrist, and an expensive-looking watch with a navy blue nautical theme on the other.

It could only be Gilbert Ethingham, whom her father had perfectly described for her just a little while ago.

As Doc had said, Gilbert was rarely seen around town, so his presence here today was something of a surprise. But she imagined a dead man in the museum's archives was enough to draw him out of his cozy environs, for he, too, was a member of the museum's board.

As was the third individual, sitting between Gilbert and Edith.

He was even more of a surprise.

Plymouth Palfrey was the only one in the room who didn't seem irritated by her sudden appearance—and was perhaps even thankful for it, by the look of his indulgent smile. He sported a head of thick white hair, a red face, and a stylish goatee, which made him look more like a Southern gentleman than a rural Mainer. He had a subtly scholarly appearance, as befitting his role as a book publisher, and looked like a man who could command a room, but just as easily spend days all on his own, immersed in some book project, without a thought for the rest of the world.

Her surprise at seeing him here had as much to do with the distance he must have traveled this morning as anything else. The trip eastward along the coast from Boothbay Harbor, where he currently lived and worked, took almost three hours, she figured, meaning he probably left his place before dawn—or drove eighty miles an hour the entire way.

It was, she thought as her gaze took them in, a relatively formidable group, augmented in no small way by Owen himself.

Word must have spread quickly, she thought. *The powers that be are gathering. They're circling the wagons.*

No doubt discussing what to do in response to the discovery upstairs. Which made this meeting fairly important— and she'd just waltzed her way right in.

Nice job, Candy!

Still, she reminded herself, she was here for a reason.

It wasn't her intent to step on a bunch of powerful toes. Best, she thought, to find out what she needed and make a hasty retreat without antagonizing them any further.

"Hi, I hope you'll excuse me," she said to the three board members, "but this is really important, and I'll only be a second." Resting her hand on the doorknob, she leaned inward and spoke in a loud whisper to Owen, as if in confidence. "I wonder if I might have a few words . . . in *private*?"

He looked more confused than aghast. "What? Now? We're in the middle of a *meeting*!" The last word almost came out through gritted teeth.

Again, she thought of retreating, but she was committed, so she plunged on. "Yes, I can see that, and I know you're busy, but I wouldn't ask if it wasn't important." She turned back to the three board members. "I'll hope you'll excuse us. This won't take long. We just have something to discuss briefly. I'll have him back to you in a jiffy."

She flashed an apologetic smile, hoping for a fast exit, but it didn't work out that way.

"What is this all about?" Edith Pring asked in a low, coarse growl. Her tone of voice could be as intimidating as the rest of her.

"It's a personal matter," Candy said vaguely, "between Owen and myself. I just want to check something with him."

"If this has anything to do with the death of Julius Seabury," Gilbert Ethingham interjected with a slight quiver of his upper lip as he shifted around toward her, "maybe it's something we all need to hear."

"Yes, what about that?" Edith asked. "You were up there last night when the body was discovered. In fact, from what we've heard, you're the one who found him. What's behind all this? What was he doing up there by himself when the place was closed? That in itself was highly inappropriate."

Candy answered quickly and honestly. "I don't know, but I do know it was quite a shock."

Gilbert chuckled, though there was no humor in it. "Well, that's an understatement. A murder, here on the grounds of the museum? It's a disaster, in more ways than one."

"It certainly is." Owen nodded emphatically in agreement.

"It could affect the museum's reputation—and its revenue streams," Edith added, somewhat coldly.

"And, of course, the passing of Julius is a major loss for the museum itself, for the director and board members, and for the community as a whole, given his contributions to the town's historical record," said Plymouth Palfrey in a more placating tone.

"Well, that's certainly true." Momentarily mollified, Edith folded her hands in her lap. "He will be missed by us all."

There was silence around the room. Finally, Candy said, "Yes, I'm sure he will." She paused. "I don't suppose any of you know what his schedule was for the last few days?"

"How would any of us know that?" Owen asked, his face turning red.

Candy shrugged. "I'm just curious."

Edith's jaw tightened. "It wasn't our job to keep tabs on Julius's comings and goings."

"I can't even remember the last time I saw him," said Gilbert. "Our paths didn't cross that often."

"No, I suppose not," Candy said as she looked around the room. "What about the rest of you? Do any of you remember the last time you saw him?"

They all looked uncomfortable. Finally Edith said, "I'm not sure I approve of this line of questioning."

Plymouth uncrossed his legs, recrossed them in the opposite direction before he spoke up. "I don't think Candy means any of this as an accusation," he said, and he gave her a stiff, almost reptilian smile. "You don't, do you?"

Again, Candy was quick to respond. "Oh, no, of course not. It's nothing like that. I just thought, since we're all here together, it might be helpful to try to establish Julius's itinerary over the past few days—prior to arriving here at the museum. It might help us figure out who he talked to, and what he was doing up there last night."

"Isn't that something the police would do?" Owen asked.

"Yes, I suppose so." Candy noticed all their eyes on her—again—and decided maybe it was best to drop that line of questioning.

"Rest assured, Candy, we're doing all we can to cooperate with the police," Plymouth said by way of clarification. "The crime scene investigators are upstairs right now, attempting to find out what happened. The whole floor is sealed off. None of us have been able to get up there to make sure they're not damaging anything—and believe me, we've tried. I've talked to the police personally, but so far they haven't been forthcoming with any answers. So we'll all just have to sit tight until they're done and then soldier on through this as best we can."

"I agree," Owen said. He bent forward, scanning a number of documents in front of him on the desk, as if dismissing her. "Now if you'll let us get back to . . ."

But he was interrupted by a disembodied voice that seemed to emanate from somewhere around Owen's desk.

"Perhaps it might be a good time to take a short break," the voice said.

Candy felt a chill go through her. Definitely a male voice. And one she was certain she'd heard before.

"Who's that?" she asked, her eyes searching for the source. Her gaze quickly alighted on the black speakerphone on Owen's desk.

"Why, it's me, Miss Holliday," said the voice over the phone. "I couldn't be there in person this morning, unfortunately, since I'm stuck here in Boston at the moment. But I wanted to make sure I was part of this conversation, since it concerns the museum's future. So I called in to offer my support and my services in any way I can, given this very difficult time for all of us."

There was a pause, and Candy suddenly had an overwhelming urge to sit down. Her head was beginning to spin and her neck felt hot.

"Now, you and I have never had a chance to meet in person," the voice over the speakerphone continued in a lighthearted way, "but I know you by reputation, and I'm pretty sure you've heard of me. My name is Porter Sykes."

FOURTEEN

Herr Georg Wolfsburger was in love.

He was in love with baking, his chosen profession. He loved making wedding cakes and German pastries—and when fresh fruit was in season, blueberry muffins, strawberry strudel, apple turnovers, and one of his own creations, raspberry rumbles, based on an heirloom recipe he'd found in an old book. He was incredibly proud of his baked goods; of his shop, the Black Forest Bakery on Main Street; and of the reputation he'd built over the past decade, not only in Cape Willington, but throughout the state and the Northeast. He loved getting his hands deep in flour, and the smell of cinnamon in the morning, and a flaky, buttery, perfectly baked piecrust.

He was in love with this coastal village, his adopted home. He loved the quaint streets and active downtown, the opera house and Town Park, the lighthouses and seagulls, the rocky shoreline, the deep blue of the ocean and the powerful crash of waves.

He loved the people who came into his shop, villagers and tourists alike.

But most of all, he loved Maggie Tremont.

He'd known her casually for the better part of a decade, mostly due to her friendship with Candy Holliday. But he'd become completely entranced by her once they'd started working side by side at the bakery. It had been like a dance of sorts right from the beginning, and difficult for him to hold in his passion for her. He was taken not only by her physical beauty but also by her inner spirit, her contagious laugh, her seemingly endless energy, her quirky sense of humor, and her generally sunny disposition, which meshed so well with his own.

He'd felt, right in those first few days, that he'd finally found his soul mate, his partner in life—and a partner in business as well.

She'd been a fast learner and an eager student in the shop, absorbing all the nuances of the bakery business and finding ways to enhance revenue. She was wonderful with the customers, and had seemingly infinite patience when fulfilling their myriad requests. She always maintained a lighthearted disposition, even on the busiest, most stressful days. She kept things tidy, helped stock the shelves, and willingly worked beside him in the kitchen, eager to perfect her pastries, muffins, and pies. She'd even taken an interest in candy making, something new to his shop. She'd started simply enough, experimenting with chocolate-dipped blueberries and strawberries, and lately branched out, adding items like caramel crunches, chocolate truffles, and rich, creamy fudge. And she'd discovered a newly acquired love for making German-style pretzels, which they'd also added in a countertop display. They'd become a popular item with customers, and usually sold out quickly.

Over the past couple of years, she'd become an invaluable addition, not only to the bakery, but to every aspect of his life. Getting married was the next obvious step in their relationship. The trip to the altar had been a long one, but that day was nearly here.

He couldn't be more excited. . . .

Or more worried.

Georg was not a worrier by nature. Rather than let problems fester, he preferred to face them straight on and take care of them before they got out of hand. Those that were out of his control he tried to deal with as best he could. That usually removed the need to worry.

But this latest development was more than he could ever imagine. And he didn't quite know what to do about it.

He still couldn't believe Julius was gone. It seemed so sudden, a cruel and abrupt end to their long friendship. They'd seen each other just last week, when they'd met for lunch at a little sandwich shop down by the docks overlooking the English River. It was a place geared more toward locals than tourists, with a decidedly maritime feel. Julius had loved the place, for he reveled in hearing the stories of his fellow diners, who were fishermen and dock workers, laborers and old salts of the sea, and always quick to bend his ear with tales of their adventures or those of their relatives and ancestors.

That lunch had started out simply enough. Both he and Julius ordered the usual—lobster rolls with meat fresh from the boats, accompanied by homemade potato salad and fried pickles. They'd washed it all down with a good local beer. And they'd talked, as always, about many things—the upcoming wedding, of course, which had been their main topic, but they'd also chatted about the oncoming tourist season, new dining establishments in town, how some of the local businesses were faring, and, of course, the weather.

But when Herr Georg had inquired about Julius's recent activities and research, the conversation had taken an unexpected turn.

Herr Georg still couldn't quite believe what he'd heard—or what had happened next. Julius had said it was only a precaution, but had sworn the baker to secrecy, which Herr Georg had honored—so far. But he wondered if he was doing the right thing by keeping what he knew—and possessed—to himself. Especially after what had happened last night. He'd been tempted to go to the police, but so far he'd held back.

He was not one given to indecision, but in this case, he was uncertain of the proper course of action. And it nagged at him.

Julius had been somewhat reserved that day, and his moments of lightheartedness had seemed forced. At the time,

Herr Georg had attributed Julius's mood to simple pre-ceremony jitters. But he now knew that something else had been going on—something serious enough to result in Julius's death.

As he thought back over that day, Herr Georg wondered if he'd missed something. He tried to recall the details of their conversation but could remember only bits of it. Most had been left behind in the quick passage of the recent days, squeezed out by all the other thoughts on his mind. He'd done as Julius requested, and hadn't heard from him since. He'd assumed they'd catch up at last night's dinner party. But Julius never made it.

And Herr Georg felt partly responsible.

He'd been stunned to learn that one of the bottles of champagne he'd personally ordered had made its way from the inn to the museum, where it allegedly had been used as a murder weapon—and he'd told the police as much when they'd interviewed him last night, and again when he'd talked to them briefly this morning. There were too many questions he didn't have answers to. How did the bottle get there? Why was it used for such an unthinkable purpose? Was it a random occurrence—the choice of bottles—or something with a more sinister purpose?

There was a possibility, he knew, that the murderer had used a bottle of his champagne for a specific reason, but he had a hard time imagining what that might be. To blackmail him? To send a message of some sort? To delay or derail the wedding?

During the sleepless night before, the baker had racked his brain to think of anyone he knew who would want to do any of those things—or murder Julius, for that matter. He'd considered a few remote possibilities, but none of them made much sense, and ultimately he came up empty-handed.

So he tried a different approach. He worked out various scenarios in his head, trying to explain how the bottle might have made its way from the inn to the museum. As far as he could determine, there were only a few possibilities.

One: Julius had taken the bottle over to the museum himself.

It was certainly the most likely explanation, but Georg dismissed it almost at once. Julius wouldn't have taken a bottle out of the case without asking first, and so far no one had indicated that he'd done so. No one had seen him around the inn yesterday; in fact, it seemed few people had seen him at all over the past few days.

Besides, why would he have taken a bottle with him to the museum, especially if he was intent on doing research up in the archives? Julius was not a drinking man. He might have had a beer or a glass of wine now and then, but guzzling down a full bottle of champagne? That image seemed out of character for him.

Two: Someone working at the inn could have taken it over there—someone who worked in the kitchen, perhaps. Herr Georg had heard word that morning that the police had already spent some time at the inn, questioning the staff, trying to figure out what had happened, but there was no word yet on whether they'd turned up anything, or anyone, interesting.

Then there was the matter of the unconscious waiter, whom Maggie had discovered last night. What had happened to him? How did he wind up lying on the floor in that storage room? Herr Georg didn't even know the waiter's name, or if he might be linked somehow to the bottle's disappearance from the inn. Had he seen something? Did he know who took it? Is that why he'd been knocked unconscious?

Of course, the other possibility was that someone unconnected with the inn or the wedding—perhaps someone none of them knew—had crept in there, stolen the bottle without being seen, and used it to strike down Julius, for whatever reason.

The problem was, Georg knew, he himself was an obvious suspect. He'd had access to the bottles of champagne. He knew Julius and could get close to him easily. Georg could account for much of his time yesterday, but he'd run home for a while by himself in the afternoon, and he'd been in and out of the inn during the couple of hours prior to the party, seeing to preparations, before he'd settled in for the evening.

Logistically, he easily could have made a trip to the museum during that time. So although he had a fairly strong alibi, he had what the police liked to call "opportunity."

Herr Georg didn't like that word. He didn't like the supposition that he'd contributed in any way to Julius's death. He resented the suggestion, though, as was his way, he kept that thought to himself.

But it worried him. And he knew he had to figure out what was going on, somehow, if he wanted to protect his reputation, his shop, his upcoming marriage, and everything he loved so dearly. But more than that, he simply wanted to find out why his friend had been murdered in the first place. It seemed the least he could do in Julius's memory.

He knew he had to face this problem as he had all the others in his life—straight on. So he'd decided to do a little snooping around, on his own, to see what he could find out.

He'd told Maggie he wanted to work in the shop alone that morning, to make their wedding cake. The place would be closed to the public for another ten days or so as they finished preparations for the season. They still had some ordering to do, a few upgrades to complete, schedules to work on, and shelves to stock. But he'd set up everything in the kitchen. He was ready to go. He knew what he was going to bake and how long it would take him. And he planned to get started on it . . . soon.

But right now he had another task on his mind. So, with his head full of a jumble of thoughts, he removed his apron, slipped into a spring jacket, grabbed his favorite green felt Tyrolean hat, complete with tall side feathers, from its spot on a clothes tree near his office desk, and locked up the shop before heading down the street.

FIFTEEN

The town seemed sleepy today, as if resting up before the busy season ahead, reserving its strength for the time when it would need it. During the summer the town took on a faster-paced, more festive atmosphere, but today it felt like any average coastal village in Maine on a warm spring day. Folks were running into and out of the hardware store and the beauty salon, which were across the street from each other, and dashing into the diner. Down along Ocean Avenue, the shops showed signs of waking up, with lights on inside and bodies moving around, making preparations, just as he was doing at the bakery. And more than a few, he noticed, already had OPEN signs in their windows.

Herr Georg waved to people he knew, and smiled as warmly as he could, but he didn't pause to talk to anyone. He wanted to get this over with, so he could move on to other things.

The Lightkeeper's Inn looked stately as always when glimpsed against the shimmering blue sea beyond. The inn's staff was taking advantage of the improving weather, opening windows, airing out furniture, sweeping down the porch, and washing windows. A landscaper, whose name Georg thought was Mick Rilke, was out on the property, edging the flower beds and putting in carnations and marigolds along the walkways to add color as the crocuses and bulb plants began to fade and die off. Toward the rear of the building, another worker was hosing down shutters, which were leaned up against a whitewashed wall. Everyone looked busy.

Hands in his pockets, trying to appear more casual than he felt, Herr Georg waved to a few folks as he climbed the steps to the porch and entered the inn through a side door. He headed straight for assistant innkeeper Alby Alcott's office, halfway along the carpeted hallway he'd stepped into.

Not surprisingly, Alby wasn't in his office today; he was probably out overseeing the spring cleaning activities. Also missing was his receptionist, whose desk was abandoned. Georg hesitated for a few moments in the doorway, unsure whether to wait here or try to track Alby down somewhere else in the building or on the grounds. But he felt that was an uncertain quest, so he decided on another option.

Turning on his heel, he headed farther along the hallway, toward the lobby. Again, Alby wasn't behind the front desk, nor anywhere that Georg could see. So he turned right, toward the dining room and the kitchen at the back of the building.

Georg knew the way; he'd been here often enough over the past week or so, and he'd eaten here more times than he could count. He walked with a certain confidence along the hallway past the dining room, which was nearly empty, since breakfast was over and the lunch crowd had yet to arrive. Only a few lingerers remained over cooling cups of coffee, reading the paper or engaged in low conversations.

At the far end of the hall, Georg pushed through to the kitchen and took an immediate right, to a small warren of offices at one side. He stepped into the first one he came to, and here he actually found someone he was looking for.

Colin Trevor Jones, the inn's executive chef, was talking on the phone. When he looked up and saw the baker, he waved him in, motioning to a chair, before turning his attention back to the phone conversation.

"So no one knows what happened to him?" Colin said into

the phone after a few moments, his face showing his concern. "How is that possible? Wasn't someone keeping tabs on him?" A pause. "Maybe he just went home." He listened again, then said, "Yes, of course, we'll watch out for him. I'll let you know immediately if he shows up."

After a few last words, Colin hung up and looked over at the baker, his expression troubled, his thoughts still obviously on the phone conversation. "Herr Georg, good morning. What a surprise. I thought you'd be getting ready for the wedding this morning."

"Oh, I've been doing that," the baker said, settling into a chair. "But I decided to step out for a little while. I hope I'm not interrupting, Colin. I know you probably have a lot to do this morning. But after the events of last night, I thought I should stop by and follow up. See how things are going here."

"Well." Colin leaned back and ran a hand through his curly dark hair. "Things, as you probably can imagine, have been a little crazy. For some reason Oliver decided to turn everyone out today to clean the inn, while the police are in the middle of conducting their investigation. I told him it's not a good idea but I couldn't convince him otherwise. He's just got his mind set on it, and says the police can do whatever they have to do while we do what we have to do. We had officers out here first thing this morning, quizzing our people. They spent two hours just here in the kitchen, talking to my staff."

"And have they learned anything valuable?" Georg asked, unable to contain his interest.

Colin hesitated before he answered. "Well, of course, they haven't shared their findings with any of us, at least not that I've heard. And I don't expect they will anytime soon. But . . . well, it seems we've run into a bit of a snag."

Herr Georg leaned forward in his chair. "And what's that?"

"Well, it's this young waiter we have here—Scotty Whitby."

"Whitby?"

Colin nodded. "He's the young man Maggie discovered last night, unconscious in the storeroom. He's been working here for a year or two—nice kid, does a good job. I had hopes he'd stick around for a while."

"What do you mean?"

"Well, he's gone," Colin said, spreading his hands in a gesture of frustration. "After they found him unconscious in that storeroom, they took him to the hospital last night. He was supposed to be there overnight while they checked him out. But this morning he's nowhere to be found. The police went to the hospital to see him but his bed was vacant. His clothes are gone. They've searched all over town for him, but can't find him anywhere."

Colin pointed to the phone. "That was Oliver, asking if Scotty had turned up here in the kitchen. But I haven't seen him anywhere on the grounds this morning."

He paused, his concerned gaze shifting from the phone to the baker. "It appears that our unconscious waiter, who could be connected to that champagne bottle of yours, has disappeared."

SIXTEEN

Porter Sykes.

Oh, no, Candy thought. *Not him.*

Scion of the Sykes family. Successful entrepreneur and real estate developer from Boston. And her largely unseen nemesis, who she knew was behind much of the chaos that had plagued the town over the past few years.

She took a deep breath.

What have I gotten myself into?

She felt for a moment like a deer caught in oncoming headlights, unable to move, unable to speak. Her arms had gone numb and she heard a strange low buzzing sound in her ears. But she was able to blink, so she did that several times as she struggled to reclaim her thoughts. It was a momentarily difficult endeavor, since her mind seemed to have gone completely blank.

She shifted and swept her gaze around the room.

They were all looking at her, waiting for a response.

Okay, keep cool, you can do this.

Her eyes flicked from one face to another. She had to think of something to say right away. Something smart and appropriate, perhaps even witty. Something that wouldn't dig her in any deeper. But at the moment she couldn't think of anything like that, so she turned back to the phone and simply said, "Umm, hi?"

Internally she winced, but it was the best she could do under the circumstances. Fortunately, Porter spoke up to fill the awkward silence.

"I probably should have announced myself earlier," he said in an offhanded manner. "I don't want anyone to think I was eavesdropping on your conversation."

"Oh, no," Edith put in, making a face. "No one would ever think that."

"Of course not," Owen echoed, just to emphasize the point.

"Thank you both for your support." Porter sounded gracious enough, but Candy thought she detected an edge of sarcasm in his tone. It turned more serious as he continued.

"While I have a moment, I would like to add my condolences on Julius's death. I had the chance to meet him only once or twice, but he seemed like a wonderful gentleman. And obviously he was a very talented and beloved individual. I'm sure everyone there at the museum, and throughout the community, will feel his loss greatly."

"I'm sure," Candy repeated, looking for a graceful way out of this situation.

She should have realized Porter might be part of the conversation. He was on the museum's board, after all, just like the others, and had been for the better part of a decade, even though he was rarely in town. But he had family roots here—deep roots, going back generations, as Doc had pointed out earlier today.

That's why Porter kept a finger in local affairs. It's why he occasionally showed up around town, though he currently didn't own a residence here.

But, she thought, there was another reason he kept close tabs on local events and activities.

He was after something.

Something here on the cape. Something that had to do with the historical archives and the museum.

The deeds. The ones that had once belonged to Silas
Sykes and had allegedly been in his treasure box, found by
Miles Crawford shortly before his death. The ones that had
since disappeared.

It all fit. Porter was after those old deeds. Julius had been
researching deeds in the archives when he died. A list of
names, including that of the Sykes family, had been on a piece
of paper stuck into a book up in the archives—possibly put
there by Julius, since it fell out of a book he'd been using for
his research.

The connections seemed obvious.

The Sykes family had been looking for those deeds for
years, going back to the death of an elderly villager named
James Sedley. Mr. Sedley had been killed because he possessed a recipe book, which contained a secret recipe for his
award-winning lobster stew. But it also supposedly contained
details about a lost treasure, and a lost set of deeds.

Various factions had been chasing those deeds ever since.
It's what the Sykes family had been after all these years, as
well as Candy, her father, and Neil Crawford, Miles's son. So
far, no one had been successful in finding them. But maybe
Julius *had*. And maybe Porter Sykes had known it. Who knew
what spies he had around this place?

From Candy's experience, the current generation of the
Sykes clan would stop at nothing to get what they wanted.
She knew that, in one way or another, they'd left a trail of
death and destruction in their wake. But they'd also been
clever, for the most part, staying behind the scenes, manipulating local events in nefarious ways without drawing too
much attention to themselves.

Now here was Porter Sykes—the elder brother—on the
phone, talking to her.

What is he up to?

Could he have had something to do with Julius's murder?
Could he have been behind it somehow? He said he was
currently in Boston, but it was only a five-hour trip in each
direction. Technically he could have been here in town last
night and back home by morning. It was certainly possible,

at least. And, she remembered, he'd done it before, one winter when they'd held an ice sculpting competition here in the village.

Maybe he wasn't even in Boston right now. She was taking his word for that. They all were. He could be anywhere, really, even right here in town, and they'd have no way of knowing it.

Or maybe he was working with someone local, who had killed Julius for him.

She looked around the room again.

Maybe someone like Edith, or Gilbert . . . or Owen.

Could any of them have had something to do with Julius's death—maybe on Porter's behalf?

Could it be possible?

She was determined to find out, for Julius's sake, and for Maggie's and Herr Georg's. But not right now. Now, she thought, it was best to retreat, regroup, digest what she'd just learned, and think about her next move.

So she said the first words that popped into her head. "Well, I hope someday we'll be able to meet face-to-face. Now, if you'll excuse . . ."

But Porter cut in. "You know, that's a wonderful idea. I believe a meeting between the two of us is long overdue—since we've never had the chance to talk in person, of course." He paused a moment to clear his throat. "And as it so happens, I'm going to be up there in Cape Willington tomorrow. Perhaps we could set something up?"

If Candy had been surprised before, she was stunned now. "You want to meet? With me? Face-to-face? For, um, the first time?"

Despite what he was implying, and she was awkwardly confirming—for the benefit of the others in the room, obviously—they *had* met before. She'd had a run-in with him a while back, though she'd kept that fact to herself. She'd never told anyone about it, since it had been so surprising and unnerving. And Porter apparently had done the same. There were times she thought that encounter, which took place at the Sykes's abandoned mansion, Whitefield, was nothing more than a dream, a mirage. The fact that the mansion burned down shortly after their meeting made it seem even more unreal.

"Yes," Porter said pleasantly over the phone. "Do you think that would be possible?"

Candy didn't know how to respond, not with the others in the room watching and listening in with great interest. "I suppose that would be okay," she said finally after another awkward pause.

Porter didn't seem to notice. "Good. Shall we say one o'clock tomorrow afternoon?"

"Tomorrow?" Candy's mind raced, thinking of all the wedding preparations still to be done, wondering if she had the time.

"Is that a problem?" he asked.

Something in the way he said it dug at her, and she remembered that someone had murdered the wedding's best man, using a bottle of champagne Herr Georg had ordered for a dinner party. Her close friends were involved in this. She was determined to solve the mystery as quickly as possible. And maybe this was a good way to do that. "No, that's not a problem. I can make it tomorrow at one."

"Then we have an agreement." Porter sounded pleased. "We can meet out at the old Whitby estate across the bay. Do you know how to get over there?"

That caught her off guard. "The Whitby place?"

"We've kept all this hush-hush up until now," Porter said, "but since all the papers have been signed, and the deal has officially closed, I guess there's no harm in telling all of you that I bought the place myself. It will serve as our summer home for the foreseeable future, and will put all of my family a little closer to those of you there in Cape Willington."

A sudden buzzing sprung up from the other board members in the room, offering congratulations verbally while exchanging sideways glances with one another. Obviously this was new information for everyone.

Except for Owen, who did not seem surprised by the revelation. In fact, he brushed the announcement aside, as if eager to get back to business. "Wonderful. I'm so glad you've worked that out," he said, with his own hint of sarcasm. "And, of course, welcome to the community, Mr. Sykes. Now, Candy, I hope you'll excuse us, but we have some fairly important business to attend to here, and we must get on with it."

That seemed to bring her part of the conversation to a close, and she began to back out of the door. But Porter spoke up again.

"As I mentioned earlier," he said, "maybe it wouldn't be a bad idea for all of us to take a five- or ten-minute break. Stretch our legs, eh? And I have a few calls to make. Candy, I believe you mentioned you'd like a word with Owen, didn't you?"

He'd given her an opening, so she took it, though again, she wondered about the motivation behind it. "Hmm, yes, that's correct. I just have a few quick questions for him."

"Of a personal matter?" Porter asked.

Candy thought it was an odd question, but answered anyway. "Something like that. It shouldn't take more than a minute or two."

Bluntly, he asked, "To reiterate what was said earlier, would these questions have anything to do with the Julius Seabury business?"

Again, Candy hesitated. But she decided she had no other choice than to be forthright. "There might be one or two questions I have in mind about that, yes."

Edith Pring leaned forward in her chair, her stern face reflecting her concern. "Is that proper?"

"I don't think there's any harm in it," Plymouth said.

"I agree," said Porter. "We all know Candy has had some success in the past solving these kinds of . . . crimes, and the sooner we get this resolved, the sooner we can get the museum's schedule back to normal. Owen, would you talk to her and see what you can do to help her out? Shall we reconvene in, say, ten minutes?"

SEVENTEEN

Out in the main hall, Owen was livid.

Candy had stepped out of his office first, grateful to finally make a retreat. Owen followed, practically stomping his way across the wooden floorboards and pulling the office door closed behind him with a slam. Candy caught a final glance back into the office as the door was shutting on the three board members. Their expressions ranged from irritated to concerned to contemplative.

Candy just hoped she hadn't made any enemies in there.

Or encountered a murderer.

"What is the meaning of all this?" Owen demanded after he'd marched several steps away from the door before planting his feet and crossing his arms, his face florid. She could practically see the steam coming out of his ears. As he spoke, he struggled to keep his voice down, so he wouldn't be heard by the board members through the door, but his words were quick and sharp. "In case you hadn't noticed, I'm talking to some very important people in there." For emphasis, he jabbed toward the office door with his finger. "Their time is very valuable, and so is mine. I really can't afford to waste a moment on this kind of tomfoolery."

Candy raised an eyebrow but let the comment pass. *Best not to fan the flames.*

"I'll keep this brief then," she said as calmly as possible. "It's about the list of names you found upstairs last night, when you picked up the book off the floor. You remember it, right?"

"You mean that worthless slip of paper?"

Candy nodded. "I'm trying to determine if that 'worthless slip of paper' was actually a note written by Julius."

"Julius?" Owen's gaze narrowed. "Is that what this is all about?"

Candy pulled out the book she'd tucked under her arm and flipped it open to the title page. She turned it around and held it out to show Owen. "This is one of the books Julius wrote, and he signed it. That's his handwriting." She pointed to the inscription with the finger of her other hand, to make it easy for him to follow. "I'm wondering if it matches the handwriting on that note you saw last night. If we can match the handwriting, then it means it was written by Julius, which could be important."

Owen looked at her incredulously. "You're serious?"

She nodded, tight-lipped, and pointed at the inscription again. "So does this look familiar? Could the person who wrote this—Julius—also have written that note?"

"How in the world would I know that?"

"Because you saw it. As far as I know, you're the *only* person who saw it—up close, I mean—unless you've handed it over to the police."

Owen's silence told her he hadn't—just as she'd suspected. His mouth turned down at the corners. Finally he said, "Why is this important?"

"Because it could be a clue."

"To what?"

"To Julius's death. To finding out who struck him over the head with that bottle of champagne."

At this somewhat graphic description, Owen visibly flinched. He looked for a moment like he wanted to forget entirely about the murder at his museum, but also seemed to reluctantly accept that it wasn't possible.

Best to pass the buck.

"Ms. Holliday—Candy. There are plenty of experts involved in solving this . . . unfortunate crime, so there's no need for any of us to get involved. In fact, I would strongly recommend against it. My job, as I see it—"

Candy tried to interrupt but Owen talked over her, forcing her to stop while he continued.

"—my *job*," he emphasized, "is to discuss the current situation with the board members and decide how best to proceed at this difficult time, while cooperating fully with the police investigation and ensuring the stainless reputation of this institution, until this case is resolved, in whichever way that happens. And that's exactly what I intend to do. Nothing more, nothing less."

He paused, his expression as hard as New Hampshire granite. "I *do* hope I've made myself clear. Now, if you'll *please* excuse me . . ."

With a firm nod of his head, he turned on his heel and started back toward his office.

But Candy wasn't ready to give up just yet.

"Where's the note, anyway?" she called after him. "Do you have it with you? We can compare the handwriting right now. It will only take a moment."

Owen's shoulders stiffened as he slowed, then stopped. He took a deep, dramatic breath and turned back toward her, his gaze menacing. "You *are* persistent, aren't you?"

"It's one of my better traits," she said with a reassuring smile.

He was silent a moment, as if thinking it over. "Very well," he finally breathed out with great effort. "Perhaps it's best to just get this over with." He patted at his jacket pockets on both sides, and dipped a hand into the inside pockets as well. When he didn't find what he was looking for, he pressed his eyes closed and shook his head, as if suddenly remembering.

"I don't have it on me," he informed her. "I changed jackets this morning, as I now recall. I must have left it at home."

"Can you check on it?" Candy asked. "Later, when you get back to your place? And let me know?"

In response, Owen rolled his eyes. "*If* I remember," he said, obviously with great effort to maintain his composure. "But as you may realize, I have other, more pressing matters on my mind today."

Candy held out the book toward him. "Would you like to take this with you? So you can compare the handwriting?"

Owen looked down at the book warily, as if it were something distasteful. "That's not the only book he signed, you know. Now, if you'll excuse me, I need to get back to my meeting."

Candy took a last-minute different tack. "Did you know Porter Sykes bought the Whitby place? What's that all about?" she asked in a loud stage whisper.

Owen just glared at her and, without another word, turned and walked the rest of the way to his office, opened the door, and disappeared inside. Candy could hear murmuring voices briefly as he entered, but they faded to nothing as Owen closed the door firmly, shutting her out.

A moment later, she thought she heard a faint click.

Had he locked the door behind him? To prevent any further interruptions?

By her?

"Well, the nerve!" Candy said with an indignant shake of her head. "I guess *that* didn't go as well as I'd hoped."

She wasn't quite sure what to make of Owen's behavior. No doubt he was under a great deal of stress, especially when dealing with the board members. There'd been a murder in the building he managed. No one knew how long the police would have the place shut down. Money would be lost. Employees might not get paid. Owen might even be thinking his livelihood was in jeopardy. Certainly enough to account for his uncooperative behavior.

But why was he neglecting to hand the note over to the police? Did he really not understand its possible value?

Or was he trying to hide something?

Standing all alone in the dim room, eyes cast downward, Candy thought back over the encounter she'd just had with him and the board members. She'd learned a few things this morning, like the fact that Plymouth Palfrey was in town, and Gilbert Ethingham had been drawn out of his nest. And she'd learned that Porter Sykes was involved in this, which was interesting—and not unexpected, once she thought about it.

But she hadn't accomplished what she'd come here to do. She hadn't verified that the note found by Owen had been written by Julius. For the moment, however, she decided to assume it was, though she knew the evidence to support her theory was sketchy.

Owen was right about one thing—that note could have been written by anyone. It could be of unknown age, just a forgotten slip of paper tucked between the pages of a book, like so many others, only to be discovered again by whoever turned those pages years later. If that was true, then there was no point in suspecting Owen of anything. It was a nonissue.

But it had fallen out of a book Julius had been using for his research. The book must have been sitting on the table before being thrown to the floor, probably during the struggle between Julius and his attacker. It was probable, even likely, that he'd written the note and left it in that book to remind himself of something. A note about his research.

But she thought it was more than that.

She thought it could have something to do with his death.

She thought back over the names on the list: *Bosworth, Ethingham, Whitby, Rainsford, Palfrey, Sykes.*

Curiously, she'd encountered members of three of those families in the museum director's office just now. And a fourth family name was involved, through the Whitby place across the bay.

That in itself was incredibly suspicious. But what about L. B.? And Foul Mouth?

How did it all tie together?

With that question in mind, she turned and was about to leave the Keeper's Quarters when she heard footsteps coming down the wooden stairs from the second floor. A few moments later, a man and a woman whom Candy didn't know, dressed in dark blue uniforms, emerged from the side exhibit room, still wearing light blue booties and each carrying a black suitcaselike container of equipment. They walked past her through the main room, nodding as they went without saying anything to her, and exited the building through the front door. As they left, she saw the words STATE POLICE stenciled in large yellow capital letters on their backs.

They were soon followed by a young Cape Willington police officer whom Candy had seen around town. Apparently not noticing her, he made a beeline for Owen's office and rapped loudly on the closed door.

"We're busy!" Candy heard a muffled voice shout through the door, obviously Owen. "Please go away!"

The police officer looked mystified for a moment, tried the door handle, and found it locked. He knocked again, and when he received no response, he turned and spotted Candy.

"Is the museum director in there?" he asked.

She nodded. "He's in a meeting with the board members."

The police officer hesitated for a moment, then shrugged and approached her. He pointed up. "We're all done on the second floor for the moment," he said. "Would you let them know?"

"Of course," Candy said.

"We're going to leave the crime scene tape up for another day or so, just to make sure we don't need anything else. We'd appreciate it if you kept the museum closed for the rest of the day."

"What about tomorrow?" she asked.

"We'll let you know. I'll call the director later in the day with instructions."

"I'll be sure and tell him that."

"If he has any questions, he can call Officer Blackburn over at the station."

"Officer Blackburn. Got it." She repeated the name as if to lock it in her memory, and noticed his incredibly blue eyes and strong, dimpled chin. "Is there anything else I should let Owen know, Officer Blackburn? Anything about the investigation?"

She resisted batting her eyes. She had to be subtle. She knew she was fishing, but it never hurt to try.

The officer didn't take the bait, however, and gave her a typical canned, impassive response. "We're not releasing any of that information right now, ma'am, but we'll keep you posted."

"Oh, well, thanks for letting me know. And please tell Chief Durr that Candy Holliday said hi."

That caught him off guard momentarily, but he quickly recovered. "I'll be sure and do that, ma'am."

Moments later he was gone as well.

"Ma'am." Candy rolled the word around in her mouth, trying to make it sound like he'd said it, with the kind of low drawl police officers seemed to favor. She failed. "Hmm."

She was all alone in the dimly lit room again. Owen and his group were still talking behind a locked door. They'd probably be in there a while longer, she thought.

Enough time to give her a chance to dash upstairs and take a quick peek around. If she did it quickly and quietly enough, she reasoned, no one would ever know.

She hesitated and bit her lip as she weighed her decision. She didn't want to get herself in hot water again, just minutes after being on the receiving end of the Wrath of Owen. But she quickly decided the potential reward was worth the possible risk, so off she went.

EIGHTEEN

Cautiously.

She crept up the stairs in her stocking feet, shoes cradled in her arms. She made sure she stayed toward the outside of each step, tight against the side wall, to avoid the creakiest parts of the old wooden staircase. No point alerting the folks downstairs to her wanderings, though she reasoned that if they heard anything up here, they'd no doubt assume it was the investigative team still poking around—which was exactly what she intended to do.

She paused at the top of the staircase, wondering if she was pushing her luck too far. But then she reasoned that Officer Blackburn with the piercing blue eyes and cleft chin hadn't specifically said she *couldn't* have a look around up there, so she wasn't breaking any laws—at least, she didn't think so.

Of course, she'd never really *asked*.

Best do this quickly, before she was discovered—or lost her nerve.

Forcing herself to move again, she stepped lightly across the second-floor landing and stopped just outside the door to the archive room, where she'd found Julius's body.

The place looked much as it had the night before, but it *felt* different. There was an unsettling vibe in the air. The light through the windows seemed to shimmer in an odd way, and the smells were all wrong, as if an alien from a distant planet had camped out here.

Or a couple of crime scene investigators.

The doorway was now partially blocked off with yellow police tape, so she stood just outside as she surveyed the room beyond.

Books were gone, she noticed; there were none on the table, and empty spots on the shelves indicated where a book had been removed but never replaced. She couldn't quite tell what matched from the night before, or didn't. She imagined the police had taken the books on the table and some off the shelves as evidence.

Julius's notebooks were gone as well. The table was once again centered, and the chair had been set upright and put in its proper place. A taped-off, vaguely body-shaped area on the ground indicated where Julius had lain. There was another smaller marked-off area a short distance away, to indicate where the bottle of champagne had come to rest. Like the books and notebooks, the bottle was gone, obviously locked up in an evidence room somewhere inside the Cape Willington Police Department, or on its way to the state's forensics lab in Augusta.

Shelves and window ledges, as well as the overhead light, looked as if they'd been well dusted. The entire place seemed to have been scrubbed clean, every item picked over, tested, or collected.

At least the forensics team had been thorough.

Too thorough. She doubted there was much left for her to check. They'd probably taken everything that might be remotely helpful.

But after she thought about it a moment, she realized that if there was anything of interest here, it would be in the volumes on the shelves. They still might hold a few secrets, like the slip of paper that had fallen from the book. Had the forensics team checked all of the books? Possibly, but the task would have taken hours. Of course, they'd been up here for hours, possibly through the night. Still, it was worth a look, right?

Taking a deep breath, she stepped gingerly through an open spot in the tape crisscrossing the door, paused just inside to gather herself, and then crossed toward the shelves on her right. Eyes moving quickly, she scanned the titles. Typical volumes on Maine history, some covering centuries, others targeting more specific events and periods of time. Books on boatbuilding, sailing ships, steamboats, schooners, and paddle-wheelers were numerous. She also spotted a significant collection on the state's geological features, like its rivers and mountains, up in a far corner of the shelves.

Her eyes moved over the spines and old lettering quickly, looking for anything that stood out, but so far nothing caught her attention.

She shifted to another shelf, along another wall. Here were biographies, which looked more interesting to her. She shuffled in closer for a better look.

There were quite a few books devoted to famous Mainers, past and present. One shelf was devoted to political figures from Maine—people like Hannibal Hamlin, who served under Lincoln during the Civil War, and Nelson Rockefeller, who was born in Bar Harbor. She saw quite a few volumes about John D. Rockefeller, and remembered that he was among the driving forces behind the creation of Acadia National Park on Mount Desert Island. There was a sizable representation of books devoted to Maine-based artists and writers, like Winslow Homer and Edna St. Vincent Millay. And she wasn't surprised to see nearly an entire shelf devoted to Henry Wadsworth Longfellow, a native of Portland.

And then there was a section devoted specifically to Down East Maine, and Cape Willington in particular. The region's role in the state's development. The town's history, including its settlement and growth through the years. And, on a lower shelf, its founding and prominent families.

She crouched down and zeroed in on those.

She saw quite a few books devoted to the Pruitts. That was

a given, since they'd had a significant influence on the town's development. A number of buildings around town, including the Pruitt Opera House and the Pruitt Public Library, were named after them. Pruitt Manor, out on the point by Kimball Light, was still the family's summer home, frequented by Helen Ross Pruitt, the clan's current matriarch, and her children and grandchildren.

Moving on, her gaze alighted on a group of thin, older volumes, similar in size and design, all shelved together. She tilted her head so she could get a better look at the angled, faded printing, her eyes flicking from one book to another. The names on the spines were instantly recognizable.

Bosworth.

Ethingham.

Whitby.

Rainsford.

Palfrey.

Sykes.

She blinked several times. There they were, all in a row, just like on the list Owen had found last night.

She wondered what it could mean. But almost immediately she knew.

The list of names on the slip of paper and the lineup of books on the shelf in front of her corresponded perfectly. That was *too* much of a coincidence to be random. Right?

It could mean only one thing: Someone must have arranged the books purposely in that order.

And Julius Seabury was the most likely candidate.

He must have placed the books on that shelf, and written the names on that slip of paper, in a certain order for a reason. Had he just been researching them in that order? Or was he trying to send a message of some sort?

Would the investigative team have noticed those books, arranged in that specific way?

Probably not, she thought. There was nothing unusual about the way the books were shelved—at least, not to the normal eye. No one would notice the order without having seen the note—which Owen still had, tucked away in the pocket of a sport jacket hanging in his closet at home, or thrown over the back of a kitchen chair.

She wanted to take a look inside the books but hesitated to touch them. She didn't want to leave her fingerprints behind—at least, not more than she already had.

When she'd left the house that morning she'd pulled on a cotton mock turtleneck shirt with long narrow sleeves. Because the sleeves were a little long, she'd rolled the cuffs up about an inch. Now she unrolled her left sleeve and gathered the edge around her fingers, as a sort of glove. Reaching up, she touched the top of one book's spine with a cloth-covered index finger and tipped the book out. It dropped into her hand.

It was the first book in the lineup of thin volumes. The title on the cover read, *A Family History: The Bosworths, 1809–1980*. At the bottom of the page, in smaller faded yellow type, was the author's name: Lucinda P. Dowling.

Candy had heard the Dowling name around town. There was a family of that name living out past Maggie's house, she recalled, beyond Fowler's Corner on the other side of the river.

Not too far from Julius Seabury's place, come to think of it.

She opened the cover and flipped back through the pages. She half expected to find another note stuck somewhere inside, or maybe a code or a secret message or something that might point her in the right direction, give her some clue as to who killed Julius. But she found no such magic message. The book was published in 1999, she noticed from the copyright page, and the title page was signed by the author with a fountain pen in a flowing script, which looked as old and faded as the book itself.

She scanned through the volume and spotted Judicious F. P. Bosworth's name in the final pages. He'd been born in 1967 to the Honorable and Mrs. Rutledge Howard Paul Bosworth in Bangor. She quickly did the numbers and determined that Judicious would turn fifty next year.

There was no additional information about him, but she noticed he had an older brother, someone named Marshall Bosworth, born in 1963. She'd have to ask Judicious about that the next time she saw him. He never spoke much about his family, and she'd never known he had a sibling.

Other than that, there was nothing significant about the book.

Same thing with the other family histories she checked, devoted to the Ethinghams, the Whitbys, and the Rainsfords, although there were some interesting historical photos of the Whitby estate, which she studied for a few moments. But she found nothing useful.

She was just reaching for the volume on the Palfrey family when she heard muffled voices from below and realized the meeting in Owen's office might be breaking up.

Time to go.

She didn't have time to check the other two books, so on an impulse she pulled out the one devoted to the Sykes family, tucked it under her arm, and pushed the other books on the shelf closer together to disguise the fact that she'd taken one of the volumes. She'd bring it back in a day or two; she just wanted to take a little more time to look through it.

Back downstairs, the main exhibit room was still deserted. She hurried across, but on the way out she swung behind the Long Desk, her eyes searching for the sign-in book. It was a tradition for visitors to the museum to sign in, and there was a logbook for the volunteer staff as well. She assumed there was a staff schedule somewhere but thought that might be in Owen's office, inaccessible to her at the moment.

But the sign-in books were gone. The crime scene investigators must have taken those as well, to see who had been in the building recently.

Before she left, she found a blank sheet of paper and scribbled a quick note to Owen, telling him about the message from Officer Blackburn concerning the schedule for the Keeper's Quarters. She thought of leaving it just outside his office, but before she could do that, she heard a creak of hinges and twisted her head around. The door to Owen's office was beginning to open.

She didn't want to be seen by him, since she wanted to avoid another confrontation, so she simply laid the note on the top of the counter. Then, staying low, with her shoes still off, she crept along the back side of the Long Desk to the end, zipped out the door, and left the building.

Outside, the sun was bright and the ocean glimmered. Seagulls whirled above, searching for sustenance on the rocks. Moving quickly, she headed up along the sidewalk toward the parking lot, checking her watch.

Suddenly she knew where she had to go next.

It was time to pay a visit to Wanda Boyle at the *Cape Crier*.

NINETEEN

In the short drive from the museum to the center of town, the general mood around her changed abruptly. The dim, solemn rooms at the Keeper's Quarters quickly gave way to the more relaxed atmosphere up along Ocean Avenue, and Candy felt a wave of relief.

She'd hurried up the pathway from the museum to the parking lot so fast she never had time to put her shoes back on. Now, as she pulled into an open parking spot halfway up the avenue, right in front of the Pruitt Opera House, she still wasn't wearing them. She'd driven with her stocking feet on the pedals.

After she shut off the engine, she finally took a few moments to slip the shoes back onto her feet. Laced up and once again fully dressed, she stepped out of the Jeep and took a quick look around.

Town Park, down the street to her right, was abloom, the trees unfolding their lime green leaves, buds springing out on the low shrubs and bushes. Across the street, the staff of the Lightkeeper's Inn was out in full force, tidying up the place for the summer season. Store windows and doors along both sides of the street were thrust open, allowing in the sea breezes, airing out from the long closed-up winter and spring months. The villagers were out, too, winter coats left behind, chatting and enjoying the unexpectedly warm morning.

The town was waking up from its winter sleep, and things would only get busier for all of them as they headed into the next few weeks.

But she'd deal with the summer season when it arrived. At the moment, the next few days held her immediate and complete attention. Not just this afternoon's gathering out at the farm, or the wedding walk-through and rehearsal dinner tomorrow, or the ceremony itself on Saturday, just two days from today. But also her upcoming encounter with Porter Sykes tomorrow afternoon at one.

Porter Sykes.

Grandson of the family matriarch, Daisy Porter-Sykes, now in her mid-nineties. Brother of Roger, and Morgan, his sister, who lived in New York City. Descendant of one of Cape Willington's most notorious founding families.

And now a local property owner.

Apparently moving into the Whitby house, which he said he'd just bought. And she was supposed to meet him there . . . presumably alone.

During their previous encounter a few years ago, he hadn't precisely threatened her, but he had told her in no uncertain terms that he wanted to make the town pay for its past treatment of his family.

"I'm putting Cape Willington on notice," he'd told her at the time. *"For too long my family has been disgraced by the people of this town. Those days are over. . . ."*

He hadn't given her any specifics, and they'd never come face-to-face since, but she'd felt his manipulative fingers in other events that had occurred around town recently. And now it seemed as if his plan—whatever it might be—was beginning to unfold.

Candy wasn't a paranoid person by nature. She doubted

Porter would threaten her or harm her in any way if she kept her appointment with him tomorrow. But she wasn't about to head over there without knowing what she was walking into.

That's what brought her here, to the offices of the *Cape Crier*, and its new managing editor, Wanda Boyle.

Candy crossed to the opposite side of the avenue at mid-street and started up the stairs to the newspaper's second-floor offices. For years she'd walked up and down these same stairs dozens of times a week, when she'd served as the paper's community correspondent, and then its interim managing editor. She'd been given the chance to remove the "interim" part from her title and become the paper's permanent editor, but she'd never accepted the offer, uncertain that's what she really wanted to do. She'd finally realized her interests lay elsewhere and made the very difficult decision to leave the paper as a full-time staff member.

Just a couple of months earlier, at the start of maple sugaring season, she'd finally turned her title, and her office, over to Wanda Boyle and headed off into the snowy woods to tap maple trees and collect sap buckets. Hard as it was, she never regretted her decision.

But her involvement with the paper had not ended completely. She was always looking for ways to augment the income she and her father made from the farm, so she'd come to an agreement with Wanda to start writing a regular gardening column during the planting, growing, and harvest seasons, and switch to a food column with occasional restaurant reviews during the winter. The topics overlapped quite a bit, so she could mix things up when she wanted to. She sometimes wrote about food during the summer and fall, visiting restaurants up and down the coast with Maggie. They had fun sampling each establishment's cuisine, and when Candy wrote her reviews, she usually submitted them on a timely basis, rather than holding them for a specific season. She also helped out at the paper during busy times, though one day she'd realized that, much to her consternation, they seemed to operate most of the time just fine without her.

She found Wanda in the managing editor's office,

redecorated to suit her tastes. Wanda had framed and hung a number of awards she'd won, prominently displayed along one wall. There were also a few trophies artfully arranged on the credenza below the window ledge. Shelves held photographs of her with every person of note in town, up and down the coast, and throughout the state and region. Wanda with the governor. Wanda with a famous actor who had a summer house nearby. Wanda with friends and family, members of the town council, schoolteachers and firemen.

Wanda got around. And she'd done a good job with the paper in the few months she'd been running it. The readers seemed to like what she delivered, circulation and revenue were up slightly, and the paper's owners were happy. Wanda seemed happy, too, at least on occasion. It was, she said, what she loved doing. She'd started to soften her sometimes sharp demeanor, at least when it served her best interests, but underneath she was still the same old Wanda—driven, determined to make herself heard, rough-edged, and distrustful.

To get her scoops, she relied on a fairly extensive network of spies, informers, and gossips, who helped her keep her fingers firmly on the village's veins. She usually knew which way the winds were blowing. She knew the secrets, too, though she was discreet enough to keep those to herself—mostly.

If anyone would know what was going on with local real estate transactions, it was Wanda.

As Candy entered the office, she didn't waste any time getting to the point. "What do you know about the Whitby estate?"

Wanda had been clacking away at the keyboard of her desktop computer, pencil clenched firmly between her teeth, red hair frazzled, her desk strewn with papers and files. At the interruption, she raised her eyebrows, her gaze following Candy into the room. "Hmm?"

"The Whitby place," Candy said, plopping down into a chair. "What's the latest you've heard?"

It took a moment for Wanda to shift gears, but she seemed to sense something was up, given the most recent murder in town. She took on a thoughtful look as she swiveled her chair and removed the pencil from between her teeth. "Does this have anything to do with Julius Seabury?"

"I don't know yet," Candy said honestly. "The Whitby place?"

"Right. That." Wanda considered the question before she continued. "Well, I know it's been sold."

"When did it sell?"

Wanda shrugged. "A few weeks ago, far as I know. The closing's either just taken place or it's about to take place, in the next few days."

"Who's the buyer?"

"Don't know that yet. I've been asking around but nobody's talking. It's very hush-hush. I'm on it, though. Supposed to hear back from my sources any day now."

"Then I think I might have a scoop for you."

"About what?"

Instead of answering directly, Candy changed the subject. "What do you know about the Sykes family?"

Wanda's brow furrowed. "The living ones or the dead ones?"

Candy responded with a noncommittal shrug, so Wanda continued, drawing facts from her memory. "I've only met one of them personally—the younger brother, Roger Sykes—but none of the others, though I know Porter is on the board of directors over at the museum. I've requested an interview with him a number of times but never got a response. I read a lot about him, though, when he was building that development down in Portland. I know the family has pretty deep roots in town. I've heard a few rumors about Silas Sykes and that alleged treasure box of his they found a while ago, but I haven't followed up on it. It's old news, far as I'm concerned. I mean, they're not really in town much, and they don't own any property around here anymore, not after Whitefield, their old mansion, burned down a few years ago and they got rid of the place. Sold it at the bottom of the market, from what I heard. Let it go for a song. There's a pretty extensive file on them but it hasn't been updated in a while." She paused and gave Candy a suspicious look, realizing how much she'd just revealed, though most of it was common knowledge. "Why?"

Candy hesitated before answering, just to make sure she was doing the right thing. But she needed Wanda's help, so there was no way around it. "I've heard they're moving back into the area—or, at least, Porter is."

That got Wanda's interest. "They are? What have you heard? What are they buying?" But she put the pieces together before Candy could tell her. Wanda could be quick; it was one of her assets. "The Whitby place?"

Candy nodded.

Wanda sucked in a breath. "Porter Sykes is buying it? Are you sure?" And then, her suspicion returning, she asked, "Where'd you hear that?"

Candy told her about the meeting of board members over at the museum.

Wanda couldn't help but flash a look of jealousy. "I went over there this morning and they wouldn't let me inside. How come they let you in?"

"I don't know. I just walked through the door."

"And Porter Sykes told you this personally?"

"Personally," Candy confirmed. "While I was in Owen's office. Porter was on the speakerphone. Some of the other board members were in there, too, so they heard the whole thing."

"Which ones?" Wanda turned, threw down her pencil, picked up a ballpoint pen, and reached for a writing pad. She began to scribble furiously.

"Edith Pring, Gilbert Ethingham, and Plymouth Palfrey."

That got Wanda's carefully plucked eyebrows to rise into her moisturized forehead. "Palfrey's in town?"

"He is. I just saw him over there."

"If those three know, then it will be around town in hours. Minutes."

"Seconds," said Candy. "Edith Pring is probably burning up the wireless networks as we speak."

"This is huge news," Wanda said. "I'll have to confirm it, of course, before I can run it on the website and in the paper." She paused only momentarily to cock an arm, checking her watch as her mouth twisted unglamorously. "But why would he want the *Whitby* place?"

"Good question," Candy said. "That's exactly what I've been asking myself ever since I heard."

"I mean, it's not a *bad* place. But it's old, it needs work, and it's somewhat isolated. It takes twenty-five minutes or so to get over there by land, since you have to go north six or eight miles before you can cut over to the next peninsula. It's about the same by boat, I'd guess, if there's a dock over there. And the roads aren't very good either. It has some history, and presumably a decent view of the bay, but not much else. I'm not sure why he'd be interested."

"Maybe it's something else," Candy said.

"Something else? Like what?"

"I don't know yet."

Wanda quickly caught the drift of the conversation. "You want me to help you find out what he's after?"

"Something like that. I wonder if you've heard anything through your sources. Or—"

"Or if I could make a few calls and see what I can find out?"

"Yes, that, and I'm trying to establish a timeline for Julius. See if I can find out who saw him last, when and where. I thought the volunteers at the lighthouse might be a good place to start, but I don't have that list of names and numbers. Not anymore, at least."

"Ah, so that's why you came here." Wanda's look told Candy, *There's always an angle, isn't there?*

"Kill two birds with one stone," Candy admitted. "It might lead to a pretty big story for the paper . . . and it might just help us find a killer."

Wanda puzzled all that out for a moment. "Tell you what—I'll help you out and touch base with my sources, if you tell me about this champagne bottle. Darned curious murder weapon. What's up with that?"

TWENTY

Herr Georg pushed the green felt hat up off his forehead, clutched the steering wheel more tightly in his hands, and leaned forward as far as possible, so he could look up and out the windshield of his car as the building came into view.

It looks cold, was his first impression.

Cold brownstone, cold, smoky blue windows, sitting by an outcropping of cold black rocks near a misty point at land's end, a dozen yards or so above the restless sea. The place looked dark and shadowed, due in part to the thick stands of trees that squeezed in close by the house on two sides, to the north and behind it to the east. The entwining brownish-black limbs were so dense and tangled that Herr Georg doubted a single ray of sunshine could penetrate the suffocating canopy in the summer months, but he also imagined the place looked quite spectacular during the autumn, framed against a backdrop of blazing color.

The building was two stories tall with a slate roof, plus a half-story dormered attic at the top, with squat, narrow windows that wouldn't allow in much light. But from the inside, those windows would provide spectacular views to the south and west. They were dark now, too, showing no signs of life behind them, no lights, no movement.

A meandering dirt driveway led up to the building, terminating in a rectangular graveled parking area, where a front yard or garden might have been. The parking area was empty. No cars or any other vehicles in sight. No sign of anything or anyone around.

Which was not totally surprising, since he'd heard the place was for sale—and had only just sold. There'd been plenty of buzz around town about it, and intense curiosity about the new owner or owners, whoever they might be. Georg had talked to a dozen people or more about it just in the past few days, walking down Main Street to or from his shop. It was the end of an era, the villagers were saying, for the place had been in the hands of a single family for generations. And a founding family at that, with roots on the cape that went back two hundred years or more.

The Whitby estate.

He'd debated coming out here. He knew it was a long shot that he'd find anything, but in the end he'd decided to make the trip anyway. Scotty Whitby had disappeared, or so Chef Colin had said. No one at the inn seemed to know what had happened to him. Phone calls to him had gone unanswered. They'd checked his apartment and found it empty. What had happened to him? Where was he? Was he safe? Was he in hiding? But more important, what did he know about the events of the night before? How had he wound up in the storage room where Maggie had found him, knocked out cold? Had it been an accident, or had he been attacked?

And, perhaps most important, did he know anything about the champagne bottle that had wound up at the museum, next to the body of Julius Seabury?

Herr Georg had plenty to do. He was getting married in two days. He had a cake to bake. He didn't have time to go gallivanting around searching for a lost waiter. But he felt personally involved in this situation. His best man was gone. A bottle of his champagne had been used as a murder weapon. He had to know the answers to the questions rolling around in his head. And he thought the Whitby place might hold some of those answers.

He didn't know if there was a connection between Scotty Whitby and the old house that bore his family's name. Maybe he was only distantly related. Maybe he was from a different branch of the family entirely. But Herr Georg had to check it out, to ease his own mind.

The drive over from town had taken less than half an hour as he'd first proceeded north along the Coastal Loop, then cut east across the top of the bay before turning south again, but he felt as if he'd driven into the hinterlands of Maine. He saw few cars on his way over, and once he'd started down the rugged peninsula on which the estate stood, the roads had turned narrow and pockmarked, with low, broken shoulders and tight turns. In the last few miles, the asphalt had petered out and the road had become just dirt, marked by ruts and rough ridges and strewn with small rocks and pebbles. The tires and suspension on the Volvo had been severely tested, but he'd driven as carefully as possible and made it without incident.

Now that he was here, he was uncertain what to do next.

He slowed the car to a crawl. Should he park in the gravel lot and knock on the front door? Drive around the property a little? Honk the horn? Drive past and just ignore it?

After some hesitation, he decided on the first option.

Still leaning forward, watching the house cautiously through the windshield, he inched the car off the meandering dirt road he'd just traveled and into the parking area. The tires crunched over the gravel as the car moved forward. Halfway in, he pulled off to one side opposite the front door, came to a stop, and shut off the engine.

With his hands still on the steering wheel, he listened, watching the front door, waiting for something to happen. When nothing did, he moved the hat back down on his forehead, opened the driver's side door, and stepped out.

It was cooler here on the point, and damper. The wind was gusting as it came over the rocks and through the trees, tugging at his hat and jacket. Off to his left, still-naked tree branches clapped together noisily, and a few dry, brown leaves left over from the fall blew across the parking area.

He could hear the churning sea off to his right, beyond the edge of the land. He turned and looked in that direction. It was indeed a magnificent view, out across the narrow bay. He saw quite a few boats out on the water today, long white streams of churning wakes behind them. Across the bay, just a little to the south and almost due west, was the mouth of the English River and the twin lighthouses of Cape Willington. The land veered away from there, turning back and around. It was, he thought, a curious view of the village, one he'd never seen before.

He turned back toward the house as another gust of wind blew past him, threatening to lift the hat off his head. He reached up absently with a hand to keep it settled in place.

His gaze shifted back and forth and up and down as he studied the front door, and the windows, and the building's facade. He noticed that a narrow gravel road led around the far side of the parking lot, looping back behind the building. He imagined there might be a garage back there, maybe a carriage house. The place looked old enough to have such a thing. Maybe a few outbuildings as well—a workshop or a gardening shed.

He should check those out as well.

For some reason, again, he was hesitant to move. This sort of thing really wasn't his cup of tea. His friend Candy was much better at this type of work. Georg considered himself a genteel person, a baker and an entrepreneur, at home in a kitchen, not out here on this windy point, acting as some sort of crime investigator.

The very thought was ludicrous.

Nonetheless, he believed in getting things done, and getting them done quickly. He was here with a purpose in mind, so he might as well get on with it.

Stepping smartly, he crossed the gravel parking area and approached the main set of double doors. They were painted black, though they hadn't been painted in a while, he noticed. Now that he was closer, he saw that the place looked a little shabby. The windows were unwashed. The paint on the sills was peeling. The exterior stone looked dingy. The property was in desperate need of some maintenance.

Perhaps that's why the Whitbys had sold it. It had simply become too much for them to manage.

There was an ornate though dull brass knocker attached to the door. Georg reached out toward it and rapped loudly several times.

The muffled sounds of the knocker seemed to echo hollowly inside the building.

Georg thrust his hands into his jacket pockets and waited.

A few seconds passed, then a few more. No one came. No one answered the summons of the door knocker.

He tried again, a little louder this time, a few additional raps.

Again, he waited. No response.

Georg took a few steps away from the door and tilted back his head, looking up at the building.

Same as before. Dull brownstone, shadowed blue-gray windows, no signs of light or movement.

He was about to head around the far corner of the house, to check on the outbuildings, when he heard another car approaching on the dirt road, coming pretty fast. At first it was just a faint engine purr, but then he could hear the quick crunches and snaps of the car's tires on the gravel and pebbles.

A few moments later, the vehicle shot into view through the trees.

Herr Georg knew right away, by looking at the slanted chrome grille with its distinctive multicolored badge perched in the middle, that it was a Cadillac sedan, and a fairly new one at that. The car was black, with large wheels, angled headlights, and a long, sleek shape. Probably an XTS, he thought. A good-looking car.

Not many cars like that around here. In fact, he couldn't remember seeing a single one in town recently. Folks around Cape Willington preferred trucks and wagons and SUVs, leaning more toward the functional than the luxury-oriented side when it came to car buying.

Probably not someone from around here then. An out-of-towner?

The car didn't slow as it left the dirt road. It swooped into the parking area in front of the house and came to a fairly abrupt stop as it pulled up alongside Herr Georg, not too far from the front door. The engine revved for a second or two before it shut down. A cloud of dust arose around it. After a few moments, the door popped open and a tall, well-dressed man, perhaps in his early fifties, emerged from the driver's seat.

He looked at Herr Georg curiously. He had dark hair, combed back and graying at the sides, and a sharp nose and intelligent eyes. "Hello," he said in a noncommittal sort of way. Then he flipped around, opened the car's back door, and pulled out a leather briefcase before shutting both doors and approaching Georg. "I don't suppose you're one of the family members?"

"Family?" Georg asked.

That brought a glance of suspicion from the new arrival. "Are you looking for someone?" he asked, changing his tactic.

Herr Georg waved toward the building. "I just wondered whether anyone was around. I'm looking for someone who seems to have disappeared. A young man by the name of Scotty Whitby. I thought he might be out here."

"He doesn't live here, as far as I know. Never has. Are you a friend of the Whitbys?" the dark-haired man asked, his mouth tight.

Georg shrugged. "Just a concerned citizen, checking up on him. I thought he might be around. He's . . . Well, no one has seen him in a while."

"Oh, I see," the man said, shifting the briefcase and car keys from his right to his left hand and pulling another set of older keys from a pants pocket. "I doubt he's out here. No one's been around here in months, maybe longer. This place has been closed up while it was on the market, as far as I know. I just came out to check on it before the new owner arrives tomorrow. I'm his attorney. Well, the family's attorney, that is."

He walked to the front door, jabbed a battered brass key

into the door lock, and twisted it. He pushed the door open but turned back to Georg before he entered. "We can check real quick to see if anyone's around, if you'd like, but as I said, the Whitbys haven't lived out here in quite a while. The papers were all signed yesterday, down in Boston. Mr. Sykes is arriving in the morning to have a good look around the place."

Herr Georg couldn't hold back his surprise. "Sykes?"

"Haven't you heard? I thought it'd be all around town by now. Porter Sykes bought the place. As I mentioned, I'm representing the family."

The attorney reached into a shirt pocket and pulled out a business card, which he handed to Herr Georg. "The name's Bosworth," he said, holding out a hand with well-manicured fingernails. "Marshall L. Bosworth."

TWENTY-ONE

Candy had a lot on her mind as she drove up the dirt lane at Blueberry Acres. She'd spent most of the past two hours tucked away in her old office at the paper. Located in the warren of hallways and rooms near the back of the old building's second floor, it once had been her second home, and she'd spent countless hours in there, running down stories and crafting columns. Vacated now, it was stripped of any sort of decoration or personality. It had a phone, though, and a desk, and a place for her to sit and make calls.

From somewhere deep in her files, Wanda had scrounged up a typed list of museum volunteers, with associated phone numbers and e-mail addresses. It was a couple of years old, and some numbers and names were crossed off, and some new ones written in. But it was a starting place, so she sat down at her old desk and began to dial.

She kept her conversations as upbeat as possible. She was working on a tribute story about Julius for the paper, which was true—Wanda had assigned it to her; it was to be part of a larger section in the next issue devoted to the elderly historian, appearing alongside Julius's obituary, along with several photos and a column Wanda intended to write—so Candy was looking for anecdotes, remembrances, and comments about his life, his books, his work at the museum, and his place in the community. It also gave her a chance to ask the one question she thought was more valuable than any other right now: "When was the last time you saw him?"

As it turned out, the day before his death was the last time he'd been seen by anyone. He'd been upstairs at the museum two days ago, on Tuesday morning, digging into the archives, scribbling away at his notebooks. Several people saw him but none spoke to him, other than to say a quick *hi* or *hello*. One of the volunteers, Doris Oaks, said she'd seen him later that day (or it might have been Monday; she wasn't quite sure, as her memory wasn't what it used to be) walking from the rocky shore toward the Keeper's Quarters while she'd been on her way out to the parking lot. He'd looked windblown, she told Candy, and had a pair of binoculars hanging on a strap around his neck. He'd seemed distracted, and hadn't returned her wave when she called out to him. In fact, he never looked up from the ground as he made his way into the red-roofed cottage, failing to notice her.

Daniel Brewster, assistant librarian at the Pruitt Public Library, reported that Julius had been seen around the library a couple of days earlier, pulling out old books on Maine history. Daniel had chatted briefly with him, but again, Julius had seemed distracted and didn't respond much. And Elvira Tremble, a haughty villager who took great pride in the fact that she was the cofounder of the Cape Willington Heritage Protection League, was somewhat miffed because Julius had missed his scheduled shift behind the Long Desk yesterday— Wednesday, the morning of the day he died. It had put her in quite a bind, she informed Candy with an undisguised tone of exasperation, since she was responsible for keeping track of the volunteers this month. So she'd had to step in and fill the shift herself, until she'd finally located someone who agreed to come in and relieve her. She took no joy in greeting the public, which was a major responsibility of the position. She was a behind-the-scenes person, she claimed, and had better things to do with her time. "Of course," she'd finished, "we're all so sorry to hear what happened to him. He did a lot for this village. It's a great loss for all of us. And you can quote me on that."

And so it went. Candy made it through only half the names on the list when she glanced up at the old clock on the wall and realized she had to get moving. So she'd slipped the list into her tote bag and hurried down to her Jeep.

She could make more calls later on, if she had the time. And Wanda was checking with her sources to see if she could find out anything else about Julius's final days.

Now, as she pulled up to the house, she tried to push any thoughts of volunteers and schedules and champagne bottles and unconscious waiters out of her mind. She had just enough time for a quick bite to eat before everyone arrived for the afternoon wedding setup session.

She didn't see her father's truck in its usual parking spot next to the porch, so she guessed he was still at Duffy's Main Street Diner, his usual weekday hanging-out spot. But she knew he'd show up soon. He was probably just caught up in a conversation with his trio of golfing, card-playing, and jawing buddies, who Candy sometimes collectively thought of as "the posse"—retired ex-cop Finn Woodbury, classic car admirer William "Bumpy" Brigham, and eBay entrepreneur Artie Groves. She often hung out with them at the diner, but she'd never had a chance to stop by today. Still, she'd see them all shortly, since they were helping out with the setup, and made a mental note to quiz her father when he got home to find out if he'd learned anything interesting.

Before she stepped into the house, she headed around the barn to check on her chickens. As usual, they were clucking contentedly away, scratching and pecking at the ground in abrupt, comical movements, doing what chickens did. She made quick work of tending to them before she headed inside.

Five minutes later, she was piling lettuce, thin slices of tomato, and tuna salad on two slices of toasted bread when she heard a vehicle coming up the driveway. She looked out the kitchen window, expecting to see her father in his truck, headed home from the diner. But instead she spotted a vintage red Saab wagon in need of a good washing, and knew her first guests of the afternoon had arrived.

It was Neil Crawford, the local strawberry farmer, with his big shaggy dog, Random.

Candy couldn't help but smile. The day had suddenly turned much brighter.

Leaving her sandwich behind for the moment, she went out to greet them.

Neil and Random had moved to town permanently a year ago, after Neil had inherited Crawford's Berry Farm from his deceased father. They'd all been good friends ever since. They visited often and helped out whenever they could at each other's farms. Neil and Random were frequent dinner guests at Blueberry Acres, and Candy and Doc spent quite a bit of time at Neil's farm, learning about hoophouses, cherry trees, and the finer points of strawberry farming.

Neil also had contributed copious amounts of time and labor last fall and again earlier this spring, when Candy and Doc finally put up their own hoophouse, a half hoop–shaped greenhouse with an elevated internal temperature. It would help them extend the growing season, expand their crops, and increase their annual revenue. They'd started in October, with Neil's help, clearing the spot they'd selected, just east of the barn along the dirt driveway, and assembling the galvanized steel frame, setting the bows four feet apart for the hoophouse's forty-foot length.

Then, once the snows melted in early April, they'd finished the rest of the work, covering the steel frame with double plastic sheeting, installing the removable wood-framed end walls, and putting in the trickle irrigation system. They didn't have mechanical heating and ventilating systems in place yet; those would come later. But, for now, their unheated hoophouse would keep plants from freezing during the spring and give them a head start on a number of crops.

They'd started by planting seeds for cold-tolerant plants, like carrots, scallions, radishes, and spinach. These they would transplant to the garden just after Memorial Day. Tomatoes, peppers, and beans were next on the list.

They had other plans for the blueberry farm. They wanted to start a small grove of cherry trees, and when they had a little extra time, clear out some acreage at the top of the far western ridge to expand their barrens.

But one step at a time, she'd often told herself.

Random was the first to greet her, leaping out of the car almost before it stopped, bouncing across the driveway in long, lazy gaits, and skipping to a stop at her feet. When she'd sufficiently showered him with praise, to his great content, she turned her attention to Neil.

He wasn't as shaggy as he used to be; he'd trimmed his beard and cut his hair a little shorter in an effort to tame it. But he had the same earthy look, with a weathered face, a quick smile, and flashing eyes. Today, though, he was more serious.

"Sorry I didn't come over sooner. I heard what happened. You doing okay?" Despite his somewhat earthy exterior, faded ball cap, rough hands, and farmer's work clothes, his voice was smooth and surprisingly refined, with a nice back-of-the-throat rumble on the low notes.

Candy nodded. "I'm doing okay. Even better, now that you and Random are here."

That brought out his smile, at least for a moment. It was a good smile, she thought, warm and inviting. "So, are you on the case?" he asked.

Candy squared her shoulders. "Whatever do you mean?"

He laughed. "You know exactly what I mean."

Random barked at something in the distance, and started off through the fields at a dash, while Candy and Neil started toward the house.

"Well," Candy said as they walked, "I feel like I owe it to Julius, to at least look into it and try to find out what happened to him. *Something* brought about his murder last night—some event or activity, or something he discovered up in those archives. Or he found out what someone was up to, and that certain someone didn't want word to get around."

"Who?" Neil asked.

"I don't know yet."

"Do you think it has anything to do with that treasure box we found out at the strawberry farm a couple of years ago, or those missing deeds that were supposed to be in it?" Neil asked, his sun-bleached brows lowering in concern.

Candy nodded. "It could all be tied in, yes. How, I don't know yet. That's what I have to find out."

"Then I think I can help you out. I have some information that might be of interest to you," he said as they both stepped up onto the porch.

As Candy pulled open the screen door, she stopped and turned back toward him. "What kind of information? What have you heard?"

"I stopped by the police department and told them this morning, and I don't suppose there's any harm in telling you as well."

"About Julius?"

"Julius," Neil confirmed, and waited until they were inside, standing in the kitchen, to continue. "He called me yesterday afternoon, a few hours before he died."

"You talked to him?"

Neil shook his head. "I was out in the fields, so I didn't have my phone with me. I didn't know he called until I got back to the house later in the afternoon. The time stamp said he phoned at three thirty-four P.M."

"Did he leave a message?"

"He did. He said he had something to tell me about the deeds, but he wanted to meet me in person, since he couldn't discuss it over the phone. He said he'd call me back later, but he never did."

They were both silent a moment, before Neil continued, "There was something else he mentioned in the message. I couldn't quite make it out, and I'll let you listen to it. But it sounded like he said 'Foul Mouth.' I don't have any idea what that means, but I was hoping you might."

TWENTY-TWO

Foul Mouth.

There it was again—that name, those words. In this case, specifically spoken by Julius in a phone message to Neil Crawford. But what was it? A place? A person? Something else?

Whatever it was, Candy realized one thing: Julius's message to Neil, including his mention of Foul Mouth, was an important link in the mystery, since it confirmed with almost certainty that the note found in the book last night by Owen had indeed been written by the elderly historian.

It was too much of a connection to be coincidental, and seemed to verify that Julius had created that list of family names himself, and jotted down the words *Foul Mouth* and the initials *L. B.* as well.

And, by extension, it proved that Julius had arranged those books by Lucinda P. Dowling on the shelf in that particular order.

By why? It must have been a message of some sort—possibly about the deeds, since he mentioned those in his phone call to Neil. What had he planned to tell Neil about the deeds? And how were they linked to Foul Mouth?

Another thought came to her, one that rattled her a little: If Julius left those clues hidden in the books up in the archives, then he must have felt threatened in some way, since the creation of the list and especially the arrangement of the books in a specific way indicated premeditation.

But whom had he felt threatened by? It was a threat he'd obviously taken seriously enough to create the clues he'd left behind. Who had been after him? What had he stumbled into?

Maybe the answers she sought were right there in that list of names.

She could feel her heart ticking just a tad faster.

"He didn't give you any idea as to what it is—this Foul Mouth thing?" she asked Neil.

The strawberry farmer shook his head. "Nope, that's all he said."

"And the police know about this?"

"They do."

She nodded. "That's the right move. I should probably follow up with them. And with Owen." And briefly she told Neil about the list of names Owen had found, with the words *Foul Mouth* written on it, and had stuffed into his coat pocket. "He needs to find that list and take it over to the police as soon as possible."

"Do you think this list has anything to do with those deeds? Or with Julius's death?"

"I do. I think they're all connected," Candy said as she considered the issue for a few more moments, pondering her next move. She thought of pulling out her phone right then and there and making a few calls, but decided to listen to Julius's message first.

Then she looked over and caught Neil's gaze. He looked hungry, she thought, like a man who hadn't had a good meal in a while.

Despite all that was on her mind, she allowed herself to smile. Maybe it was time to turn her attention back to her guest, at least for a few minutes, as she thought everything through.

She glanced over at the sandwich she'd been making for herself, then looked back at Neil. "Have you eaten?"

"Not since breakfast."

"You like tuna fish?"

"Love it."

"I think I have a jar of pretty good pickles I can open, and I can maybe scrounge up some potato salad from the fridge. Why don't we eat and then we can try to figure this out?"

"Works for me."

While she made him a sandwich, her mind going over all the new information she'd just learned, Neil plopped down into a chair at the kitchen table by the window, doffed his ball cap, and ran a hand through his unruly hair. Once settled, he pulled out his phone and scrolled through it until he found what he wanted. He hit the speaker button and held it out toward her, so she could listen to Julius's message from the previous day:

Neil, it's Julius Seabury. I wonder if you might have time to meet with me this afternoon, or perhaps early this evening. There's something important I need to discuss with you about the deeds. I can't go into any details right now, over the phone, but I have some information that might be of interest to you. I've also come across a reference to something called Foul Mouth. I don't know if that means anything to you, but I'll explain when we meet. I'll call you back later.

That was it.

She listened to the message a second time as she set two plates down on the table, and then a third time as she sat herself, picking the phone off the table and holding it to her ear while Neil gobbled down his sandwich. But she left hers largely untouched as her mind worked.

She was just about to pull out her own phone when she

heard another vehicle coming up the driveway, and suddenly everyone was there, and she was swept away into other things.

They all arrived within five minutes of one another, coming up the dirt lane in a variety of cars and trucks, leaving low clouds of dust in their wakes. Doc came first, pulling up next to the porch in his pickup truck with his buddies in tow, driving three separate vehicles. They were followed in short order by Maggie with her mother in the Subaru, Herr Georg in his Volvo, Amanda and Cameron in a separate pickup truck, and finally their nascent wedding planners, Malcolm and Ralph, in a small convertible import sports car with a large yellow rented cargo van right behind them.

As the parking lot filled with cars and trucks, it also became filled with the sounds of meetings and greetings, handshakes and backslaps, smiles and solemn words about the absence of Julius, before they got down to business.

Two workers who arrived with the van opened up the back doors and started to unload folding tables, chairs, plants, and long white aisle runners, rolled up like giant scrolls, which they planned to put down over the barn's recently swept and hosed-off cement floor and out past the back barn door to the reception tent. Doc, Neil, Cameron, and the boys—Finn, Artie, and Bumpy—pitched right in, helping to carry and set up, while Maggie and Candy started pulling out potted plants and setting them down near the entrance to the barn. Ellie, meanwhile, headed into the kitchen to start making lemonade and treats for the workforce, and before turning their attention to other tasks Herr Georg went off with Malcolm and Ralph for a quick tour of the property and potential parking spots for wedding guests.

They worked for most of the afternoon, as the sun went behind a bank of clouds and the day turned a little cooler. Candy took a few minutes to walk through the hoophouse with Neil, who gave her some pointers, and they pulled a few seedlings out of the back of his Saab, taking the plants into the new structure. And she finally found the time to make a few phone calls, though she came up empty. Owen didn't answer, and Chief Durr was currently occupied. She left messages for both of them to call her back.

She also tried to spend as much time as possible with Maggie, who told her about the groom's cake she was baking. "It's going to be fantastic," Maggie said, her hands moving as she talked. "It's going to be chocolate, since that's traditional for groom's cakes, but I'm going to make it from scratch, naturally."

"Naturally," said Candy.

"I'm going to frost it with chocolate blueberry frosting and then decorate it with candied pansies and blueberry blossoms, which I've already made. I've got them tucked into a container in the back of the fridge, where Georg wouldn't find them if he came over. Round, two layers, with this gorgeous cake topper I found at Malcolm and Ralph's store. It will be my most inspired creation to date! I'm going to bake tomorrow morning, if you want to come over to help."

"I wouldn't miss it for the world. It'll be fun. You're all set with Freda at the House of Style, right?"

Maggie gave a quick nod. "Hair and makeup, first thing Saturday morning, by special appointment. She's opening the shop early just for us—and Amanda and mom, of course. Plus Piper, she'll be here by then."

"Your sister-in-law, right? And your brother, Jack? They're from Presque Isle, right? When are they coming in?"

"Tomorrow afternoon. They'll be here in time for the wedding walk-through and rehearsal dinner, so she'll go with us Saturday morning. We'll make it a girls' beauty breakfast!" She brightened at the thought of that. "Georg says he's making Viennese apple strudel for us, from scratch! He's even going to spike it with a little bit of rum—just to, you know, help calm our nerves . . . well, help calm *my* nerves!"

Candy laughed. "Sounds yummy. I can't wait to try it—and a little bit of rum first thing in the morning will definitely get the day started in the right direction. What about the groom's gift?"

"I'm glad you mentioned that!" Maggie said, her eyes

going wide. "It's finally ready. He called a couple of days ago but I haven't had a chance to make it up there yet. So I thought I'd drive up there this afternoon to pick it up. He closes up his shop at six, so I have to leave soon!"

Over the past few months, Maggie had fretted endlessly about an appropriate groom's gift for Herr Georg. She'd considered a number of ideas, like an old and valuable cookbook, or family photos of his ancestors from Germany, but nothing felt quite right to her. "I want to give him something special," she'd told Candy, "something that he'll always remember."

She'd finally settled on an antique gold pocket watch that had once belonged to her grandfather. Ellie had come up with the idea, and Maggie liked it.

"It's something personal, and somewhat valuable, and it will help welcome him to our family," Ellie had said, according to Maggie. "It was your grandfather's retirement watch. I've held on to it this whole time, but I think it's time to pass it along to someone like Herr Georg, who I know will love it."

The only problem was that because of its age, the watch needed maintenance and cleaning, so they'd found a jeweler in Ellsworth with experience in such watches. He'd had it for two weeks now, and had just finished working on it.

"You want some company on your trip up there?" Candy asked.

"Mom's going with me. And Amanda." Maggie glanced around to make sure no one else was listening in before she continued. "And there's actually something else you can do for me here."

"What's that?"

"Will you cover for me while I'm gone? You know, run interference, in case someone comes looking for me?"

"Like Herr Georg?"

"Right. I don't want him to know where I'm going."

"Of course. Don't worry about a thing. I'll cover for you like a blanket covers a bed. So when do you think you'll be back?"

Maggie raised her gaze toward the sky and put her hands

on her hips as she thought out loud. "Well, let's see. It's close to an hour each way, give or take a few. And I'll need some time in the shop, to make sure everything looks right with the watch, especially with the new engraving I've had made. We'll call it two and a half hours round-trip—depending on traffic, though that's a relative term here in Maine."

Candy knew what she was talking about. "More likely you'll get stuck behind a tractor than encounter heavy traffic, right?"

"Or a slow-moving eighteen-wheeler, or a lumber truck, which are much more likely here than a traffic jam. Have you *seen* those lumber trucks? I hate getting behind them on those old two-lane roads! Those things are *scary*. Have you seen how high they stack those logs on there, held on by only a few narrow forks or bands or whatever? I *hate* it when I get behind them—or have to pass them! I just zip around as quick as I can. Imagine what it would be like to have some of those logs come crashing down on you!"

"Definitely uncomfortable," Candy acknowledged.

"Anyway, Mom usually gets hungry early, so we might stop on the way back to get something to eat. And that means"—she checked the time again—"around sevenish or so? Maybe a little later? Something like that?"

"Sounds good. And don't worry about a thing here. I'll take care of everything, and I've got plenty of people to help me out."

Maggie leaned forward then and gave Candy a big hug. "You're the best friend ever!"

"Why don't you and your mom and Amanda slip away right now while no one's paying much attention?" Candy continued. "I'll make up some excuse if anyone spots you. And I'll hunt up Malcolm and Ralph and go over the wedding checklist again with them. We'll figure out what still needs to be done and divvy it all up, so we make sure everything gets done in time. I imagine Georg will want to head back to the bakery soon, so he might not even notice you're gone. And if you hurry, you'll still have time to meet him later for dessert."

Maggie's eyes brimmed over with gratitude, but then her expression turned sly. "Someday I hope we'll be doing all this for *you*, for *your* wedding! And, of course, I'll be your maid of honor—or matron of honor, I guess!"

"Of course! That goes without saying . . . if it ever happens, which I'm sure it probably will someday," Candy said noncommittally. "But you're first. So let's both get going."

TWENTY-THREE

Twenty minutes later, Candy almost ran headfirst into Herr Georg.

She was just leaving a conversation with Malcolm and Ralph, where they went over the wedding-day timeline and discussed last-minute details, and came away with a list of calls to make, including one to the caterer and another to the Reverend James P. Daisy, just to touch base with him a final time. She'd also talked to Neil, who was headed back to his place to do his evening chores while it was still light outside.

She was walking across the driveway toward the house, her head turned back toward the barn to see how much progress they'd made inside, and the baker was coming out of the house and down off the porch, looking back over his shoulder toward the blueberry fields. They both noticed each other at the very last moment and came to jerky stops before nearly colliding with each other.

"Candy, there you are!" Herr Georg exclaimed, his eyes bright and his white mustache twitching excitedly as he spoke. "I've been looking for you."

She pointed back the way she'd come. "I was talking to

Malcolm and Ralph over by the cars. We were going over the wedding checklist and timeline."

"Oh, *wunderbar! Wunderbar!* They've done such an excellent job so far, as I'm sure you've noticed. It's all coming together quite nicely. And your father and the others have been so helpful, and creative! Have you seen what they've done inside the barn?"

"Not yet, but I'll check it out shortly. I have to make a few phone calls first, before it gets too late."

"They've transformed the place, I don't mind telling you!" Herr Georg continued. "It looks like a palace in there—well, a rustic one, of course, but what they've done with the lighting and drapes and potted plants and overall setup is quite impressive. Maggie will be so thrilled when she sees it!" He glanced around, his eyes searching. "Where is she, anyway? I haven't seen her in a while."

Candy had hoped to avoid the question completely but she had a ready response at hand. "Oh, she just had to dash off to run a quick errand. She shouldn't be gone too long. I'm sure she'll be back before you know it."

"Oh . . . yes, I see . . . hmm. Lots of secrets, eh? Wedding related, I imagine." Herr Georg's expression was more thoughtful than playful. "Well, since you and I have a few moments alone together, I wonder if the two of us could talk?"

"Sure. About what?"

Again, Herr Georg's eyes darted back and forth, this time in a more surreptitious manner. When he spoke, he lowered his voice so only she could hear. "It might be better if we discussed this someplace a little more private." And in an even quieter tone, he added ominously, "It's about Julius."

"Oh! Of course." She looked around as well, before pointing toward the house. "Why don't we talk inside? We can use Dad's office."

Herr Georg nodded. "You lead the way," he said, and together they walked onto the porch and in through the kitchen door.

Once they were settled, with the office door closed behind them to ensure their privacy, Herr Georg came right to the point. "I have to admit," he said, talking quickly now in a long stream of words, "that I'm not used to this sort of thing, by any stretch of the imagination. I'm not an investigator at heart, as you quite obviously are, and I don't have the instincts of a supreme detective of any sort. But since I'm intimately involved in this unfortunate business, and since a confounded champagne bottle I ordered *myself* was used as a murder weapon, raised against my own *best man*, well, I believe I was *compelled* to act, right? I mean, I had no choice in the matter, don't you see?"

He paused, his eyes open wide and his face reddening as he looked expectantly to Candy for some sort of response.

She blinked a time or two, uncertain of what to say. "Well, yes, I suppose I can understand that."

Appearing relieved, he went on. "So that's why I went down to the inn, to talk to Chef Colin, because I was trying to find out what happened, and I thought he might be able to point me in the right direction. Which he did, of course. He provided some very helpful information. That's why I went over to the Whitby place."

"You were at the Whitby place?" Candy asked, surprised.

"Um, yes." He seemed a little unsettled by her reaction. "I drove out there this morning, right after I talked to Chef Colin. Shouldn't I have?"

Candy considered her response. "Well, I don't know, really. I was toying with the idea of going over there myself, but I wound up doing other things." She paused and shook her head. "But I think I'm missing something here. Why don't we back up a little bit? What did Colin tell you in the first place that made you go out to the Whitby estate?"

"Well, it was because of that waiter, of course. The young man Maggie found in the storeroom last night, unconscious," he clarified. "Chef Colin told me his name. It's Scotty Whitby."

Candy's eyebrows rose. "Whitby? The old family name?"

She was quiet for a moment as her mind worked over this new bit of information, wondering what it might mean. "So that's why you went over there, to the Whitby place—to try to talk to him? So you could ask him if he knows anything about that champagne bottle?"

"Something like that, yes, but there's more to it, you see. I went there because he's disappeared—Scotty Whitby has— or at least that's what Chef Colin told me," Herr Georg explained. "From what I've heard, after Maggie found him unconscious last night, they took him to the hospital to check him over. He was supposed to stay overnight for observation, but later they found his room was empty. He'd vacated it when no one was watching him. So far, there's no sign of him anywhere. No one knows what's happened to him."

Candy looked concerned. "Do the police know this?"

Herr Georg nodded. "I believe they're looking into it, but I thought I might conduct a little investigation of my own. So that's why I went over there—I was hoping I might find someone at their family estate who would know where he's gone."

"And did you find anyone? The house has been closed up for a while, right?"

"Yes, well, that's just it. You're right. The place was deserted, because it's been for sale, I suppose. I thought I might get lucky, but no one was around. I was going to have a quick look about the place, but then someone else arrived, and I learned something else, something curious. That's what I wanted to talk to you about. I found out who bought it."

Candy nodded. This bit of information she *did* know, but she waited for confirmation from Herr Georg.

"His name is Porter Sykes," the baker continued. "I learned this from his attorney—a man by the name of Marshall Bosworth, who came by the estate when I was out there looking around."

"Marshall Bosworth?" It took her a moment, as the name rang a bell, and then she remembered where she'd seen it— in Lucinda P. Dowling's book on the Bosworths up in the archives that morning, when she'd been sneaking around. "Judicious's brother!" she exclaimed.

"Yes, I believe it's the same family, though Marshall didn't say so specifically. They're all in the legal profession, isn't that correct? Judicious was an attorney also, wasn't he, before he went off to Tibet?"

Candy nodded. "Their father is a judge—the Honorable Rutledge Howard Paul Bosworth, if I remember correctly—but I don't know much about him, or the brother, except he's about four years older than Judicious."

"He gave me this." Herr Georg reached into a shirt pocket, located a business card, and handed it over to Candy. It read:

> Marshall L. Bosworth
> Attorney-at-Law
> Bosworth & Bosworth, LLC
> Bangor Portland Bar Harbor

Her brows furrowed. "Marshall L. Bosworth?" she said to herself, more than to Herr Georg. She tilted her head thoughtfully, and read it again.

Marshall L. Bosworth.

L. Bosworth.

L. B.?

The same initials Owen had read last night, written on that slip of paper. Could they refer to the same person—or was she reaching too far?

"What did he say to you?" Candy asked, looking back up at Herr Georg, her gaze narrowing.

"That he was the legal representative for the family. That he'd helped put together the real estate deal for the Sykes family, who live in Boston. He said they wanted to expand their holdings in the area, and were looking for a place near the village."

"But why that place? I would think they'd want something closer to town. It's nearly a thirty-minute drive over there, isn't it?"

"About that, yes. And from what I could see, the place appeared to be in a state of disrepair. Quite honestly, it needs some work. It's isolated, out on that point all by itself. And the roads over there are all dirt into the place. I realized the property probably has some historical value attached to it, and the view is quite incredible out over the ocean. Perhaps that's why they bought it . . . for the view."

"Hmm," Candy said thoughtfully. "Yes. For the view. I'm sure it's quite amazing."

She thought of the binoculars Julius had been carrying around, and the sand on the bottoms of his shoes.

Was that what he'd been looking at, across the bay—at the Whitby place? Had he known Porter Sykes had bought the place? And that Porter had been after the deeds for years? Had Julius learned something else, possibly about Porter, something that caused his death?

"What exactly can you see from that point?" Candy asked, instinctively turning her head to the right, eastward, as if she could see through the walls and out over the land to the ocean, and beyond.

"Well, the house faces west," Herr Georg said, "so you can see parts of Cape Willington, of course, the lighthouses and the docks along the English River."

"And Pruitt Manor, I bet," Candy observed.

"Oh, yes, it's almost a direct view across the bay—point to point, you might say."

"Yes, you might say." The wheels in her brain were beginning to turn more quickly. "Well," she said finally, softly, almost breathlessly, "isn't *that* interesting?"

TWENTY-FOUR

Something had clicked in her brain, an almost physical thing. For the first time since she'd found the body of Julius Seabury upstairs in the archives, she could see how the disparate bits of information she'd collected over the past twenty-four hours were beginning to fit together, intersecting in neat ways. Like a spiderweb slowly being spun, one silky strand at a time, the wider design, unidentifiable at first, was beginning to reveal itself.

And Porter Sykes, it seemed, was the spider at the center of that web—an ominous, shadowy presence, lurking, waiting, ready to pounce at some unexpected moment.

Why the Whitby place? she wondered. *What could his interest be in that old broken-down estate?*

What was he up to?

Was he planning to spy on the village from his vantage point across the bay? Specifically, on the Pruitts? Or on the comings and goings at the museum and lighthouse? It was certainly something he could do from that estate.

But why? What was he hoping to achieve?

Julius had mentioned the deeds in his phone message to

Neil. What had he wanted to tell Neil about them? And what about Foul Mouth? Did it have anything to do with the Whitby place?

Candy didn't know yet if Porter was responsible for Julius's death, but she knew he'd been the catalyst behind, if not directly involved in, at least two other deaths that had taken place in the village a few years ago, and members of his family had been involved in other murders since she'd been in town. She knew that for a fact. It seemed the Sykes family had a few dark strains of DNA in their chromosomes. He'd revealed as much to her during their brief, surrealistic encounter in that abandoned mansion a few years ago. More recently, she'd crossed paths with other members of his family, who also had murder on their minds. The Sykes family, she knew, had malicious intent when it came to Cape Willington and its villagers, and she wondered what other family members might show up someday soon to cause more trouble.

It was a disconcerting thought, but she pushed it aside for the moment, so she could fully focus her thoughts on Porter.

Despite what she knew about him, or suspected, she couldn't prove he'd done anything illegal. He'd been careful. He'd always worked in the background, always let others take the fall for him, rarely revealing himself or making himself known.

Until now.

He was finally showing himself, and beginning to make his move—whatever that might be. He was inserting himself back into the village his ancestors had once inhabited, and helped establish. He'd been a part of the conference call this morning at the Keeper's Quarters, and it was about to become common knowledge that he was the buyer of the Whitby place—which just so happened to have excellent views of the town and, intriguingly, Pruitt Manor across the bay. No doubt he'd start popping up more often around the village. He was raising his public profile, and tapping into his family's legacy.

And, for some inscrutable reason, he wanted to meet with her.

There must be a plan, a design of some sort, behind all his machinations. She could vaguely see several possibilities of how it all might unfold, but nothing definite. There were too many unanswered questions, huge gaps in her understanding of what was going on. She had to do more work to solve this mystery—and, if Porter Sykes was involved, put an end to his family's influence and intentions once and for all.

"So what should we do?" Herr Georg asked anxiously, breaking into her musings.

"Hmm?"

She realized she'd been gazing out the back window of her father's office, absently studying the blueberry barrens and the trees in the distance, her thoughts drifting away with the clouds.

"About Porter Sykes?" Herr Georg said. "And the Whitby place? Do you think he's after something?"

Candy pulled her attention back to the moment. It was a curious comment from the baker, one that echoed her own thoughts. She sensed he knew more than he was telling her. "Like what?"

There was an odd look in his eyes, and he hesitated only briefly before he continued. "I've heard the same rumors you probably have—about the Sykes family, and how they're looking for some missing documents that used to belong to one of their ancestors. Apparently they're some old land deeds. . . ."

His words trailed off, and his mouth clamped shut so tightly it made his mustache bristle.

Candy looked at him curiously. "So what have you heard about these deeds?" she asked, prompting him with a twist of her head.

"Well, just that they supposedly once belonged to this fellow named Silas Sykes." He was talking rapidly again, as if in a hurry to get everything out before he changed his mind. "The story is, they're the original deeds for properties here on the cape, and were apparently lost long ago, but what if . . . ?"

Again, he let his words hang in the air, like unpopped balloons.

Candy waited for him to continue, but he seemed to be

holding something back, and she couldn't help but brace herself for what he might spring on her next. "Herr Georg," she said softly but firmly, "if you know something about those deeds, you should tell me now. So, please continue . . . *what if . . . ?*"

His gaze shifted back and forth as he considered his next words, and he swallowed hard a couple of times before he finally turned his gaze to her, his mouth set firm. "Well, what if they're not lost?"

"Not lost? You mean they've been found?"

"And what," the baker continued, ignoring her question for the moment, "if *he* knows that?"

"Who? Porter? But how would he know?" She felt a sudden chill. "Herr Georg, what are you saying? Do you know where the deeds are?"

Again, the baker hesitated. But he'd made up his mind, and knew it was time to tell her the truth.

"I do," he said. "I have them."

TWENTY-FIVE

"You!"

The word came out in a propulsive rush of energy and disbelief. She said it so loudly Herr Georg had to shush her, verbally and by using his hands, motioning for her to keep her voice down.

"This is top secret!" he said in a hoarse whisper, looking around in both directions, but they were still alone in Doc's office, with the door closed. One of the windows was cracked open but he could see no one outside within hearing range. He shifted his gaze back to Candy. "I don't want word of this to get out. You know how the villagers can be."

"But . . . but . . . but." Candy hardly knew where to start. With some effort, she finally managed to form a few more words. "But . . . why haven't you said anything about this before? Neil and I have been looking for those deeds for years—but we kept it to ourselves. *No* one was supposed to know about them, other than me and Neil and Dad . . . and Julius, come to think of it. So how did *you* find them?"

"Well, that's just it," Herr Georg said. "I didn't *find* them, per se. Julius *gave* them to me."

"Julius? But where did *he* get them?"

"Well, from Miles Crawford, I guess." The story came out quickly then, in rapid, hushed sentences. "Julius got the deeds from Miles, you see—indirectly, as it turns out. Apparently, after Miles found them in an old treasure box he unearthed on his property, he sent them to the museum, where they wound up in Owen Peabody's office. But because they arrived anonymously, with no explanation of what they were, they were treated with some skepticism. So they were shuffled around for quite a while and eventually were sent upstairs for examination and cataloging. I suppose they must have been there for months, maybe even a year or more, sitting in a dark cabinet, until someone eventually pulled them out again. Then, one day, they came to the attention of Plymouth Palfrey, who was upstairs researching another project—a historical book he's publishing, I believe. And *he's* the one who asked Julius to have a look at them, and perhaps determine their authenticity."

"So they've been floating around the museum this whole time, and nobody knew what they were?" Candy almost laughed at the simplicity of it all. She'd never really thought of checking there, though now in hindsight it seemed the most logical place to start. "And Julius gave the deeds to you?"

"He did. Well, not the original deeds—I believe he kept those for himself. But he gave me copies of them, as a backup, I suppose."

"Copies? But why?" It took Candy a moment to realize what he meant. "In case something happened to the original deeds? Or to him?"

The baker looked uneasy. "I don't know for sure. If he was worried for his safety when he gave me the copies, he didn't show it—or, at least, not that I can recall, though he did seem distracted that day. To be honest, I didn't think much about it at the time."

"Did he say anything about who might be after the deeds?"

"No, not in so many words, but he did mention Porter Sykes by name. That's why I made the connection when I heard Porter bought the Whitby place."

"What exactly did Julius say about him?"

"Only that Porter expressed an interest in seeing the deeds when Julius had finished researching them—and that others at the museum were suddenly interested in them as well, though he didn't mention anyone else by name. But he told them his research was incomplete, so he wasn't ready to give them up just yet."

"Then why would he give you backup copies, if he wasn't certain of their authenticity?"

Herr Georg shrugged. "Julius could be a little eccentric at times. We all know that. I admit I thought it was a rather strange request, but it was a favor for a friend. I readily agreed to it. I had no reason to question his motives. He just asked me to hold them for him, to lock them away somewhere, and that's what I did."

"So where are the deeds now—the copies?"

"At the bakery, locked in the safe in my office, in the back of the shop."

"And Julius kept the originals?"

"As far as I know, yes."

So, Candy thought, *Julius must have had the original deeds still in his possession yesterday—possibly with him last night upstairs in the archives at the Keeper's Quarters, when he'd apparently been researching them.*

A definite motivation for murder.

And Porter Sykes had expressed an interest in seeing them. How had *he* found out about them?

Most likely through either Owen or Plymouth, she thought, since both of them had apparently seen the deeds before handing them off to Julius. Obviously they hadn't known what the documents were initially, or they wouldn't have treated them so casually, but they might have found out later. The topic had possibly come up in one of their board meetings. Porter could have called into a meeting when the deeds were discussed, just as he did with the conversation earlier today. Is that how he'd learned about them?

And how hard had he pressed Julius about them? Had his requests been polite, or not so polite? Had threats been made?

Was that why Julius felt it necessary to leave behind those clues in the books? Had he felt he was being threatened? Maybe he thought someone was trying to take, or steal, the deeds from him—and he refused to give them up.

Candy took a deep breath. Out loud, she asked, "So when did this happen? When did he give the deeds to you?"

"Well, just a few days ago."

"You've had the deeds—the copies—for only a few days?"

"Less than a week," Herr Georg confirmed. "Julius gave them to me last Friday, when we had lunch together. He didn't tell me how long I should hold on to them. But I didn't really think that much about it . . . until last night."

"Did he say anything else to you about them?"

"Just what I've already told you—although there was one other thing. As we were leaving, he pulled me aside and insisted I say nothing about them to anyone. No one was to know I had the copies. He was very adamant about that. I did as he asked—until now, of course. But after all that has happened, I felt I had to talk to you about them, get your advice. I'm not quite sure how to handle this. So what do you think I should do?"

Candy fell silent for a few moments as she thought this through. Finally, she answered honestly. "I don't know yet."

"Should we take them to the police?" Herr Georg persisted. "Or give them to someone else? Owen, maybe? Or Plymouth, since he gave them to Julius? Or even to Neil, since his father found them in the first place?"

She tugged absently at her chin with her index finger and thumb as she considered his questions. "We could do any one of those things, yes. But Julius also could have done any of them. He could have given the deeds to the police, or back to Owen or Plymouth, but he didn't—because he was being cautious, I think. He held on to them, saying his research wasn't complete. But I think he knew what they were. He must have determined they were real, not fake. He knew what they could do in the wrong hands."

"Is that why he was murdered?" Herr Georg asked.

"It's starting to appear that way, isn't it?" Candy admitted.

Herr Georg looked aghast. "So someone really is trying

to get those deeds? To, what, gain control of the land around Cape Willington?"

"It's seems very possible that's exactly what's happening, doesn't it?" Candy said. "And, from the evidence I've heard so far, Porter Sykes sounds like the number one suspect."

Herr Georg looked like he was about to be ill. "But if that's true, and the deeds really do affect the legality of property ownership in Cape Willington—it would cause absolute chaos, wouldn't it? We could all lose our homes, our businesses, our livelihoods. It could be the end of Cape Willington as we know it."

"Exactly," Candy said, "if Porter decided to pursue that course. We don't know for certain what he would or wouldn't do. But he certainly has a legal claim to the deeds, since he and his lawyers can probably prove that the original documents belonged to Silas Sykes."

"Yes, but how do we know he had them rightfully?" the baker asked. "From what I've heard, Silas was a scoundrel and a thief. How do we know he didn't steal them in the first place?"

"I don't think it matters," Candy said. "The courts would probably award the deeds to the Sykes family. Which is why we should keep everything we've just talked about between us, for now, until we figure out our next move."

"Which is?"

"Well, we just have to follow the clues—figure out what happened to the original deeds. Make sure they didn't wind up in the wrong hands. Because if Julius had those deeds with him last night when he died, and the murderer now has possession of them, we could all be out of luck."

TWENTY-SIX

Absolute chaos.

That's what they all were facing, as Herr Georg had said—*if* the deeds were authentic, *if* they were for property in the village, and *if* they were now in the possession of Julius's murderer.

Somehow, she had to find out what was happening—and she had to do it quickly. With an impending wedding and honeymoon, and with both herself and possibly Herr Georg under suspicion due to the use of the champagne bottle as a murder weapon, she felt that time was running out.

After the baker headed back outside to check on the wedding setup, Candy sat alone in her father's office, trying to figure out her next moves.

For the moment, she decided, it was best to leave the copies where they were. They were safe, and only the two of them knew where the copies were, or even that they existed at all. There was plenty of time to turn them over to the police, or to someone else, if that's what they decided to do. She didn't want to make the mistake of putting the copies into the hands of the wrong person.

Until she learned otherwise, she was going to assume Julius had the original deeds in his possession and was murdered because of them. Porter Sykes was an obvious suspect. But so, too, were Owen Peabody and Plymouth Palfrey. Both of them knew about the deeds, which had been floating around the museum, where they'd been sent anonymously by Miles Crawford. Plymouth, if not Owen as well, knew Julius had them. Owen himself was around the Keeper's Quarters last night, although as far as she knew, Plymouth had still been at his home in Boothbay Harbor, which gave him an alibi.

So, at least she had a starting place. But there was still a lot she didn't know.

First, where was Scotty Whitby, the young waiter Maggie found unconscious in the storeroom last night? Why had he disappeared from the hospital? Could he, like Julius, have felt threatened in some way? And why? Possibly because he'd seen someone at the inn taking away a bottle of champagne. That seemed to make the most sense. But where had he gone? What had happened to him?

It was a question that required an answer.

Suddenly compelled to movement, she reached over to her father's desk, picked up a legal pad and pen, and wrote at the top of the first sheet: *Find Scotty Whitby*. He might solve the mystery of the champagne bottle.

That led her to another question: Why use a bottle of champagne in the first place? Was it an attempt to frame Herr Georg? If so, why? Or was it something else—an accident, a mistake of some sort?

She let that question percolate while she considered others that were swirling around her head.

She looked down at the business card Herr Georg had handed to her, the one given to him by Marshall Bosworth.

Marshall *L*. Bosworth, she corrected herself.

He had come out of nowhere. She'd never known about any other Bosworth siblings until today. How come Judicious never mentioned his own brother? Why didn't Judicious talk about his family at all? What could they expect from this Marshall? Was he someone they needed to watch out for? And why was he working for the Sykes family? She hadn't been aware of that connection. It was one that needed to be checked out.

There was a relatively easy way to get some answers. On the pad, she wrote, *Talk to Judicious.*

And what about the books lined up on the shelf upstairs at the Keeper's Quarters, the ones devoted to various founding families, with the names arranged so they matched the list of names on the piece of paper that had fallen out of the book Owen had picked up? Could that have any significance? Could Julius have arranged them in that manner for some reason?

One person might know, if she was still alive: the author of the books.

Candy wrote, *Find and talk to Lucinda P. Dowling.*

Then there was the issue of sand on the bottoms of Julius's shoes. Had he been out on the beach, perhaps looking across the bay at the Whitby estate? What had he suspected was going on over there? And why the binoculars? Had he seen something that resulted in his murder?

And, finally, what was Foul Mouth?

She jotted down these last few questions, just to keep them fresh in her mind, then turned to her other task: making the phone calls on her list.

She had a brief but pleasant chat with the Reverend Daisy, who told her how much he was looking forward to Saturday's event, and how sorry he was to hear of Julius's passing. And she confirmed menus, arrival times, a setup time, and a head count with local café owner Melody Barnes, who'd be hosting the rehearsal dinner on Friday night and catering the Saturday-afternoon reception in the party tent they'd set up behind the barn.

She made a few additional calls, then keyed up the number for Wanda over at the paper. "Have you ever heard of a woman named Lucinda Dowling?" Candy asked. "She's a local author. She wrote a number of books about the town's founding families."

"I remember them. They're upstairs in the archives," Wanda said, sounding distracted. Candy could hear the clacking of a computer keyboard in the background. Wanda was writing while she was talking. "You can check them up there."

"I'm looking for the author," Candy clarified. "Do you know if she still lives around here?"

"Why?"

"Research."

"For the story on Julius?"

"Sure, for that."

Wanda hesitated. The clacking slowed, and Candy could sense she was thinking it through, wondering if it was a lead she herself should be running down. But she seemed to finally dismiss it, willing to let Candy chase after it. "I don't know. I can ask around. Call over to the historical society. They might know."

"Okay, thanks."

After she ended the call, Candy sat for another minute or two in the silence, gazing out the back window, working out her next moves in her head. Then she tore off the front sheet from the legal pad and began to fold it up as she headed back outside.

TWENTY-SEVEN

Once out the front door and down off the porch, lost in her thoughts, she made a beeline for her Jeep, parked at the far side of the driveway. But she was almost immediately sidetracked.

She noticed a number of people standing over by the barn, including Herr Georg talking to her father, with Cameron and the boys of Doc's posse hovering nearby. As she passed by them, she heard her father call her name and looked over. He pointed toward the open barn door behind him. "Want to take a look inside?" he asked.

She smiled, nodded, and headed in his direction.

"Things are just about wrapped up in there," he told her as she approached, and as she reached him, her father put his arm around her and guided her toward the barn door. "Come on in and take a look," he said. "Prepare to be amazed."

And she was.

The barn had been transformed. It was like something out of a design magazine, a magical place of light and scents and things of beauty.

The moment she walked in, her gaze was drawn upward.

Around the dark wood rafters above, they'd strung long, twirl-ing strands of white Christmas lights, which made the whole place glow warmly. From one rafter near the back of the barn hung an elaborate vintage-style chandelier, positioned so it illuminated the spot upon which Maggie and Herr Georg would exchange their vows. That spot had a raised platform covered in white velvet, and was framed by long, thin white drapes that reached from the bottom of the chandelier to the side and back walls, creating a sort of illuminated tent under which the bride and groom would stand.

White drapes had also been hung from the side walls, helping to lighten the barn's dark interior. Arranged around the raised platform and along the sides, large pots of plants added some greenery. She also noticed there were pots with small cinnamon trees in them, the plants no higher than a foot or two. They'd put out the cut flowers, including pale cinnamon iris, white hyacinth, and tulips, on the morning of the wedding, she knew, which would add even more color.

Baby blue and cinnamon-colored accents were every-where, in small twists of dried flowers and ribbons, as well as candles on intricate stands in the corners and along the sides. The chairs set up in front of the raised platform were decorated with cinnamon-colored ribbons for the bride and blue for the groom. On the floor down the center ran a long white runner, and back where the runner started, at the oppo-site end from the raised platform, was a decorative portal through which the bride and groom would enter. It was hand-made from carefully selected and cut tree limbs, intertwined and joined together to form a tall arch. It, too, was festooned with white, blue, and cinnamon-colored dried flowers and ribbons, as well as vines that twisted around it, and it was topped with sprigs of blossoming blueberry flowers.

"It's breathtaking," Candy said in awe, taking it all in. She looked over at her father, whose eyes sparkled with reflected light as he watched her, and then turned toward Herr Georg. "Maggie will be beyond thrilled! She'll be ecstatic! You've all done an amazing job."

"Oh, we just helped out," the baker said. "Malcolm and

Ralph are the real geniuses behind this. They're the ones who designed everything."

Candy looked around but didn't see the two wedding planners. "Where are they?"

Doc pointed out the far side of the barn. "In the reception tent, finishing up in there."

"Well, then, I have to go tell them personally how impressed I am with everything they've done."

"We'll go with you," Herr Georg said. "I'd like to thank them again myself."

They spotted Malcolm first. He was a tall man, slight of build, with a mop of unruly strawberry blond hair and dove-gray eyes. He was positioning some of the potted plants, arranging them with practiced hands.

"Malcolm," Candy said as she approached him. As he turned toward her, she gave him a tight hug. He responded with an easy smile. "The barn looks amazing," she told him. "Better than I ever could have imagined. Maggie will love it."

"I love it as well," said Herr Georg, standing behind her, beaming.

Malcolm took the compliments easily. "Thank you, all of you!" He turned to Herr Georg and shook the baker's hand. "And thank you, Georg, for putting your trust in us, since we're neophytes at this sort of thing."

"You're far beyond that," the baker said. "You're masters at this! I will heartily recommend both of you in all your future endeavors."

"Your recommendation would mean everything to us," Malcolm said earnestly. "We're still trying to get this second business off the ground, as a side project of the store."

"I'll definitely do all I can to help you become established," the baker said. "Of course, since I make wedding cakes, I have quite an extensive array of contacts I can send your way. There's a great need for planners with your talents, especially in this area of the coast."

They found Ralph at the back of the tent, straightening tables and arranging chairs. He was a bit more reserved when he received his hug from Candy, but still seemed pleased with the recognition. Shorter than Malcolm, and darker, he had a neatly trimmed beard, green eyes, and a strong, angular jaw. The others thanked him as well. Malcolm walked over to join them, and for a few minutes they discussed the remaining tasks and itinerary for the following two days.

"We'll be back out here tomorrow, putting the finishing touches on everything before the walk-through," said Malcolm, "and, of course, we'll be at the rehearsal dinner tomorrow night."

"Melody's Cafe," Candy reminded them. "Seven P.M. sharp."

"And we'll be back out here bright and early Saturday morning," added Ralph, "and we'll stay until the last guest leaves, to make sure everything goes smoothly."

"You two are the best," Candy said. "I'm so glad you're doing this."

"As am I," the baker added. "Best decision I ever made, hiring the both of you—other than asking Maggie to marry me, of course!"

They laughed, shook hands all around, and then left the two wedding planners to finish up their tasks.

As Herr Georg fell into a conversation with Cameron, and Finn, Artie, and Bumpy went off to make a final tour of the property to see if anything else needed to be done, Candy took her father by the arm and led him aside.

"Maggie's off picking up the groom's gift for Herr Georg," she told him in low tones, "and I actually have to leave as well to, um, run a few errands. Maggie should be back around seven, but I'm not sure how long I'll be. Will you be okay with everything around here until I get back?"

She noticed some wariness behind her father's eyes as he responded. "Well, I'm sure I'll be just fine, pumpkin. There's not much left to do today. I was about to break out some beers for everyone. But what about these 'errands' of yours? Would they have anything to do with Julius?"

She gave him a reassuring smile. "They might, Dad, but I promise I'll be careful."

He didn't appear convinced. "You know I worry about you."

"I know, Dad. And I appreciate it. There are just a few

people I have to talk to. It's really nothing more than that. I'll do my best to stay out of trouble."

That seemed to reassure him just a little, and his expression softened. "Trouble does seem to follow you around, doesn't it?" he said with a chuckle. "Guess it always has, ever since you were a little girl."

She gave him a sideways smirk. "I wasn't *that* bad, was I?"

"No, not really, but you were always adventurous. You had this need to know what was going on, and why. You hated being left out of things. I think you got some of that from your mother, God rest her soul. There were a few adventurers on her side of the family, you know."

Candy nodded. She'd heard the stories when she was little, and she had a flash of her father as a much younger man, full of vigor and the quest for knowledge. On an impulse, she leaned up and gave him a kiss on the cheek. "Are *you* okay? Are you comfortable stepping into the best man's shoes at the last minute like this?"

"Oh, sure, it's a big responsibility and an incredible honor. I'm sorry Julius can't be here, but I'll do my best to carry on the tradition."

"I'm certain he'd be happy to know you're standing in for him. Well, I have to get going." She gave him a wave. "I'll be back later."

He nodded. "I'll keep an eye out for you. Call if you need anything."

Before she left, she remembered to dash behind the barn to check on her chickens, and she fell into a brief conversation with Finn, who'd heard from his secret source at the Cape Willington Police Department but had nothing new to report. "They're following up on a bunch of leads but haven't closed in on the murderer yet," he told her.

"What about fingerprints on the bottle of champagne? Did they find anything there?"

"The jury's still out on that one. Last I heard, they're already checking it out in the crime lab."

She thanked him for the information and was just climbing into her Jeep when she heard footsteps hurrying across

the driveway after her, and she shifted around to see Herr
Georg approaching.

"Candy!" he said, holding up a finger when he caught her
eye. "A moment, please!"

She waited for him to cross the rest of the distance to her,
watching him expectantly. "Herr Georg, did I forget something?"

"No, no, it's nothing like that," the baker said, waving a hand.
"I understand you're heading off to do some sleuthing."

"Well, I wouldn't put it quite like that, but yes, I need to
talk to a few people."

"Good," the baker said with a firm nod of his head. "I'm
going with you."

"You are?" She pulled her head back at this sudden
announcement.

"Absolutely. Your father just said something to me about
it and, well, I think it's important that I accompany you."

"But I'll be fine. And you have too many things to do
here, and at the shop, don't you?"

"It doesn't matter. There's a murderer on the loose, and I'm
not going to let you face any possible dangers alone, as you've
done in the past. Besides, I'm just as involved in this thing as
you are. So it's only proper that I see it through to the end."

"I appreciate that, but I'm not sure how long it will take, or
when I'll get back. I'm not even totally sure where I'm going."

"Then we'll figure it out together. Besides, to answer your
questions, they're just about finished up here, and I'm not
ready to start baking yet. I have too much on my mind to fully
enjoy the creative process, and I refuse to compromise on
something I've been planning and anticipating for years. I
must help finish this other business first, and clear both our
names. Then I can focus on other things. Plus, I haven't heard
back from Maggie yet. So, for the moment, I'm a free man."

"Hopefully not for too much longer, if we solve this murder,
and everything else goes as planned," Candy said, trying to
add a bit of levity. "To be honest, I'd appreciate your company.
And you're right—I don't really know for certain what I'll run
into."

"Should we bring a weapon?" he asked, leaning in to whisper, his eyes wide.

"No, I don't think that's necessary. We'll make do. But before I agree to let you come along, I have one condition."

"And what's that?"

"You drive. Your car's more comfortable than mine."

The baker chuckled, and his mustache fluttered like a caterpillar in the wind as he spoke. "Agreed. So which way are we headed first?"

TWENTY-EIGHT

Judicious F. P. Bosworth was a man of mystery to many around town. The son and grandson of judges, heir to a family fortune and legacy, groomed with lofty ambitions for an illustrious career in the legal field, he'd eschewed all of that, throwing it away, in the eyes of some, and headed off to discover himself and find his place in the world. Over a period of years, his journey of exploration and illumination had led him across Europe and Asia to a mountaintop in Tibet, where he'd settled in at a Buddhist monastery, seeking inner peace. When he'd finally returned to Cape Willington many years later, he'd been firmly convinced of his mystical powers, including his ability to make himself invisible at will.

Though few villagers believed he could actually do such a thing, they tended to humor him, often commenting to each other about it, saying things like, "Is Judicious being seen today?" or "I haven't talked to Judicious in a while. When is he going to make himself visible again?" He'd even garnered some minor fame locally, thanks to a regular feature in the *Crier*, which kept track of his visible and invisible days. Numerous folks around town contributed to the report,

sending texts and e-mails to the paper when they spotted
him, and noting when he was absent from the sidewalks,
shops, and events. Typically, his invisible days outnumbered
his visible ones, though many attributed it to the fact that
he was simply a bit of a recluse, and could deal with crowds
and social occasions only in limited amounts.

Today, it appeared, he was not being seen.

On the way over, Candy had explained her reason for the
visit to Herr Georg, who was driving his Volvo wagon, with
Candy in the passenger seat. "We're going to stop by and
see Judicious Bosworth first," she told the baker. "I want to
see what we can find out about this brother of his."

"Right. Marshall Bosworth," Herr Georg commented.

Candy held up a finger. "Marshall *L.* Bosworth," she said,
emphasizing the middle initial.

The baker glanced over at her. "Is that significant?"

"It could be." And briefly she described the list Owen had
discovered the previous night, with the initials *L. B.* written
on it.

"You think those initials could refer to Marshall?" the
baker asked.

"That's what we're going to try to find out. Maybe he's
linked to this whole thing somehow."

Judicious lived on the outskirts of town in an isolated log
cabin on family-owned property along the river. Candy had
visited the place a few times before but had never been inside.
She'd heard it had a comfy décor, with easy chairs, a large
stone fireplace, and bookshelves everywhere, housing a fairly
extensive library favoring nature, religious, and New Age
titles, as well as books on law, politics, and government.
Though he rarely engaged in legal or political matters himself,
and tended to stay on the periphery of the gatherings he
attended, he kept a close eye on community events, like its
festivals, cook-offs, bashes, and fairs. He also had a knack
for showing up at opportune moments, especially when
Candy was in a tight spot and sorely in need of a diversion or
helping hand.

The sun was falling toward the tops of the trees to the west as Herr Georg made the turnoff onto a single-lane dirt road that led down to the river. It was a tight fit, through low trees and dense shrubs, which pressed in from either side. The canopy of branches and leaves overhead was beginning to fill out, shading them in a ladderlike strobe effect as they followed the road's twists and turns. It bottomed out at one place and became rougher and more pockmarked, but soon it was rising again. Up ahead, through the dark tree trunks and blossoming foliage, a small log cabin came into view.

Judicious had no car, so the parking spot in front of his place was empty; he walked wherever he needed to go, or hitched a ride when he could. He also had a bike, which was now propped up against the side of the house, next to the fishing poles, ladder, tree trimmer, and a variety of shovels, hoes, and other garden equipment.

The old rocker on the porch was empty too. The front door was closed. The windows were dark. No sign of Judicious anywhere.

After Herr Georg stopped the car, Candy climbed out, stepped up onto the porch, and knocked on the cabin's door, but wasn't surprised when no one answered. She stepped down off the porch and walked around the side to see if he was behind the house, but he was nowhere to be seen.

"His bike's still here," she told Herr Georg as she climbed back into the Volvo. "He could still be around here somewhere, in the woods or down by the river, or he could have walked into town—or he really could be just about anywhere, I suppose."

"So what should we do?"

"I think," Candy said, her gaze shifting back and forth to the woods on either side, "we should wait a few minutes and see what happens. I have a feeling he just might turn up."

And he did. Fewer than five minutes later he came walking along one of the paths that wound back through the trees behind the house, materializing bit by bit like an apparition emerging from a mist, so that at first they weren't certain it was actually him, until he stepped out onto the narrow dirt lane and approached the car.

He was wearing a great floppy hat and hefted a walking stick in one hand, taller than he was. For some strange reason, he reminded her of Gandalf, though he had only short stubble on his jaws instead of a full beard. His dark hair had grown out and was as long and lanky as he was, slipping from under the hat and puddling at his shoulders.

Candy waved at him and leaned out the window. "Hi, Judicious. Hope we're not disturbing you."

He shook his head. "No, not disturbing. Not disturbing. I've been expecting you," he said as he approached. His mouth was working a little, as if he were chewing over the words. "I heard what happened to Julius Seabury. Very sad. I suppose that's what this is about."

"It is," Candy confirmed. It was best to be straightforward with Judicious.

He stopped a few feet from the car and planted the bottom end of the walking stick into the dirt. "And I've heard my brother is in town," he continued, addressing them both through the open driver's side window without leaning down to look at them. "I'm guessing one of you has run into him."

"Yes, I have," said Herr Georg, leaning over so he could look up at the newcomer. "Out at the Whitby place this morning."

That actually got a reaction out of Judicious, a slight movement of his typically stoic features, and in the brief silence that followed, Candy added, "We didn't know you had a brother, Judicious. So we wanted to talk to you about him, too, if that's okay."

He gave the slightest nod of his head. His eyes were thin, dark slits, recessing into his head, as if he were deep in thought. "You want to talk about the family, then, and how we're tied into the Sykes clan."

"You're reading my mind," Candy said with a reassuring smile. "I wasn't aware your family *had* ties to the Sykeses. But, yes, that could be important."

"Then you're trying to find out who killed Julius—and why."

Candy's response was brief. "Yes."

Again, silence, as the wind rattled tree branches and leaves. "Well, you'd better come in then. I'll put on the tea. We have a lot to talk about, and we don't have much time."

"Why not?" Candy asked, uncertain about his last few words.

"Because if I'm guessing correctly, I'd say the situation surrounding Julius's death is still fluid. The murderer still wants something, and hasn't achieved it yet. And *that* means someone else in town could die—possibly sooner rather than later."

TWENTY-NINE

Once they were inside, Judicious disappeared, though not in a supernatural sense. He ducked into a back room, and when he emerged, he'd changed into black shorts and a black T-shirt. The hat was gone, the walking stick left by the side of the front door. He made a quick stop in the kitchen to put on a kettle, and finally returned to the cluttered living room. He was barefoot as he sat down, tucking his feet up underneath him, assuming a sort of lotus sitting position. It took him a few moments to get settled, and to start talking, but when he did, he told them what they wanted to know. As he spoke, his eyes darted around, rarely alighting on his guests, and he frequently gestured with his hands.

"This all goes back generations," he said when all the preambles were out of the way, "to the turn of the twentieth century, when the Sykes family still had a number of principal holdings in the area, including their mansion. They also owned a few businesses along Ocean Avenue, and a good share of the warehouses along the river, and were heavily invested in a small line of steamboats that took passengers up the English, Penobscot, and Kennebec rivers. Back then, they were wealthy and successful—until their fortunes began to fail. They suffered from a series of setbacks over a period of a few decades."

"Why, what happened?" asked Herr Georg, intrigued.

Judicious shrugged, bony shoulders showing through his T-shirt. "Bad decisions, in part, and some back luck. Railroads came along and took a large part of their transport business, and then the advent of the automobile made river steamboats obsolete. But they also encountered resistance and opposition from the more powerful Pruitts."

"Ah, yes, the local family feud," Candy said. "Our version of the Hatfields and McCoys."

Judicious gave her an enigmatic smile. "That's a pretty good analogy. The disagreements and clashes between the two families went on for decades, and their animosity for each other could turn quite vicious at times." He paused and pointed toward his bookshelves. "Some local writers have speculated that many of our current troubles stem in part from those old, lingering hatreds between the two families, with the rest of us caught in between."

"You're talking about all these murders we've had over the past seven years or so," Candy said, making it more of a statement than a question. "Is that what Julius thought?"

Judicious twisted his head toward her oddly, like a baby bird. His gaze was suddenly piercing. "Him, and others. Don't you feel the same way?"

Candy hesitated before she responded, but she had to admit he was right. "It does seem like there's something larger going on around here, yes. So what did you mean when you said someone else is about to die?"

"I don't have any hard evidence," he admitted. "It's more of a feeling, or perhaps more accurately, a speculation. I believe Julius wasn't killed because of who he was, or what he was doing, but because of what he *knew*."

Candy nodded her agreement. She felt the same way.

"He discovered something during his research," Judicious continued. "And someone else found out what he'd learned. That someone—the murderer—had to stop him from doing whatever he was planning. Maybe Julius found something in one of those old books he was using for his research, or possibly he overheard a private conversation when he was upstairs at the museum. Maybe he got in someone's way, or refused to give up the information he knew. And that means there's something else going on, something larger—and another target."

"But who?" Herr Georg asked, his eyes wide.

"I don't know that yet."

"Someone at the museum?" Candy prompted. "Someone in town?"

When Judicious responded with a shake of his head, she tried a different angle. "So how did your brother get involved with Porter Sykes? Marshall told Herr Georg he's representing the Sykes family, which is news to me. Why them instead of the Pruitts?"

Judicious's expression darkened. "Ah, Marshall." The word came out in the most ferocious tone Candy had ever heard from Judicious, who typically displayed a more genial manner. "I don't agree with everything my family does, I should make that clear. It's why I left, why I went to Europe and Asia. It's why it took me so long to come back, why I'm in Cape Willington instead of Bangor or Portland. It's why I'm not in the family business. It's why I live here, like this, a hermit of sorts. You could say I'm the black sheep of the family, the one who went in a different direction, much to my father's dismay. But I don't see it that way."

The kettle whistle blew, and he rose then, walking to the kitchen. They could hear him clinking around in there. He returned a few minutes later with mugs of a good strong tea for all of them, which he handed around. As he settled back into his seat, legs crossed, his expression was lighter. He absently dunked his tea bag into the mug of hot water as he continued.

"To answer your question, our family represented both the Sykes and Pruitt families for a while, generations ago, until we were forced to make a choice between the two—or, rather, my great-grandfather, Stanton Harlan Hay Bosworth, was.

We in the family often refer to him simply as 'H. H.' He's the one who set the tone for the generations that followed. He had a falling-out with Horace Roberts Pruitt at one point over something to do with the Sykeses—though it was a clash of egos more than anything else, really, and had been building for a while—and was given an ultimatum by Horace: them or us. Unfortunately, H. H. didn't respond well to veiled threats, no matter who they came from. He abruptly terminated the family's association with the Pruitts. This was just after the turn of the twentieth century. The head of the Sykes clan at the time, a rather sour man by the name of Thaddeus Montgomery Sykes, tapped H. H. as the family's primary attorney, confidant, consigliere, and executor of the family's estate and assets the very next day. We've been in league with them ever since."

"In league?" Candy thought it was an odd choice of words.

Judicious moved uncomfortably in his chair. "Some of the endeavors of the Sykes family have been, should we say, in gray areas—though they don't see it that way, of course, and neither do the other members of my family."

"Were there repercussions from the Pruitts?" Herr Georg wondered.

"Over the years, yes, numerous times. But we survived, in part by being canny, and in part by remembering that money motivates all business decisions."

"And now your brother carries on the tradition with the Sykeses," Candy observed.

"He does," Judicious said simply. "He's their gofer, to be blunt about it. But a very well-paid one."

"That's what he was doing this morning when I met him," Herr Georg said. "Checking out the Whitby place before Porter Sykes arrives tomorrow."

Judicious nodded knowingly, as if already aware of this information. "I'd heard Marshall was in town—or Lex, as we used to call him when we were younger. But I didn't know why. I suppose it all makes sense now."

Candy's ears perked up. "Lex?"

"His middle name: Marshall Lex Bosworth. *Lex*, as you might know, is the Latin word for 'law.' It's a tradition among my family to use some type of legal term or the name of a prominent attorney or judge somewhere in our names. That was his, in part. He's named after John Marshall, who was the secretary of state under John Adams and the fourth chief justice of the Supreme Court. Stanton, Harlon, Hay, Rutledge—they're all taken from noteworthy lawyers, many of whom sat on the Supreme Court."

"So your brother was commonly known as Lex Bosworth?" Candy pressed.

"For most of his life and to his close friends, yes, though professionally he uses his first name these days."

"What kind of connection did he have with Julius?"

"Julius?" That seemed to stump Judicious. "I'm not sure they had much of a connection at all. I'm not sure they even knew each other."

Candy decided to reveal a key bit of information. "I believe Julius wrote a note before he died, perhaps containing a number of clues, including the initials *L. B.* I'm wondering if it might be a reference to your brother."

"In what context was this?" Judicious asked.

"It was associated with a list of names of the town's founding families—your family, plus the Ethinghams, Whitbys, and Rainsfords, as well as the Palfrey and Sykes families. Could there be any significance in those names, other than their ties to the cape?"

"Sure," said Judicious almost at once. "My family has represented all those families at one time or another—and still does, some of them, I believe."

Candy turned to Herr Georg, her eyes twinkling with excitement at this new discovery. "That's the link then. Marshall Bosworth. L. B."

"Do you think he has something to do with Julius's death?" the baker asked.

For an answer, Candy turned back to Judicious. "What do you think? Could Marshall do something like that? Is it possible?"

If Judicious was offended by the suggestion that a member of his family might be associated with a murder, he didn't show it. "I don't think he's that brave—or that crazy. Or that stupid, for that matter."

"Do you two plan to get together while he's in town?" Herr Georg asked.

"No."

Judicious didn't elaborate, and neither Candy nor Herr Georg pressed further. "I have just a few more questions," Candy said after taking another sip of tea, "and then we'll get out of your hair and let you get back to . . . whatever you were doing."

Judicious nodded as he glanced out the window to gauge the light. He seemed anxious to move on, to head back outside, so she quickly asked her questions. "Have you ever heard of a place called Foul Mouth?"

He turned back to her and thought a few moments before he answered, "No."

Candy nodded at his response. She hadn't expected much. She tried again. "You mentioned local historians earlier. Have you ever heard of a woman named Lucinda Dowling?" She held up her index finger and thumb, about half an inch apart. "She wrote these thin histories of some of the town's founding families, including those I mentioned earlier."

Here, his response was more positive. "I have. She also wrote a two-volume history about the Pruitts, and books on others, like the Kimballs, the Libbys, the Trembles, and the Frosts."

"Really? I didn't see all those on the shelves up in the archives."

"Oh, they're there somewhere," Judicious said. "I have copies of some of them here, if you'd like to see them."

Candy set down her mug of tea and flashed him a smile. "Actually, I would . . . if it's not too much trouble."

Judicious seemed mildly surprised by her response, but he didn't seem to mind complying. "No trouble at all."

He pushed himself up out of his chair. Candy rose as well, and the baker followed suit, though hesitantly.

Judicious motioned with a hand. "This way."

It was a small cabin but efficiently laid out and furnished. He took them through the kitchen and then into his bedroom in the back, which doubled as a study. Two tall windows looked out at the woods behind the house. A single bed covered with a multicolored quilt was pushed into one corner and flanked by two low wood dressers. In the opposite corner, two worktables pushed together and arranged in an L shape were filled with stacks of books, which overflowed onto the floor and surrounding floor-to-ceiling shelves. In addition, the shelves were filled with mementos and knick-knacks, magazines and photographs. Candy wanted to take a closer look but held herself back. She didn't want to appear as if she was snooping.

Judicious paused in front of the shelves, studying them as he sought the specific volumes in question, then pointed to a spot on one of the lower shelves. "Here they are."

He crouched down, and Candy did also. She saw them right away. They had the same look as the ones she'd seen upstairs in the archives—thin, older volumes of similar size and design, though there were more of them, and they were arranged in a different order. Alphabetically, she noticed, which made sense. And there were other family names mixed in. Abbot was first, then Bosworth and Delano, followed by the Frosts, Kimballs, and Libbys, before the Pruitts, Rainsfords, Trembles, Wendells, and Whitbys.

"Twelve volumes," Candy said, counting them quickly, including the two Pruitt volumes, "and none devoted to the Sykes family, or the Ethinghams, for that matter."

"There might be a few missing," Judicious admitted. "I'm not sure I ever had a complete set."

"That means there are at least fourteen or fifteen in the set, maybe more. Lucinda must have written a whole series of them. But why are there only six in the archives at the museum?"

"I'm sure they must have a complete set somewhere. Maybe only a few are out in circulation."

Candy pondered that for a moment. "Maybe." She

pointed to one of the spines. "What do you know about the writer? Lucinda P. Dowling?"

Judicious shrugged. "I met her a while ago. She still lives around here, and she's still alive. I don't know if she's still writing, though. She was a librarian by trade, and wrote the books as a side project over a period of years."

"The Dowlings live out past Fowler's Corner, right?"

"On Lookout Lane, off River Road, about ten or twelve minutes out of town, on the other side of the river."

"I think I know the place. It's an old New England–style house, set back from the road, near the coastline."

She turned to look back over her shoulder at Herr Georg. "Our next stop."

THIRTY

On the way she got a call from Wanda Boyle at the *Cape Crier*'s office.

"I did some more checking," Wanda told her with quick breaths, as if she was walking hurriedly somewhere, which she probably was, "and heard from a couple of my sources. It sounds like a bunch of your suspects have alibis for the time of Julius's death."

"Which suspects?"

"All of them, really."

"*All* of them?"

"Well, most of them. Let's see." Wanda was silent for a moment as she apparently referred to her notes. "Brandon, the bartender at the inn, tells me that last night, Wednesday night, he saw four gentlemen at a back table in the lounge. I've verified that with a second source, a waitress who works there. It took a little time but we managed to identify three of the gentlemen, since they're not regular patrons—in fact, no one I talked to can remember ever seeing them in the place. So it must have been a special occasion of some sort."

"And who were the three?"

"Owen Peabody, Plymouth Palfrey, and Gilbert Ething-ham."

"Board members," Candy said. "What time was this?"

"Closest we can come is around six or six thirty P.M., though there are some conflicting accounts on the time."

Candy's mind quickly ran through the implications. "But that means Plymouth was in town last night." She remembered thinking, earlier in the day when she'd been at the Keeper's Quarters, that Plymouth must have risen before the sun to drive all the way from Boothbay Harbor to Cape Willington for the morning meeting of the board members. But now, according to Wanda, there was evidence he'd been in town last night, so he'd been able to spend an extra few hours in bed this morning before heading over to the museum.

It also meant he'd been at the inn when Scotty Whitby had allegedly been attacked in the back room. And, she thought, he easily could have slipped out of the lounge for ten or fifteen minutes, long enough to make a quick trip across the street to the museum and swing a bottle of champagne at Julius Seabury's head.

He would also have had access to the cases of champagne in the back, Candy thought. All of them had. Perhaps, she thought, it was some sort of conspiracy. Perhaps they were *all* involved in Julius's death.

"You don't know who the fourth person was yet?"

"Not yet. Still checking on it."

"Do you have a description?"

Again, Wanda took a moment to refer to her notes. She was breathing more regularly now. Apparently she'd slowed her pace or settled into a chair. When she spoke again, it was as if she was reading from a list. "Well dressed, smelled good, nice manicure, catchy smile, a bit of a flirt, dark hair graying at the sides, acted like a lawyer or a doctor."

Candy repeated the description as she looked over at Herr Georg. At first he seemed a little confused, until he realized who she was describing. "Marshall Bosworth," he mouthed.

Candy nodded. "Thanks, Wanda. Let me know if you find out anything else."

"You close to solving this thing?" she asked before they hung up.

"Don't know if I'm close, but I'm working on it."

"I'm guessing you want to have this wrapped up by Saturday. It'd be a shame if this interferes with the wedding."

"You're right about that." Candy could have said more, but she was being diplomatic, always a good approach with Wanda, especially when she was trying to get off the phone with the other woman.

"How are things going out at the farm?"

"We're mostly set up. As long as the good weather holds, we should be fine."

They talked a few more moments, and Candy keyed off the call. "You caught most of that, right?"

"Marshall Bosworth was at the inn last night with three of the board members. At around the same time we were there. Funny we didn't see them."

"Yes, isn't it?"

"What do you think they were talking about?"

Candy shook her head. "I wish I knew."

Herr Georg gave her an encouraging look. "Well, think positive! We've discovered a lot so far. Perhaps the other answers we seek lie just ahead!"

Candy smiled at that, and looked expectantly out the windshield at the road ahead. "Perhaps they do."

THIRTY-ONE

The Dowlings lived in a weather-beaten two-story house with white siding, small single-pane windows, and faded blue trim. There was no porch, only three wooden steps leading up to the front door. With no exterior decorations or enhancements of any sort, it was a rather plain place, and like many coastal homes in this part of the state, built to withstand the punishing weather that could come off the restless sea, rather than stand out aesthetically.

It sat on a flat piece of land close to the rocky shore but not right on it, surrounded by low coastal vegetation, scrubby brown trees, and a few evergreens. Winding sandy paths led through the tangled thigh-high brush to the water's edge.

And the sea itself was magnificent today, broad, bright, and an uncommonly deep rich shade of blue. A few boats bobbed out on the water, smaller craft used for work or pleasure, including a sailboat or two. As they drove along the narrow lane, Candy and Herr Georg could see past the house and shoreline, all the way across the bay, to the low, gray peninsula and rocky point on the far side, including the spot upon which the Whitby estate stood. From here, though, it was mostly hidden behind a curtain of trees and shrubs.

Anyway, Candy realized, you couldn't really see much of it regardless, unless you had a good pair of binoculars, since it was so far away.

Right. Binoculars. Just like Julius had in his car. If that's what he'd used them for—to view the comings and goings at the Whitby estate across the bay—she doubted he'd have been able to see much detail, unless he had a high-powered pair. But with the pair he had in his car, he certainly would have been able to see more than he could with the naked eye.

As they approached, Candy shifted her gaze back to the Dowling property. There was no garage, just a gravel driveway and a couple of cars pulled up beside the house. Fortunately, it appeared someone was home. Herr Georg parked the Volvo next to one of the cars and they both got out.

The wind was stronger here, by the sea, and it blew around Candy's hair, so she had to take a few moments to regain control of it. Herr Georg, noticing the weather, dipped into the backseat and pulled out his green felt Tyrolean hat, which he plopped tightly onto his head over his white hair. He nodded toward the front door. "You're the expert in this type of thing," he said with an encouraging smile that showed off the gap in his front teeth. "I'll follow your lead."

Together they approached the house. Herr Georg remained on the dirt driveway while Candy climbed the stairs and knocked. They waited. No answer, though she thought she could hear someone moving around inside. She knocked again. For a few moments she thought she'd been mistaken—despite the cars, it appeared no one was home—until she heard a lock turn and the door creaked open. An eye peered out. "Yes?"

"Hi, my name is Candy Holliday, and this is Georg Wolfs-burger of the Black Forest Bakery," she said, pointing behind her. "We hope we're in the right place. We're looking for an author by the name of Lucinda P. Dowling."

The door pulled open a little farther and Candy saw the

face of a fairly plump middle-aged woman, who gave her a curious look. "You're Candy Holliday?"

"That's right."

"You're looking for Lucinda?"

"I am. We just have a few questions we'd like to ask her . . . for an article," she added, almost as an afterthought.

"Ohhh," the woman said, pointing at Candy, as if suddenly realizing who she was. "You're from the paper! You wrote about all those murders!" Her eyes went wide, as if she were meeting a celebrity.

Candy took it all in stride. "Well, yes, I did cover all kinds of topics when I was working full-time for the paper. Now I just write a gardening column and an occasional restaurant review, although sometimes I write other types of articles. And I'd like to talk to Mrs. Dowling for a tribute article I'm currently working on—if she lives here. As I said, I'm hoping we have the right place."

"Oh, you have the right place, all right. Lucinda will be thrilled to meet you! Come on in. She's right through here. Mind the clutter. We have two growing boys."

The woman pushed open the door a little wider, inviting them in as she started back through the house, talking as she went.

"I'm Jenny, by the way, Lucinda's daughter-in-law, though sometimes I just call her Lucy for short, but she prefers Lucinda. She says it sounds more distinguished, and I guess it does. She lives here with me and Jeff. That's her son, by the way. He's my husband, you know, so we're all Dowlings here." She laughed a little, a nervous twitter. "The kids are over at a friend's house today, so you lucked out. It gets pretty noisy in here sometimes. But Lucinda doesn't mind. She says they keep her young. She doesn't get around as well as she used to, so we set up a first-floor room for her. It's got a great view of the ocean. She likes to get up early and watch the sunrise. We get the earliest sunrises in the country here, but I'm sure you already knew that."

Candy responded with a series of *ohh*s and *umm*s but

couldn't get another word in edgewise, so she didn't try. Herr Georg followed her silently.

The house was well lived-in, typical of a busy family, with unfolded laundry on the sofa, a television set to low volume, and cooking smells coming from the kitchen. But Candy paid it little attention as she and the baker followed the woman toward the back of the house. Jenny soon came to a door that was half-closed and peeked in. "Just give me a minute to make sure she's awake," she said with a wink, and ducked inside.

She was back quickly, holding the door open for them. "Come on in, she's right over here," said Jenny, and she led them to a big wicker chair set over by the windows. Sitting amongst the pillows and warming under a colorful throw was an older woman, perhaps near eighty, with a hardback book open on her lap. A mystery novel, Candy noticed as she approached.

Lucinda held out a welcoming hand, and they shook. "Candy Holliday," she said with a strong voice that conveyed genuine warmth. "I've heard so much about you, and of course I've been reading the paper for years. It's so nice to finally meet you."

"Likewise, Mrs. Dowling. I didn't realize you lived so close, or I would have stopped by sooner."

"Oh, I've been hiding out here for a while. Jenny and Jeff have been taking good care of me, and it's nice to live around the grandchildren. They're so energetic!" She turned to the baker. "Herr Georg, it's nice to see you again. I've been in your shop, of course, but I'm afraid it's been a while."

"Of course, I remember now," the baker said, brightening as he shook her hand delicately. "I neglected to put the face with the name, and I pride myself on knowing my customers. I apologize."

She waved a hand and made a clucking sound with her tongue. "Don't even think about it. Most people couldn't pick me out of a lineup," she said with a soft chuckle. "I'm usually just Lucinda around town, when I have a chance to get around, and far from somebody you'd recognize. I was a librarian in

Bangor for most of my adult life before coming here to live with my son and daughter-in-law. So I'm probably not as well known around town as the other villagers."

"But you've contributed quite a lot to the history of Cape Willington," Candy said. "I saw the volumes of family histories you wrote, up in the historical society's archives at the museum."

"Oh, yes, those little books of mine. My side project, as I used to call it. I had quite a lot of fun writing them, though I finished them up a while ago. . . ." She paused as Jenny brought in a couple of folding chairs, and Candy and Herr Georg sat down by the windows near Lucinda's wicker chair. Once they were settled, she continued.

"My husband, Jim, was originally from Cape Willington, though he's gone ten years now. But he had both a Rainsford and a Libby in his family tree, so that got me interested in the cape's history and its original landholders and founding families. I researched the books here in town and in the state archives in Augusta, as well as at the state historical society in Portland and in Bangor—anywhere I could find the resources I needed, really. I also did some local interviewing, though this was many years ago, when I still had the energy to do that sort of thing. I turned up a number of interesting stories—the true stories behind the legends, you might say."

"How many books did you write?" Candy asked, deciding it was best to start at the beginning before she got down to the nitty-gritty.

"There were sixteen in all, written over a period of almost two decades," Lucinda said, "including two volumes on the Pruitts. I intended to write more books about them, since they were so influential in this area, but I never finished their story. I guess I just got sidetracked with other projects. Those books are mostly forgotten now, I believe, though Julius seemed to have taken an interest in them lately, didn't he?" She gave Candy a knowing smile. "I suppose that's why you're here, isn't it?"

"It is," Candy admitted. "Sometime over the past few days or so, he was doing some research using your books. But it sounds like you're already aware of that."

"I am . . . or, at least, I suspected as much."

"Do you know what he was researching?" Candy asked.

"As a matter of fact I do, because I talked to him in person, not more than two weeks ago."

"You did? You went to the museum?"

"No, he came here to the house, to pay a visit, he said. He was a very friendly and endearing gentleman. We'd met a few times before, but I hadn't seen him in a while, so it was nice to have him visit. We had a very interesting chat that afternoon. We were sitting right here by the windows, just as you and I and Herr Georg are doing now."

"And what did you talk about?" the baker asked.

"Well, a number of things. We're both authors, of course, so we shared some stories about the general travails and triumphs of our chosen avocation. Typical stuff, you know. We discussed some of our common areas of research, and of course we talked about the town's history, especially its founding families, since he was apparently researching the topic himself for a book."

She paused as her face took on an odd expression. "And then, strangely enough, right out of the blue," she said, "he asked me about a place called Foul Mouth. I guess I must have looked surprised when he said it, hearing that name after so long. But I surprised him right back when I told him I knew exactly what it was."

THIRTY-TWO

"You've heard that name before?" Candy asked, her shoulders rising and her ears perking up. She felt like she'd just tapped into a gold mine. "Two words, right?"

"Oh, yes, two words. Julius was quite clear about that fact," Lucinda said, her hands fidgeting absently in her lap. "But I knew exactly what he meant, as soon as he said it. Still, he insisted on spelling it out for me, so I wouldn't mistake it for the towns with a similar name."

"And what did you tell him? Where have you heard of it?"

"Well, I wrote about it, of course!" Lucinda said, her eyes widening. "Many years ago. I never thought much about it, not at the time, and I'd honestly forgotten about it until Julius brought it up. It was just one of those small historical details one uncovers while reading old diaries and talking to folks who have lived in town a long time. I wrote it down in my notes, put it in a book, and then it went right out of my mind."

"It's in one of your books?"

"Two of them, actually. The volumes on the Whitby and the Sykes families."

"Why those families?" Herr Georg asked.

"Because it was on land they owned—Foul Mouth, that is. It's not called that any longer, of course, but it was commonly used back in the eighteenth and nineteenth centuries, and even into the early part of the twentieth. I've seen it occasionally in old land deeds and in wills. The Native Americans originally named it, in their language, in something unpronounceable to the early English settlers, but it sounded like they were saying Foul Mouth and it stuck—for a while, at least, until cooler heads prevailed and someone decided the name was a little too offensive, so they came up with something more acceptable."

"And where is it?" Candy asked, so excited in anticipation that she realized she wasn't breathing.

Lucinda pointed out the window. "Well, it's largely forgotten now. I'm not sure anyone remembers it. But it's right there, across the bay. I look at it every day."

In unison, as if they'd rehearsed their movements, both Candy and Herr Georg rose from their chairs to look out the window, eastward, in the direction Lucinda indicated.

It was the point of land upon which the Whitby estate stood.

"Whitby Point?" Herr Georg asked, turning back toward Lucinda with a confused expression on his face.

"Yes, that's how we refer to it these days, but that's a relatively new name. I've seen it referred to in various sources as Pine Point, Sykes Point, and even Rocky Point, though there were already plenty of those around the region, so it became confusing to sort everything out. And I've also seen it listed on an old map or two as Smuggler's Point."

"Smuggler's Point? Why was it called that?" Candy asked.

"Well, from what I've read, as that name implies, it once was a common hangout of smugglers and privateers along the coast. They were quite prevalent around here a century or two ago." She nodded out the window, at the point of land across the bay. "There's a small harbor around the other side of the peninsula, farther up toward the main land mass, though because of the tides and the rocks it was considered too treacherous to navigate, to be of any real use. But with the surrounding vegetation and the isolation of the peninsula, it was a popular transition point for contraband. Supposedly there's a cave over there—this place called Foul Mouth—where the smugglers stored their stolen booty until they were able to get rid of it. I've even heard rumors, which I haven't been able to verify, that there's a secret passage leading from the cave up into the Whitby estate itself—which, as you probably know, was originally built by a member of the Sykes family."

"No, I didn't know that." Candy pondered this latest revelation as she settled back down into her chair, though Herr Georg remained standing, staring out the window.

"Oh, yes, but this was a long time ago, back at the early years of the last century, when the Sykes fortune was still humming along, before they fell on hard times. Just a few years after they built it, they lost the estate somehow, possibly in a poker game or something like that, and the Whitbys have owned it ever since. They've kept it in the family until just recently, when it sold to a new owner."

"And do you know who bought it?" Candy asked.

When Lucinda shook her head, Herr Georg told her. "It's Porter Sykes," he said quietly. "I heard it from Marshall Bosworth, the family's attorney."

"Oh my," Lucinda said, and she scrunched up her face as if she'd just caught a whiff of a particularly bad smell.

"Porter is headed up from Boston tonight or in the morning, possibly as we speak," Candy said, "and he's going to be out there tomorrow. It appears, from what you've told us, that he's bought back a property his family once owned."

"I hadn't heard anything about that," Lucinda said, her voice quivering just a bit. "It hasn't been in the paper, has it?"

"Not yet. I don't believe it's been officially announced, but that should happen shortly."

"Well," Lucinda said, "I just hope they don't resort to their old ways, and that they're able to maintain the peace around here. There's been some animosity over the years between the Sykes and the Pruitt families, you know."

"So I've heard."

"It turned quite violent at times," Lucinda continued. "I tell some of those stories in the books. Did you know that at one point, during an escalation of the feud, they shot cannonballs back and forth at each other across the bay, from the Whitby estate—the Sykes estate then—toward Pruitt Manor, and back?"

"No, I didn't know that either," Candy said.

"Can you imagine?" Lucinda seemed pleased with herself for revealing this bit of information to an ace reporter. "Some of those old cannons could shoot as far as two thousand yards, which is more than a mile. But of course the bay is a few miles across, so all the shot went into the water. The echoing booms could be quite deafening, though. I've heard they could shatter windows here in town. Thank goodness those two families didn't live closer! They could have destroyed each other's houses. I read about it in a very old edition of your paper, the *Crier*, which I found in the historical archives."

"If you'll forgive me," said Herr Georg, settling uneasily back down into his chair, "this is all very interesting, but I'm not quite sure why this place called Foul Mouth caught Julius's attention."

"Well, I wondered the same thing," Lucinda said, her voice rising in agreement. "I thought it was such an odd inquiry for him to make, the way he came out of the blue with it like that. That's why I mentioned it to you."

"And what did he say when you told him about it?" Candy asked.

"Well, he didn't say much of anything, really. He just nodded and made a few notes. That was about it. But it stuck in my mind, especially after . . . well, after what happened to him."

"Do you think there's a connection?" Herr Georg asked.

Lucinda shook her head. "I don't know that for sure. If I did I would have gone to the police by now. It's just . . . well, it's been bothering me, that's all. I had to tell someone about it—someone who might know how to use that information in the proper way."

"There's another question you could answer that might help us out," Candy said. "You say you wrote sixteen books in all, covering fifteen families, with the Pruitts getting two volumes. Is that correct?"

Lucinda proudly nodded a confirmation, and Candy continued. "When Julius was here, did he ask you about any of the other families—the Bosworths, for instance, or the Ethinghams, or the Rainsfords, or the Palfreys?"

Lucinda thought a moment, then shook her head. "Not individually by name, not that I can recall."

"Are there any specific connections between those families—the Bosworths, Ethinghams, Rainsfords, and Palfreys, as well as the Sykes and Whitby families? Anything that might tie them together?"

"Well, yes, I suppose there could be a number of things. Some of them intermarried, for instance, and some were involved in various endeavors together. Cape Willington is a small community, you know. It would have been impossible for them all to live here and not have had some connections between them."

"Anything specific you can think of?"

"In what way?"

"Well, is there any sort of thread that links the families, perhaps an incident or person or an event, something like that?"

"Well, I don't know." Lucinda abruptly went quiet as she considered the question. "I suppose there could be, but nothing jumps immediately to mind. I could research it, of course, see what I can come up with—if you think it's important."

"It might be," Candy said, "but let me ask you this: In what order did you write the books? Did you start alphabetically, or chronologically? Which family did you start with?"

"Oh, that one's easy to answer. I started with the Rainsfords and the Libbys, of course, since they were both part of my husband's family tree. And then I moved on to the Pruitts, who were the first unrelated family I wrote about. Even though there are a number of histories about them, I thought I had to include them in any collection of the town's founding families, since they were the most influential, as I said."

"Are all those books you wrote in the museum's archives at the Keeper's Quarters?"

Lucinda seemed a little surprised by the question, but nodded her head. "As far as I know, yes. Why?"

"Because I was up there recently," Candy said, avoiding any mention of the actual timing of her visit to the archives, "and I saw only a few of them on the shelves."

"Well, that's interesting." Lucinda leaned forward slightly in the wicker chair, absently rearranging the throw around her legs. "Which ones, dear?"

Candy recited the names quickly from memory: "Bosworth, Ethingham, Whitby, Rainsford, Palfrey, and Sykes."

"That's all you saw?"

Candy nodded. "They were all on the shelves in a row, in that order."

"Where are the rest?"

"I don't know. That's why I thought I'd ask you."

"Well, I suppose they could just be shelved in a different area, though that wouldn't make much sense, would it? Maybe you just missed them somehow."

"Maybe. Is there anything significant about the order of those families?"

Again, Lucinda didn't seem quite sure how to respond. "Significant? In the order? No, I don't think so."

"They're certainly not shelved alphabetically," Candy pointed out, "and from what you've just said, not in the order in which they were written. Maybe there's another reason? Date of publication?"

Lucinda blinked several times, and it appeared as if she was tiring. "Maybe they were just shelved in a random order?" she said helpfully.

Candy acknowledged that was a possibility, though the order matched the names on the list that had fallen out of the book Owen picked up. But she left that part of the mystery unspoken, and when she saw Lucinda stifle a yawn, she realized they wouldn't learn much more today. But there was just one more question she had to ask.

"Who published your books?"

"It was a small imprint for the University of Maine Press."

"Not the Kennebec Press? Not Plymouth Palfrey?"

Lucinda waved a hand as her mouth puckered. "No, not him. He hadn't started his publishing business yet, of course, though I've talked to him since about other histories. But I don't think I'd ever publish with him."

"Why not?" Candy asked.

"Well, because we just don't get along. We have different ideas about what makes a good history book. He tends more toward popular subjects, while I prefer those that are more scholarly. And he uses a lot of, well, coarse language at times. I'm not comfortable with it."

A short time later, out of questions, they thanked Lucinda and Jenny, said their good-byes, and headed back out to the baker's car.

"So," Herr Georg said as they settled inside, "did that help?"

"Yes, though I haven't figured out how yet."

"What do you think we should do next?"

Candy thought back over all she'd learned just in the past few hours—and hadn't learned. They now knew the location of the place called Foul Mouth, they knew the Sykes family had once owned the Whitby place, and they knew Porter Sykes had recently bought it back from the Whitbys. They knew Scotty Whitby was missing. She knew Julius had kept a pair of binoculars in his car, and that he'd had sand on the bottoms of his shoes, which meant he might have been out on the narrow beach, staring out across the bay with the binoculars.

What—or who—had he been searching for?

She checked her watch. Not quite six P.M. Maggie wouldn't be back for another hour or so, and it was probably a good idea to keep Herr Georg distracted, so he wouldn't think too much about his fiancée's absence.

And she still had some investigating to do. Might as well kill two birds with one stone—something she'd been successful at doing today.

"I think, if you're up for it, we have one more stop to make before we head home."

The baker nodded, inserted the key into the ignition, and pulled on his seat belt. "Where to?"

"Across the bay. To the Whitby estate."

THIRTY-THREE

"It's like déjà vu all over again," Herr Georg said as they approached the Whitby place on the pockmarked dirt road nearly half an hour later. "I was just here this morning, but it feels like ages ago."

"It's true," said Candy, peering out the windshield as the house revealed itself through the trees and rising road dust. "A lot has happened in a short period of time. We've made some good progress, and I feel like we're closing in on some real answers."

"About the Whitby estate? And Foul Mouth? You think they're the keys to this whole mystery? About what happened to Julius?"

"Yes, those. But also Marshall Bosworth and Porter Sykes, and Scotty Whitby and that bottle of champagne. And that list of names Owen found. And those deeds of yours, and their connection to Foul Mouth. You know, Judicious Bosworth made an interesting comment when we were talking to him. He thought Julius might have found out something in one of those old books he was researching, or possibly overheard a private conversation when he was upstairs at the museum. But I think it could be more than that. He certainly could have run across the words *Foul Mouth* in one of Lucinda's books. But I'm wondering if he also found that reference mentioned when he was reading through the deeds."

The baker's eyes widened. "But that makes perfect sense! It would link the deeds and Foul Mouth together."

"It would. It's certainly possible—even probable—that the Whitby estate and this Foul Mouth place would have been mentioned in those deeds. And if Julius made inquiries about what he'd learned, it might have put him in dangerous territory, especially if what Judicious said is true—that there's something larger going on."

"I suppose that's what we're here to find out," Herr Georg said, looking out at the house in front of them. As he surveyed the property, he added, "Marshall Bosworth must have left. I don't see his car in the driveway. The lot is empty again, just like this morning when I drove out here."

Candy was a little surprised she didn't see Porter Sykes's car in the driveway, although she had no idea what kind of car he drove. If he was planning on meeting with her tomorrow, he must be on his way here. Would he arrive later tonight—or in the next few minutes, while they were snooping around the place?

She definitely didn't want to be seen here if he should suddenly show up. It would be, at the least, very awkward.

"We probably shouldn't stick around too long," Candy said, thinking out loud. "Technically we're trespassing, although I'm sure no one would press charges if someone found us out here." She paused. "Mostly sure." She paused again. "Okay, I'm not sure at all. Let's just not stick around too long."

"I'm all for that," the baker said as he pulled the car to a stop in the graveled parking area. "A quick look around and then back to town?"

"Right. Good plan."

As Candy opened the car door and stepped out, her cell phone rang. She fished it out of her pocket and studied the screen.

The Cape Willington Police Department was calling.

"It must be Chief Durr, responding to that message I left for him," she said, and swiped at the screen. "Hello?"

Their conversation was relatively brief, as the chief was somewhat abrupt—obviously a man with a lot on his mind at the moment. So she quickly told him about the list of family names Owen had found and how she thought it might help with his investigation.

"What makes you think that?" the chief asked, sounding suspicious.

"I saw Neil Crawford this afternoon. He played the message Julius left for him on his cell phone. Julius mentioned something about Foul Mouth, which was also written on that list of names. I think it was created by Julius before he died."

The chief took down the information and turned away from the phone for a few moments to talk to someone else. When he came back on the line, he sounded distracted. "Why didn't you tell me about this list before?"

"I didn't know if it was significant or not."

The chief grunted at that. "We'll look into it," he said, and quickly ended the call.

As Candy slipped the phone back into her pocket, she realized that Owen had never called her back. Not surprising, she thought. They probably weren't on the best of speaking terms at the moment. She decided to let the police follow up with him, and turned her attention back to the matter at hand.

She stood for a few moments staring up at the facade of brownstone and dark windows before her, studying it, searching for any signs of movement or activity. But it looked lifeless, deserted. Her gaze darted back and forth, to the trees on either side, and to the half-seen outbuildings around the back. She was struck by the building's stateliness, but also by its isolation out here, all by itself on this lonely spit of land.

But then she turned, and was transfixed by the view out over the bay.

It was spectacular, she thought, and she instantly knew

why they'd chosen to build upon this spot. The water before her stretched out to the west and south like fine glass, glistening in the bright sun, moving and wiggling gently like a living thing. And it had a voice as well; she could hear the muted sound of waves breaking on rocks below, the calls of the gulls above, and the distant thrum of boat engines, chugging north and south on the bay.

And, on the far shore, stood the low buildings of Cape Willington, with its twin lighthouses, the mouth of the English River, and Pruitt Manor clearly visible.

"It's magnificent, isn't it?" Herr Georg said as he joined her.

"I've never been out here before. I didn't realize what an amazing view it has of the town."

"Yes, well, if you wanted to keep a close eye on the comings and goings in our little village, you could do so easily from here—with the help of a good telescope, perhaps."

"Or a pair of binoculars," Candy said thoughtfully. She turned to scan the property again, wondering what Julius might have been observing, but nothing jumped out at her.

Finally, she started back toward the house. "Let's see if anyone's home."

Not surprisingly, given the absence of vehicles out front, their knocks on the front door went unanswered.

"Should we have a look around back?" Candy wondered.

"I had intended to do that this morning when I was out here," Herr Georg said, "but I never had a chance."

"Well, we have a chance now."

The baker flashed her a smile and made a motion with his hand. "After you, detective."

Candy was amused by his comment but said nothing. And despite his suggestion, she didn't start off immediately. Instead, she hesitated as she craned her neck out so she could see as far around the side of the house as possible. "Okay, just . . . keep an eye out."

"I assure you, I will be doing exactly that."

Together they headed off, their shoes crunching on the gravel as they rounded the side of the house, following the lane that looped around the building. The wind had been gustier out in front but here it died down. It was as if the house and trees were serving as a sort of windbreak. The sounds of the boats and the sea ebbed as well, muted by the foliage.

The lane widened again at the back of the house, and Candy saw a large carriage house with a two-stall garage, a side building that looked like it might be a workshop, a separate storage building, and a gardening shed, surrounded by piles of empty clay pots and a weather-beaten wheel-barrow.

No cars. No people. Nothing out of the ordinary.

Candy looked out through the trees, behind the outbuildings, and thought she saw some blue back there. "We're close to the point," she said. "The ocean isn't too far in that direction."

She spotted a dirt path that meandered off through the trees. It appeared to lead to the right, toward the headland. It made sense, she thought. There was probably a spectacular view in that direction as well, off to the south and southeast.

Oddly, the path looked churned up, as if it had been trodden on recently.

Crossing her arms in thought, Candy moved in closer for a better look. That's when she spotted the footprint.

It looked fairly fresh, though she was no real judge of these sorts of things.

She saw another one a little farther on.

"Someone's been along here recently," she said, pointing.

Herr Georg was right behind her. He saw the footprints as well. "Maybe it was just Marshall Bosworth checking out the property, or a gardener, or something like that."

"Maybe," Candy said. "Did you notice what kind of shoes Marshall was wearing when you saw him this morning?"

"Shoes? No, not really."

"He was dressed up, right? Business attire?"

"Yes, that's correct."

"Then we can assume he was wearing some type of dress shoes, and not sneakers, right?"

The baker nodded, and Candy pointed again. "These footprints have a pattern, like on the bottoms of sneakers. Dress shoes are usually smooth on the bottom, with no patterns." Her gaze intensified as her head shifted and her eyes followed the dirt path.

"Let's see where this leads."

THIRTY-FOUR

At first, it seemed, the trail led only to the water's edge—
though it was quite a magnificent edge.

They stopped a few feet from the craggy drop-off and
learned forward as far as they dared, peering cautiously down
to the sea far below, where the waves slapped sometimes
gently, sometimes violently against unforgiving black rocks,
often creating deep gurgling thuds they could hear up top.

The land curved away from them on both sides, disappear-
ing to the north on their left and to the west on their right.
The ocean stretched away to the south, and they could see
the faint outlines of hazy islands to the south and west. Far
out on the horizon, a tanker ship plowed through the relatively
calm waters, a mere rusty smudge balanced on the fine, nearly
indistinct line that separated sea from sky.

For several long moments they both studied the pan-
orama, until Herr Georg finally doffed his hat, scratched
absently at his head, and said, "Nothing down there."

"No, it appears not."

They dawdled a little longer, hesitant to leave, taking a

last long look, and were just about to turn back when another gurgling burp echoed up toward them along the rocky face.

"What was that?" Candy asked.

Herr Georg wasn't quite sure what she meant. "What was what?"

"That sound."

The baker took a step closer to the edge and stretched his neck to look down over the side. "The waves? Hitting the rocks?"

"Yes, but that hollow sound." She turned toward him. "You've been to Thunder Hole over on Mount Desert Island, right?"

"Yes, though it's been a few years."

"It's a long, narrow, natural inlet in the rock," Candy said. "When the waves come in there at some speed they say it sounds like clapping thunder."

"Yes, but . . ." Herr Georg inched a little closer to the edge and listened.

There it was again, sonorous and intermittent, like large bubbles emerging and popping out of the ocean, different from the rest of the sounds made by the slapping waves.

The baker retreated a few steps before he turned toward her. "What do you think it is?"

Candy shook her head. "I don't know for sure, but if I had to guess, I'd say it's that cave Lucinda mentioned—the one the smugglers used to use."

The baker's face was a mixture of curiosity and wariness. "Could it be?"

And she spoke the words that were lurking in both their minds. "Foul Mouth," she said.

"Down *there*?" He pointed in an animated fashion, as if horrified by the fact that she actually might want to check it out.

"Whatever it is, there's something below us, down among the rocks." She looked up and around, checking the sky to the east. "Sunset today is around a quarter to eight, I think. We still have some light left, though it could be dark if we're going into a cave." Another pause as she glanced at the baker. "You don't happen to have a flashlight in the car, do you?"

"As a matter of fact, I have two in the back. I always like to be prepared."

"Just like a Boy Scout, right?"

His grin returned, and the gap between his front teeth. "I was a bit of an explorer in my youth, and yes, I've been into a few caves." Again he looked over the edge. "Not one as hard to get to as that place down there, though. Do you really think it's possible to reach it?"

"There must be a way," Candy said. "Why don't you grab the flashlights and I'll have a look around. I just wish I'd brought my boots."

The baker waggled a finger at her. "Ah, see, it pays to be prepared! I might have an extra pair of rubber winter boots in the car too. I'll see what I can find."

Less than ten minutes later they regrouped, Herr Georg carrying a black backpack on his shoulder.

"There does seem to be a way down of some sort, over in that direction"—Candy pointed to her left—"though I'm not sure how safe it is. We'll have to exercise the utmost care if we're going to attempt this. We don't want the groom to have to limp down the aisle on a twisted ankle—or a broken leg."

"Or the maid of honor!" he responded. "Step carefully then. And as always, I'll follow your lead, my brave blueberry farmer!"

Again, Candy smiled. She was glad he'd come along. She would never have attempted something like this alone, and she honestly wasn't sure it was wise to do it with someone. But they were trying to solve a murder, and she knew they needed to follow up on this possibly important discovery.

She led him to a spot she'd scoped out earlier. It was a cleft in the cliff wall, a narrow but not too deep gash that carved a more gently sloping path down off the top. The cleft was rock strewn and cluttered with some low vegetation and small, hardy, knobby-branched trees, bent to sharp angles by the fierce winds off the sea. It gave them something to cling to as they cautiously began their descent.

It was slow going. Candy went first, taking great care where she put her feet. Herr Georg followed right behind, in her footsteps. Once or twice she misplaced her footing and slipped, sending down a cascade of rocks and pebbles that disappeared over the side. Fortunately she was able to find a handhold on a tree or clump of weeds to keep her from sliding farther down. At those times she'd glance back up at the baker, to gauge his demeanor, but he seemed to be holding steady so far, so she went on.

Slowly and safely, they moved farther down the cleft, until it came to an end. From there, they spotted a narrow ledge that ran along the cliff face, sloping gently downward, so they continued their trek in that direction. It led them to a series of steps, which seemed to almost have been cut by human hands, though she supposed some of them could have been natural, and those led them down close to the water's edge.

Here they stopped and surveyed the landscape. The hollow gurgling was louder now, close by, but Candy still couldn't quite see the source, hidden behind an outcropping of rock. *Somehow*, she thought, *we have to get around that*.

Behind her, Herr Georg was breathing heavily from the descent, but when she looked back at him, he seemed exhilarated and as game as ever, with the backpack now looped over both shoulders to make it easier to carry. "Okay," he said, brushing some dust off his pants, "where next?"

She pointed ahead. "The way is blocked. We've got to get beyond those rocks."

It was the baker who discovered the solution. "Up this way," he said, pointing and heading off on his own, back up the slope a little. "I think we can get across here."

The baker removed the backpack and tossed it upward, then scrabbled partway up a steep escarpment, finding handholds and footholds in the face of the rock, pulling himself upward with some effort, until he reached an arching plateau, across which he started moving laterally. He stopped only briefly to retrieve the backpack and wave to Candy. "Come on, I think we're almost there!"

And he was right. The rock archway they followed led

them across the cliff face and up over the area where the hollow, intermittent belches were coming from.

"It's right underneath us," Herr Georg said when he was halfway across, pointing downward as they paused, but looking down they still could not see an opening in the rocks below.

"Lead on," Candy said, and on the other side of the arch they found a narrow path down to the edge of the sea. There, they were rewarded for their efforts.

To their left was a low opening, partly flooded due to the oncoming waters, but a definite break in the cliff face, possibly leading into a cave of some sort. The rocks around it were rough but somewhat smoothed by the endless ocean, though there were still some jagged bits they'd have to watch out for. It looked, in some way, like the opening to the gates of hell.

"Foul Mouth," Candy breathed.

They studied the uninviting opening for a few moments, until Herr Georg asked, "But how do we get in there?"

"The same way the smugglers did long ago. We walk."

THIRTY-FIVE

The baker drew a face. His earlier enthusiasm seemed to quickly dissipate. "But we'll get wet."

"Yes, we will. There's no other way."

He took a deep breath and seemed to steel himself. "Very well, if we must do it to solve this mystery, then we must. But we should go in well equipped."

He dropped the backpack down off his shoulder, zipped it open, and started pulling out the items he'd stuffed inside. There were two flashlights, two pairs of rubber boots, two pairs of old work gloves, a length of wound clothesline rope, which he shoved up onto his shoulder, and a pocketknife, which he slid into his pocket. "Just in case," he said as he looked up at Candy.

The boots were big for Candy but they fit well enough over her sneakers. Herr Georg slipped on his, which reached to his calves, and tucked the cuffs of his pants inside. He'd clapped the Tyrolean hat down more firmly onto his head, and handed Candy a yellow ball cap with a food industry manufacturer's logo on it. "I get these from time to time at conventions and such," he said. "I have many of them. Keep this one."

Candy nodded her thanks as she pulled on the gloves and hefted the flashlight, then studied the sky one more time before they entered Foul Mouth. She checked her watch. "We have only an hour or so of light left. And the tide will start to come in soon. We should stay inside no more than thirty minutes—or less."

"Good point," Herr Georg said as he flicked his wrist out of his sleeve. "Fortunately, I wore my diver's watch today. I have it merely because I like the design, of course, since I'm not a diver myself. It's a beautiful timepiece. And it's waterproof, which makes it appropriate for today, and has a rotating bezel." He turned the bezel to mark off a time period of twenty-five minutes. "Okay," he said when they were all suited up, "I'm ready. Let's go."

Candy took the lead again, crawling down carefully, almost on her hands and knees, across the rocks toward the low opening just above the water's surface. As she approached it, another tall wave came in and sloshed into the opening, narrowly missing her and creating that hollow gurgling sound they'd heard from above. It was louder here, and deeper in tone, and seemed to reverberate through her ribs.

She turned back to Herr Georg. "Keep an eye out and let me know if you see another one of those waves coming in," she said.

He nodded. "I'll give you as much fair warning as I can, if I can spot them."

"That's all I ask." She felt she'd probably emerge from this adventure looking like a drowned rat, but there was no turning back now. Whatever happened, happened.

Cautiously she put a rubber-booted foot down on the bottom front lip of rock, the water sloshing over her foot. She ducked her head down low, held the flashlight out in front of her, and took a few tentative steps into Foul Mouth.

She knew instantly where the place got its name. There was a nose hair–curling stink coming from inside. It smelled like dead fish and rotting seaweed, with a heavy tinge of brine, and a few other unsavory things she preferred not to know about. She hesitated, wondering if she should go any farther.

Maybe there were things inside she didn't want to encounter—a critter of some sort, with big teeth and sharp claws. Or, worse, the ghost—or skeleton—of some old pirate left over from a previous era, also with big teeth and sharp claws.

Neither was a very comforting thought.

She went on.

As she took a few steps forward, the rock walls on either side closed in on her, compressing into a narrow, low tunnel.

She heard a shout from Herr Georg, who was still outside the cave, and a moment later a great wave of water washed over her, reaching almost to her waist and nearly pushing her off her feet. Her gloved left hand went out to the rock wall as she struggled to stay upright, and she heard the hollow gurgling sound behind her now, like some sort of sucking wound. Moments later the water withdrew again, threatening to pull her back out with it, but she held on, and when the tunnel had once more dried out, more or less, she was soaked.

"Are you all right in there?" she heard the baker call to her.

"I'm okay," she said, and took a quick peek behind her before she turned the flashlight forward again.

"I'm coming in!" the baker said, and the tunnel darkened as he dropped down into the opening behind her, blocking out the light. He caught up with her quickly, shining the beam of his flashlight into her face. "What is that *horrid* smell?"

"Dead things from the sea."

"Delightful. Let's hurry before the next wave arrives."

And they did, moving quickly now, through the narrow gap and, within another dozen paces or so, into the dark, swelling cavern beyond.

Here they found a side ledge upon which to stand to get out of the way of the onrushing waters, and took a few moments to survey their surroundings.

It was larger than they expected, a high dome of glistening black rock, rancid seaweed hanging and clinging everywhere. It was under their feet, creating a sort of cushion upon which they stood. Candy held two fingers to her nose, pinching it and breathing through her mouth. "Hopefully it won't be this bad farther inside."

"Are we going farther inside?" Herr Georg asked, shining his flashlight around.

She didn't know. She searched with her flashlight also, trying to determine their next step.

That's when she spotted the blanket.

It was on a higher ledge, above them and to their left, along with an old green oil lantern and what looked like a discarded pair of sneakers, a jacket used as a makeshift pillow, a hat, empty crumpled bags of potato chips, a bottle or two of water, a few scattered food packages, and the remnants of a fire within a small circle of rocks.

She guessed that if she checked the pattern on the bottoms of those sneakers, they'd match the footprints they saw on the path above.

She was suddenly spooked. "Someone's in here," she said softly.

Herr Georg caught her uneasiness. He literally cringed and his head twisted nervously in either direction. "Where?"

"I don't know. Somewhere. Look around."

They both fell silent then as their lights played across the interior of the cave in questing motions, often crossing over each other, until one of the lights caught a slight illumination in a back corner of the cave, in a recess a few yards above the waterline.

Candy pointed. "There!"

Both lights focused on the small points of illumination— a pair of eyes, they both realized, looking out from a narrow, human face.

It was a young man, huddled into the recess in the rocks, in a sitting position, knees up and tucked into his chest, arms wrapped tightly around his knees. He looked waterlogged and uncomfortable. He had a pale face, prominent cheek-bones, and longish dark hair. He was wearing black pants and a white shirt, much like something a waiter might have on.

Candy knew instantly who it was.

"Scotty Whitby," she said, the disbelief evident in her tone.

THIRTY-SIX

Much to Candy's surprise, the baker took immediate control of the situation. "You, young man!" he called out in a booming voice. "Scotty Whitby! What are you doing up there? Get down here immediately!"

The young waiter sat unresponsive, frozen, as if frightened out of his wits, staring down at them in disbelief, eyes wide.

In a more calming tone, Candy said, "Scotty, I'm so glad we found you. We're here to help. Are you okay? Are you hurt?"

No answer from Scotty.

"We've been looking for you everywhere," she added. "Why did you disappear from the hospital like that? Everyone around town is worried sick about you."

She knew that last part was a bit of hyperbole, and the young man seemed to know it too. In a soft, quiet voice, he finally said, "Nobody cares about me."

"I don't believe that for a moment," the baker said adamantly. "Of course people care about you. *We* care about you. The whole town is out looking for you."

"No, they're not!" the young man said with sudden vehemence. "No one cares where I went."

"That's just not true," Candy replied, trying to reassure him. She could see how conflicted and upset he was, and didn't want to push him too hard.

Herr Georg seemed to sense the same thing. He let out a long breath, as if the frustration that had been building in him for the past day or so was leaking out of him. In a more pleading tone, he said, spreading his hands wide, "Scotty, just tell us what's going on here. Why are you hiding out in this cave?"

But the young waiter shook his head violently and refused to speak.

Candy tried again. "Tell us what happened to you at the inn last night. How did you wind up in that storage room? Who attacked you?"

Softly, so they could barely hear, he said, "I don't know. It was too dark."

"Do you know anything about the death of Julius Seabury?" Herr Georg asked. "Or about the champagne bottle that was found near his body?"

"I didn't have anything to do with that," Scotty Whitby said. Then, more vehemently, he added, "I think *they* did it. *They* were there last night."

"They?" Candy felt a chill as she latched on to his comment, her eyes going wide. "Who do you mean? Who's *they*?"

Scotty finally moved a little, raising a hand to jab at the air off to the side, pointing back across the bay toward Cape Willington. *"Them.* Their conspiracy."

"What conspiracy? What are you talking about?" the baker asked, his voice rising again, as if his patience was running out.

"Them. All of them. They're all in on it."

"Who?" asked the baker, clearly becoming agitated.

Candy was about to warn Herr Georg to take a softer, more compassionate approach, but apparently his harsher words did the trick.

Scotty finally started naming names. "Those men in the lounge last night. There were four of them, though I didn't really know who they were. But one of the other waiters told me. They're from the museum—Owen somebody, and Gilbert somebody, and a couple of others I can't remember."

"Plymouth Palfrey?" Candy asked, filling in a name.

"Yeah, I guess that sounds right. Maybe. I don't know." The young man ran a hand with long, thin fingers through his hair, which only made him appear worse.

Now it was Candy's turn to sound frustrated. "Scotty, none of this makes any sense. Why don't you come down here so we can get you out of this place, get some food into you, warm you up, and get you checked out? You must be cold and hungry. We can talk about all this later. Right now, we need to take care of you."

That seemed to finally get through to him, and he started to move more, unhooking both arms from around his legs and stretching them out. "Okay, okay, hang on, I'm coming down."

Despite the fact that he appeared to have been hiding out in a cave for most of the day and the previous night, he seemed remarkably agile once he was on his feet. He descended from his perch in quick, easy movements, finding foot- and handholds in the rock with little problem, as if he'd done it a hundred times. He slipped down onto the cavern floor and started coming toward them, sloshing through inches-deep water that had not yet drained off the rocks. He was wearing some sort of misshapen rubber boots, Candy noticed, thick and heavy and well-worn. Apparently he'd abandoned the sneakers he'd come in with. He was carrying a small black day pack on his shoulder.

Instinctively and subconsciously, both Candy and Herr Georg backed up a little as he approached, giving the young man some space. He took advantage of their movement by shifting away from them, toward the tunnel that led out of the place. His eyes were quick, darting about the area.

And before they knew what was happening, he'd scrambled along the wet rocks right in front of them and made a mad dash for the exit. He moved so fast there was no way they could stop him or get in front of him. With a young person's speed and agility, he slipped out through the tunnel, sloshing through the water toward the sea.

In their surprise, all they could do was watch him go. In a matter of a few quick moments, he was lost to their view.

Before they knew what had happened, Scotty Whitby was gone.

Candy and Herr Georg were alone in the cave.

Neither of them quite knew what to think. Several seconds passed before they turned to each other, slightly bewildered.

"What just happened?" Candy asked.

"I think our lost boy has just disappeared . . . again!"

"I wonder what that's all about. We should go after him, I suppose—though I have a feeling whatever we do, he'll outrun us."

Herr Georg checked his watch. "We have to get out of here anyway. Our time's up. We're going to lose our light."

It took them some time, since neither of them moved as quickly as Scotty Whitby had, but they traversed their way back through the tunnel to the opening of Foul Mouth and slowly, painstakingly began to make their way up the cliff face, which proved not as difficult as their descent had been.

By the time they reached the top once again, the day's light was fading in the west, and they needed to use their flashlights to find their way back through the woods, past the house, and to the car.

They saw no sign of Scotty Whitby anywhere, though they searched fervently for him the whole way back. They were hesitant to call out to him, lest they give themselves away if anyone else was around, but realized their words would probably be lost anyway, since the wind had picked up and was rushing through the trees around them, creating a great rustling sound that reminded Candy of the crash of waves.

Before they left, they made a final search around the house and checked the front door, but it was locked. Scotty Whitby was nowhere to be seen.

He had slipped from their grasp and disappeared into the gathering night.

THIRTY-SEVEN

They drove back to Cape Willington in silence. Both were lost in their thoughts—and still damp from their adventure in the cave. Herr Georg turned on the car's heater to help dry them out, but said little, until his cell phone buzzed as they were approaching the village.

The baker's demeanor changed immediately when he heard who it was. "Ah, my beloved! It's so good to hear your voice. I've missed you today!"

Must be Maggie on the other end, Candy thought as she listened to the baker softly purr into his phone. *She's back from her trip to Ellsworth, with perfect timing.*

Herr Georg listened then, nodding, smiling, now completely relaxed, and adding a comment or two of his own, when he could. "That sounds fine, my dear," he said after Maggie had apparently discussed the evening's plans with him. "I'll drop Candy off and head right over—although I must stop and change first. I'm quite disheveled at the moment! I'll explain later. I can't wait to see you again, *mein Liebling!*"

After he'd keyed off the call, he told Candy, "We're going

to meet at the inn for dessert and a nightcap. I certainly need a drink after this busy day!"

"It has been rather eventful, hasn't it?" She hesitated a moment, then added, "Herr Georg, I'm not sure I'd talk too much about where we were just now—or what happened."

"But we found Foul Mouth! And Scotty Whitby!"

"Yes, that's true. But we were also technically trespassing, since we had no one's permission to be there. That could get both of us in hot water. I think it's probably okay to talk about it with Maggie, and I might discuss it with Dad, but for the time being, until I figure all this out, let's just keep it between the four of us."

The baker thought about this for a moment before he said, "I'll do whatever you believe is best. You're the expert in these sorts of investigations. But I'm not sure we should keep this information to ourselves for too long."

"I agree," Candy said, and as they took the turnoff toward Blueberry Acres, she began to gather her things, including her wet sneakers, which she'd removed on the way back. They were still damp, but wearable. "Just give me tonight to figure it out. We'll talk more about it tomorrow, okay?"

"Okay," the baker said with a firm nod.

A short while later he pulled up beside the barn, and Candy jumped out as the car came to a stop. She gave him a quick good-bye and wave, and then he was gone in a cloud of dust, a twinkle of anticipation in his eyes.

"Well, Candy," she said to herself as she stood in the driveway watching him go, enjoying the cooling night air and the silence that surrounded her, "I sure hope you know what you're doing."

She'd debated it on the way back, trying to decide if she should tell the police they'd found Scotty Whitby. She knew she should. It was important to the case. But she hesitated. She wasn't sure what to do at this point. She hadn't thought it all through yet. She just needed some time to figure it out, and right now she was too tired and too hungry to think straight.

Deciding she needed to clear her mind, she walked

toward the barn. Against the backdrop of the oncoming night, it was illuminated by an interior glow that made it look magical, like something from a fairy tale. The rafter lights and chandelier were still on, and the doors were still opened wide, so she wandered inside. They'd done a little additional work while she'd been away, but they'd apparently finished for the night. Everyone seemed to be gone now. She wandered back into the reception tent, then looped around to check on her chickens before she headed into the house.

Oddly, the place seemed vacant. She heard no sounds inside, heard no one moving around.

She checked upstairs, with the same result. No one up there.

She changed into dry clothes before heading back down. After a quick stop to peek into her father's dark office, she walked back through the kitchen. She was about to head outside but realized she hadn't eaten anything since the tuna fish sandwich at lunch with Neil—and even then, she'd had only a few bites. She was famished.

She made a quick dip into a plastic storage container on the countertop to grab a blueberry muffin, which she'd baked a couple of days earlier, and went back outside.

The oncoming night was clear and cool. As she stood on the porch, taking a bite of the muffin, her gaze roamed around the place.

Her father's truck was there, in its regular spot, so he must be around somewhere.

She found him on the back side of the house, sitting in a weather-beaten Adirondack chair, gazing out over the blueberry barrens. There were two chairs, a few feet apart and angled toward each other. The chairs sat out here in all seasons, except during the snowiest parts of the winter.

He heard her as she came around the corner and waved a hello. "Evening, pumpkin," he said gently. "Glad you're back home. Everything go okay with your 'errands'?"

She dropped into the chair beside him. "Yes, better than expected. But I'll tell you about it later." She leaned back and gazed out over the darkening fields. "So how's everything going around here?"

"Going just fine. The boys just left a little while ago, followed shortly by Malcolm and Ralph. We got a lot done, but it's nice to finally have a break. I was just enjoying a little peace and quiet."

"It has been a hectic day, hasn't it?"

"That it has. Been a lot going on."

"And we still have a lot ahead of us. Two very busy days."

"The busiest for us in a while, that's for sure. I'm meeting with the boys in the morning and picking up my suit at the dry cleaner's. Then back here to finish the preparations before the wedding walk-through, and the rehearsal dinner tomorrow night, and the wedding on Saturday. So I thought I'd sit here for a while, take a little breather while I can, and enjoy the night."

"Sounds like a wonderful idea."

They talked a little, about the wedding, and about Julius. They both shared their memories of him, some humorous, some melancholy. And they talked about the farm, which was an ongoing topic of conversation. Later on, Candy ducked into the house to get a sweater and mugs of tea for the both of them, and then they sat in silence as the darkness settled like a warm cocoon over Blueberry Acres, and the bright stars began to light up the night sky.

THIRTY-EIGHT

Restful sleep did not come easily to her that night. Candy tossed and turned into the early-morning hours, and when she finally did fall asleep, the events of the previous two days kept showing up in her dreams. When she woke, she still hadn't decided what to do about Scotty Whitby and the police.

The problem, she realized in one of those moments of clarity right after dawn when her brain was awake before her eyes would open and her body would move, was that she wasn't sure she *should* say anything to the police. And that, she realized, was at the center of her conundrum.

If she told the police about Foul Mouth and their discovery of the young waiter, she'd have to explain what she and Herr Georg were doing out at the Whitby estate in the first place. And why they'd gone so far as to climb down that cliff and search the cave. She'd been warned by Chief Durr numerous times not to do any snooping around on her own, and she'd tried as hard as possible to comply, but for some reason she kept finding herself pulled into these investigations, often because they involved someone she knew. He'd be extremely upset with her if he found out what she and Herr Georg had been doing yesterday afternoon, and she wasn't sure she was ready to face his wrath this morning—not with all the wedding-related events they had lined up through the day.

But should she delay in telling them? If so, for how long? Should she go over there right now? Or should she contact the police anonymously? Something like that?

Should she say anything at all about what she'd learned? Or, instead, should she keep the information to herself, for now? Sit on it and see what happened next?

Maybe flush out a killer?

The other issue that weighed on her was the upcoming meeting this afternoon with Porter Sykes out at the Whitby estate. She still wasn't sure what to do about that. And then there was the revelation from Wanda, and from Scotty, about the four men in the lounge at the Lightkeeper's Inn the night Julius was killed—Owen Peabody, Plymouth Palfrey, Gilbert Ethingham . . .

And Marshall L. Bosworth.

Was it a conspiracy of some sort? That's what Scotty had called it.

Had one of them killed Julius Seabury? Or had all of them been involved?

Their gathering that night certainly seemed suspicious. What had they been talking about?

Difficult questions, and ones she didn't have the answers to. As she pondered the problem, she jumped into the shower. Afterward, still undecided, she dressed in one of her nicer casual outfits and headed downstairs.

Her father was in his usual place, out on the porch, reading the paper and sipping on a cup of coffee. She grabbed a muffin and a cup of coffee and joined him.

They talked for a while, and Candy was just about to tell him of her dilemma concerning Scotty Whitby, when her phone chirped with a text from Maggie, who was getting ready to bake. Candy texted her friend back, saying she was on her way. She rose and was about to head back into the house to gather her things when Doc said, "You never did tell me what happened yesterday after you left here."

Candy gave him a knowing look. "No, I never did, did I?"

"You know," Doc said, rising as well, "my offer is always open if you ever need my help. I'm a good listener."

"You always have been." She paused. "You going to see Finn this morning at the diner?"

"Sure. I'm headed over there now. He'll be there."

"I wonder if you could give him a message for me," she said, and she proceeded to tell her father about their encounter with Scotty Whitby the day before. She didn't tell him everything—there was just too much to cover—but she gave him the basics and explained her dilemma. When she'd finished, Doc anticipated her request.

"You want me to ask Finn what *he* thinks you should do?"

"No, more than that. I wonder if you'd ask him to contact his source inside the police department and relay a rumor he's just heard—that Scotty was spotted out at the Whitby estate sometime early last night. Sort of an anonymous tip, but coming from him it might have some weight to it. Like a back-door-channel type of thing. That way they'd know about all this at the station, but, well, it would . . ."

"Keep your name out of it?" Doc finished.

Candy smiled. "Yes, exactly. For now, at least."

Doc thought it over a moment before he nodded. "I'll talk to Finn and see what he says, and we'll deliver the word to the police, one way or another. Of course, you know it won't take Chief Durr long to figure out where this rumor came from. He's a pretty smart guy, you know."

"I know, and that's fine. I'll deal with the repercussions when I get to that point." She leaned forward and gave him a quick hug before she pointed at the Jeep. "But for now, I have to run, and help the bride-to-be bake a cake!"

THIRTY-NINE

She found Maggie in the kitchen of her home in Fowler's Corner, up to her elbows in flour. Ellie was hovering nearby, helping out wherever she could but mostly trying to stay out of the way.

"For some reason I decided to make it from scratch," Maggie said with a look of mild dismay. "Is that crazy of me?"

Candy patted her friend reassuringly on the shoulder. "Well, maybe just a little, with everything that's going on today, but you wanted it to be special, so I completely understand. We'll all work on it together. So"—she rubbed her hands together—"where are we?"

Maggie quickly returned to an upbeat mood. "Well, as I mentioned yesterday, it's a chocolate groom's cake with blueberry cream frosting, decorated with candied flowers. I've already made the flowers with sugar syrup, so they'll be edible, of course. They're in the fridge."

"What color are the pansies?" Candy asked, surveying all the items Maggie had laid out on her countertop in preparation for baking.

"White and a sort of a bluish purple, like a blueberry—as close as I can get to the color of Georg's eyes."

Candy looked around for an apron. "Okay, what can I do to help?"

They divvied up the tasks and spent the next two hours working together in Maggie's kitchen, mixing, melting chocolate, beating, pouring, baking, cooling, assembling, frosting, and decorating. Amanda showed up mid-morning and pitched in, and the whole process went as smoothly as possible. And when they were finished, they had something marvelous.

Maggie surveyed their handiwork. "Do you think he'll like it?"

"I think he'll love it," Candy said.

"He'll be thrilled," Ellie agreed.

"It's beautiful, Mom," Amanda added, admiring their handiwork.

Maggie beamed. "It did turn out pretty amazing, didn't it? As good as I'd hoped. Of course, it's not quite up to Georg's level of achievement."

"You're getting there," Candy said supportively.

"A few more years and you'll be outbaking him!" Ellie put in.

Leaning closer to Candy and speaking in a stage whisper, Maggie asked, "Have you been over to the shop to see what he's baking?"

"I haven't. He hasn't told me anything about it, except what he said at the dinner party, about it being from an old family recipe."

"I heard he was in the shop at five this morning," Maggie said.

Candy arched her eyebrows. "Where'd you hear that?"

Maggie gently bumped her friend in the hip. "I have my sources, you know. Wanda Boyle isn't the only one around here with spies."

"I'll keep that in mind. It might come in handy someday."

"I'm sure he's whipping up something wonderful, just like we did," Amanda piped in.

As they were putting their final touches on the cake and

starting to clean up, their conversation turned to other matters.

"How goes the investigation?" Maggie asked.

"It's going," Candy said, and she checked her watch.

"Close to solving it?"

"I might be. I'll let you know this afternoon."

"Why, what's happening this afternoon?"

Candy didn't reply right away, and for a moment an awkward silence filled the kitchen. But Amanda quickly figured out what was going on. She'd heard enough about Candy's investigations from her mother. Discreetly she cleared her throat and turned to Ellie. "Umm, Grandma, why don't you and I take a break? Maybe a short walk? It's beautiful outside right now."

"Why, what's happening?" Ellie asked, looking slightly confused.

Maggie said, "Mom, Candy and I just need a few minutes together . . . to talk about something. You know, bride, maid of honor, that sort of thing. Girl talk. Why don't you go on a quick walk with Amanda and we'll press on with the rest of the preparations when you get back."

Ellie didn't quite understand what was going on but complied. And when they were gone, Candy proceeded to tell her friend all that had happened over the past day or so—her encounter with the members of the museum's board yesterday afternoon, including the disembodied voice of Porter Sykes; his invite to meet at the Whitby estate at one P.M. today; the fact that three board members plus Marshall Bosworth had been spotted at the inn on Wednesday night, lending credence to a possible conspiracy of some sort; Candy and Georg's discovery of Foul Mouth and Scotty Whitby; and the young man's sudden disappearance into the night.

Maggie whistled. "Wow, you've been busy! And you've been keeping my fiancé occupied, which I appreciate—although I'm not crazy about that rock-climbing part. And I'm not sure what to do about Scotty Whitby. But you're not going back out to that place again this afternoon, are you?

Not alone? Not after what you told me about Porter Sykes in the past."

"I don't know," Candy said. "I really don't have any sort of plan in mind. I should probably go to the police with all this. That would be the proper thing to do, but . . ."

"You don't want to get into a tussle with the chief?"

Candy nodded. "That's certainly part of it."

"But you don't want to get accused of withholding evidence?"

"That would get me deeper in hot water, yes."

"Sort of damned if you do and damned if you don't?"

"Exactly. I've asked Dad to talk to Finn about it. That should buy me a little time."

Maggie thought for a few moments. "You know," she finally said, "if you could just find the murderer yourself, that would get you off the hook, right?"

"Not entirely, but it would probably help. At least the water I'm deep into wouldn't be quite so hot."

"True. So," said Maggie excitedly, "let's see if we can solve it!"

They talked about the suspects then, and the long trail of clues Candy had followed so far. "I can't help but think that it all goes back to the list of names Julius left for us to find in the books. I'm ninety-nine percent sure he made that list, and I think he must have been trying to tell us something. But I can't for the life of me figure out what it is. If I could just crack that code, it might be the piece I need to finally solve this thing."

"Well, let's have a look at this famous list of yours then," Maggie said. "Two heads are better than one, right? Maybe we can figure it out together before you head over to the Whitby place. At least maybe we can come to a conclusion, one way or another, about Porter Sykes, before you put yourself at his mercy."

"I don't have the list with me," Candy said as she looked around for something to write on. "Owen had it, and hopefully the police have it by now. But I can re-create it from memory."

Maggie found some paper and a pen for her, and Candy wrote down the list of names Owen had recited that night in the archives.

Bosworth.

Ethingham.

Whitby.

Rainsford.

Palfrey.

Sykes.

She also added the initials *L. B.* and the words *Foul Mouth* at the bottom of the page, but told Maggie, "I think I've solved these two parts. L. B. refers to Marshall Lex Bosworth, and I've told you about Foul Mouth, but it's these names that have me stumped." She ran her finger down the list. "As far as I can tell, they're not in any particular order. They're not alphabetical, or arranged by publication date, or follow any sort of format that I can figure out."

"What makes you think they're important?"

"Well, because the list was repeated. It was on the slip of paper Owen found two nights ago in a book up in the archives, and yesterday I found books about these families arranged on a shelf in this particular order."

"So you think this slip of paper with the list of family names, and the books on the shelf, could have been put there specifically by Julius as a message of some sort?"

Candy acknowledged that was her theory.

Maggie rubbed her chin as she studied the list again, leaving a small smudge of flour behind. "Well, then, if he was leaving a message for you—because, let's face it, you're the only one who could discover something like this, and he probably knew that—then the answer to whatever he might have been trying to say is staring us right in the face."

"How do you mean?" Candy asked.

"Well, you said it's a code of some sort, right?"

Candy looked back down at the list. "That's what it seems like. What do you suppose it means?"

"Well, I don't know. Something with the names, right? Their order?" She was rubbing at her chin again, thinking. "Let's try something simple," she said, and stepped away briefly, returning with a folded slip of paper, which she put over all the letters in the names except for the initial capitals:

B.

E.

W.

R.

P.

S.

Candy leaned in for a closer look as Maggie read out the letters:

"*B-E-W-R-P-S.*"

"Bewerps?" Candy said, trying to pronounce the word Maggie had revealed. She leaned back and scrunched up her face. "But that doesn't mean anything. It's just gibberish."

"No," Maggie said. "It's a code, like you said. Look at it again."

And they both did.

"Draw a line between the *R* and the *P*," Maggie suggested.

Candy finally saw it. "*B-E-W-R. Beware!*"

"Right! He was trying to tell you to beware of something. But what?"

Candy studied the last two letters, and gasped. She could feel the blood suddenly pounding through her. "That's it! You figured it out!" And she pointed at the initials with her finger. "Palfrey. And Sykes." She looked up at her friend. "*P-S!* He was trying to tell me to beware of *Porter Sykes*!"

FORTY

Maggie wouldn't let Candy leave for the Whitby place without having some sort of backup in place. "If you're wandering into the house of a possible murderer, someone Julius took the time to specifically warn you about, you *have* to take someone else with you." She paused. "I'd go myself, of course, but . . ."

"No way." Candy waved a hand in the air. "I'm not putting you in a potentially harmful situation on the day before your wedding. I did that last night with your fiancé, and we were lucky we escaped with no injuries, but I don't think I should do it again. Besides, I'm sure you still have plenty to do around here to get ready for tonight and tomorrow."

"It's true," Maggie said, "but I'm not letting you waltz into that place all alone."

"I'll try not to *waltz* in," Candy said with a half smile, "but honestly I don't see any other way. I have to find out what he wants, and I don't think he'll talk if I bring someone along with me. Of course, that doesn't mean . . ."

Her mind worked for a few moments before she pulled

out her cell phone and placed a call to Finn Woodbury. He was still at the diner with her father, and he'd already had a conversation with Doc, so he had a good idea why she was calling. But she had another request for him. It took a little convincing, but finally he agreed to do as she asked.

"Just backup," she clarified. "Don't come in with your guns blazing."

"Unless you need my help."

"Right. Unless I need your help."

"I've got you covered," Finn said. "Don't you worry about a thing. You just do what you have to do."

"What did he say?" asked Maggie, who had overheard Candy telling Finn her plan.

"He's in. If anyone has to back me up, Finn is the guy," she said as she began to gather her things. It was nearly twelve thirty, and she had a twenty-five-minute drive over to the Whitby estate. It was time to leave if she wanted to be there on time.

Maggie gave her a hug. "You be careful. Take care of yourself!"

"I'll be back as soon as I can."

With that, Candy headed out the door and toward her Jeep. As she fired it up and turned the steering wheel north and east, she still wasn't certain she was doing the right thing.

Her uncertainty continued as she drove out of Cape Willington and up the road along the bay, before crossing over to the next peninsula. As she turned south again and the roads deteriorated to dirt, she decided that, whatever happened, she was doing what she had to do, just like Finn said.

She had to find out what was going on, and right now Porter Sykes was the person who held all the cards—at least, she hoped so.

One way or another, she'd find some answers soon.

The Whitby estate looked different this morning than it had the day before, when they'd been out here chasing down mysterious footprints along a dirt path. On this bright, clear afternoon, the place didn't look so gloomy, thanks to the sunlight filtering down through the trees. The brownstone looked more elegant, the windows not so dark, the landscape around it not as looming and claustrophobic.

And there were cars in the driveway this time—three of them, including what looked like a fairly new Cadillac.

Candy pulled the Jeep to a stop in the gravel driveway in front of the house. She shut off the engine, grabbed her tote, and climbed out.

Holding the tote close to her chest, she stood for a few moments beside the Jeep, taking deep breaths, preparing herself for what might come next. Then, as determined as she'd ever be, she walked up to the house and knocked firmly on the front door.

The knock seemed to resonate inside, making the building sound hollow and un-lived-in. Which, she imagined, it was—or had been until this morning.

She thought she heard a distant, deep thudding noise from somewhere inside, possibly toward the back of the house. It was there briefly and then gone.

She waited, trying to calm the uneasiness she felt. She was just about to knock again when she heard echoing footsteps from inside, approaching the door. A few moments later, a lock turned and the door creaked open.

A tall, fiftyish man with a sharp nose, intelligent eyes, and dark hair graying at the sides stood before her. For a moment he looked surprised to see her, but he recovered quickly and held out a hand. "Hello there, I'm Marshall Bosworth. How can I help you?"

"Oh, hi, Marshall," Candy said as casually as possible. "I know your brother, Judicious." She watched for a reaction from him but saw none. "I'm Candy Holliday. I believe I have a one o'clock appointment to meet with the new owner, Porter Sykes."

Marshall's eyes widened. "Oh, right, I think he mentioned something about that. They haven't arrived yet, but why don't you come on in and you can wait for them. They should be here any minute."

He checked his watch as he opened the door a little farther, and she was about to ask who "they" were, when she heard the sound of an engine coming along the dirt track into the parking lot behind her. Both she and Marshall turned toward the sound.

It was a black town car, the kind often used as a limousine, with a driver and two passengers. It did a wide circle of the parking area, coming around 180 degrees, so the right side was aimed toward the door, toward Candy and Marshall, as it came to a stop.

A face looked out at her from the front passenger seat. It was a man who looked to be in his mid-forties now, with thick brown hair and an aristocratic nose on his rugged face.

He nodded in greeting, and smiled at her through the window.

Candy recognized that devious smile. She knew right away who it was.

Porter Sykes.

But it was the face of the second passenger, the one in the backseat, that drew her attention. It was the visage of a much older woman, frail-looking, dressed impeccably, right down to her pillbox-style hat and gloved hands.

Porter jumped out of the car and came toward Candy first, his hand outstretched. "You must be Candy Holliday," he said, that unsettling smile never leaving his face. "How good it is to finally meet you in person. Sorry for our delay, but we got a late start. Grandmother had a few things to take care of before we left Marblehead—and, of course, she wanted to make sure she looked her best for her grand entrance back into Cape Willington society"—he paused to look around the place—"such as it is."

He walked back to the car, opened the rear door, and held out a hand. "We're here, Grandmother. Come say hello to Candy Holliday."

It took a while, but the elderly woman finally managed to extricate herself from the backseat, with her grandson's assistance. She leaned on him heavily as she came forward, and it was clear she was having trouble walking. But she was determined to make it, and she did, crossing the short distance to the house, where she stopped in front of the other two people.

"Marshall, Candy," Porter Sykes said by way of introduction, "I'd like you to meet my grandmother, Daisy Porter-Sykes."

FORTY-ONE

"So this is what you bought with your own money?" the Sykes family matriarch said as she eyed the place with some disdain, her mouth twisting slightly. "A pile of brownstone on a pile of black rock, miles across the bay from Cape Willington? Not exactly the height of style, is it?"

"It needs some work, that's true, but it should be no problem," Porter said easily. He was obviously used to dealing with Daisy's cantankerous moods, and she appeared to be in one now.

"It's certainly a fixer-upper. When will the furniture arrive?"

"Later this afternoon, although I've asked Marshall here to arrange for some chairs and a table for us until everything gets here."

"Is there tea?"

"Of course, Grandmother. We wouldn't deny you the comforts of home."

She eyed the place again. "It's hardly what I would call home—not like our old mansion up here."

"Trust me, a few months from now we'll be all settled

into our new summer place here in Maine. Come inside and have a look around. The building has good bones, as you'll see, and should have plenty of room for us—and it was a good deal."

The elderly woman smacked her lips, as if she'd just eaten something tasty. "Yes, I'm sure it was, after that leverage you used." She almost cackled, though it came out as an extended cough.

Together the two of them entered the building, chatting between themselves, and with an exchange of glances, Marshall and Candy followed, though she still had no idea what she was doing here, or what these people wanted from her.

"I've us set up in the dining room," Marshall said, scooting around Porter and his grandmother and leading the way toward the back of a long, dark hallway. "I've opened up some windows to air out the place, and the cleaners are here. They're working on the second floor right now."

"How many?" Daisy asked.

"I hired two for today, Grandmother," Porter said.

"Not enough. You'd need a battalion to clean this place."

"We can bring in more if we need them," Porter said. "Let's get through today and see what happens. We'll go from there."

Daisy just grumbled under her breath about that. She seemed to Candy like a hard woman to please.

The churning feeling in the pit of her stomach worsened.

Soon, they were all seated around a wooden table in a sunny, airy room. Marshall, apparently serving as host for the day, brought out a kettle of tea with a small plate of cookies, and Daisy seemed to settle in to the point where a conversation was possible.

"So, Ms. Holliday," the matriarch said, turning to Candy, "I'll bet you're a little surprised to see me here."

Candy knew something like this was coming. She answered carefully. "Yes, well, obviously I've heard a lot about you, Mrs. Porter-Sykes, and your grandsons, of course, but I never thought we'd have a chance to meet in person. This is an unexpected . . . pleasure."

"I doubt it's that," Daisy said honestly, "but there *is* a reason for this meeting. We do have something we'd like to discuss with you."

"And what might that be?" Candy did her best to keep an open mind, but mentally prepared herself for the worst.

When Porter spoke up, his request was completely unexpected. "To be honest, we'd like to hire you," he said as he reached into an inside pocket and produced a silver flask. He unscrewed the cap and poured a small amount of its caramel-colored contents into his tea, spiking it a little.

Candy was surprised. "Hire me? To do what?"

"To solve all these murders, of course," said Daisy with a touch of impatience. "They're destroying the village's reputation. You should hear how people are talking about the place. And now that we're homeowners in the area again, we're going to try to put an end to them, once and for all."

"But—" And Candy almost said, *Your own grandsons were responsible for some of those murders.* At the last moment she held her tongue, though, knowing that would be the wrong way to proceed. Instead, she said, "Unfortunately, I don't have a license. I'm not a private investigator or a detective or anything like that. So I'm not really available for hire—at least, in that sort of capacity."

"But you've worked for the Pruitts, correct?"

How did she know about that? Again, a careful answer. "Yes, that's true, they hired me a few years ago, in sort of an informal way, though we did have a verbal agreement." She was referring to a time when Helen Ross Pruitt, the matriarch of the Pruitt clan, hired Candy to find an old book that had been stolen from the family's private library.

"Then we'll forge the same arrangement," Daisy said. "On or off the books, I don't really care. We can pay you cash if you'd prefer to handle it that way." She motioned impatiently to her grandson. "Porter, give this woman some money."

"No, no!" Candy held up her hands, waving them in the air. "We should talk about this first, just so I know what you're expecting from me. And as I said, I can't really do it anyway."

Daisy waved dismissively. "You're right, of course. We should let Marshall handle all the details anyway. That's what he's here for. Marshall, take care of this, would you, and see that Candy has all the information she needs to make an appropriate decision."

"Yes, of course, Mrs. Porter-Sykes," Marshall said, dipping his head a little as he pulled out his phone to key in a few notes.

Porter lightly slapped his knee. "Well, now that that's all taken care of, we can move on to other things. Shall we talk about the liaison issue next?"

Daisy grimaced as she took a sip of her tea. She set it down uncertainly. "Of course. Let's get on with it."

"What's the liaison issue?" Candy asked, a concerned look on her face.

"I have some details on that," Marshall said, and he dipped into his briefcase, which he'd positioned on the floor near his feet. He dug around for a moment, pulled out a manila folder, opened it, and peeled off the top sheet inside. He slid it across the table toward Candy.

"Essentially, we would like to hire you as a liaison between the family and the villagers, specifically the Pruitts. We'd like you to help us set up a meeting—a summit, if you will—between the two families. There's been bad blood between the two groups for generations, as I'm sure you know. We'd like to put an end to all that, and see if we can reestablish some sort of mutually beneficial relationships between the Sykes and Pruitt families."

Candy picked up and scanned the sheet Marshall had sent in her direction. It looked formal. She hesitated.

"I . . . I just don't know. I'm not really qualified to do any of these things. I work on a blueberry farm. I'm not a diplomat." She set the paper down and slid it back across the table to Marshall, her mind working, but she'd already come to a decision. "I'm afraid I have to decline. I'm just not the right person for any of this. I'm sure there are plenty of people around—you, Marshall, for instance—who could do a much better job than I could at something like that."

"But you know the Pruitts, quite well, I believe," Porter pressed. "You could talk to them on our behalf. I believe Mrs. Pruitt usually arrives in town with her entourage right around the Fourth of July, if not earlier. The timing would be ideal. We should have the place fixed up by then—at least the worst parts of it. Maybe you could help us arrange a meeting out here."

Candy wasn't quite sure how to respond. The whole thing sounded crazy. Not what she was expecting at all. She thought of trying to extricate herself from the situation as quickly as possible, but decided she might as well try to get some information out of them before she made her way back to Cape Willington.

"Maybe. I'll have to give it some thought. But I wonder if I might change the subject briefly. I've heard Julius Seabury was writing a book about Cape Willington's founding families. I was just wondering . . . had he contacted you about that in any way? I know he was doing some research up in the archives about the Sykes family." And here she reached into her own tote bag, withdrawing Lucinda Dowling's book on the family, which she'd taken from the archives. "This was one of his sources, among a few others, including volumes on the Bosworths, Ethinghams, Whitbys, Rainsfords, and Palfreys. So, did you hear from him in the days leading up to his death?"

That seemed to stop the conversation cold. Candy waited patiently. If she and Maggie were right about the code Julius left behind, apparently pointing a finger directly at Porter Sykes, then she hoped he might slip up, and she might learn something new—as long as she didn't get herself killed in the process.

"Julius?" Porter said finally, uncertain at the change of topic.

"You said it yourself," Candy pointed out. "The goal is to put an end to all these murders around town, once and for all. Any information you might have could help us do that."

Porter nodded and cleared his throat. "Well, to answer your question, no, to the best of my knowledge, none of us talked to Julius. And as I said on the phone yesterday, we're all extremely sorry to hear of his loss. He will be greatly missed in the village. And—"

He was interrupted by a great thudding sound that seemed to come from nearby—the kitchen, maybe. His head shot around. "What's that?"

Marshall's alertness had also picked up. "I don't know. I heard it earlier and couldn't figure out what it was. I believe it came from the basement, but I can't get that door open. It's apparently locked on the other side. It sounds like someone's . . . *banging.*"

Daisy nervously set her teacup down on the table as Porter pointed with his head in the direction of the kitchen. "Go check it out."

Marshall was on his feet and gone in an instant.

There was another thud, this one beneath them, vibrating through the floor. Candy could feel it in her shoes. "Someone's under us," she said to no one in particular.

"It's the building!" Daisy cried in a quickly elevating tone. "It's falling apart around us!"

Porter was on his feet now as well, rounding the table toward his grandmother. He motioned to her. "You sit tight. Don't move. I'll find out what's going on."

He never got any farther, for he was frozen in place.

He'd looked up and toward the kitchen, and Candy followed his gaze.

Marshall was emerging through the door—and there was a dark figure behind him, someone none of them could make out at the moment.

But it struck Candy quickly, and she knew. She knew from the slim figure and lanky build, the dark hair, and the still-wet boots that were planted firmly on the floor behind Marshall.

Much to her shock and surprise, she realized it was Scotty Whitby.

FORTY-TWO

The young waiter grabbed Marshall by the collar and brutally shoved him into the dining room with the others. Marshall stumbled a little before he caught his footing and abruptly dropped into his chair with a grunt, his face pale against his darker hair.

But at the moment no one was watching Marshall. They were all focused on the intruder.

Scotty's eyes were wild, flashing around the room. He carried a black pistol in his right hand, which he waved in a menacing fashion at those seated or standing around the table.

"So, you're all here, right?" he said in a voice that cracked a little. "All of you who have stolen my family's place from us. And now you're all going to pay."

He was still dressed in black and white, wearing the same thing he'd had on the day before. His pants were damp and clingy, the shirt smudged and untucked, his face streaked with dirt. And he still carried the small black day pack on his shoulder. He looked like some sort of wraith that had risen from the dark sea.

He came up through the basement, Candy thought as she watched him. He'd found the back entrance into the house— the one through Foul Mouth, which Lucinda mentioned yesterday.

Is that what he'd been doing down in the cave when we found him? Scoping out the entrance that would lead him up into the house?

He wasn't hiding out when we found him, she suddenly realized. *He was casing the joint!*

Almost as if in response to her thoughts, Scotty's gaze shifted to his right. He caught sight of Candy then, and looked surprised. At first he didn't seem to recognize her, but he quickly put it together.

"It's you, isn't it? I saw you in the cave yesterday, right?" he said. "When you interrupted me. I put on a pretty good act for you, didn't I? Probably had you convinced that I was just a lost, lonely kid. But what are you doing here now? I thought these criminals were all up here by themselves, hatching their latest plot to take over the village."

Candy forced herself to give him a casual shrug. As lightly as possible, doing her best to defuse the situation, she said, "I guess I wandered into the wrong house at the wrong time."

"You wander into a lot of places at the wrong time," he said in a dark tone.

But Candy didn't let his words distract her. "Scotty, what are *you* doing here? I don't know you that well, but this doesn't seem like you. Put down that gun and let's talk."

"How do you know what I'm like?" the young waiter responded, but he seemed to waver a little, until Porter spoke up.

"She's right," he said, motioning toward Candy with a hand. "There's no need for things to turn violent. We're all rational people here. Whatever your issues might be with us, we'll work it out. I promise you."

That brought Scotty back to the moment, and he swiveled the pistol so it was pointing directly at Porter's chest. "I don't believe you. Hands up, Mr. Sykes."

"What? What are you talking about?"

Scotty flourished the gun. "Just do as I tell you or I'll end it all right here."

Reluctantly, Porter complied, making a somewhat feeble attempt to hold up his hands. "Okay, you got me. Now what?"

"*Now* what we're going to do is bring you to justice. Because *you're* the one behind all this, aren't you? *You're* the one who convinced my uncle Elliot to sell you this place for a song, because he thought the deed had gone bad and he was about to lose the land underneath it. He thought the place was almost worthless, because *you* told him that, through your lawyer lap-dog here."

Still holding his hands up, Porter started to protest, but Scotty cut him off, licking his lips in an almost animalistic fashion. When he spoke again, the tone of his voice had lowered a few notches, almost to a growl.

"But *I* knew you didn't have those deeds, because *Julius Seabury* had them, didn't he? You knew that but lied to my uncle, because even though you didn't have them yourself, you knew they existed. You *hounded* Julius for them, maybe even threatened him, but he wouldn't give them to you, would he? Because he knew what you'd do with them."

"That's completely preposterous!" Porter snapped. "I knew he had them, yes, but I never *hounded* or *threatened* him. I just asked him politely if I could have a look at them when he was finished with his research."

"You're lying!" the young waiter spat out. "I overheard your friends talking at the inn that night. They said you were after the deeds! They said you wanted to destroy the town! I knew right away what they were talking about, because my uncle told me about it. He didn't want to sell the place. I might have inherited it myself! But now it's gone, because you swindled him out of this place. All because of those deeds Julius had!"

"Scotty," Candy cut in, trying to catch up after his outburst, "how did *you* know Julius had the deeds?"

The young waiter's gaze shifted to her, and he hesitated before he spoke. "I didn't at first," he said, "not until I heard those men talking about it the night before last."

"Who exactly?" Candy pressed.

"Them—the ones who were in the lounge that night. The heavyset one, and the other one, with white hair and a goatee."

"Owen Peabody," Candy said, "and Plymouth Palfrey."

"They were all by themselves, just the two of them, talking back in the hallway when I passed by them carrying a tray with plates of food," Scotty went on, as if she'd never interrupted him. "They didn't even seem to know I existed. But I heard what they said. They were talking about *you*"—he indicated Porter with vehemence—"and said Julius had the deeds, and you were after them, so you could use them to take over the town. That's when I knew what you'd done."

Again, he waved the gun at Porter and Marshall, and then at Daisy. "And you, I guess. You're probably involved in this too. Just as guilty as the rest of them."

"Young man, you're out of line," Daisy said with a tone of exasperation. "I come from a very respectable family. We didn't steal this place from you—your family stole it from *us*, long ago. We lost it in a dubious poker game, and it was *your* ancestor who cheated, not mine. We're just reclaiming what's rightfully ours."

"It's not yours!" Scotty spat. "It's called the Whitby estate. It belongs to *my* family. And now it's gone, because of you!"

"That's nonsense!" Daisy countered. "No one *forced* your uncle to sign anything. He signed it willingly." She swept an arm around her. "Look at this place. It looks like a slum. Your uncle hasn't done any upkeep on the place in years, because he didn't have the money. Now he's got a little money, thanks to the sale of this place. We actually helped out your family, young man. They might even have enough money to send you to college now. That's what you want, isn't it?"

This news was obviously unexpected, for it struck Scotty like a hammer. He stumbled backward, as if he'd been pushed. Marshall was out of his chair almost instantly, reaching for the gun, but Scotty veered away, brandishing the weapon at them, his finger curling around the trigger. They thought it was going to go off. Daisy screamed, Porter shouted, Marshall flinched, and Candy sat where she was, stunned.

After a few moments Scotty seemed to regain his senses, though he kept the pistol pointed at them. "Don't try that again," he said, motioning Marshall back to his seat. "I should just get rid of all of you, right here and now. Because none of you are telling me the truth. You're just telling the same old lies you've told a thousand times before."

It was clear he was close to his breaking point, so rather than get angry at him, Candy appealed to him with a softer tone. "Scotty," she asked quietly, "don't push this any further, until something terrible happens. Why don't you put the gun down and let's talk?"

"No!" he shouted. "I can't. It's too late."

"Too late?" Candy repeated, watching his eyes, his manner. He looked distressed, upset about something. He was shaking, she noticed. And then it suddenly struck her, and she knew what must have happened—why Scotty had run, and why he looked so wild and scared now.

"Scotty," she said quietly, feeling goose pimples running up her arms, "what happened that night after you heard Owen and Plymouth talking in the hall?"

The young waiter visibly swayed at the question, and his eyes closed for a moment. Candy thought he might faint, until his eyes opened again. "Julius called," he finally said softly.

Candy was surprised to hear this. "Julius Seabury? He called you?"

"He called the inn," Scotty clarified, "and I just happened to pick up the call, because it rang back in the kitchen, and there was no one else around to answer it."

"And what did he say?" Candy asked, fascinated by this revelation.

"That he was delayed. That he was over at the museum. That he was doing research. And that he'd be joining the dinner party as soon as he could. He said I was supposed to tell them."

"So you knew he was at the museum?" Candy confirmed. And a moment later, she realized that at that point, Scotty

Whitby was perhaps the *only* person who knew where Julius was. "So did you do as he asked? Did you deliver his message?"

Again, the young waiter hesitated and swayed a little, until he finally shook his head.

"What happened after that?" Candy pressed in a hushed tone, and everyone else in the room was still and silent, listening to their exchange.

Whatever state he'd been in, Scotty seemed to snap out of it, and his anger returned. "I knew he had those deeds," the young waiter said, now talking quickly, "and I knew I had to get them from him, before someone else did. So I went into the back room and picked up a bottle of champagne."

"To do what?" Candy asked.

"I don't know! I needed a reason to go over there to talk to him, so I took that champagne bottle with me. I figured it would give me a way to explain why I was there. I told him it was from the party, it was a gift for him. But he just waved it off. He said he didn't want it."

"And what happened next?"

Scotty's eyes glazed over a little, as if he was remembering the events of that night. "I . . . I guess I surprised him up there. He hadn't expected anyone to find out what he was doing."

"He was researching the deeds, right?" Candy prompted.

Scotty nodded. "He had them laid out on the table in front of him. I knew right away what they were. They were so old and crinkled, like they'd been around for hundreds of years. He tried to hide them from me but . . . I told him I wanted them. I wanted to destroy them."

"And what did Julius do?" Candy asked, her voice now barely above a whisper.

Scotty barked a laugh at that. "He refused, of course! He tried to stuff them under some books. He told me I didn't know what I was talking about."

"So . . . what? You tried to take them from him?"

"I tried," Scotty admitted, nodding his head slowly. "I tried."

"And he fought you, right?"

Scotty pointed at his head. "I'm not quite sure what happened. It got crazy. He grabbed the bottle of champagne and hit me in the head with it for some reason. Not hard, but enough to leave a lump. So I took it from him, and hit him back, just like he hit me. . . ."

"And then what?"

Scotty shook his head. "He fell. I don't know if he was alive or dead at that point. I told him I was sorry." His eyes were glistening now, and his mouth was moving oddly. "It all happened so fast. I didn't want to leave him there but I didn't know what else to do. So I took the deeds and ran back to the inn."

"And what happened when you got there? How did you wind up in that storage room?"

Scotty raised his hand to his head again. "I heard someone had been looking for me, so I ducked into one of the storerooms to try to figure it out. And my head hurt, because I'd been hit with that bottle. I figured I'd just lie there for a while, until someone found me, and then . . ."

Candy knew the rest. "Then they'd think *you* were the one who had been attacked by someone—someone at the inn, someone who had taken the bottle of champagne."

Scotty nodded.

Candy was silent for a moment as she digested all she'd just heard. So were the others. No one spoke.

Finally, Daisy cleared her throat. "Well, that's a very interesting story, young man, but why are you here now, harassing us like this? Why aren't you running for the hills? The police will certainly find out what you did, because we'll tell them. And then you'll go to jail for the rest of your life."

"No, I won't," Scotty said, his anger rising again, "because you're not going to tell anyone what I've just told you. None of you. I knew all about Foul Mouth. My uncle told me about it years ago. I used to explore down there when I was a kid, though the passage that led up to the house was closed off long ago. So I had to break it down and sneak up here, because I wanted all of you to know what happened before I kill you."

"Killing us won't help," Candy said. "You won't get your property back."

"Maybe not," Scotty said, and he indicated the black day pack he had on his shoulders, "but *he* won't be able to do this to anyone else in town—because *I* have the deeds now, right here with me."

The young waiter turned toward Porter then, who still had his hands up, though not very high. "I've heard the rumors," Scotty said in an accusatory tone. "They say you're behind all the murders that have taken place around here for the past few years, but no one's ever been able to prove it. You just keep getting away with things. So it was time for someone to take the law into his own hands and put an end to it, once and for all."

He leveled the pistol at Porter one last time, and from the look on his face, he'd made a decision.

"Mr. Sykes," he said ominously, "you've been found guilty in *my* court of law. And now, it's time to carry out the punishment."

His finger started to squeeze the trigger. Daisy screamed again, and Porter flinched. But all of a sudden there was another movement, behind Scotty. Someone came out of the kitchen fast and violently knocked the youth down. Scotty fell awkwardly and the gun went flying out of his hands, skidding across the floor. Porter made a sudden scramble for it but a loud voice yelled, "Don't anyone move!"

Candy's eyes shifted from the fallen waiter to the newest arrival, and her eyes went wide.

It was Plymouth Palfrey, with a pistol of his own. And it, too, was pointed right at them.

FORTY-THREE

His sudden appearance was so unexpected that Candy audibly gasped. But Porter Sykes didn't seem surprised to see the newcomer.

"About time you got here," he said evenly, and finally lowered his hands. "Things were just about to turn ugly." Again he made a move for the gun Scotty had dropped, but Plymouth spoke up in a calmer tone.

"As I said, no one move. That includes you, Porter. Stay right where you are."

Porter's expression changed abruptly to one of anger and confusion. "What are you talking about?"

Candy followed this exchange with growing awareness. "You two have been working together?" she blurted.

"I wouldn't call it that," Plymouth said with a grim smile. "But we both had a mutual desire—to get our hands on those deeds."

"You said you had this all taken care of," Porter accused the newcomer.

Plymouth sneered at that. "I'm here, aren't I? I just saved your miserable life. You're lucky I kept a close eye on this

kid. I knew he went over to the lighthouse the night Julius
died. I spotted him while I was having a conversation in the
hallway with Owen, and got suspicious he'd overheard us.
I saw him take that bottle of champagne and head out the
inn's back door. And when he came back without the bottle,
and I heard what had happened, I figured out what he'd done.
And I also suspected he took the deeds from Julius. But I
had to make sure he had them."

He turned toward Scotty then, still sprawled on the floor,
and held out his hand. "The bag, kid."

Porter protested. "You were supposed to get the deeds
for *me*," he emphasized. "That's what we agreed on. It's
what I *paid* you for."

Plymouth laughed, and in that moment Candy realized
where she'd made her mistake.

She'd read the code wrong—the one Julius had left behind.

Bosworth.

Ethingham.

Whitby.

Rainsford.

Palfrey.

Sykes.

And her mind focused on the first letters of each name:

B.

E.

W.

R.

P.

S.

But she got it wrong. Julius had changed the format on

her. She'd taken the first letter of all six names as the code, but he had spelled out the last two for her. It wasn't "beware of Porter Sykes," but "beware of Palfrey *and* Sykes"!

That's why Julius had left the messages behind. The two had both been watching him. Julius must have suspected they were after the deeds—and in some way he'd felt threatened by them. Rightly so, as it turned out.

But in the end, the attack had not come from either of them, but from a third, unexpected person.

It had been, she now knew, an unplanned act of anger and desperation by Scotty, not a premeditated murder. It had been a misguided effort to restore his family's property, and perhaps its prestige in town. But his plan had gone horribly wrong, and an innocent man had died.

With great effort, Candy shifted her gaze from Plymouth to the young waiter, now pulled into a tight huddle on the floor. "Scotty, where are the deeds?" she asked.

"They're in that backpack of his," Plymouth said, pointing, "or maybe he's lying, and they're still stashed down in that cave. Is that where they are, kid?"

Scotty wiped his mouth with the back of his hand and gazed at the newcomer with fury in his eyes. "How do you know about the cave? No one outside the family is supposed to know about it."

"Because I've been there. I checked it out myself a few days ago."

"But how did *you* know about it?" Candy asked, her gaze shifting back to Plymouth.

He gave her a sly smile. "Julius wasn't always as cautious as he should have been with his research. He tended to leave his papers lying around the archives at times."

Candy doubted that's what had happened. "You spied on him, didn't you? You knew he had the deeds, because *you* gave them to him at some point. At the time you didn't know what they were, but you eventually found out. Porter probably told you about them, right? So you tried to get them for yourself, even though you told Porter otherwise."

Plymouth just shrugged at her accusations. "I kept an eye

on what Julius was doing, yes. I thought those deeds were worthless at first, and never even took a close look at them. When I finally found out what they were, I told him I wanted them back, but he refused. He said he wasn't finished researching them. After that he got weird. He kept them under wraps. Didn't show them to anyone, as far as I know. But I saw his notes. I saw his references to Foul Mouth and the Whitby place. So I did a little research of my own."

"And that's what Julius was doing out on that beach? Watching you dig around the Whitby place, searching for Foul Mouth?"

Plymouth shook his head. "I don't know anything about that, but it doesn't matter now, does it? All that matters are the deeds themselves."

He shifted the pistol from Porter to the young waiter. "Time's up, kid. I'm out of patience. Give me the backpack now, and you'd better hope the deeds are inside, or else you'll suffer the consequences." Again, he held out his hand.

"And what do you plan to do with them?" Porter demanded to know.

"Same thing you were going to do. Make some money with them."

"Money?" Candy said in an accusatory tone. "Is that what this is all about?"

Plymouth glanced at her with a hard look. "Times are tough. The publishing business has some pretty thin margins. I need the money, and those deeds could be worth a lot."

"But they belong to my family," Porter insisted, "and we can prove that in court."

"You can try. But possession is nine-tenths of the law. Those deeds belong to me now." He waggled his hand impatiently as he turned back toward Scotty. "Toss me that backpack. Let's see what you've got in there."

Reluctantly, his eyes still glistening with anger and emotion, Scotty pulled the day pack down off his shoulder. He hesitated a moment, but finally tossed it to Plymouth. "Here you go. They're inside, like I said. But you're wrong about one thing."

Plymouth grabbed the pack eagerly and started to open it. "And what's that, kid?"

"Those deeds don't belong to anyone anymore, because they're gone."

Plymouth had unsnapped the day pack's top flap and looked down into it. For a moment his expression was one of total confusion. Then his brows fell and his gaze shot over to Scotty. "What's the joke here? What have you done?"

"What someone should have done long ago," Scotty said proudly.

And Plymouth scowled as he turned the day pack upside down, allowing the contents to spill out.

Ashes. Nothing but gray ash fell out.

Porter looked shocked. "You *burned* them?"

"Down in the cave," Scotty confirmed. "They're gone forever. Now no one can use them to steal property from people."

"But those were important historical documents!" Porter said, almost screaming, his face turning red.

"You little weasel!" Daisy spat out, equally furious. "How could you do such a thing?"

For a moment, no one spoke. Then suddenly bodies were moving, and there was a scuffle as both Scotty and Porter lunged for the pistol that still lay on the floor between them. Marshall made a move for it as well, Daisy screamed again, and Plymouth shouted something, waving his gun around.

The house seemed to rattle then, as if it were coming alive. Doors burst open, windows were thrust up, and Finn Woodbury strode into the room, closely followed by Chief Durr and a number of Cape Willington's finest.

"Freeze, everyone!" the chief called out. "Plymouth Palfrey, drop your weapon! No one move a muscle! We've got you surrounded. It's all over, folks!"

And it *was* over. Plymouth looked like he was about to make a run for it, until he saw the officers surrounding him. Finally realizing he was beaten, he let the gun slip from his hand. It dropped to the floor, while Scotty let out a cry of despair. One of the officers reached out with a foot and kicked both weapons out of the way. Plymouth and the young waiter were quickly swarmed by officers, who took them into custody.

Her carefully constructed facade completely gone, Daisy Porter-Sykes was crying, and her grandson was at her side, comforting her.

Meanwhile, Marshall L. Bosworth sat in his chair, to which he'd returned after attempting to get the gun. He appeared stunned at what had just happened, and was apparently unable to move again.

Finn rushed over to Candy, slipping a pistol he'd been carrying into a side holster. "Are you all right?" he asked.

"Yes, I'm fine. And thanks. But your timing was a little off. For a few moments there, I thought we were all goners."

"We got here as soon as we could," Finn said. "It took me a while to round up the troops."

"Did you hear Scotty's confession? And Plymouth's?"

Finn shook his head. "We swarmed the place as soon as we arrived. The situation looked pretty intense. Didn't have time for a stakeout."

"Well, at least you made it," Candy said, sounding relieved, "and for that I'm eternally grateful."

Finn spread his arms wide. "Hey, that's what I'm here for. Told you I had you covered. And to be honest, I knew you'd handle the situation like an expert—which you obviously did. And look, it all turned out okay, right? Nobody got hurt, and we caught us a couple of criminals." He smiled broadly and slapped her energetically on the shoulder. "Pretty exciting! Good times, right?"

FORTY-FOUR

Good times, indeed, Candy thought a few hours later.

Everyone in the place was in a jovial mood—or as much as possible, given the loss of one of their own party. But they were also grateful, even thrilled, that the killer had been unmasked, the conspiracy exposed, and a danger removed from their community.

Now, it was time to focus on other things.

As planned, they'd gathered at Blueberry Acres in the late afternoon for the wedding walk-through, which had gone off smashingly, and now they'd regrouped at Melody's Cafe on River Road for the rehearsal dinner. All those invited had arrived, decked out in their finest, with a heavy emphasis on the wedding's colors, cinnamon-brown and blueberry-blue. Malcolm and Ralph, who directed the walk-through at the farm, had dashed over to the café to help with the preparations, but Melody and her staff had the situation well in hand. They'd closed down the place to the public at five, and had set to work decorating for the event.

Fresh white flowers and linens adorned the tables, and

streamers flowed across the ceiling. Warm and appetizing smells emerged from the kitchen. Malcolm and Ralph, along with Maggie and Herr Georg, and Candy and Doc, greeted their guests with smiles and welcoming words, including two newcomers, Maggie's brother, Jack, and her sister-in-law, Piper. Everyone milled around for a while, chatting and sipping on white wine or a hearty German beer personally selected by the baker (he'd decided to skip the champagne for this particular get-together), and in time they all began to make their way to their seats.

As the newly designated best man, Doc took the lead again, raising his glass of beer, which still had a frothy head on it. "Welcome, everyone, to our little shindig here tonight. To get us started off on the right foot, I'd like to propose a toast!" he said. "So if you'll all join me once again in wishing the best of everything for our guests of honor and soon-to-be newly-weds, Maggie Tremont and Herr Georg Wolfsburger!"

They all cheered and drank, and the night was on its way.

Candy was dressed for the occasion, in a formfitting yellow-patterned dress with cinnamon trim, accompanied by cinnamon-colored pumps and a blueberry-blue cotton sweater, with the sleeves pushed up on her forearms. She'd spent the better half of six months looking for something just like this, to celebrate the occasion in proper style, and support the two people she loved most in the world—at least, right at this moment.

Make that three, she thought as she looked over at Finn, who was seated at a nearby table with his wife, Marti. He caught her gaze and gave her a wink and a sly smile. She responded with a raised glass and a thankful nod of her own. He'd saved her skin today, and she'd never forget it.

Both Plymouth Palfrey and Scotty Whitby, she'd heard just a little while ago from Wanda Boyle—who was still on the scene, she reminded Candy, while others were off party-ing the night away—had been taken to the CWPD station for initial booking but were already on their way to the county jail in Machias, about an hour away. It seemed they were both out of the village for good. That in itself sent a huge collective wave of relief through the villagers, especially those involved in the wedding party.

After the welcome toast, Doc introduced the wedding party, which included Cameron, Maggie's brother, Jack, and Doc, along with Finn, Artie, and Bumpy, as ushers, and Candy, Amanda, and Piper as bridesmaids.

Next came the exchange of gifts. They began with gifts for the wedding party, selected personally by Maggie and Herr Georg. Naturally, all had a German slant, including huge gift baskets with German beers, crackers, candies, and cheeses like Butterkäse and Edelpilzkäse, a blue-veined cheese, plus baked items and pretzels, most personally created by the bride and groom. Everyone also got a personalized beer stein, ordered specially from Germany, and a decorative cheeseboard from the Old Country.

Then it was time for the bride and groom to exchange gifts. Maggie insisted her fiancé go first, so Herr Georg presented her with her very own chef's coat, embroidered in cinnamon-colored thread on the chest with the words *Chef Maggie*, and her very own chef's hat, a cinnamon-colored toque that matched the embroidery on the coat. While everyone oohed and aahed over these, the baker pulled out a long jewelry box, which he presented to Maggie. Inside was a silver bracelet with cinnamon- and blue-colored gemstones, some of which he explained were stones like hessonite, a type of brown-orange garnet, and sapphire-blue stones. It literally took Maggie's breath away, and she had to fan herself for several moments to regain her composure.

Then it was her turn.

She waited until everyone in the room had quieted before she began.

"Georg, thank you so much for the gifts. They are truly amazing. But I believe I have an amazing gift for you as well. Specifically, I would like to give you a gift from my family."

Amanda handed her mother an elaborate box trimmed in black velvet, which Maggie in turn presented to Herr

Georg. He studied it for a few moments before he opened it with a dramatic flair.

"It's a pocket watch," she told him as his eyes widened, "that used to belong to my grandfather, whose name, by the way, was George. It was a retirement watch, and he treasured it for the rest of his life. Mom has held on to it all this time but, well, I wanted to give you something special, something that's a family heirloom. This way, you're now truly a member of our family!"

Herr Georg gently lifted out the watch, turning it one way and the other, studying its intricacies. He noticed the new engraving on the back and read it out loud: "To my beloved *Kuschelbär*," he said with a smile. And then, as everyone watched, he fitted the gold chain across his vest and carefully placed the watch into a small vest pocket. He patted it affectionately. "I shall treasure it always!" he said, and everyone applauded.

After that, the night carried on with a definite higher level of buzz as they ate and drank, laughed and sang, and enjoyed good times together. Candy was enjoying herself as well, though she started thinking of Neil and Random out at Crawford's Berry Farm, and wished she had invited him tonight, although he'd be at the wedding the following day.

She was deep into her dessert, a Frankfurter Kranz German sponge cake with buttercream frosting, caramel-covered nuts, and toasted almond flakes, when she looked up over her fork and saw Owen Peabody approaching her table.

FORTY-FIVE

She couldn't quite tell his mood but sensed that if he'd shown up here personally to talk to her, it couldn't be good. She wasn't ready to endure the Wrath of Owen tonight.

However, by the time he reached the table, he seemed quite contrite, and spoke to her in his best civil tone.

"Candy," he said, glancing around the table before looking back at her, "I'm sorry to interrupt, but I knew you were here and I have to talk to you. I wonder if I might have a few moments of your time . . . in private?"

Candy was in such a good mood that there was no way she was going to give him a hard time, as he'd done to her the day before. "Of course, Owen. Why don't we step outside?"

She realized after she said those words that they might sound ominous, but it wasn't her intent. Excusing herself from the table, she led the way out, with the museum director following behind.

Once on the sidewalk and relatively off by themselves, she turned back to him. "So what can I help you with?"

"Well, to be honest," he said sheepishly, "I've come to apologize. The way you solved that case was fairly impressive, and myself and the members of the board—well, the ones who are left—are grateful that we'll be able to open the museum tomorrow. So, serious crisis averted—except for Julius's death, of course!—and now we all can begin to figure out what our next step is, so we can put this tragic affair behind us and move on to other things."

Candy was going to inquire about a period of grieving, or some event to honor Julius, but she left that for later. Instead, she said, "Thank you. That means a lot. I was just trying to help."

"Well, I realize that now, though yesterday, of course, I was under quite a bit of stress when we talked, and I might have . . . overreacted." He paused, trying to swallow that thought before he continued. "I'm here for another reason as well. I came to give you this."

He reached into his jacket pocket and withdrew a folded slip of paper.

"Is this what I think it is?" she asked, taking it from him and opening it up. She saw the familiar list of names inside. She knew at once, looking at the handwriting, that it had indeed been written by Julius Seabury and stuck into that book as a way to warn others about Plymouth Palfrey and Porter Sykes.

"It is," he said. "I should have listened to you and given it to the police right away. They called this morning and said they'd send someone over to pick it up, but, well, with all that happened, it got lost in the shuffle. I wonder what I should do with it now."

She took a final look at the list, folded up the paper, and handed it back to him. "You should take it over to the police station right now, yourself. I'm sure they'll want to talk to you about it. Just tell them the truth. I think they'll understand."

He nodded as he took the note and slipped it back into a pocket. "Very well. I'll cooperate fully, of course. And next time, I'll know."

"Let's hope there won't be a next time," Candy said. "At some point these murders have to end—sooner rather than later, preferably."

"Let's hope," Owen agreed.

"So you're down a board member," she said, and Owen nodded. "Might I make a suggestion about who should fill that slot?"

"Of course!" he said. "Any suggestions you have would be welcome."

"Well, how about my father? He's a retired college professor with a lot of historical knowledge and experience. And he's working on some historical books he hopes to publish soon. I think he'd be a wonderful addition to the museum's board."

Owen thought about it a moment before he nodded. "I think it's a wonderful suggestion," he said, and looked back toward the café. "Do you think I should talk to him right now about it?"

"He might be a little preoccupied at the moment," Candy said. "We have a lot on our plate this weekend. Another day, maybe sometime next week?"

"I understand," the museum director said. "I'll give him a call first thing Monday morning."

"I'm sure he'll be thrilled," Candy said.

Owen seemed pleased by that. "Good." He nodded to her, and appeared about to start off, when she stopped him. "Before you go," she said, "I have one last question for you."

He looked at her warily. "And what's that?"

"Well, on the night Julius died, there was a meeting at the inn's lounge, and I heard you were there with some others—Gilbert Ethingham, I believe, and Marshall Bosworth, and Plymouth, of course. I wonder what it was the four of you talked about."

"Oh, that," he said. "Yes, that was a fairly disturbing meeting, to be frank about it."

"Really? In what way?" Candy said, her tone urging him on.

"I guess there's no harm in discussing this now. You could say we were a small group of concerned citizens."

"And what were you concerned about?"

Owen hesitated before he said, in a low conspiratorial

tone, "Quite frankly, we were worried about Porter Sykes. Marshall Bosworth told us that Porter had bought the Whitby place and was moving into town."

"Oh!" Candy said, and she had to think about that for a moment. "So, yesterday, when Porter told you on the phone that he'd bought the Whitby place, you already knew."

"Yes, Marshall informed us the night before at the inn, giving us a heads-up, as it were. He wanted us to be prepared. Frankly," Owen went on, his voice lowering even more, "this man Porter worries me. I've heard some of the rumors about him around town. I've never been completely comfortable around the man. It's one thing to have him call in to our board meetings, but having him and his family so close to the village—well, to be honest, I wasn't sure how it was going to work."

"That makes two of us."

"So we discussed Porter and the deeds that night. Of course, at that time I had no idea what Plymouth was up to, or what he was involved in. After our meeting, I went for a walk, through Town Park and over to the lighthouse, to try to clear my head and think it all through."

"And that's when you saw the light in the Keeper's Quarters and surprised me upstairs."

"Precisely." He actually made an attempt at a smile.

"So have you heard from Porter since the events of this afternoon? Have they arrested him?"

"Not that I'm aware of. But I did hear from Marshall a short while ago. It appears Porter and his grandmother are already headed back to Boston. According to Marshall, Daisy says she won't stay in that house another minute, after what happened there. And now that the deeds have been destroyed, Porter apparently has no more interest in the Whitby estate. He's instructed Marshall to put the place back up for sale. And Marshall says that Porter plans to assemble a legal defense team, in case he's indicted in this issue in any way."

"Well," Candy said, "isn't that interesting."

"Indeed. It seems we may have seen the last of the Sykes family in Cape Willington."

"Maybe, but I have a feeling that one way or another, we'll hear from them again."

Owen considered that. "You might be right, but let's hope it's not for a while."

"Let's hope," Candy agreed.

"As far as you and I are concerned," Owen continued, "I wonder if we might regroup and try to right our professional relationship. Get things back on track around here, so to speak."

"I'd like that," Candy said with a warm smile.

Owen seemed visibly relieved. "I'm glad to hear that. Well, then, I'll look forward to seeing you soon at the museum," he said, and he gave her a parting nod before he walked away into the gathering darkness.

FORTY-SIX

In more ways than one, it was the warmest day of the year, so far, in Cape Willington, Maine.

By noon, the temperature was headed to just over seventy degrees, a perfect day, and an hour later, Maggie Tremont and Georg Wolfsburger officially became Herr *und* Frau Georg Wolfsburger. The bees didn't come between them, nor the black flies, seeming to hold off out of respect until after the ceremony and reception. But the small flying critters would probably be out in full force come twilight. Most of the guests would be long gone before that, and the happy couple headed off on their honeymoon. But it was a day they'd always remember.

Maggie's brother, Jack, walked his sister down the aisle, as the wedding march played over the PA system. Herr Georg met her at the altar, and the Reverend James P. Daisy began the ceremony.

Maggie looked radiant in her wedding dress. She and Candy had spent a winter weekend in Boston several months ago, looking and shopping for just the right dress. They'd finally decided on a floor-length dress of ivory tulle with a sweetheart neckline. The top was sleeveless, showing off her bare shoulders, and the dress was accented by a rhinestone-beaded sash. At the beauty shop that morning, Maggie had her hair loosely pinned up with rhinestone hair clips. She'd decided against a veil.

She'd kept the dress at Candy's place, ready for her wedding day, and Candy, Amanda, Piper, and Ellie had all lent a hand getting her ready that morning. The bridesmaids all wore pale blue straight shift dresses, most at knee length, although Amanda's was shorter, above the knee. The dresses had three-quarter-length sleeves and were overlaid with lace, and they'd brought matching light linen sweaters to wear if the day was cool, but those weren't needed today.

Maggie and Georg held hands, and from there Candy didn't remember much. Sitting between Neil and her father in the front row on the bride's side, with Random roaming around somewhere out in the fields, she was overcome with emotion, and memories, at this special time for her friend, and knew neither of their lives would ever be the same. *We're moving on*, Candy thought, *to new lives, growing, changing, creating new families.*

As she looked around the barn, she saw many of the villagers she'd come to know so well. Wanda Boyle and her family had showed up, as well as Judicious F. P. Bosworth, as always decked out all in black, despite the fact he was here for a wedding. At least he'd accented his outfit with a pale blue tie. Mason Flint, the chairman of the town council, sat near the back, along with Cotton Colby and Elvira Tremble of the Cape Willington Heritage Protection League, who had brought their husbands along. Candy saw Elsie Lingholt from the Putting Food By Society, and Aurora Croft from the Pine Cone Bookstore, and local farmer Marjorie Coffin and her husband, and Lyra Graveton, who worked at the Ice Cream Shack in the summer. And she spotted the Gumms, who ran the hardware store, and some of the Watkins family, who owned the general store.

It was, she thought, a wonderful cross section of villagers, and it warmed her heart to see them all here, supporting her friend on her special day.

Both the bride and groom read personal messages to each other, said their *I do*s, and exchanged gold rings, each engraved with a personal message. Finally, the reverend pronounced them man and wife, and the two kissed, amid much applause and cheers.

Before Candy knew it, the ceremony was over.

Guests were throwing herbal rice, a creation of Maggie's. And they were on to the reception.

The cake had arrived just an hour before the wedding. Word was Herr Georg had baked through the night, into the early-morning hours, and finished in the nick of time. It was, he said, his masterpiece, a relatively simple three-layer cake, but it had been meticulously made and decorated with intricate swirls and patterns, as well as a small, delicate family crest with the initial *W* at the center. Its fragrance filled the air.

Once the guests had gathered around, glasses of champagne in hand (a different label, but also selected especially for their wedding day), Herr Georg explained his creation.

"Even though it appears to be cream colored, it is," he informed them, "actually an orange wedding cake with orange buttercream frosting. I've taken it from an old recipe of my mother's, but I made a few changes to it."

"Did you add cinnamon?" someone from the back of the crowd asked. Candy identified the voice as belonging to Bumpy.

"I did!" the baker said with a laugh. "Just a dash—and a few other secret ingredients as well. I can't wait until you try it. I promise you've never tasted anything like it in your life!"

The groom's cake was there as well, which the baker fussed over. "You have done such a magnificent job!" he declared to Maggie. "My, you are a wonderful baker!"

She nudged him. "I learned from the best."

The expression on the baker's face said everything.

They drank and sang German beer songs, opened some of their wedding gifts, and then cleared out the chairs in the barn and danced until their legs grew weary. Later, as the afternoon sun lowered in the sky, the event began to break up. Happy and satisfied, the guests started to drift away. The bride and groom thanked the reverend and his wife, Gabriella, as elegant as always. Ralph and Malcolm were weary but happy with all they'd accomplished.

In the end, everything went off without a hitch. "Or rather," as Maggie's mother, Ellie, declared to all who would listen that day, "with one!"

All agreed, as promised, that it was the social event of the season in the village of Cape Willington.

EPILOGUE

The Black Forest Bakery was buzzing with activity on the Tuesday morning after Memorial Day.

Tourists who had spent the holiday weekend in town were crowding the place. Spelt apple and Bavarian rye bread, cinnamon breakfast muffins, cheese strudels, raspberry rumbles, almond and chocolate crescents, and fruit turnovers, and as well as a variety of cupcakes, cream puffs, pastries, croissants, tarts, tortes, cakes, and pretzels, were flying off the shelves. They were going so fast, Maggie could barely keep up with her restocking efforts, running back and forth to the kitchen, while Candy worked at the cash register, her fingers moving as fast as possible. Every once in a while she looked up at the line stretched before her, which seemed to keep getting longer, then pressed her lips together and turned back to her work. In the kitchen, Herr Georg did what he did best, and the smells emanating through the shop were the best evidence possible of his culinary efforts.

By late morning the crowds began to thin a little, and the three of them finally had a chance to talk, as Herr Georg meandered out of the kitchen, wiping his hands on his apron.

"My, what a morning!" he exclaimed. "It seems the crowds are getting larger all the time."

"We might have to expand, my dear," Maggie said, sidling up to him and hugging his arm. "I heard the place next door might be available soon. Maybe we should think about buying it, knocking out the wall, and putting the gift items on that side. It would free up some space for additional shelves in here."

"Hmm, yes, a wonderful idea," the baker said. "I'll certainly look into it."

The three of them hadn't had much time to talk since the Wolfsburgers returned from their honeymoon at Niagara Falls, which they said was chilly but beautiful. They'd been busy setting up the shop, and Candy and Doc had been equally busy out at Blueberry Acres, especially in the vegetable garden, which they'd expanded shortly after the reception tent had come down. They'd also filled the hoophouse with growing plants and had cleared out a spot for their small grove of cherry trees. It was only this morning the three of them had a chance to hook up, when Maggie called the farmhouse frantically, asking for Candy's help in manning the shop.

For Candy, it was like old times. She'd worked in the bakery for several years, before Maggie took over her position behind the counter, and her old skills with the cash register came back easily. The aromas and atmosphere in the bakery reminded her of the years that had passed. They'd been through a lot in this village over the past six or seven years, she thought, including a number of murders, but she hoped the worst of it was behind them, and they could finally all get back to what they did best.

She'd heard not a word from any of the Sykes family members since her encounter with them at the Whitby estate. They seemed to have holed themselves up in their mansion in Marblehead. Finn occasionally gave her a little news about the status of Scotty and Plymouth, as well as the police investigation into Porter's possible link to the murder of Julius Seabury. But so far he hadn't been charged, and Candy wouldn't be surprised if he never was. He seemed to have escaped from justice once again.

As long as he stayed far away from the village, she was fine with that.

Her father had attended his first board meeting at the museum, and had been warmly welcomed by all. Porter Sykes had not called in during the meeting, Doc informed her when he got home, and according to Owen, had resigned his seat on the board after serving on it for nearly a decade—much to the relief of all involved, especially the museum director.

The Whitby place was vacant again. It hadn't sold, and Candy didn't know if it would for a while. But there was always a chance someone "from away" would sweep in and snatch it up. That's the way it worked sometimes along the Maine coast.

As the three of them were talking, Candy noticed that the baker was watching her oddly, and when there was a break in the conversation, she said, "Herr Georg, is everything all right? You look pensive."

"I was just thinking," he said. "It slipped my mind in all the activity of the last few weeks, but, well, it's about those copies I still have in the safe in my office."

"Ahh." Candy nodded knowingly, and she lowered her voice before she said, "The copies of those famous deeds, which were destroyed by Scotty."

"Yes, exactly. But unfortunately I still have them, so they're not really gone, are they?"

"No, but they're safe for now, and no one knows about them except us."

"So what do you think we should do with them?" Herr Georg asked.

"We've both been talking about it," Maggie put in. "I think we should have a nice bonfire some night and burn them, just like Scotty did with the originals."

"And I tend to agree," said the baker, "though I know they still might have some historical value. However, I'm afraid that if they get out into the open again, we'll be right back where we were before, with the Sykes family trying to get hold of them."

"That's true," Candy said, "and those are all good points. But I'm not sure I have an immediate answer for you. I've thought about those copies, too, and I lean toward Maggie's suggestion. It probably would be best to get rid of them once and for all."

Maggie sensed some hesitation in her friend's tone. "But . . . ?"

Candy shrugged. "But I'm not sure that's the right thing to do." She thought about it a minute. "Why don't we do this, if it's okay with you two? I'll talk to Dad about it, and maybe Neil as well. And possibly even Owen, though I'm not sure I should bring him into this. Honestly, I'm still not really sure I can trust him at all. Maybe just the five of us. And we can talk it over and come to some sort of conclusion about what to do with them."

Herr Georg thought about it a moment, and finally nodded. "Very well. But if possible, I'd like to resolve this issue as quickly as we can. I feel like I'm holding on to a hot potato, and I don't want it to burn my fingers."

Candy nodded. "I'll try to have an answer for you in a few days."

"The sooner, the better," the baker said. "The last two people who had those deeds—Miles Crawford and Julius Seabury—were both killed because of them. I don't want that to happen to me!"

"Heaven forbid!" Maggie exclaimed, and she gave her husband a quick kiss on the cheek. "Don't talk like that, my *Kuschelbär*! I don't know what I'd do without you!"

That made Herr Georg chuckle, and he patted her hand. "Don't you worry, *mein Liebchen*. I'm not planning on going anywhere for a long, long time. By the way," he said, turning back to Candy, "did I tell you that I had an idea for a new pastry when we were at Niagara Falls?"

"No, you didn't," Candy said, glad for the change in subject. "Tell me about it."

"Well, after all you did to solve this most recent mystery,

and in such a way that it didn't interfere with our wedding, I thought I should create something special to commemorate your achievements over the past few years. So I'm going to create a new pastry in your honor. It's going to be made with blueberries and cinnamon, of course, with a delectable frosting and perhaps a splash of rum. I'm going to call it the Candy Holliday Mystery Strudel!"

They all laughed at that, and got right back to work as more customers starting coming through the door.

AUTHOR'S NOTE

The story of Silas Sykes's land deeds, which has wound its way as an interconnected subplot through all of the books since the second one in the series, *Town in a Lobster Stew*, was inspired by a real-world event. In the 1990s, members of the Golden Hill Paugussett Indian Nation in Connecticut claimed to have legal rights to eighty acres in the Golden Hill area of Bridgeport, as well as to acreage in downtown Greenwich. Although the tribe eventually lost its claim to the land, the story served as a starting point for the one appearing in the Candy Holliday Murder Mysteries. Many thanks to first reader and proofreader nonpareil Mary A. Cook and her husband Joel; Kae and Jon; Leis, Bethany, Danielle, and Katherine at Berkeley Prime Crime; Teresa Fasolino for the cover art for all the novels; Ron, Jayme, and Patti, as well as Ronnie, Lucas, and Zach for the encouragement and good company; Barbara, George, and Ruby for continued support; and, as always, Mat, James, and Noah. For more information about the Candy Holliday Murder Mysteries and Cape Willington, Maine, visit hollidaysblueberryacres.com.

RECISPES

Maggie and Georg's Orange Wedding Cake with Orange Buttercream Frosting

(From an old Wolfsburger family recipe.)

Serves 12

> *Grated rind and juice of one large orange*
> *5 eggs*
> *2 cups powdered sugar*
> *½ cup cold water*
> *2 cups flour*
> *2 tablespoons baking powder*

Preheat the oven to 350 degrees.

Grease and flour 2 round 9-inch cake pans or 1 9-inch-by-13-inch rectangular baking pan.

Into a large mixing bowl, squeeze the juice from 1 large orange.

Grate the rind of the same orange into the bowl, mix well with the juice.

Add eggs to the orange mixture and mix well.

Add powdered sugar a little at a time, mixing well with a wire whisk for 10 minutes.

Add cold water.

Add flour and baking powder a little at a time, mixing well after each addition.

Split batter between 2 pans or put it all in the 1 rectangular pan.

Bake at 350 degrees for 20–25 minutes or until a toothpick comes out clean.

Cool cakes in pans for 20 minutes, then turn out cakes onto 2 sheets of wax paper until ready to frost.

When the cakes are completely cooled, set one round cake on a cake plate.

Orange Buttercream Frosting

Makes 2½ cups frosting

1 cup butter (2 sticks), softened
3–4 cups powdered sugar, sifted through a sieve or
*   with a sifter*
¼ teaspoon salt
1 tablespoon orange extract
Up to 4 tablespoons of heavy cream

In a large bowl beat the softened butter.

Mix some of the powdered sugar with the butter in the bowl.

Add salt, orange extract, and cream. Mix for 3 minutes.

Add more powdered sugar or cream to get the consistency you like.

Frost the top of 1 layer; put the second layer on top.

Frost the sides, then the top.

For a wedding cake, this would be many tiers high and decorated with vines and flowers.

Congratulations to the happy couple!

Cinnamon Raspberry Flop

Serves 8

> 2 tablespoons butter
> 1 cup sugar
> 2 cups flour
> 2 teaspoons baking powder
> 1 cup milk
> 12 raspberries, cut in half
> 4 tablespoons brown sugar
> 2 tablespoons cinnamon

Grease and dust with flour 1 pie pan.

Preheat the oven to 350 degrees.

In a large mixing bowl, cream the first tablespoon of butter.

Add sugar and mix well.

Add flour and baking powder to the mixture a little at a time, mixing well after each addition.

Add 1 cup milk and mix well.

Add the raspberries and mix well.

Fold the batter into the pie pan.

Cut the remaining tablespoon of butter into 4 small pieces and dot the batter with the butter.

In a small bowl, combine brown sugar with cinnamon.

Sprinkle the brown sugar/cinnamon mixture over the top of the batter.

Bake at 350 degrees for 25 minutes or until a toothpick comes out clean.

Enjoy!

Cinnamon Toast

Serves 2; makes 4 large pieces of toast

¼ cup honey
2 tablespoons brown sugar
1 teaspoon ground cinnamon
Dash of extract—vanilla, orange, or blueberry
Bread for toast
Butter of choice to butter toast

In a small saucepan, mix the honey, brown sugar, cinnamon, and dash of extract.

Heat over low heat for 2–3 minutes until brown sugar and cinnamon are dissolved.

Toast slices of bread in the toaster.

Butter toast as desired and put on a plate.

Drizzle the cinnamon mixture over the toasted buttered bread.

A toast with cinnamon toast! Cheers!

Chocolate Groom's Cake

As made by Maggie, Candy, Ellie, and Amanda.

Serves 12

½ cup butter (1 stick), softened
2 cups sugar
2 eggs
2 squares or 2 ounces baking chocolate, melted
½ cup buttermilk
2 cups flour

2 teaspoons baking soda
1 cup boiling water
1 teaspoon vanilla extract

Preheat the oven to 350 degrees.

Grease and flour 2 round 9-inch baking pans or 1 9-inch-by-13-inch rectangular baking pan.

In a large mixing bowl, mix the softened butter with the sugar. Beat until smooth.

Add the eggs and beat until smooth.

In a double boiler or 2 pots, 1 filled with water and a smaller pot to set inside it, melt the chocolate.

Pour the melted chocolate into the mixing bowl and mix with the other ingredients in the bowl.

Add the buttermilk, mix.

Add the flour and mix well.

Add the baking soda to 1 cup of boiling water, stir, cool slightly, and slowly add to the bowl of ingredients.

Add the vanilla, mix well.

Pour the batter in the pans in even amounts.

Bake at 350 degrees for 30 minutes or until done, when a toothpick in the center comes out clean.

Cool the cakes.

Chocolate Blueberry Frosting

1 cup butter (2 sticks), softened
3–4 cups powdered sugar, sifted
1 tablespoon blueberry extract
¼ teaspoon salt
2 ounces bittersweet baking chocolate
Up to 4 tablespoons heavy cream

In a mixing bowl, beat the softened butter until creamy.

Sift the powdered sugar and add to the butter, mixing well.

Add the blueberry extract, mix well.

Add salt, mix.

Melt the chocolate over a double boiler, or use 2 pots,

1 filled with water and a smaller one with the chocolate to
fit into the first.

Pour the chocolate into the bowl and mix with the other
ingredients.

Add 2 tablespoons of the heavy cream and beat for 3 minutes, until very creamy.

Add additional cream or powdered sugar to get the desired
consistency.

When the Chocolate Groom's Cake is cooled, frost with
the Chocolate Blueberry Frosting.

The cakes can then be decorated with the candied flowers.

Candied Pansies and Blueberry Blossoms

Granulated sugar
2 egg whites
2 teaspoons cool water
20–30 pansies, violas, or blueberry blossoms
1 small, delicate paintbrush

Cover a baking tray with sugar.

In a small mixing bowl, beat the egg whites and water with
a fork. They will get frothy.

With the small paintbrush, paint the blossoms on both sides
with the mixture, just enough to coat them.

Lightly sprinkle the painted blossoms with sugar. The
color should show through the sparkles of the sugar.

Dry the blossoms on a tray for 3 hours.

The blossoms will keep in a sealed container for several
months.

*Decorate the cake with the blossoms by pressing them
lightly into the frosting.*

A NATURAL GUIDE TO SPRINGTIME PLANTING

by Candy Holliday
Gardening & Food Correspondent
Special to the *Cape Crier*

It's hard to imagine, in the middle of winter, with so many feet of snow on the ground, that spring will surely arrive in a few months and gardens will grow again. It will, and they will!

Even in the month of May it can be cold and—*gulp!*—even snow in Maine. But instead of wondering when the cold will ever end and when you can plant, you can follow the signs in nature and let them be your guide, rather than trying to figure it all out on your own and losing precious plants in the process.

The following is the "natural" planting guide my father, Henry "Doc" Holliday, and I use every year out at Blueberry Acres. It hasn't failed us yet, and should work for you as well. (Note: All these tips are for planting outside. A greenhouse or hoophouse will change your planting schedule, but the time to transplant outside remains the same.)

- One important tip is to not plant delicate plants or annuals before the last frost full moon in May. After the full moon in May, it is safe to plant.

- One of the first flowers to bloom is the snowdrop. When you see the beautiful white flowers open, it is safe to plant your peas, onion sets, and lettuce.

- The next flower we all look forward to seeing is the crocus. When the crocus blooms, it's time to plant radishes and spinach.

- Next come those beautiful yellow, sweet-smelling daffodils! When the daffodils bloom, it is safe to plant half-hardy vegetables, which would be your chard, beets, and carrots.

- When the maple trees begin to leaf out, you can start planting perennials.

- When the fragrant apple blossoms bloom, it is safe to plant beans.

- The trees I always wait for are the lilacs. When the lilacs are in bloom, the world smells wonderful, and it is safe to plant annual flowers, cucumbers, squash, and basil.

- When the irises bloom, you can plant peppers and eggplants.

- Wait for the lily of the valley to bloom to transplant tomatoes. It's hard to wait for that one!

- When the oak leaves are the size of mouse ears, it is safe to plant your corn.

- It has to be really warm for peonies to bloom, and then it is finally safe to plant melons.

In all these cases, patience truly is a virtue, and it will save you from having to replant plants lost due to the cold. Happy spring, and happy gardening!

CHARACTER LIST

Principal Characters

Candy Holliday—amateur sleuth, runs Holliday's Blueberry Acres with her father, Doc

Henry "Doc" Holliday—blueberry farmer, retired college professor, historian, and writer

Maggie Tremont—Candy's best friend, works at the bakery, lives in Fowler's Corner

Amanda Tremont—college student, daughter of Maggie, fiancée of Cameron Zimmerman

Cameron Zimmerman—fiancé of Amanda, regional manager for an agricultural company

Herr Georg Wolfsburger—renowned baker, owner of Black Forest Bakery, Maggie's fiancé

Ellie Chase—Maggie's mother, visiting for the wedding

Jack and Piper Chase—Maggie's brother and sister-in-law, from Presque Isle

Wanda Boyle—managing editor of the *Cape Crier*, the town's weekly newspaper

William "Bumpy" Brigham—retired attorney, part of Doc Holliday's "posse"

Artie Groves—retired engineer, bespectacled member of the posse

Finn Woodbury—retired police officer, local play producer, member of the posse

Neil Crawford—current owner of Crawford's Berry Farm, son of Miles

Random Crawford—Neil's shaggy dog

Ralph Henry and Malcolm Stevens Randolph—local gift shop owners, budding wedding planners

Judicious F. P. Bosworth—World traveler and town mystic

Others in Cape Willington, Maine

Alben Alcott, commonly called "Alby"—assistant innkeeper at the Lightkeeper's Inn

Melody Barnes—owner of Melody's Cafe and caterer for the reception and rehearsal dinner

Marshall L. Bosworth—older brother of Judicious, attorney in Bangor

Daniel Brewster—assistant librarian at the Pruitt Public Library

Bob Bridges—maintenance staff at the English Point Lighthouse and Museum

Ben Clayton—former editor of the *Cape Crier*

Cotton Colby—cofounder of the Cape Willington Heritage Protection League

Miles Crawford—former owner of Crawford's Berry Farm (deceased)

Gabriella Daisy—wife of the Reverend Daisy

The Reverend James P. Daisy—pastor of the Cape Willington First Unitarian Church

Charlotte Depew—past director of the English Point Lighthouse and Museum (deceased)

Lucinda P. Dowling—librarian and local author of family histories

Gilbert Ethingham—museum board member, descendant of the Ethingham founding family

Mrs. (Rachel) Fairweather—town resident, lived in a bungalow on Shady Lane (deceased)

Mason Flint—chairman of the town council

Augustus "Gus" Gumm—owner of Gumm's Hardware Store

Colin Trevor Jones—executive chef at the Lightkeeper's Inn

Jesse Kidder—photographer and graphic designer for the *Cape Crier*

Oliver LaForce—owner and head innkeeper of the Lightkeeper's Inn

Doris Oaks—volunteer at the English Point Lighthouse and Museum, owner of Roy the Parrot

Plymouth Palfrey—museum board member, owner of the Kennebec Press

Owen Peabody—director of the English Point Lighthouse and Museum

Daisy Porter-Sykes—matriarch of the Sykes family, lives in Marblehead, Massachusetts

Edith Pring—member of the museum's board of directors

Molly Prospect—officer of the Cape Willington Police Department

Helen Ross Pruitt—matriarch of the Pruitt family, owner of Pruitt Manor

Tristan Pruitt—nephew of Helen Ross Pruitt

Alice Rainsford—member of the Cape Willington Heritage Protection League

Julius Seabury—local historian, self-published author, and tourist favorite

James Sedley (known as Mr. Sedley)—town resident and recipe creator (deceased)

Gideon Sykes—husband of Daisy Porter-Sykes (deceased)

Morgan Sykes—sister to Porter and Roger, lives in New York City

Porter Sykes—real estate developer, grandson of Gideon and Daisy Porter-Sykes

Roger Sykes—Boston restaurateur, grandson of Gideon and Daisy Porter-Sykes

Silas Sykes—ancestor of Porter, Roger, and Morgan Sykes (deceased)

Elvira Tremble—cofounder of the Cape Willington Heritage Protection League

Wilma Mae Wendell—town resident, former winner of the Lobster Stew Cook-off

Elias Whitby—previous owner of the Lightkeeper's Inn and the Whitby estate

Elliot Whitby—Poe impersonator, current owner of the Whitby estate

Scotty Whitby—nephew of Elliot, waiter at the Lightkeeper's Inn

Marti Woodbury—wife of Finn, frequent visitor to Florida in the winter (with Finn!)

For a complete character list spanning all seven books, visit hollidaysblueberryacres.com.

Keep reading for an excerpt of
the first book in B. B. Haywood's
Candy Holliday Murder Mysteries . . .

TOWN IN A BLUEBERRY JAM

Available from Berkley Prime Crime!

PROLOGUE

He was falling.

A moment earlier he had been standing on solid ground, near the edge of the seaside cliff that dropped sharply to wet black rocks below. Now here he was, his face turned toward the night sky and nothing beneath him but open air. His arms windmilled back and his legs pumped wildly as the memories of a life well lived flashed before his eyes with such speed and vividness it made him gasp.

It really did happen like that, in the moments right before death. He could attest to the fact, if he lived long enough. But he knew he'd never get the chance.

He could still feel the spot on his chest, like a hollow wound, where the hand had struck him hard, coming out of nowhere in a stab of anger. It had caught him so suddenly, so unexpectedly that he'd lost his footing and stumbled to the edge of the cliff, where he'd teetered as a terrifying surge of panic swept through him. An instant later his feet lost contact with solid ground. Now, as he fell, his mind exploded with disbelief and regret, and his face tightened as his mouth pulled back in a death grimace. And underneath it all he cursed himself. He should have seen it coming. All the signs were there. He should have been more attentive. He shouldn't have been standing so close to the edge. But he'd lost his bearings in the argument. He'd let his emotions drive the wits from him—a fatal mistake, he realized now, and his whole body shuddered at the hard, horrifying realization:

I have just been murdered!

How could this be happening? The surrealism of the moment threatened to overwhelm him, to send him into deep shock. His eyes rolled back, his fingers tingled unnaturally, and his chest felt cold, colder than he would have thought possible. His breath was pulled from him by the rushing air as he felt death closing in on him all too quickly.

In those last moments anger spewed forth from him, a hot blast of furor, and he tried to fling curse words back up at the shadowed figure that stood at the edge of the cliff above, watching him with a shocked expression, eyes wide, hands out, grasping at emptiness. But he could bring nothing forth—not a curse, not a scream, nor a grunt or even a spasm of sound. His throat constricted with preternatural fear, all words and sounds choked off, for death was racing toward him at an incalculable speed. How much time did he have left? A heartbeat? Two? Was his heart even still beating? He heard a roaring in his ears as he considered the question within the space of a millisecond. He decided to measure the remainder of his life not in heartbeats, nor in seconds, nor in the blinks of a watery eye, but in the beats of a hummingbird's wings. Surely he had a few dozen of those left, perhaps even a hundred. It would give him a small bit of time to ponder his life before it was crushed achingly from him.

And there was much to ponder, for the memories were coming lightning fast now, like rapid bursts of fire from an automatic weapon. His first remembered glimpse of his parents' faces, younger than he'd ever remembered them before. Touching tiny toes in a retreating wave at the beach. Seagulls whirling overhead. Skipping rocks on a quiet stream, fishing with his father, hockey on the ice pond, his first moments underwater in a wading pool. Then the passion that consumed him, compelled him through life, a life as a professional swimmer. Racing with his friends in the ocean's rough surf—and always winning. Indoor pools at the YMCA, his earliest lessons, and soon after, his first formal swim meet. The cheers of the crowd and the odor of chlorine in his nostrils like the breath of life. The faces of coaches and trainers and myriad competitors, every face remembered. Endless meetings and practices, the tension and excitement of race day, followed by powerful surges of adrenaline for bare moments in the water that became his sole reason for existence. Controlling his rhythm and holding back just a bit of extra energy for the finish. The roars of the crowds growing louder as the crowds themselves grew. Awards and honors, "Oh Say Can You See," feeling the tug of heavy medals draped around his neck, the way they gleamed in the spotlights. Sitting around the kitchen table, talking to his folks about the greater goal. The worry but determination on their faces as they considered the costs, the struggles, the uncertainty of such an unimaginable future. Driving in his dad's old truck to statewide meets, his first time on a plane as he flew off to Nationals, then his first trip overseas with his father, to Europe. Where he won. And continued winning, so many meets, so many wins, so many steps along the way, all laid out like pages of an aged scrapbook that flipped rapidly across his vision. Then to Tokyo and the Olympic Village and the Parade of Nations, all passing by him with such detail, such clarity that he could remember the sounds and the smells as if he stood there now. And his eyes watered as he wondered where it had all gone, how it had slipped away too fast, too fast. . . .

Back home, with the parades and speeches, the handshakes and hugs, the looks of pride, admiration, and often jealousy—those last looks were the ones he came to love the most, for they empowered him, gave him a sense of worth and accomplishment.

And the women. Lots of women. They had always come easily to him, attracted by his confidence, his skills, his lean body, his good looks, and that burst of unruly, always uncombed red hair that became his trademark. Even cut short for swim meets it was noticeable, but after his retirement he let it grow out again, and the women couldn't keep their hands off it. Through all the years of traveling, of broadcasting and commentating, of commercials and special appearances, milking his celebrity for every cent he could get out of it, his hair was his calling card.

But in the end it had not saved him. In fact, more than likely it had, in some not-so-small way, led to this moment, his literal downfall.

That almost made him laugh as the hummingbird's wings beat a few more times, and the hard black rocks raced toward him with astonishing swiftness.

He'd heard the rumors around town, the whispers, the surreptitious nods in his direction, the looks askance, and the occasional finger-pointing when they thought he wasn't watching. Folks liked to talk about the plethora of redheaded children around town, though no one ever said anything to him directly about it. And what problem was it to him anyway? Just because he never married, and made little distinction between married and unmarried women—were any of those kids his fault? But that hadn't stopped the threats, the lawsuits, the angry husbands, and sullen stares from jilted lovers. The worst were the clingy ones, who expected more from him than he ever wanted to give. Their emotions spun on a dime, moving from adoration to terrifying rage with a speed that always left him cold and confused, cautious, and ultimately uninterested in any form of intimacy and attachment.

But again, that had been part of his attractiveness, what drew the women to him. There were many who accepted him for what he was, of course, and those were the ones who figured most prominently in his final thoughts. He recalled them all fondly as he fell back, his head below his feet now, his gaze rolling up. The stars in the black sky above glowed brightly before him, so close, so distinctively sharp, elegant pinpricks in a restless infinity. Its beauty struck him with such force that he was distracted from the memories, and in the last moments those memories were lost to him, fading away like a foamy wave rolling off a sandy beach, drawn back into the greater ocean.

The ocean. Water. It had always been his sustenance, his greatest love, his only mistress. It would accept him for a final time now, and he would give himself fully to it.

But still, he had regrets. Too much left undone, too much life still left to be lived. And again, he wondered— how had this happened? How had he come to this moment?

His mind raced in those final few flutters of the hummingbird's wings, and it was only then, in the last milliseconds of his life, as his body broke on the rocks, crushing the air from his lungs and stealing away his life, that the final flash of memory and realization shot through his screaming brain. The clarity of it was striking, and he knew in that last instant who had driven him to his death. No, she hadn't pushed him off the cliff herself. Her hand wasn't the one that had struck him in the chest, ending his life. But she'd been there in spirit, in the dark shadows of motivation. Hers was the hand behind the hand, her words the whispers in the ear, her thoughts the seeds that led to this tragic end. Scheming and manipulating behind the scenes, she'd driven the killer to murder, flicking domino-block events out to this final, inexorable moment.

It had been her, he was certain of it.

His last thought was of Sapphire Vine.

From the *Cape Crier*
Cape Willington, Maine
July 23rd Edition

THE WEEKLY GRAPEVINE

by Sapphire Vine
Special Correspondent

BLUEBERRIES FOR EVERYONE!

Are you ready to par-tay? Of course you are! Once again, good citizens, it's time for Cape Willington's world-famous Blueberry Festival! As I'm sure you well know, the fabulously fruity festival is an all-day event scheduled for Saturday, July 27, and it's usually the town's busiest day of the year. (Tourists are *everywhere*!) Festivities kick off at 7:30 A.M. at Legion Hall, with other events taking place around Cape throughout the day. The Blueberry Parade begins at 3 P.M., with Olympic Gold Medal winner Jock Larson serving as the Grand Marshal (again!). Most important, the Blueberry Queen Pageant will take place at 6 P.M at Town Hall. There are many lovely contestants taking part this year, including Yours Truly—*moi*! Do wish me luck!

Don't forget to check out the many wonderful booths that will be lined up along Main Street and Ocean Avenue during the festival. There will be plenty of goodies for everyone. See you there!

CELEBRITIES ABOUND

Seems like our attractive little town has been a celebrity magnet lately. A few weeks ago we reported sightings of big-time chunky-hunky TV and movie star Patrick Dempsey (he's sooooo McDreamy!) and the lovely missus, who toddled about town with their brood and sampled the wares at a local restaurant. (Patrick was born in Lewiston, you know.) Now a more literary celeb is gracing the starstruck streets of our village—none other than Sebastian J. Quinn, he of the revered poetic tome, *The Bell of Chaos*. And we're thrilled to report that the esteemed Mr. Quinn has consented to serve as a judge at this week's prestigious Blueberry Queen Pageant. Remember, you read it here first!

ENGAGEMENTS
Little Kimmy Whitebridge is all grown up and planning to marry D. Douglas Douglass III of Cape Willington. Both are graduates of CWHS. Kimmy is currently working in hotel management at the Motel 6 up on Route 1. Douglas is employed at D. D. Douglass & Son Realtors. (I wonder how he got that job?) A September wedding is planned. Happy honeymoon, kids! Do they have heart-shaped beds at the Motel 6?

KUDOS
Once again we have to thank the amazing (and seemingly tireless) Wanda Boyle for her committee work at our local schools. In the last year, Wanda planned the teacher luncheons, the Soccer Extravaganza, and the Music Club Money-Makers Fair; worked on the planning committee for reading evaluation of our gifted children; made costumes for the third-grade play; baked cookies for the Halloween and Valentine's Day parties; chaired the PTO— and didn't miss a single meeting. (I think she even cleaned the classrooms a few times.) Wow! Have you seen your own kids lately, Wanda? Ha! Just kidding!

ATTENTION ALL GARDENERS!
Get out your trowels and dig your way to the Cape Garden Club's First Annual Flower Festival, to be held at the Cove Inn on Sunday, August 2. The theme of this very merry special event will be "Tea in the Garden." (Make mine Earl Grey, please!) You can call Lily Verte for all the flowery details. We hope this turns out to be a blossoming event for them.

THE THEATRE
Apparently Lyra Graveton can carry more than buckets of ice cream. She can carry a tune as well! We normally see Lyra at the Ice Cream Shack scooping up gobs of delicious home-made ice cream. (Have you seen those ice cream cones? They're humongous!) Starting next weekend, you can see (and

hear) Lyra belting out tunes in Cape Summer Theatre's musical version of everyone's favorite cowboy show, *Oklahoma!* Tickets are still available at the box office (though they're sure to go fast with Lyra up there on stage!). The show runs through August 12 at the Pruitt Opera House. See it, and Oh! we guarantee you'll have a beautiful, beautiful morning!

TASTY TIDBITS

Rumors that Town Council Chairwoman Bertha Grayfire will wear her outrageous Dolly Parton costume (a favorite with the kids at Halloween) when she emcees the annual Blueberry Queen Pageant Saturday night are completely FALSE! (We have heard, however, that the costume has fallen into disrepair lately. You should take better care of your assets, Bertha!). . . . My spy tells me that Melody's Café, that new restaurant up on River Road, is doing a booming business. The lobster rolls are supposed to be absolutely scrumptious! (Don't tell the tourists, though, or I'll never be able to get a seat!) My spy's only request—better desserts, please! . . . Official Judicious F. P. Bosworth sightings for the first two weeks of July—Visible: 9 days—Invisible: 5 days. Sounds like Judicious has been out enjoying this glorious Maine summer weather! Be sure to pass on Judicious sightings to the Grapevine for future publication!

ONE

Candy Holliday was standing at the kitchen sink, cleaning up after making another batch of blueberry pies, when she looked out the window and saw Doc's old pickup truck rattling up the dirt driveway way too early. Curious, she glanced at the clock on the wall over the kitchen table. Usually he wasn't back home until ten thirty or eleven, preferring to linger over his coffee cup as long as possible. But here he was at a little past nine.

She knew right away something was up.

The kitchen wasn't Candy's favorite place to be; she had never considered herself much of a domestic sort. She would rather be outside, tending to her chickens, fiddling around in the barn, taking care of the gardens, or walking the fields behind the house. But when you had a blueberry festival to prepare for, you did what you had to do.

So to stay out of her way (or perhaps just to avoid the chores that always seemed to need doing around the farm), her father, Henry "Doc" Holliday, had gone into town that morning for coffee and donuts with "the boys"—William "Bumpy" Brigham, a barrel-chested semiretired attorney with a deep passion for antique cars; Artie Groves, a retired civil engineer who now ran a bustling eBay business out of a cluttered office over his garage; and Finn Woodbury, a former big-city cop who had segued into small-town show business, serving as producer for three or four community theater projects each year, including the annual musical staged at the Pruitt Opera House on Ocean Avenue. They were golfin' and jawin' buddies, all in their mid- to late sixties, who spent their Friday nights playing poker as though it were a religion and could be found most weekday mornings holding court in the corner booth at Duffy's Main Street Diner. These freewheeling breakfast gatherings, where the latest headlines, rumors, gossip, and sports stories were chewed over like well-cooked bacon, were as addictive as coffee and salt air to Doc, who, despite his retirement, still had an unquenchable thirst for knowledge of any kind and liked to keep his finger tight to the pulse of his adopted village.

So it wasn't surprising he heard the latest shocker before Candy did.

The story had been on the front page of the morning paper, of course, but Doc always took that with him to the diner. Candy only got it around lunchtime, after it had been well pored over and thumbed through, and smartly decorated with coffee rings and swaths of smeared donut icing. And she could have switched on the TV and gotten the story that way, but for the past few days she had been too busy to waste time sitting in front of the tube. Anyway, TV watching was a winter activity around Cape Willington, Maine, where the Downeast summers were short and glorious, and so had to be enjoyed to their fullest. That meant being outside as much as possible, letting the sensual warmth squeeze the chill completely out of one's bones before winter set in again with its unrelenting timeliness.

Candy wasn't outside today, though. It was the day before Cape Willington's much-anticipated Forty-First Annual Blueberry Festival, and she had been in the kitchen since six thirty that morning, making last-minute preparations. She still had way too much to do, and now here was Doc, distracting her when she had no time for distractions.

He pulled the truck to a stop in a cloud of roiling dust; it had been a wet spring but a dry summer so far, causing them both to worry, what with the crop and all. But the upper atmosphere patterns were changing, according to the weatherman, who promised rain in the next week or so, possibly as early as next Tuesday, which could salvage this season's harvest. But she guessed Doc wasn't here to talk about the weather.

He jumped out of the truck, slamming the door hard behind him, and walked with a determined gait into the house, his limp barely slowing him down. He managed to find his way into the kitchen without tripping over any of the baskets and boxes that littered the floor. With a dramatic flourish he laid the paper out on the countertop, front page up. "Have you heard?"

She gave him a confused look and shook her head. "Heard what?"

Doc jabbed with a crooked finger at the paper's front page. "They announced it this morning. It's all over the TV and newspapers." He paused, then said in a low breath, "It's Jock Larson. He's dead."

TWO

"Dead?" At first Candy wasn't sure she had heard what she thought she had heard. Maybe her ears weren't working right. She almost smiled, thinking Doc was just playing with her, as he sometimes did. "You're kidding."

He shook his head. "'Fraid not, pumpkin." His face was stern; there was no trace of a smile to indicate a joke. "Jock's gone, that's for sure."

Candy felt a chill go through her that made her think of winter's coldest day. Suddenly hushed, she asked, "What happened?"

Doc started to speak, but his voice was low and hoarse. He paused, took a moment to clear his throat. Obviously the conversation at the diner that morning had been more spirited than usual. It must have been quite an event. *The boys are probably in a frenzy*, Candy thought. *The whole town probably is.*

Her next thought was, *This is big news. I've got to call Maggie.*

Gathering himself, his voice grave, Doc said, "Well, the information's still pretty sketchy. But what's clear is that sometime late last night, Jock took a nosedive off a cliff up on Mount Desert Island—"

"Oh my God." Candy's hand went to her mouth.

"—and fell to the rocks below, or at least that's the official version. He must have landed hard. Probably killed him instantly." Doc paused. "I've seen those rocks. I was up there just a few weeks ago." He took a deep breath. "Anyway, at some point during the night, his body must have rolled into the water and drifted out to sea. But the tides brought it back in this morning. He washed up on Sand Beach sometime around daybreak. Some elderly tourist up from Maryland found the body. Gave her quite a shock, too, or so I've heard."

"Dad, that's awful."

Doc Holliday nodded. "Yeah it is." He shook his gray-haired head. "This whole thing seems so unreal. I guess it's just hard to believe he's really gone. It sure is going to shake up this town, though."

Falling into silence, he leaned back against the counter, arms crossed and head bowed, and for the first time in a while Candy took a good look at her father. The crags on his face seemed deeper, his dark brown eyes more guarded. His clothes were as rumpled as ever, though, hanging loosely on his frame. He had never been a burly man, but he seemed thinner these days, though not frail. He was getting stronger again, she realized, after years when it seemed he would never fully recover. Despite his efforts to conceal the truth with his humor, the death a few years ago of Holly, Doc's wife and Candy's mother, had hit him hard, and it had taken him a good while to recover from the loss. In the end it had taken a major change—retirement from the university and the purchase of a blueberry farm in a small Maine coastal village, at the strong urging of his daughter—to help him start his recovery. The farm, his life's dream, had become his raison d'etre, keeping him busy and giving him purpose. He started writing again, beginning to fill the hollowness inside him with books and research and activity and friends. And he had quickly adopted this community as his own, taken its people into his heart, its history into his bones.

Now the town's loss was his loss. And it seemed to draw him back just a little into the funk he had worked so hard to pull himself out of.

Still, Candy thought, he and Jock had never been good friends. Come to think of it, they had disliked each other. A lot.

It was all because of that parking spot, Candy recalled. She hadn't lived here then, hadn't yet pulled herself out of the downward spiral in which she had, for a time, floundered herself. But she had heard the story from Maggie Tremont, her best friend in town.

Jock (Maggie had told her) was like a god around Cape Willington. That might have been an overstatement, but it was hard to deny that Jock had put the place on the map, given it a face to the rest of the world. If nothing else, he had been for decades the town's adventurous soul, its favorite son—though a somewhat immoral and often arrogant one, filled with the juice of life. He was not shy to claim his privilege, whatever that might be. For the past few years, that privilege extended to a primo parking spot in front of Duffy's Diner every weekday morning and at around noontime, when Jock stopped in for a cheeseburger and a bowl of homemade chicken noodle soup. New in town and unaware of the etiquette that followed Jock around, Doc parked in that spot one morning and had promptly been warned by both Dolores, the waitress, and Juanita, who worked the counter. Doc listened but hadn't moved his car; he wasn't about to play that game.

When Jock walked in, stomping about and complaining loudly that his parking spot had been taken by some blasted out-of-towner, and that he had been forced to park almost a half block away—an inconceivable affront to his quasi-celebrity status—Doc calmly assumed responsibility and then proceeded to tell Jock, to the horror of all in listening range, that the parking spots in town were for the general public, available on a first-come-first-served basis, and that it was foolish and downright undemocratic to assume they could be reserved for any one individual. With that, he paid his check and left, leaving stunned diners and a sputtering, disbelieving Jock in his wake.

Once they got off on the wrong foot, it had never been set right. Jock took to getting up extra early so he could get to the diner before anyone else to claim his spot, and Doc let him have it, ambling in at his usual time, around eight. Jock usually sat at the counter, so Doc opted for the corner booth. Jock had his friends, so Doc found others. After that first meeting there had been few words between the two, and there had never been any overt confrontation, but it was clear they rubbed each other the wrong way.

So why was Doc so upset now?

With a start, Candy realized there was more to the story, something he hadn't told her yet. She could see it in his eyes now; somehow she had missed it earlier, or misinterpreted it. Her mind lurched off in a different direction as she thought back over what Doc had said. . . .

He took a nosedive off a cliff and fell to the rocks below . . . or at least that's the official version. . . .

She shuddered as she was struck by a horrendous thought.

"Dad . . . was it an accident or . . . did he jump?"

Doc's gaze shifted toward her. "Suicide?"

Candy had the impression he was ready for the question but still held something back. She pressed on. "Well, it's possible, isn't it? Unless he was just trying to dive in. You know—doing something crazy. Maybe he had a few drinks in him and took it as a challenge."

Doc shook his head. "Jock pushed the limits, but he wasn't crazy."

"Well, then he either fell by accident . . . or he jumped."

But Doc wasn't buying it. "That doesn't make any sense. Jock was treated like a god around here. He never had a care in the world—got everything he wanted. No, pumpkin, I don't think he jumped. I think the real question is, did he fall . . . or was he pushed?"